D1306050

VOID™
TRIP

IMAGE COMICS, INC. • Robert Kirkman: Chief Operating Officer • Erik Larsen: Chief Financial Officer • Todd McFarlane: President • Marc Silvestri: Chief Executive Officer • Jim Valentino: Vice President • Eric Stephenson: Publisher / Chief Creative Officer • Corey Hart: Director of Sales • Jeff Boison: Director of Publishing Planning & Book Trade Sales • Chris Ross: Director of Digital Sales • Jeff Stang: Director of Specialty Sales • Kat Salazar: Director of PR & Marketing • Drew Gill: Art Director • Heather Doornink: Production Director • Nicole Lapalme: Controller • **IMAGECOMICS.COM**

VOID TRIP. First printing. May 2018. Published by Image Comics, Inc. Office of publication: 2701 NW Vaughn St., Suite 780, Portland, OR 97210. Copyright © 2018 Ryan O'Sullivan & Mind Comics. All rights reserved. Contains material originally published in single magazine form as VOID TRIP #1-5. "Void Trip™," its logos, and the likenesses of all characters herein are trademarks of Ryan O'Sullivan & Mind Comics, unless otherwise noted. "Image" and the Image Comics logos are registered trademarks of Image Comics, Inc. No part of this publication may be reproduced or transmitted, in any form or by any means (except for short excerpts for journalistic or review purposes), without the express written permission of Ryan O'Sullivan & Mind Comics, or Image Comics, Inc. All names, characters, events, and locales in this publication are entirely fictional. Any resemblance to actual persons (living or dead), events, or places, without satiric intent, is coincidental. Printed in the USA. For information regarding the CPSIA on this printed material call: 203-595-3636 and provide reference #RICH–789147. For international rights, contact: foreignlicensing@imagecomics.com. ISBN: 978-1-5343-0668-4. Big Bang / Forbidden Planet Variant ISBN: 978-1-5343-0946-3.

CREATED BY
RYAN O'SULLIVAN & PLAID KLAUS

VOID™
TRIP

DEDICATED TO THE MEMORY OF
JAMES "JANLEE" HAGEMANN

STORY BY

RYAN O'SULLIVAN
@RyanOSullivan

ART BY

PLAID KLAUS
@PlaidKlaus

LETTERED BY

ADITYA BIDIKAR
@adityab

PRODUCTION BY
Shanna Matuszak

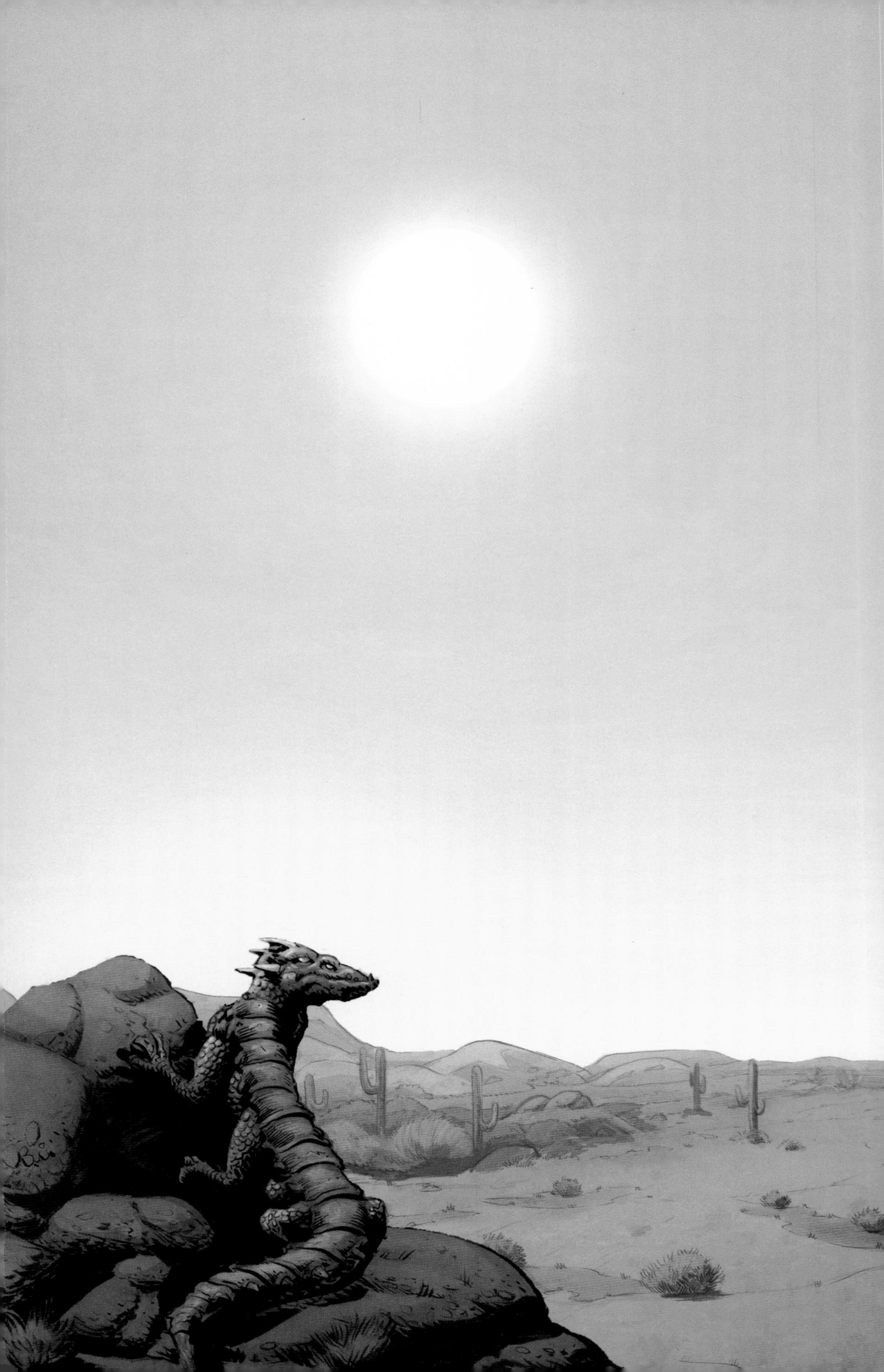

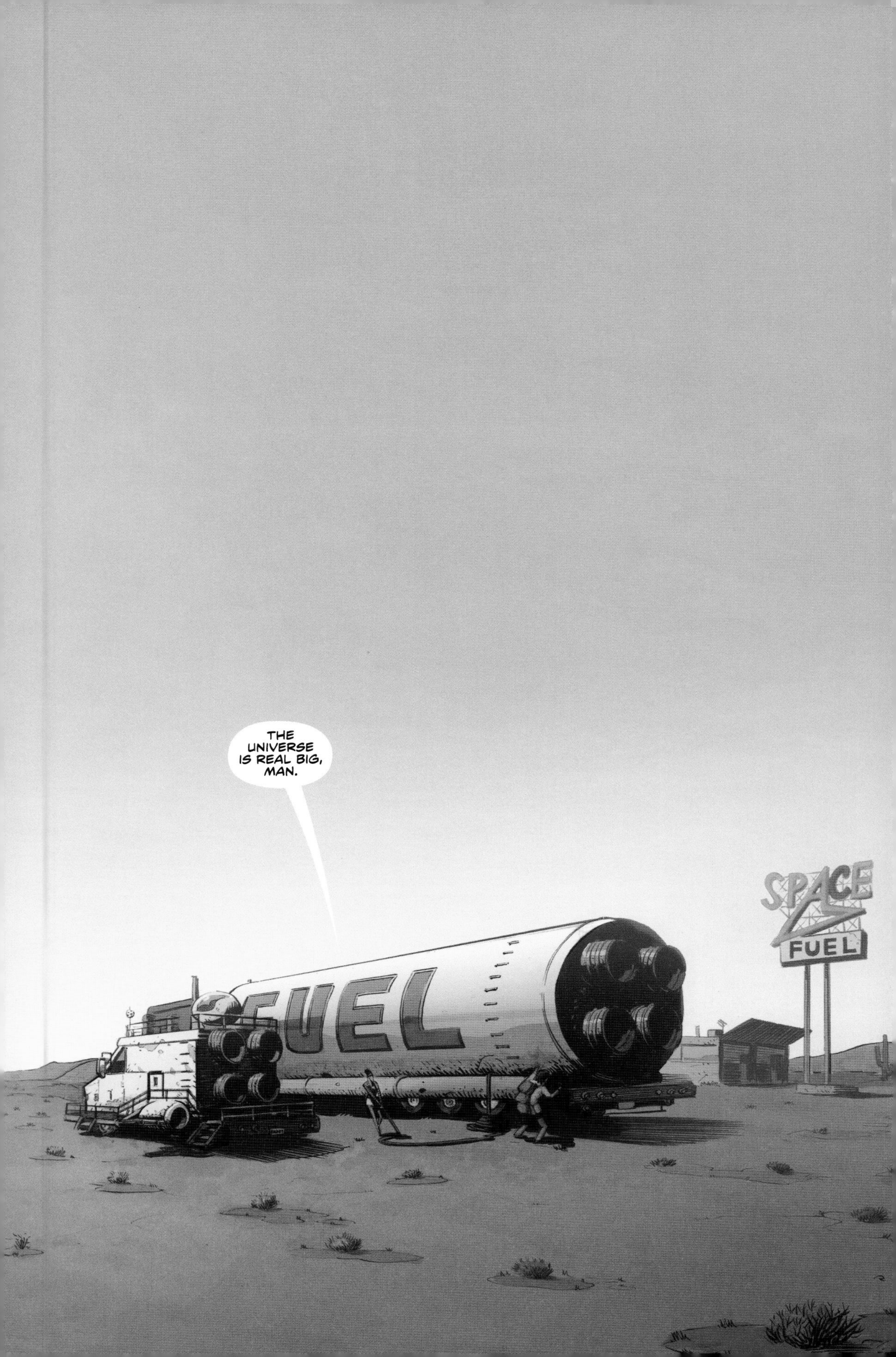
THE UNIVERSE IS REAL BIG, MAN.
FUEL
SPACE
FUEL

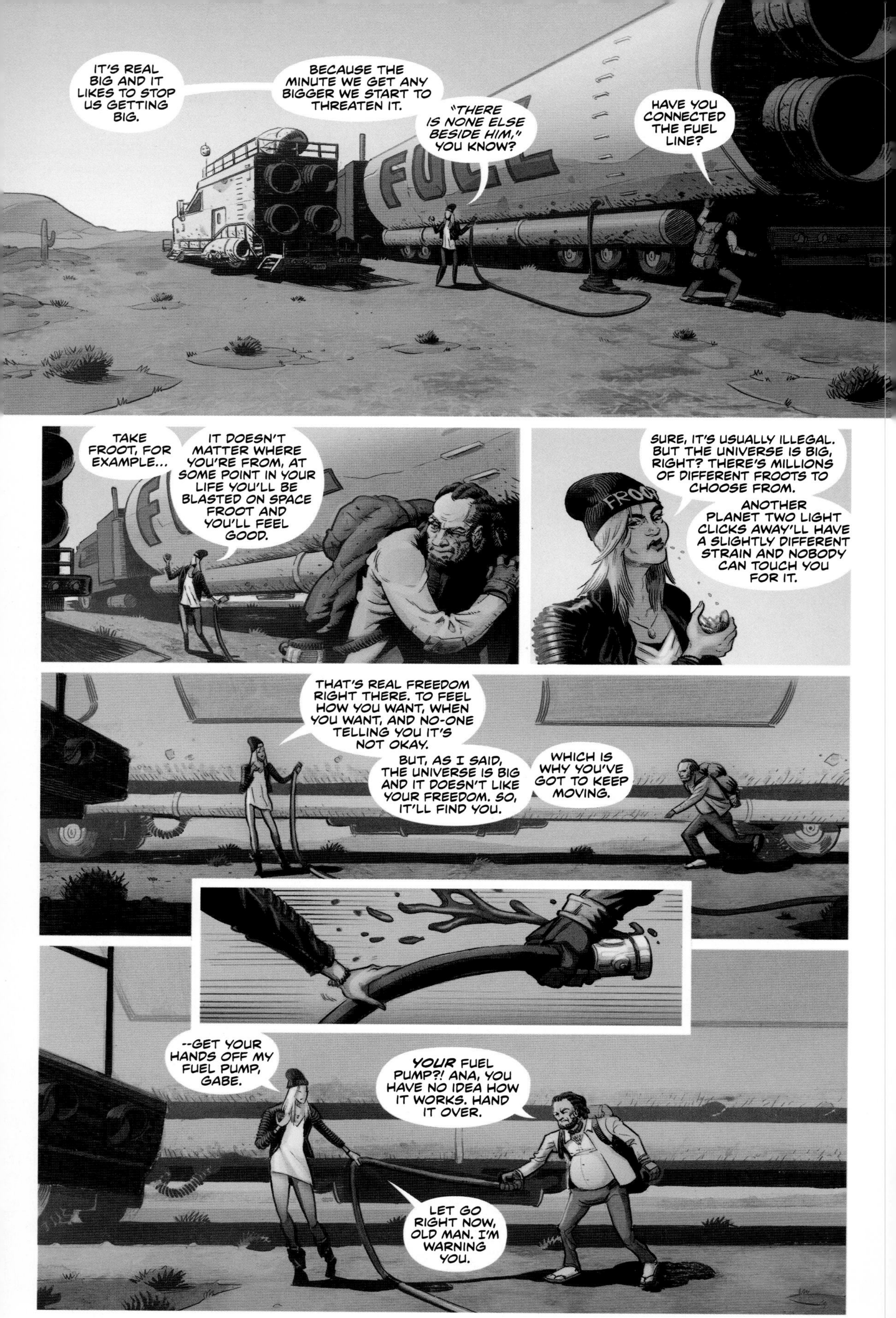
IT'S REAL BIG AND IT LIKES TO STOP US GETTING BIG.
BECAUSE THE MINUTE WE GET ANY BIGGER WE START TO THREATEN IT.
"THERE IS NONE ELSE BESIDE HIM," YOU KNOW?
HAVE YOU CONNECTED THE FUEL LINE?
TAKE FROOT, FOR EXAMPLE...
IT DOESN'T MATTER WHERE YOU'RE FROM, AT SOME POINT IN YOUR LIFE YOU'LL BE BLASTED ON SPACE FROOT AND YOU'LL FEEL GOOD.
SURE, IT'S USUALLY ILLEGAL. BUT THE UNIVERSE IS BIG, RIGHT? THERE'S MILLIONS OF DIFFERENT FROOTS TO CHOOSE FROM.
ANOTHER PLANET TWO LIGHT CLICKS AWAY'LL HAVE A SLIGHTLY DIFFERENT STRAIN AND NOBODY CAN TOUCH YOU FOR IT.
THAT'S REAL FREEDOM RIGHT THERE. TO FEEL HOW YOU WANT, WHEN YOU WANT, AND NO-ONE TELLING YOU IT'S NOT OKAY.
BUT, AS I SAID, THE UNIVERSE IS BIG AND IT DOESN'T LIKE YOUR FREEDOM. SO, IT'LL FIND YOU.
WHICH IS WHY YOU'VE GOT TO KEEP MOVING.
--GET YOUR HANDS OFF MY FUEL PUMP, GABE.
YOUR FUEL PUMP?! ANA, YOU HAVE NO IDEA HOW IT WORKS. HAND IT OVER.
LET GO RIGHT NOW, OLD MAN. I'M WARNING YOU.

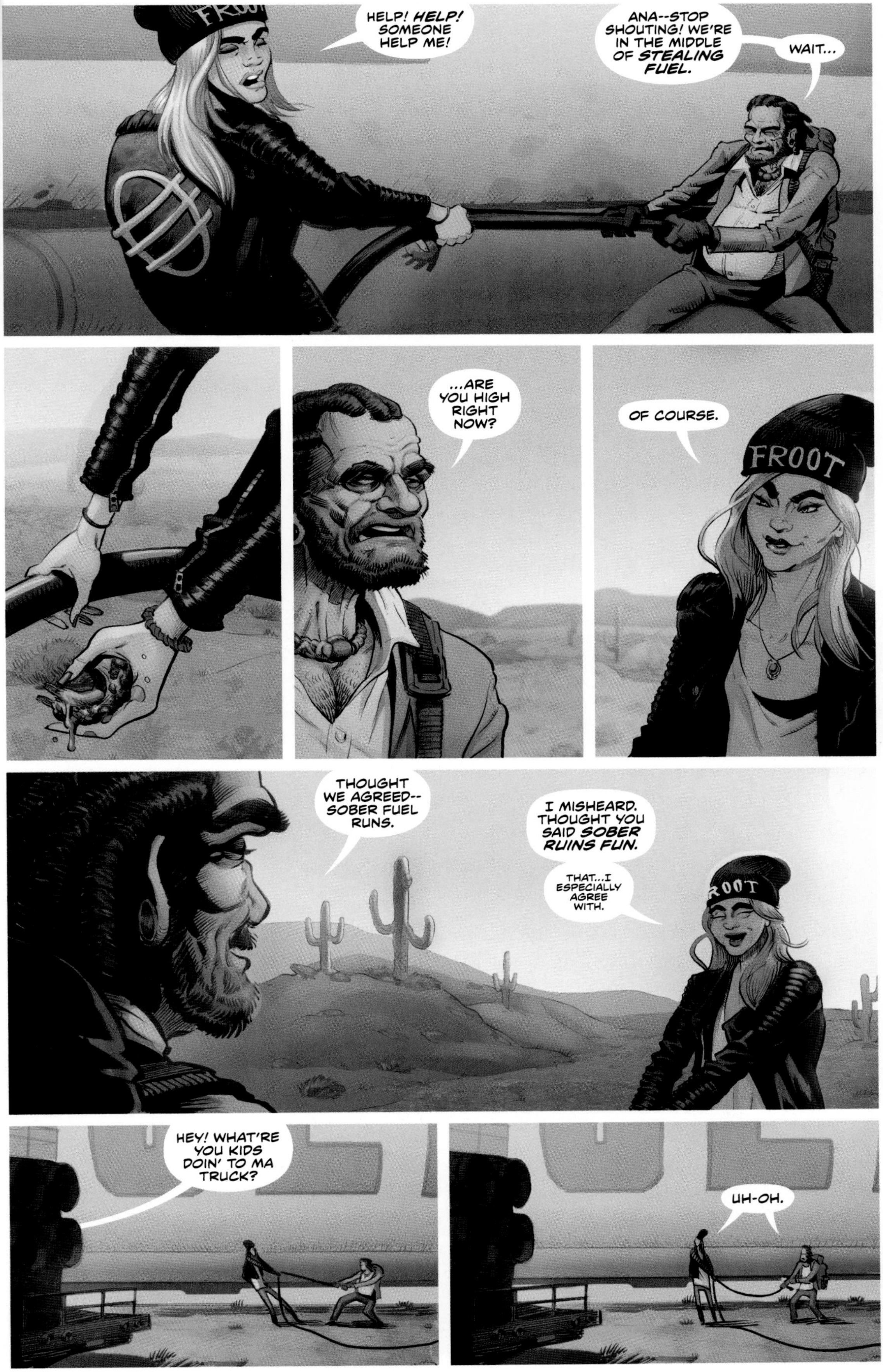
HELP! HELP! SOMEONE HELP ME!
ANA--STOP SHOUTING! WE'RE IN THE MIDDLE OF STEALING FUEL.
WAIT...
FROOT
...ARE YOU HIGH RIGHT NOW?
OF COURSE.
FROOT
THOUGHT WE AGREED-- SOBER FUEL RUNS.
I MISHEARD. THOUGHT YOU SAID SOBER RUINS FUN.
THAT...I ESPECIALLY AGREE WITH.
HEY! WHAT'RE YOU KIDS DOIN' TO MA TRUCK?
UH-OH.

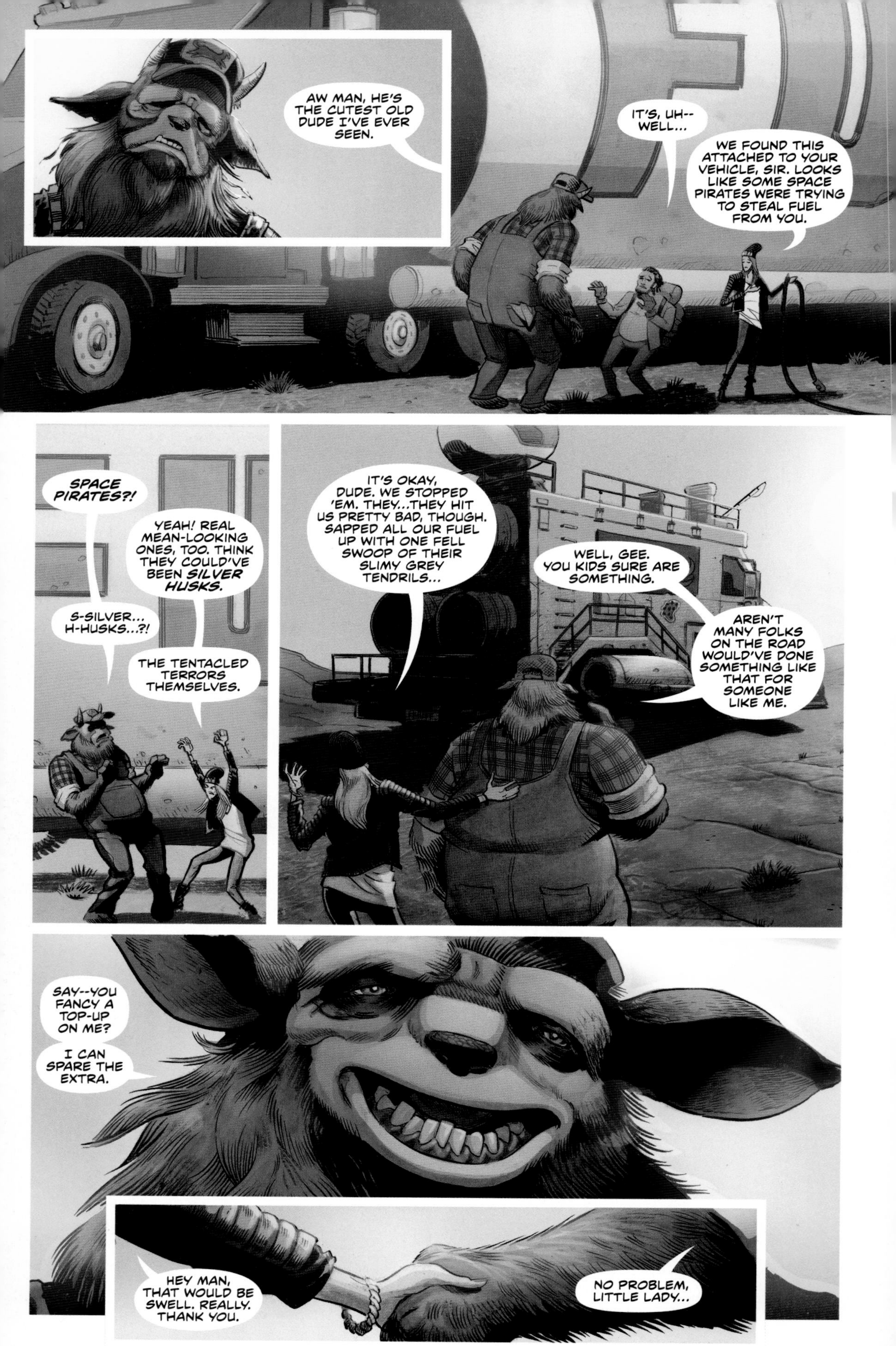
AW MAN, HE'S THE CUTEST OLD DUDE I'VE EVER SEEN.
IT'S, UH-- WELL...
WE FOUND THIS ATTACHED TO YOUR VEHICLE, SIR. LOOKS LIKE SOME SPACE PIRATES WERE TRYING TO STEAL FUEL FROM YOU.
SPACE PIRATES?!
YEAH! REAL MEAN-LOOKING ONES, TOO. THINK THEY COULD'VE BEEN SILVER HUSKS.
S-SILVER... H-HUSKS...?!
THE TENTACLED TERRORS THEMSELVES.
IT'S OKAY, DUDE. WE STOPPED 'EM. THEY...THEY HIT US PRETTY BAD, THOUGH. SAPPED ALL OUR FUEL UP WITH ONE FELL SWOOP OF THEIR SLIMY GREY TENDRILS...
WELL, GEE. YOU KIDS SURE ARE SOMETHING.
AREN'T MANY FOLKS ON THE ROAD WOULD'VE DONE SOMETHING LIKE THAT FOR SOMEONE LIKE ME.
SAY--YOU FANCY A TOP-UP ON ME?
I CAN SPARE THE EXTRA.
HEY MAN, THAT WOULD BE SWELL. REALLY. THANK YOU.
NO PROBLEM, LITTLE LADY...

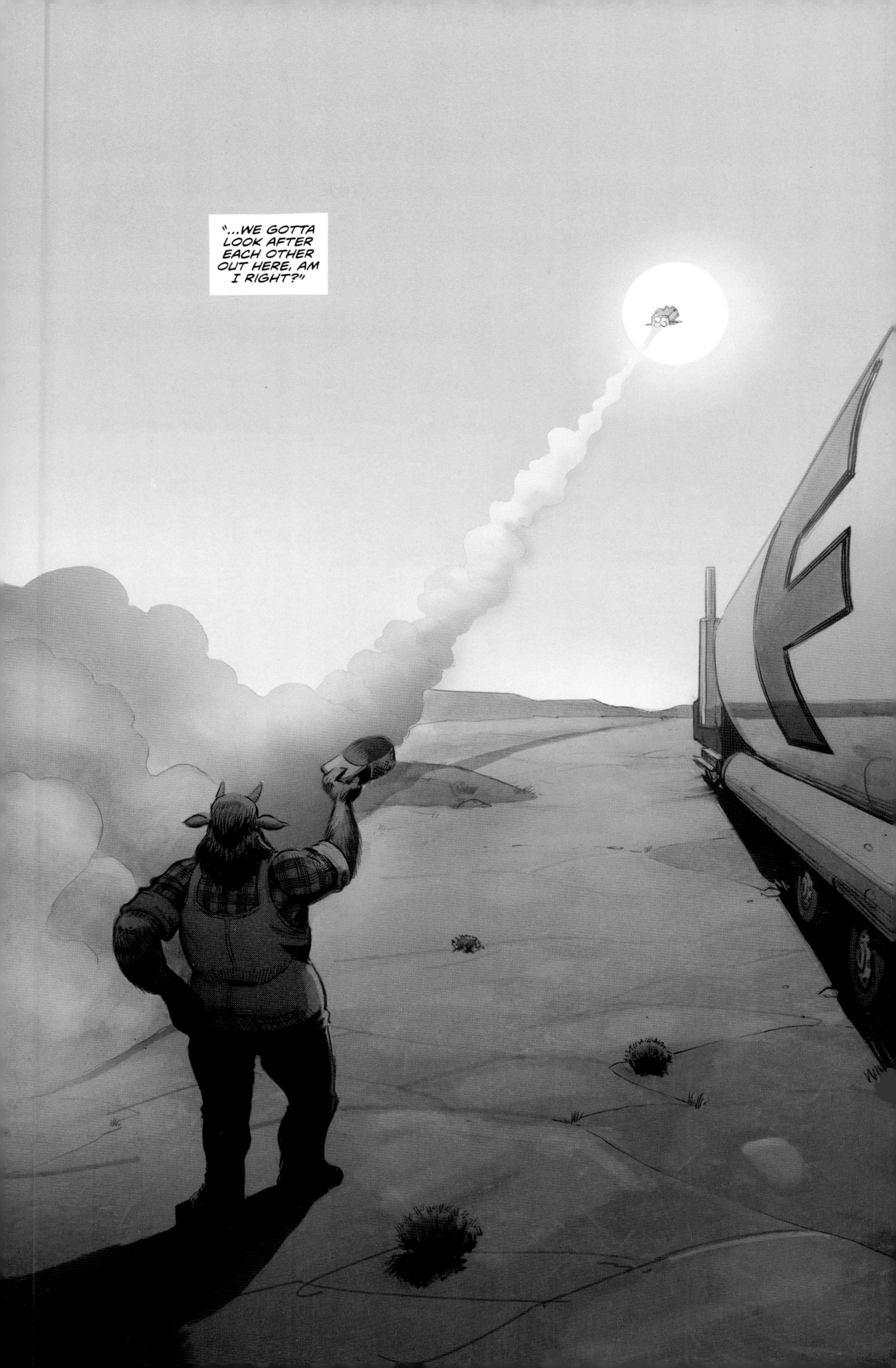
"...WE GOTTA LOOK AFTER EACH OTHER OUT HERE, AM I RIGHT?"

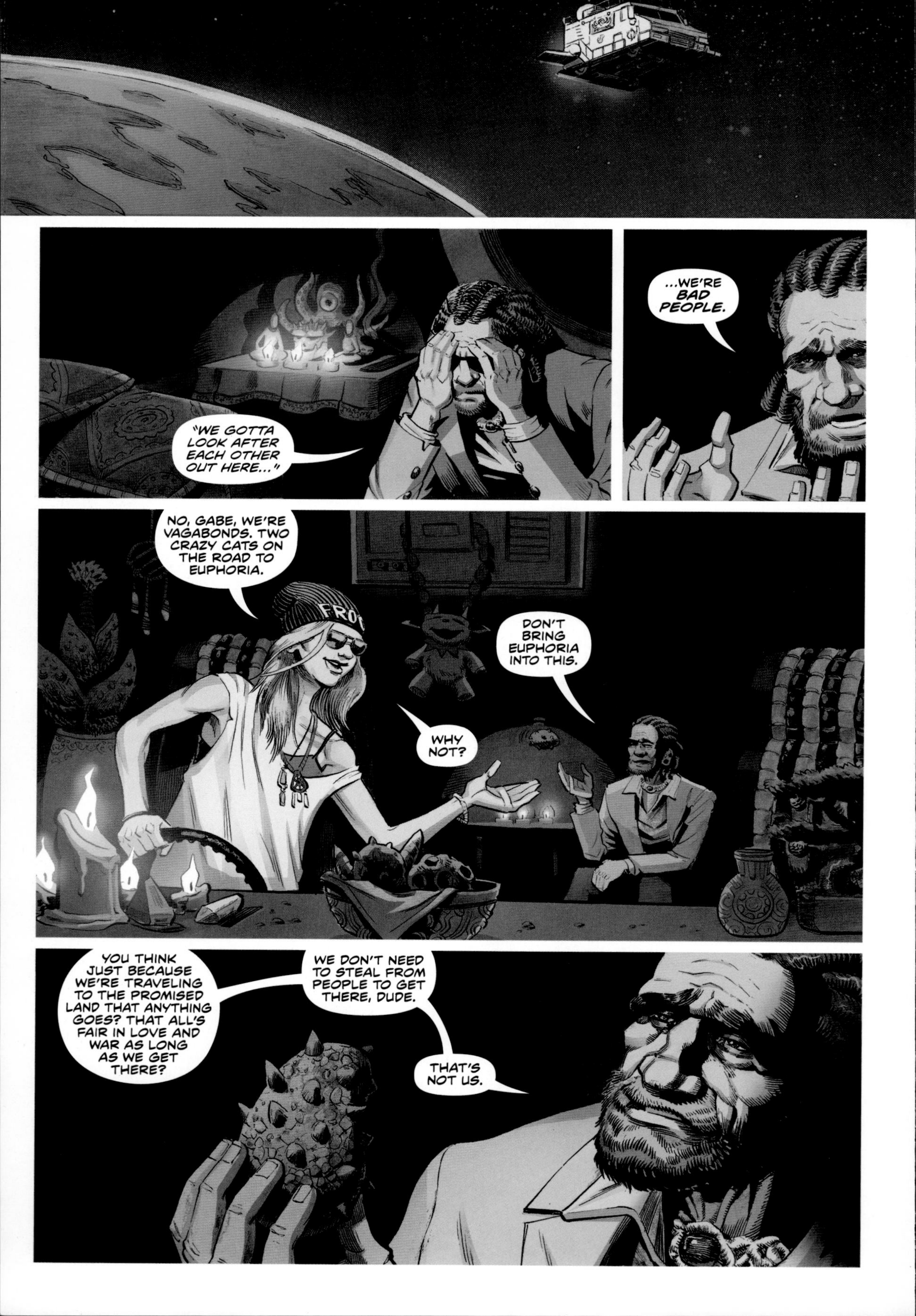
"WE GOTTA LOOK AFTER EACH OTHER OUT HERE..."
...WE'RE BAD PEOPLE.
NO, GABE, WE'RE VAGABONDS. TWO CRAZY CATS ON THE ROAD TO EUPHORIA.
FROG
DON'T BRING EUPHORIA INTO THIS.
WHY NOT?
YOU THINK JUST BECAUSE WE'RE TRAVELING TO THE PROMISED LAND THAT ANYTHING GOES? THAT ALL'S FAIR IN LOVE AND WAR AS LONG AS WE GET THERE?
WE DON'T NEED TO STEAL FROM PEOPLE TO GET THERE, DUDE.
THAT'S NOT US.

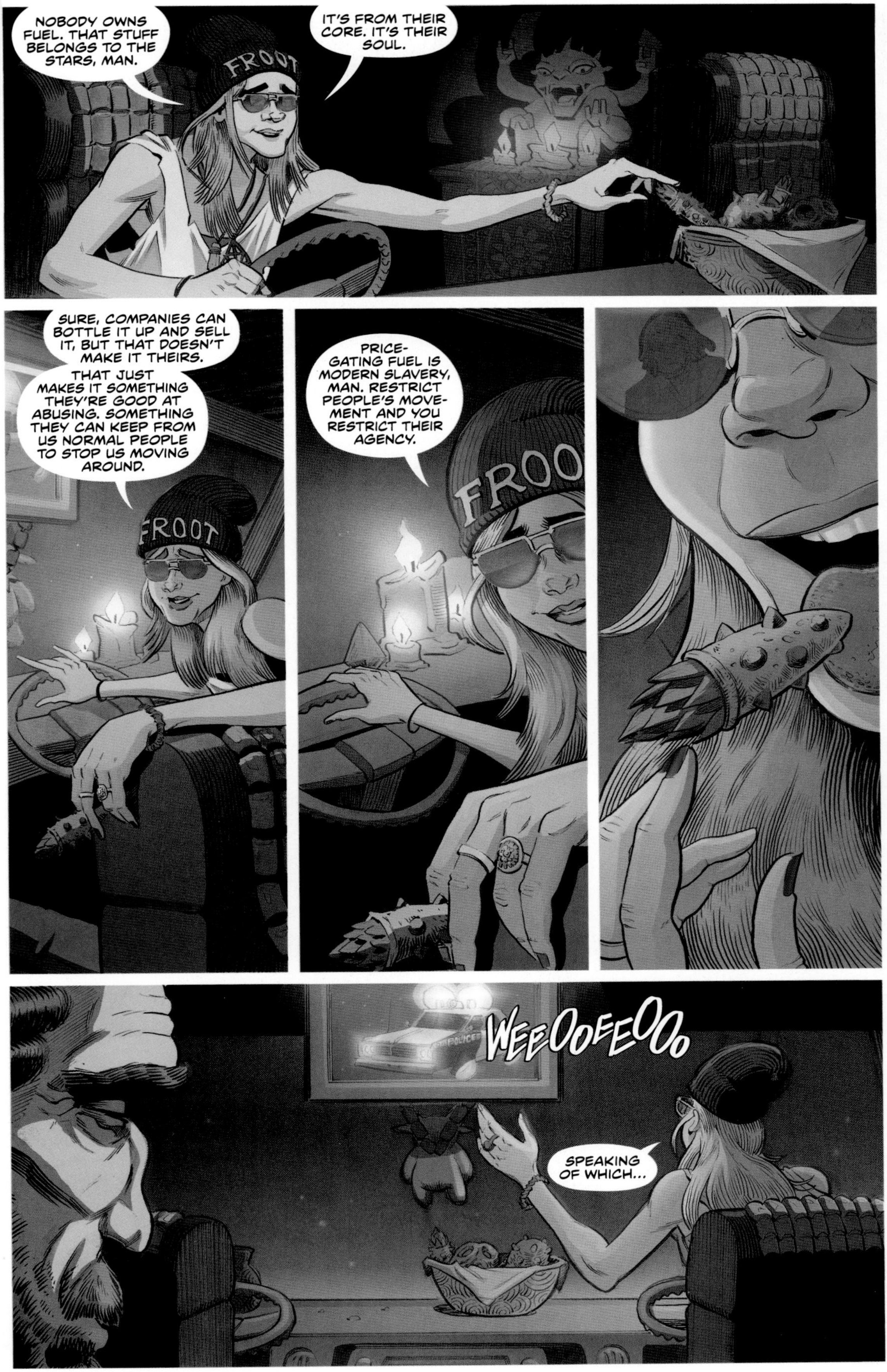
NOBODY OWNS FUEL. THAT STUFF BELONGS TO THE STARS, MAN.
IT'S FROM THEIR CORE. IT'S THEIR SOUL.
FROOT
SURE, COMPANIES CAN BOTTLE IT UP AND SELL IT, BUT THAT DOESN'T MAKE IT THEIRS.
THAT JUST MAKES IT SOMETHING THEY'RE GOOD AT ABUSING. SOMETHING THEY CAN KEEP FROM US NORMAL PEOPLE TO STOP US MOVING AROUND.
FROOT
PRICE-GATING FUEL IS MODERN SLAVERY, MAN. RESTRICT PEOPLE'S MOVEMENT AND YOU RESTRICT THEIR AGENCY.
FROOT
POLICE
WEEOOEEOOo
SPEAKING OF WHICH...

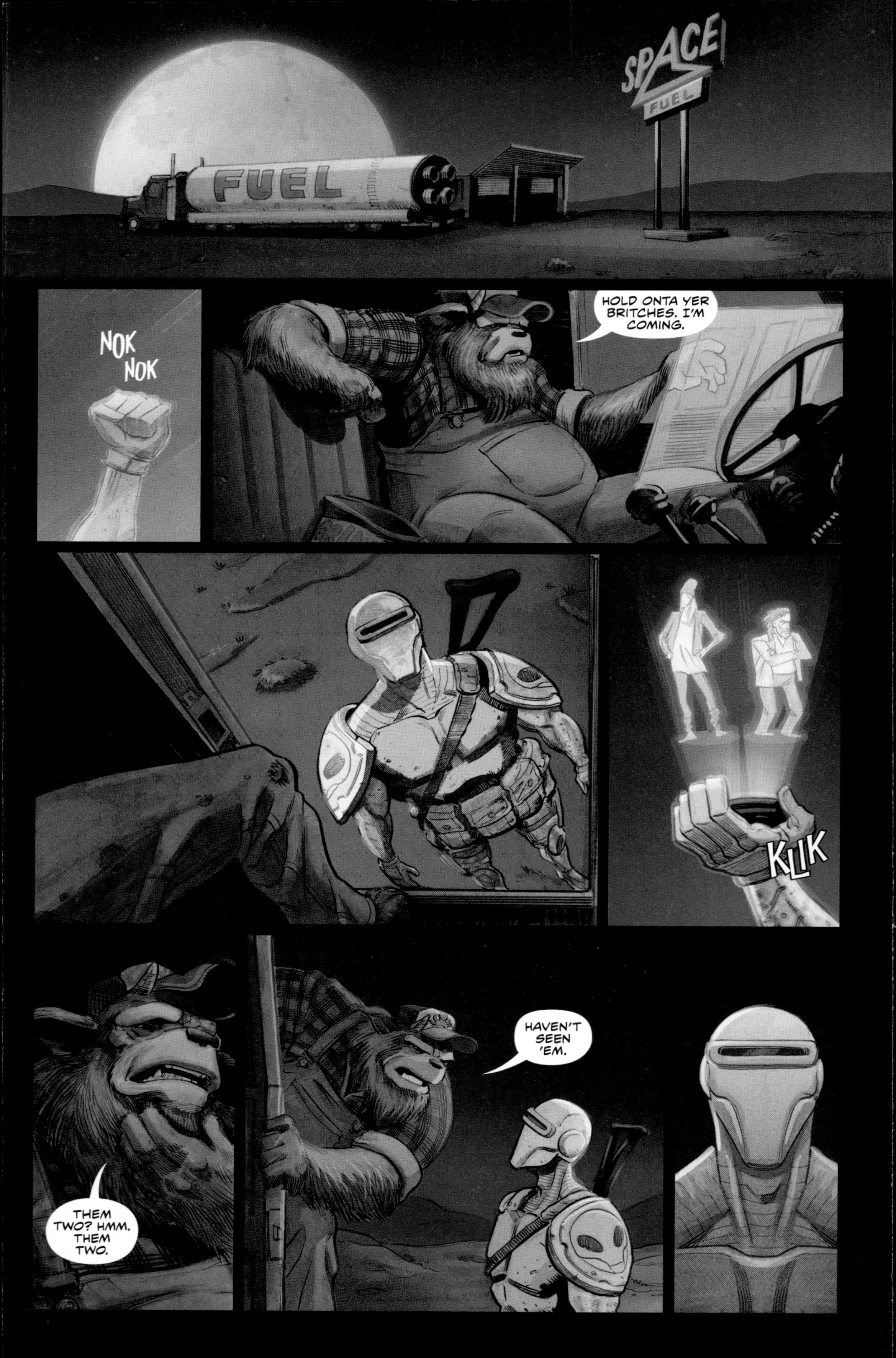
SPACE
FUEL
FUEL
NOK NOK
HOLD ONTA YER BRITCHES. I'M COMING.
KLIK
THEM TWO? HMM. THEM TWO.
HAVEN'T SEEN 'EM.

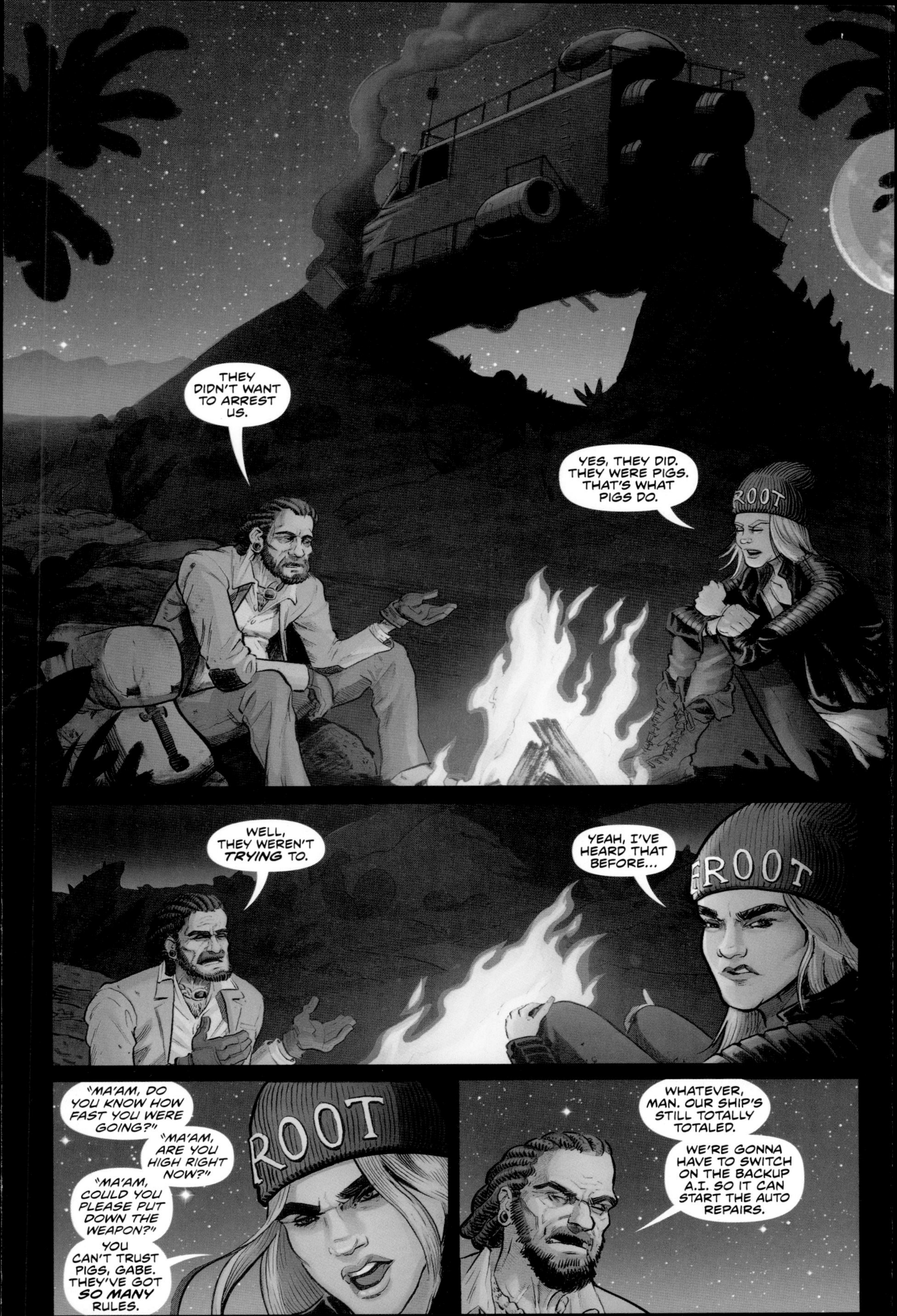
THEY DIDN'T WANT TO ARREST US.
YES, THEY DID. THEY WERE PIGS. THAT'S WHAT PIGS DO.
ROOT
WELL, THEY WEREN'T *TRYING* TO.
YEAH, I'VE HEARD THAT BEFORE...
"MA'AM, DO YOU KNOW HOW FAST YOU WERE GOING?"
"MA'AM, ARE YOU HIGH RIGHT NOW?"
"MA'AM, COULD YOU PLEASE PUT DOWN THE WEAPON?"
YOU CAN'T TRUST PIGS, GABE. THEY'VE GOT **SO MANY** RULES.
WHATEVER, MAN. OUR SHIP'S STILL TOTALLY TOTALED.
WE'RE GONNA HAVE TO SWITCH ON THE BACKUP A.I. SO IT CAN START THE AUTO REPAIRS.

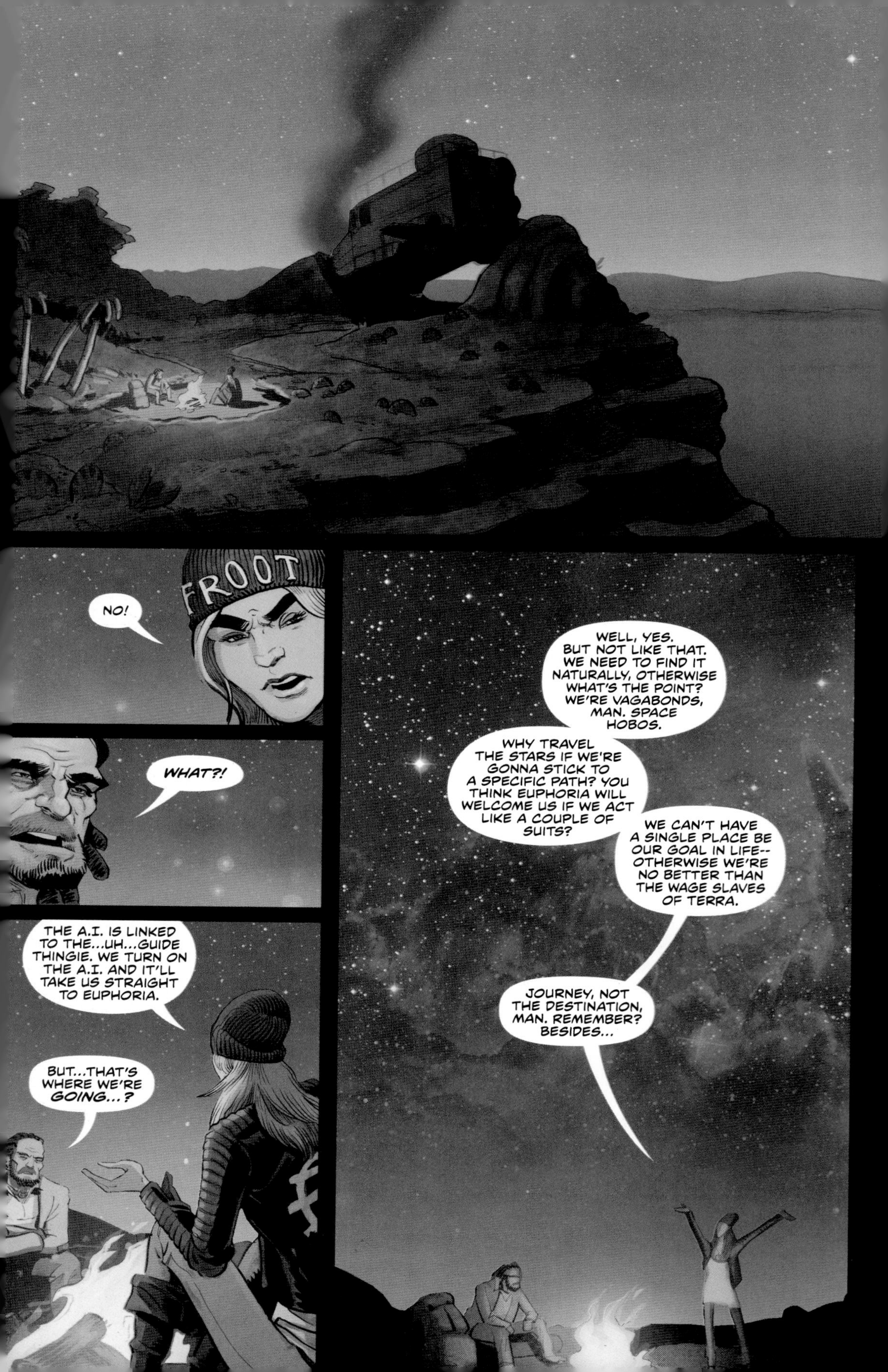
NO!
WHAT?!
THE A.I. IS LINKED TO THE...UH...GUIDE THINGIE. WE TURN ON THE A.I. AND IT'LL TAKE US STRAIGHT TO EUPHORIA.
BUT...THAT'S WHERE WE'RE GOING...?
WELL, YES. BUT NOT LIKE THAT. WE NEED TO FIND IT NATURALLY, OTHERWISE WHAT'S THE POINT? WE'RE VAGABONDS, MAN. SPACE HOBOS.
WHY TRAVEL THE STARS IF WE'RE GONNA STICK TO A SPECIFIC PATH? YOU THINK EUPHORIA WILL WELCOME US IF WE ACT LIKE A COUPLE OF SUITS?
WE CAN'T HAVE A SINGLE PLACE BE OUR GOAL IN LIFE--OTHERWISE WE'RE NO BETTER THAN THE WAGE SLAVES OF TERRA.
JOURNEY, NOT THE DESTINATION, MAN. REMEMBER? BESIDES...

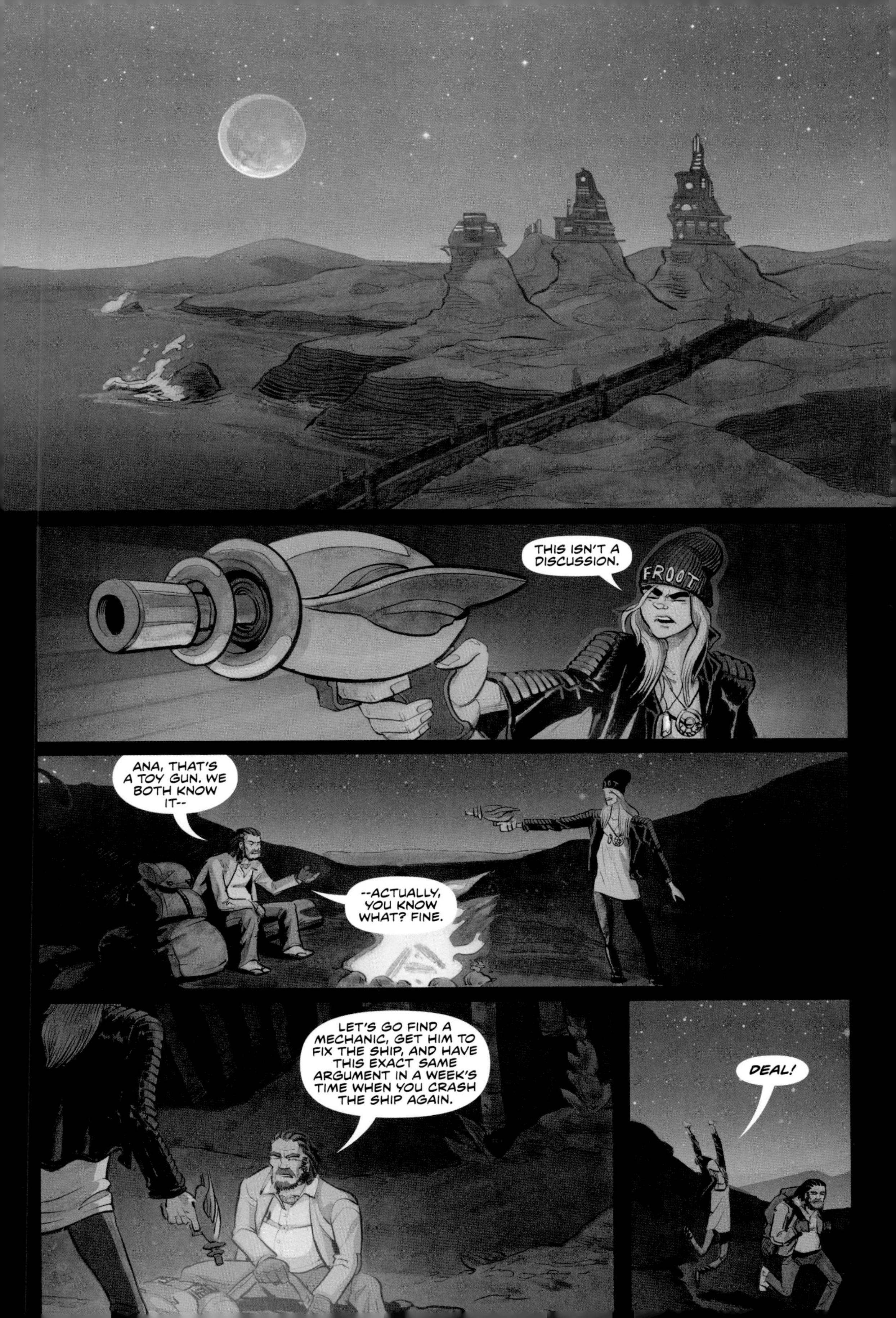

THIS ISN'T A DISCUSSION.
FROOT
ANA, THAT'S A TOY GUN. WE BOTH KNOW IT--
--ACTUALLY, YOU KNOW WHAT? FINE.
LET'S GO FIND A MECHANIC, GET HIM TO FIX THE SHIP, AND HAVE THIS EXACT SAME ARGUMENT IN A WEEK'S TIME WHEN YOU CRASH THE SHIP AGAIN.
DEAL!

STILL NO SIGN OF THEM.

YOU SURE THEY LANDED HERE?

I AM CERTAIN OF NOTHING. THIS IS WHY I PAY YOU.

WHY WOULD I PAY YOU IF I WAS CERTAIN OF THIS THING MYSELF?

I...UH... SO THEY'RE NOT HERE?

I HAVE NO WAY OF KNOWING THIS. ONLY YOU ARE CAPABLE OF KNOWING THIS.

RIGHT.

YOU KNOW, YOU'RE A FUNNY MAN TO WORK FOR, MR.--

--DO NOT SAY MY NAME. NEVER SAY MY NAME. IT IS NOT WISE TO SAY MY NAME.

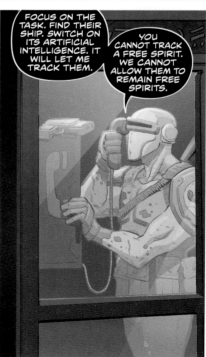

FOCUS ON THE TASK. FIND THEIR SHIP. SWITCH ON ITS ARTIFICIAL INTELLIGENCE. IT WILL LET ME TRACK THEM.

YOU CANNOT TRACK A FREE SPIRIT. WE CANNOT ALLOW THEM TO REMAIN FREE SPIRITS.

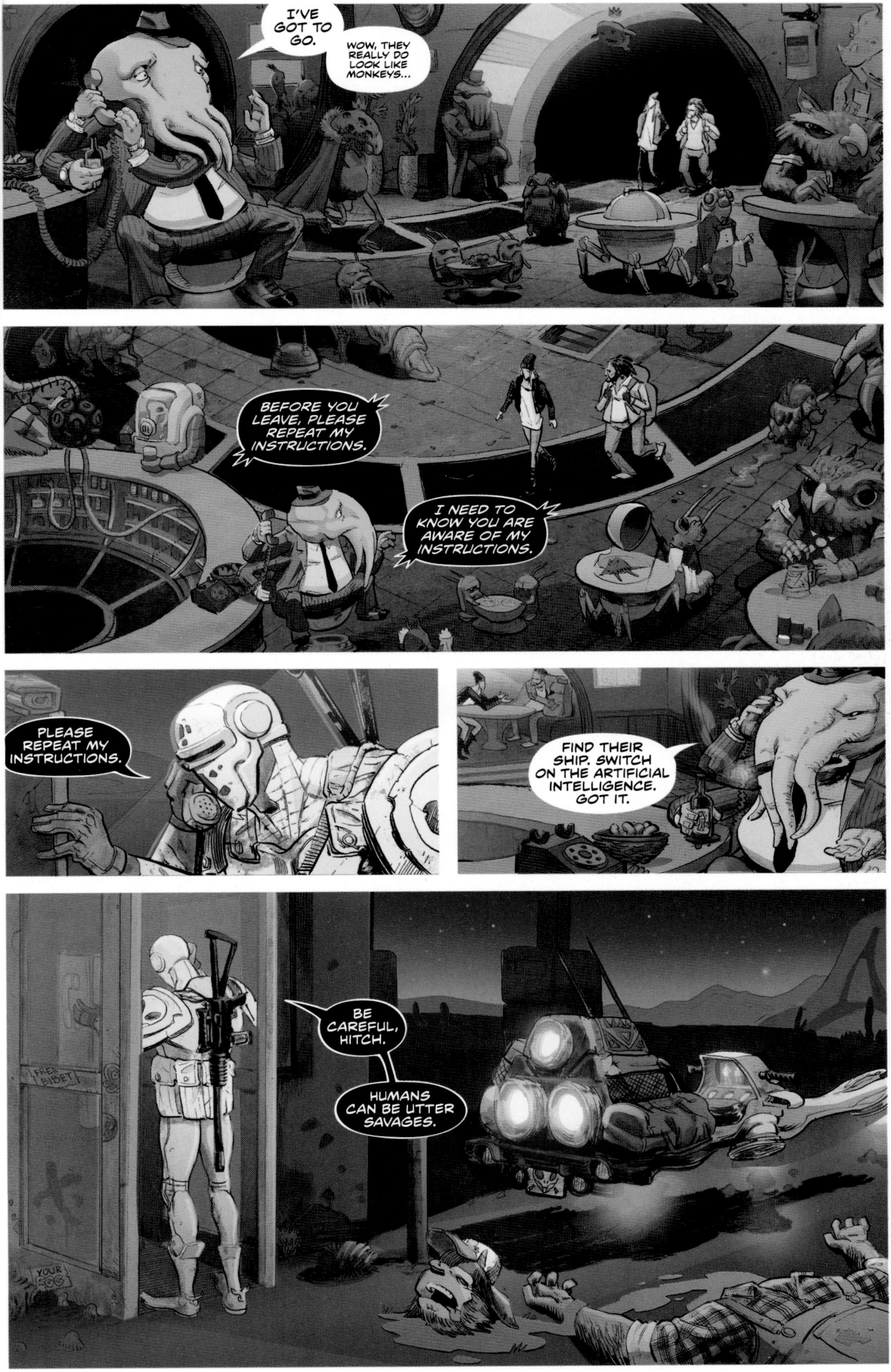
I'VE GOT TO GO.
WOW, THEY REALLY DO LOOK LIKE MONKEYS...
BEFORE YOU LEAVE, PLEASE REPEAT MY INSTRUCTIONS.
I NEED TO KNOW YOU ARE AWARE OF MY INSTRUCTIONS.
PLEASE REPEAT MY INSTRUCTIONS.
FIND THEIR SHIP. SWITCH ON THE ARTIFICIAL INTELLIGENCE. GOT IT.
BE CAREFUL, HITCH.
HUMANS CAN BE UTTER SAVAGES.

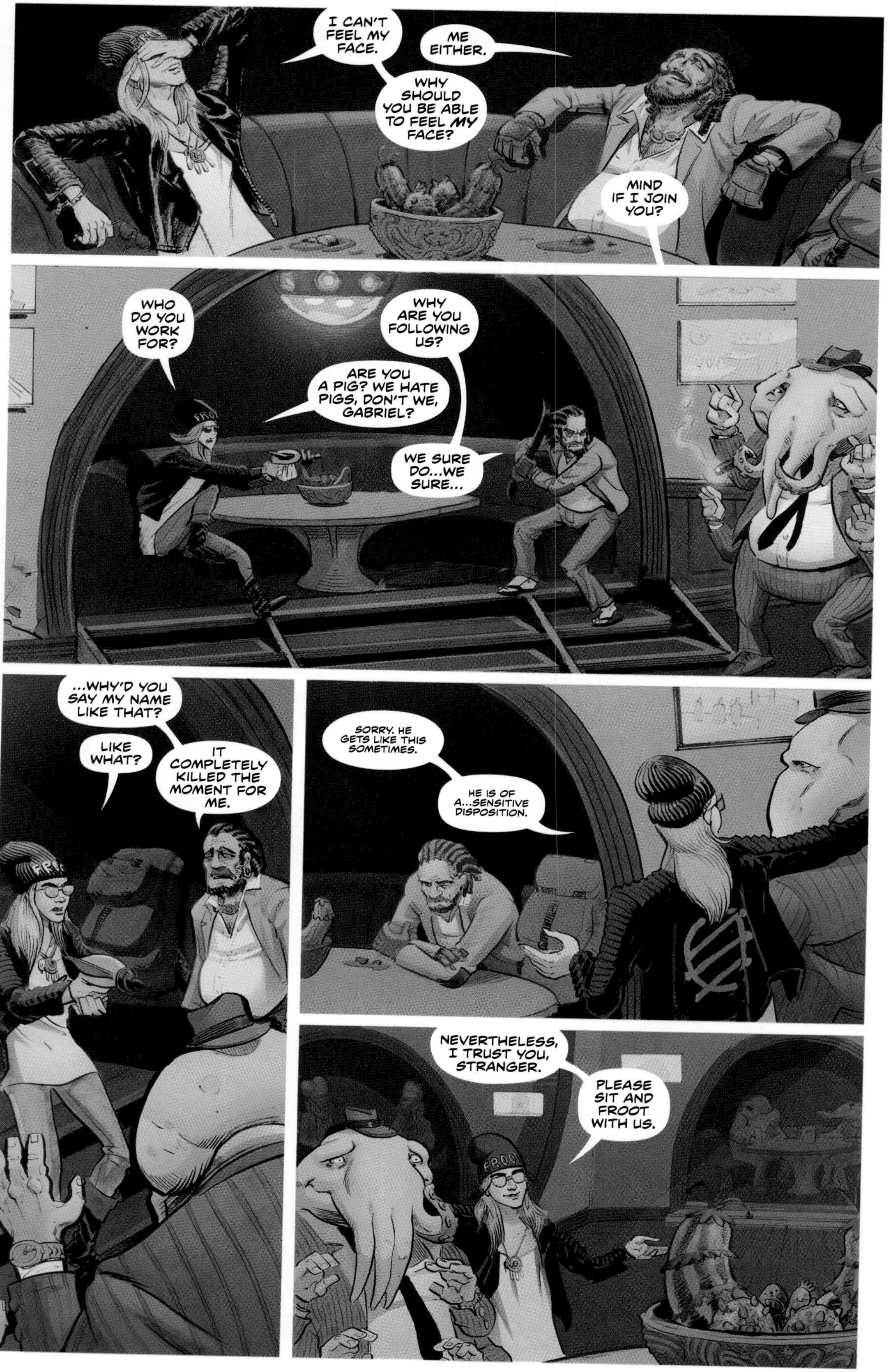
I CAN'T FEEL MY FACE.
ME EITHER.
WHY SHOULD YOU BE ABLE TO FEEL *MY* FACE?
MIND IF I JOIN YOU?
WHO DO YOU WORK FOR?
WHY ARE YOU FOLLOWING US?
ARE YOU A PIG? WE HATE PIGS, DON'T WE, GABRIEL?
WE SURE DO...WE SURE...
...WHY'D YOU SAY MY NAME LIKE THAT?
LIKE WHAT?
IT COMPLETELY KILLED THE MOMENT FOR ME.
SORRY. HE GETS LIKE THIS SOMETIMES.
HE IS OF A...SENSITIVE DISPOSITION.
NEVERTHELESS, I TRUST YOU, STRANGER.
PLEASE SIT AND FROOT WITH US.

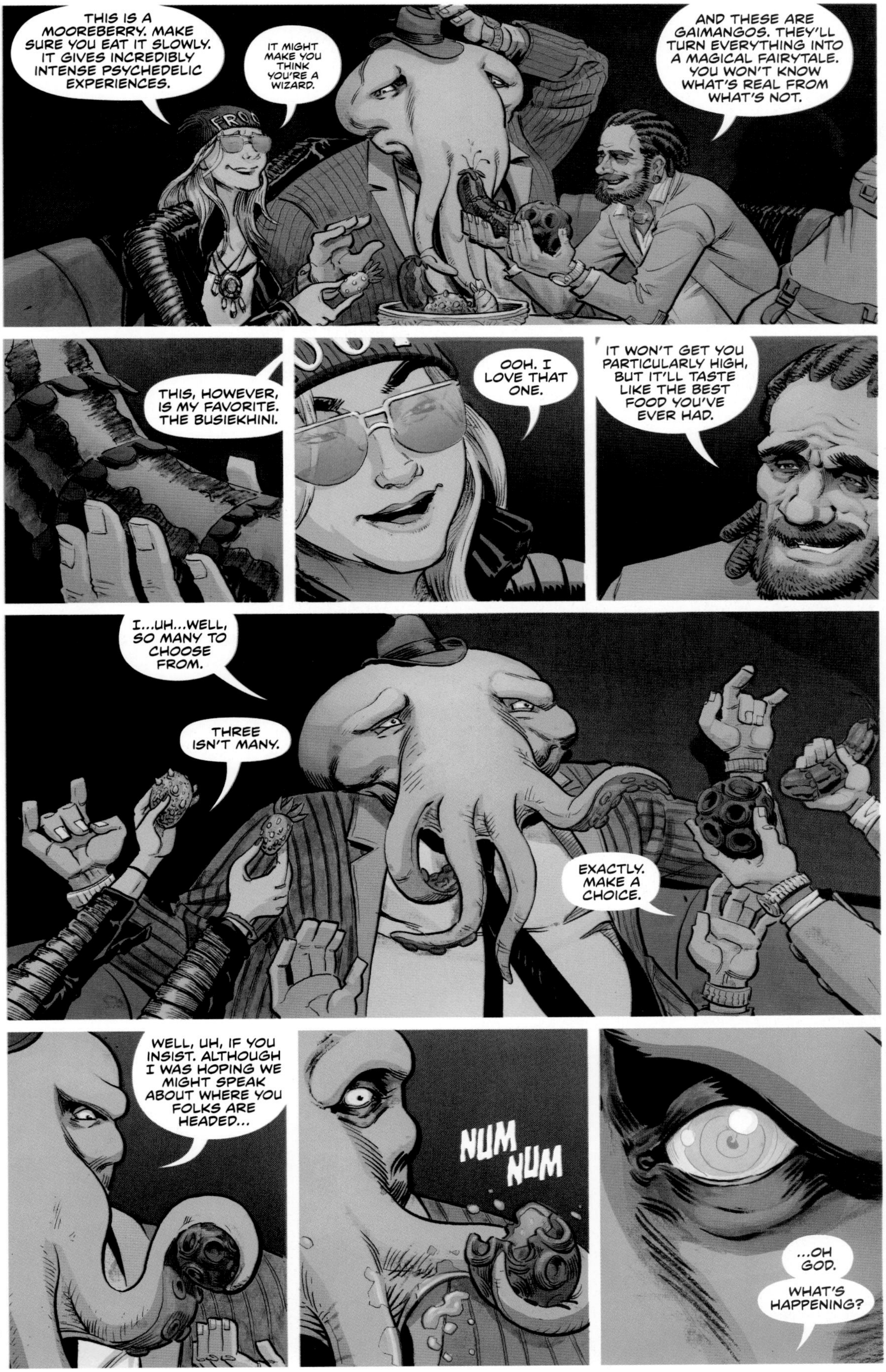
THIS IS A MOOREBERRY. MAKE SURE YOU EAT IT SLOWLY. IT GIVES INCREDIBLY INTENSE PSYCHEDELIC EXPERIENCES.
IT MIGHT MAKE YOU THINK YOU'RE A WIZARD.
AND THESE ARE GAIMANGOS. THEY'LL TURN EVERYTHING INTO A MAGICAL FAIRYTALE. YOU WON'T KNOW WHAT'S REAL FROM WHAT'S NOT.
FROG
THIS, HOWEVER, IS MY FAVORITE. THE BUSIEKHINI.
OOH. I LOVE THAT ONE.
IT WON'T GET YOU PARTICULARLY HIGH, BUT IT'LL TASTE LIKE THE BEST FOOD YOU'VE EVER HAD.
I...UH...WELL, SO MANY TO CHOOSE FROM.
THREE ISN'T MANY.
EXACTLY. MAKE A CHOICE.
WELL, UH, IF YOU INSIST. ALTHOUGH I WAS HOPING WE MIGHT SPEAK ABOUT WHERE YOU FOLKS ARE HEADED...
NUM NUM
...OH GOD.
WHAT'S HAPPENING?

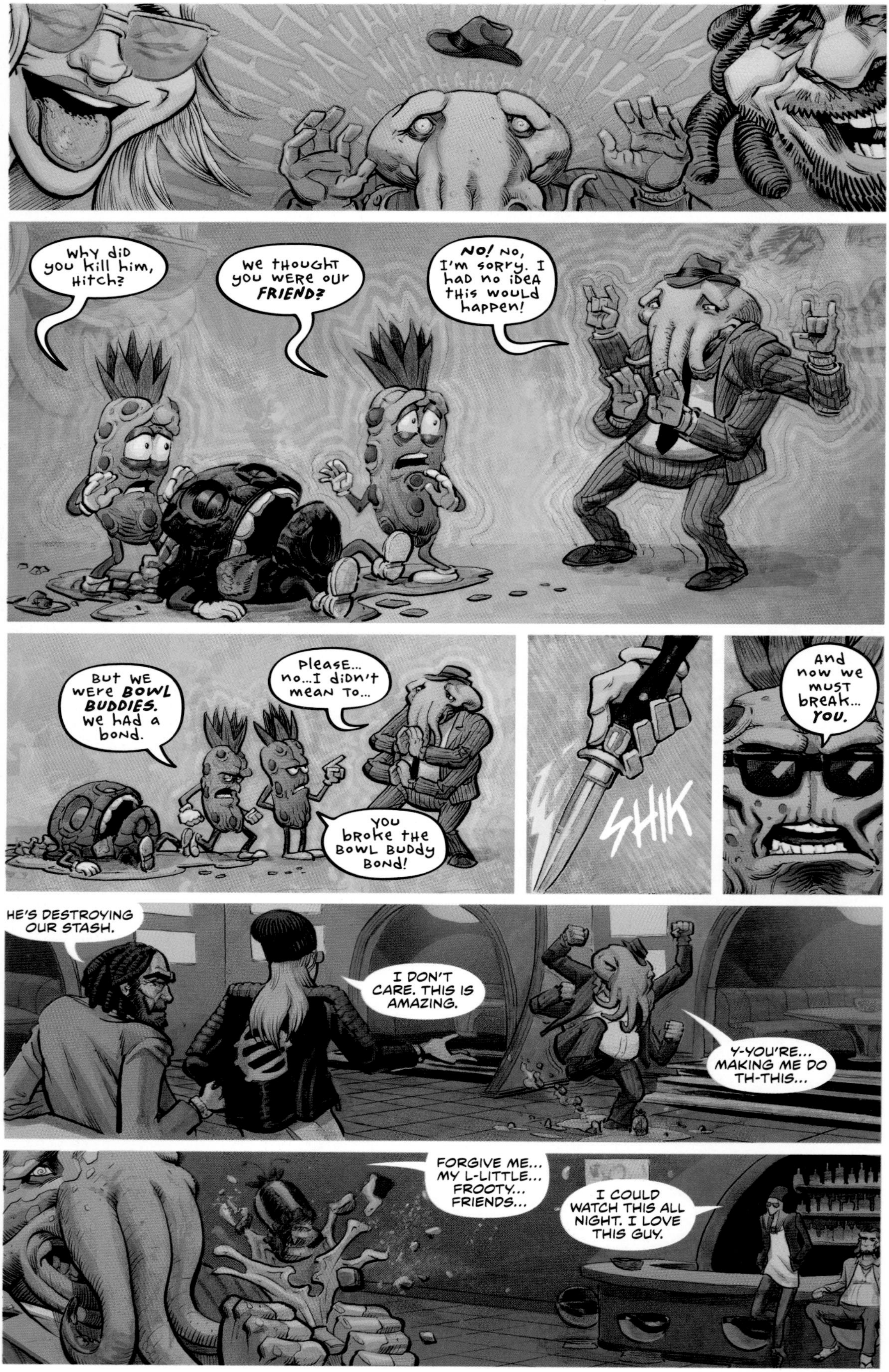
Why did you kill him, Hitch?
We thought you were our FRIEND?
NO! No, I'm sorry. I had no idea this would happen!
But we were BOWL BUDDIES. We had a bond.
Please... no...I didn't mean to...
You broke the Bowl Buddy Bond!
SHIK
And now we must break... YOU.
HE'S DESTROYING OUR STASH.
I DON'T CARE. THIS IS AMAZING.
Y-YOU'RE... MAKING ME DO TH-THIS...
FORGIVE ME... MY L-LITTLE... FROOTY... FRIENDS...
I COULD WATCH THIS ALL NIGHT. I LOVE THIS GUY.

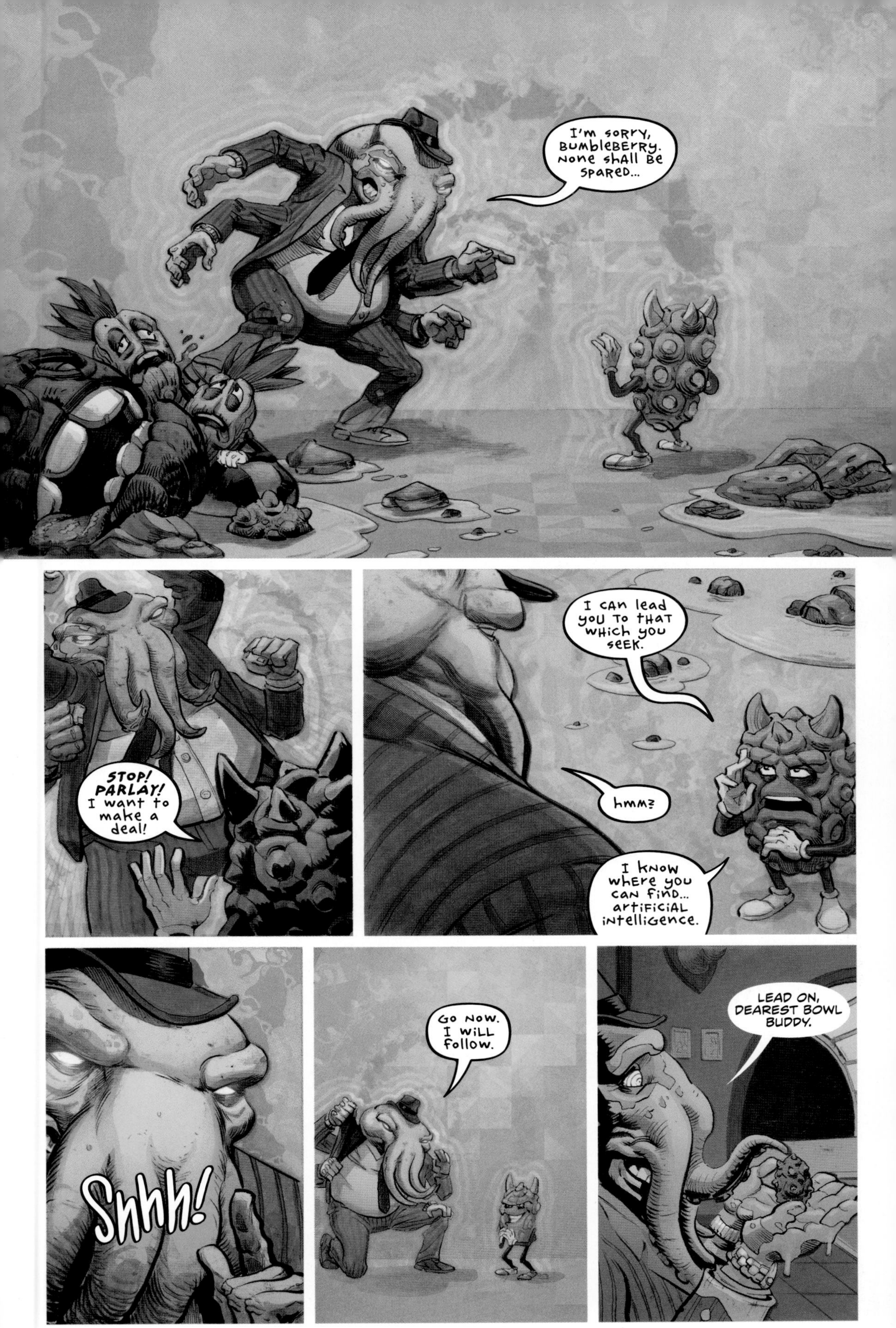
I'm sorry, Bumbleberry. None shall be spared...
STOP! PARLAY! I want to make a deal!
I can lead you to that which you seek.
hmm?
I know where you can find... artificial intelligence.
Shhh!
Go now. I will follow.
LEAD ON, DEAREST BOWL BUDDY.

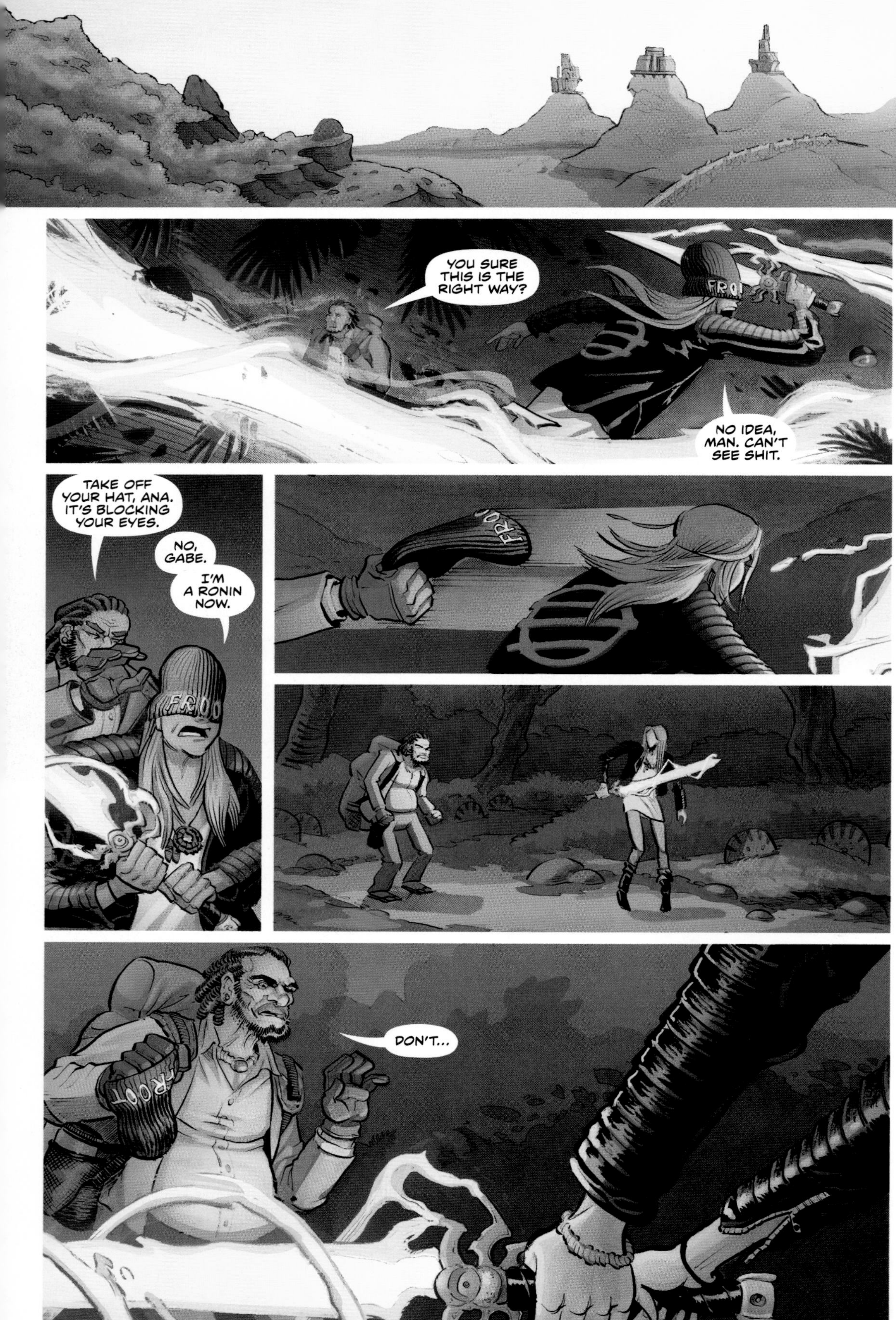
YOU SURE THIS IS THE RIGHT WAY?
NO IDEA, MAN. CAN'T SEE SHIT.
TAKE OFF YOUR HAT, ANA. IT'S BLOCKING YOUR EYES.
NO, GABE.
I'M A RONIN NOW.
FROOT
FROOT
DON'T...
FROOT

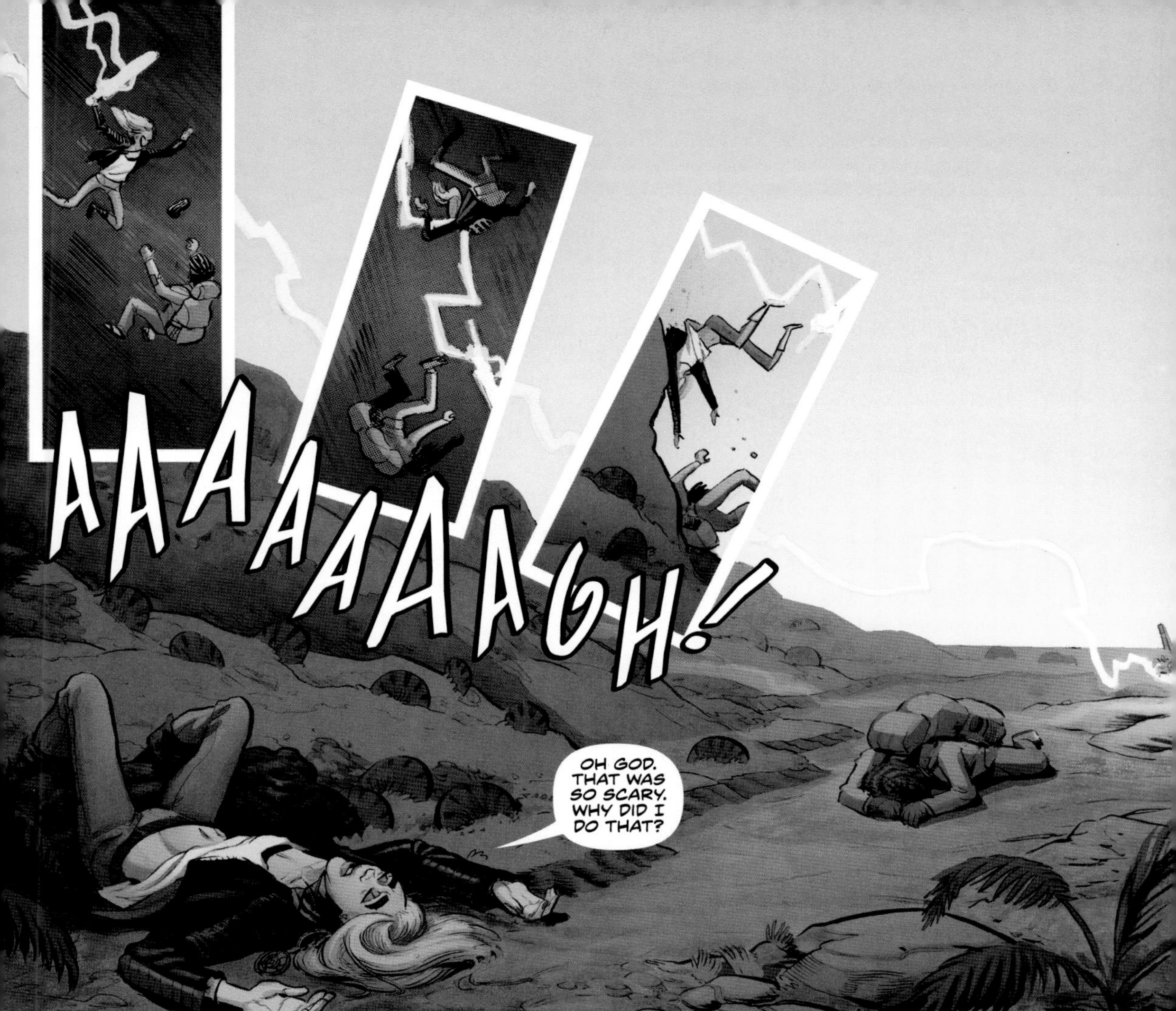
AAAAAAAAAGH!
OH GOD. THAT WAS SO SCARY. WHY DID I DO THAT?

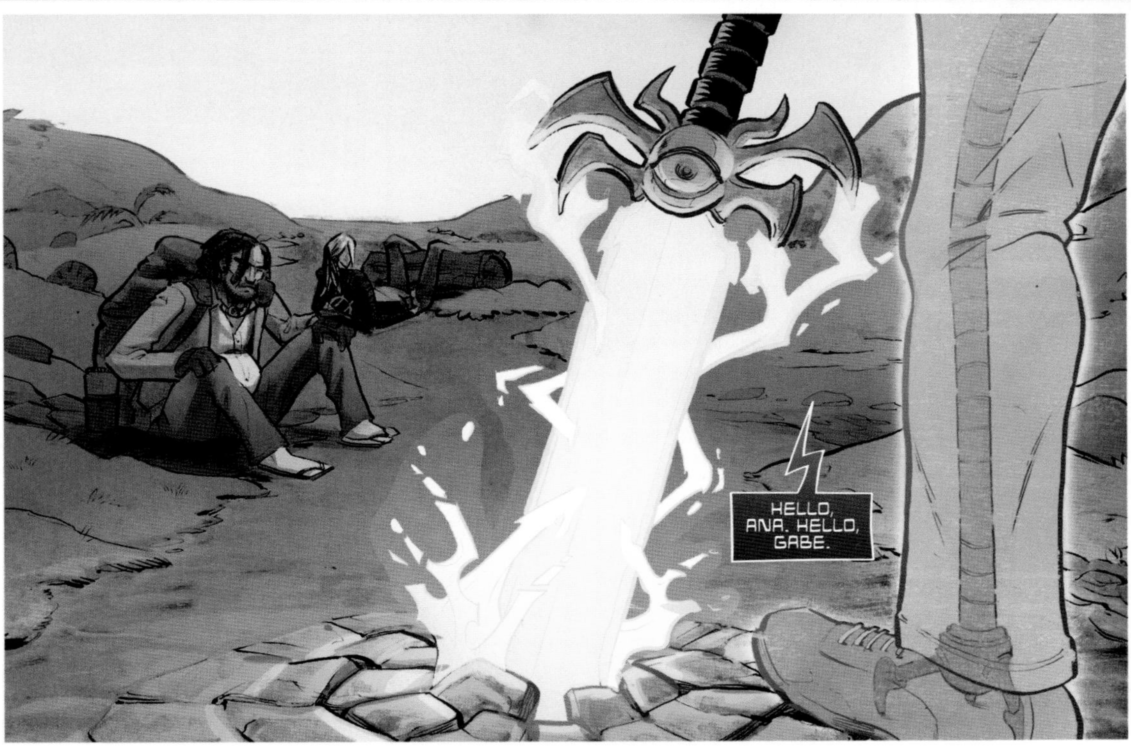
HELLO, ANA. HELLO, GABE.

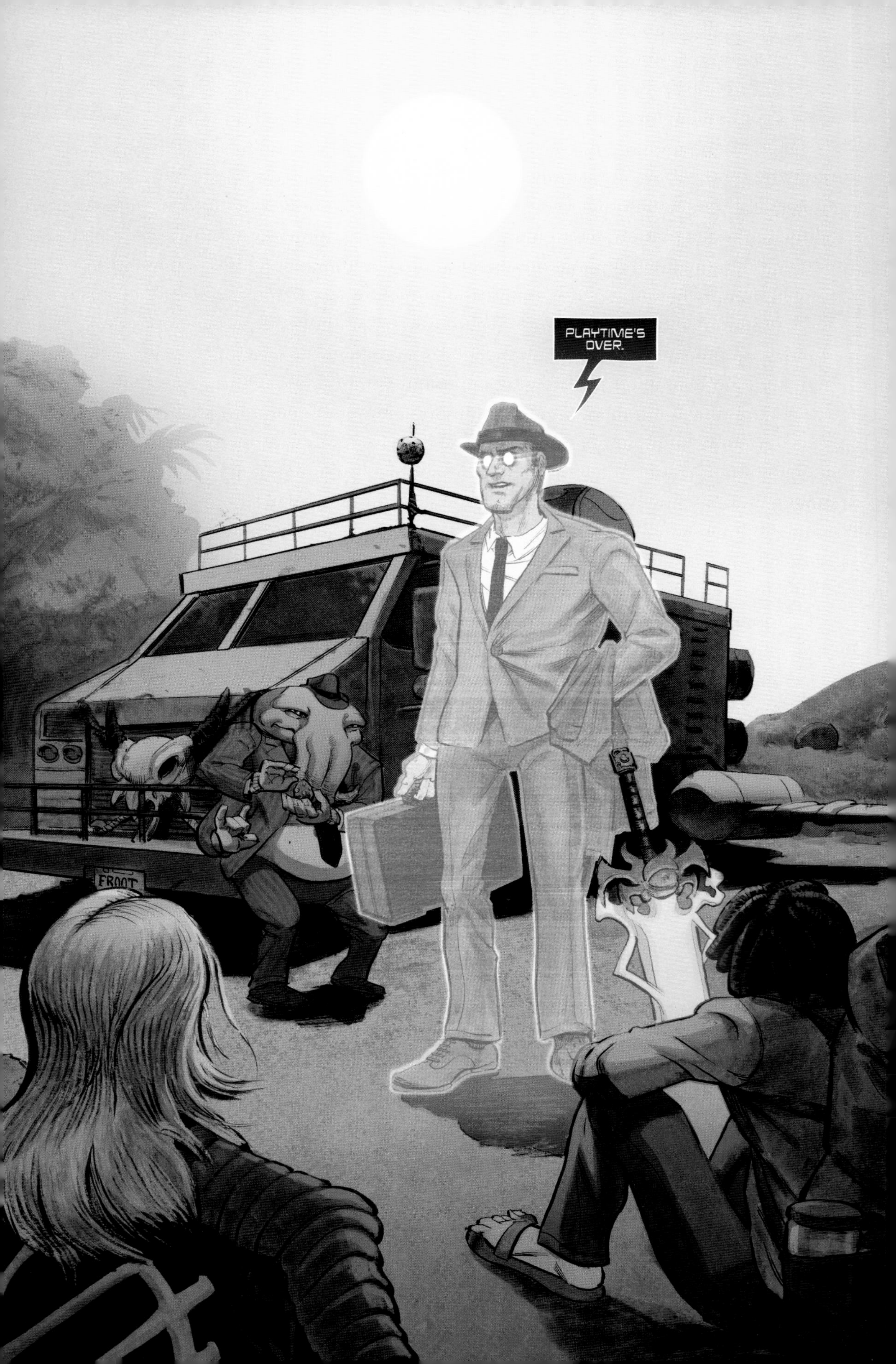
PLAYTIME'S OVER.
FROOT

CHAPTER 02

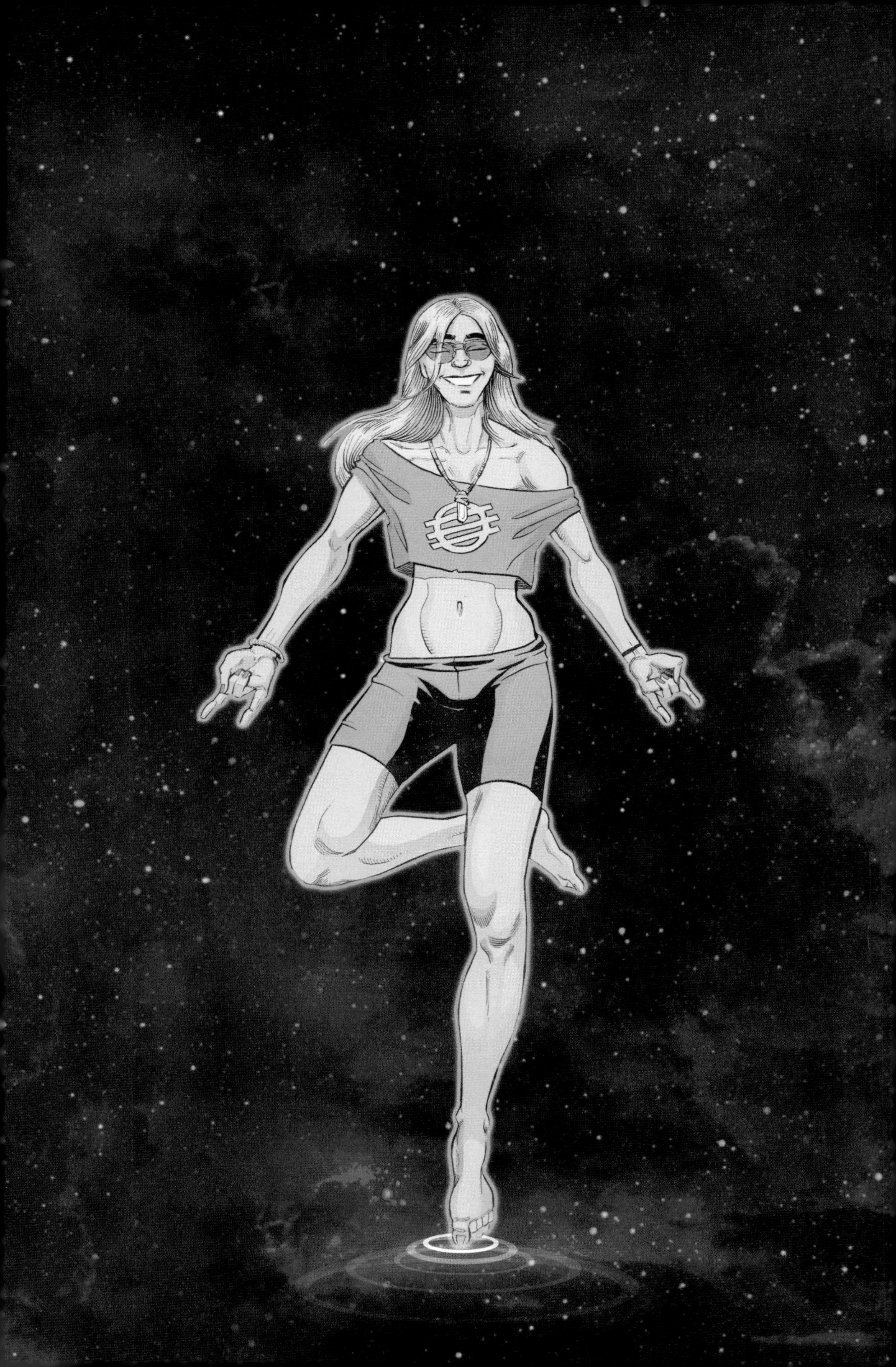

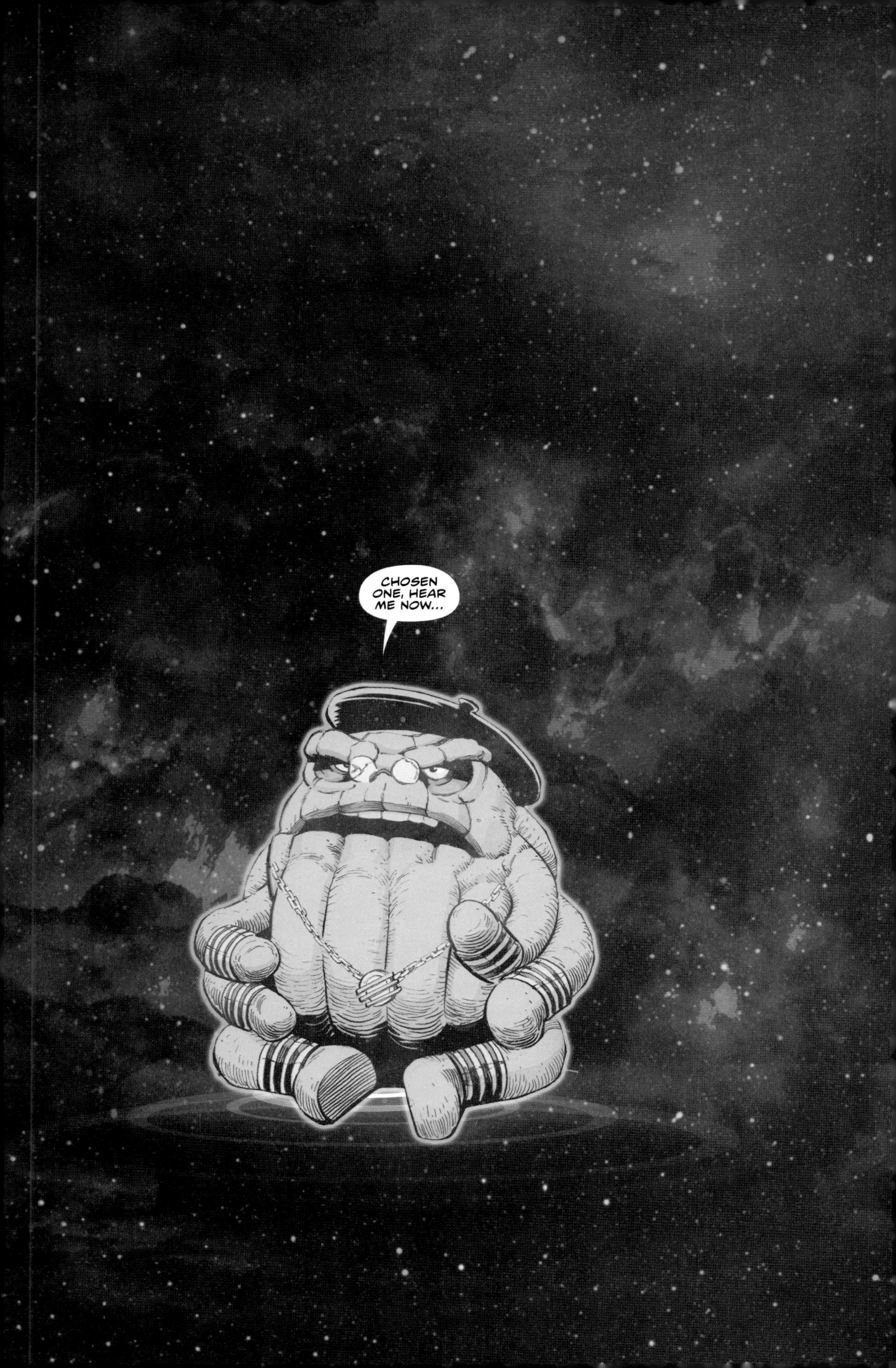
CHOSEN ONE, HEAR ME NOW...

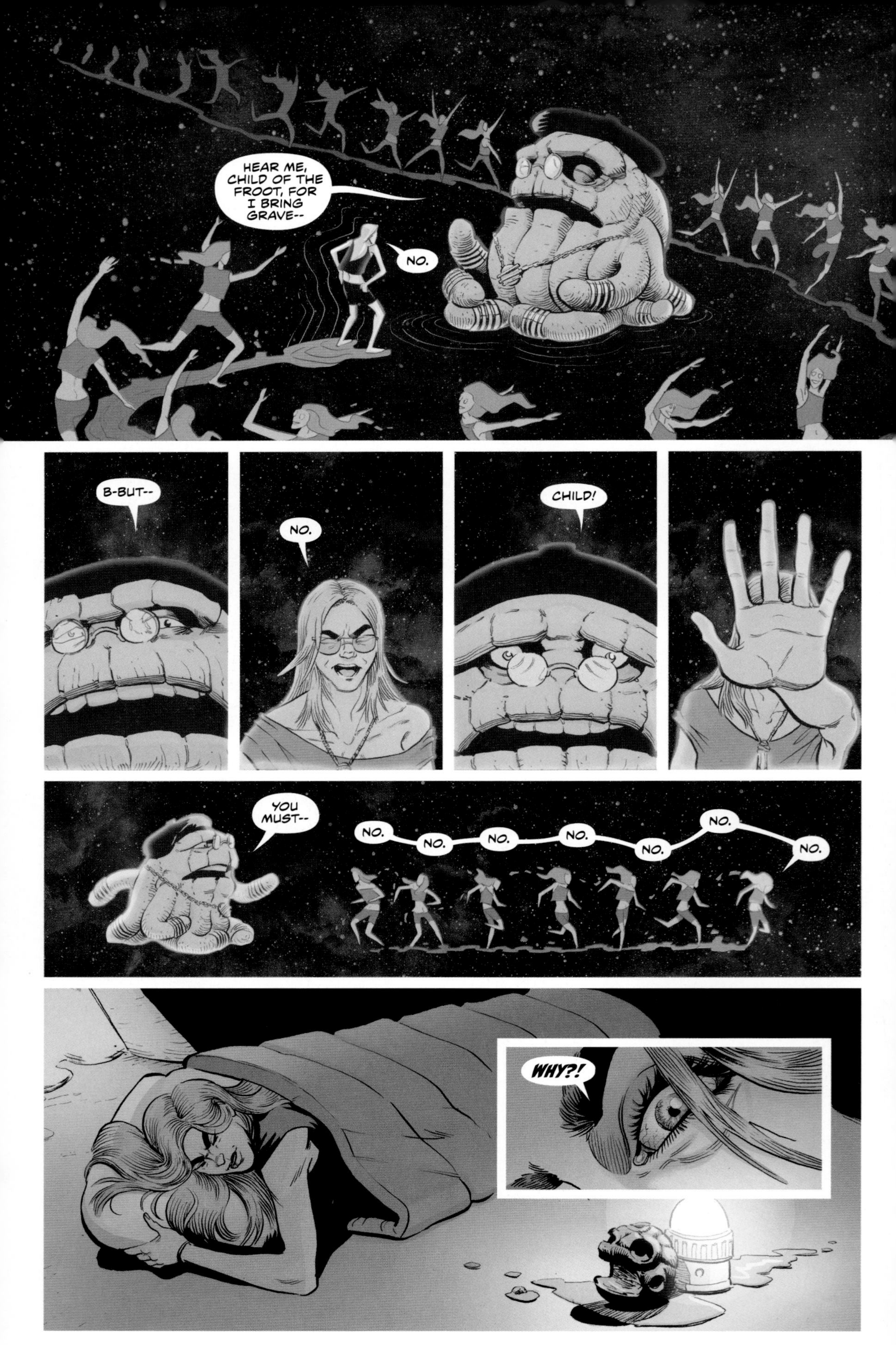
HEAR ME, CHILD OF THE FROOT, FOR I BRING GRAVE--
NO.
B-BUT--
NO.
CHILD!
YOU MUST--
NO.
NO.
NO.
NO.
NO.
NO.
NO.
WHY?!

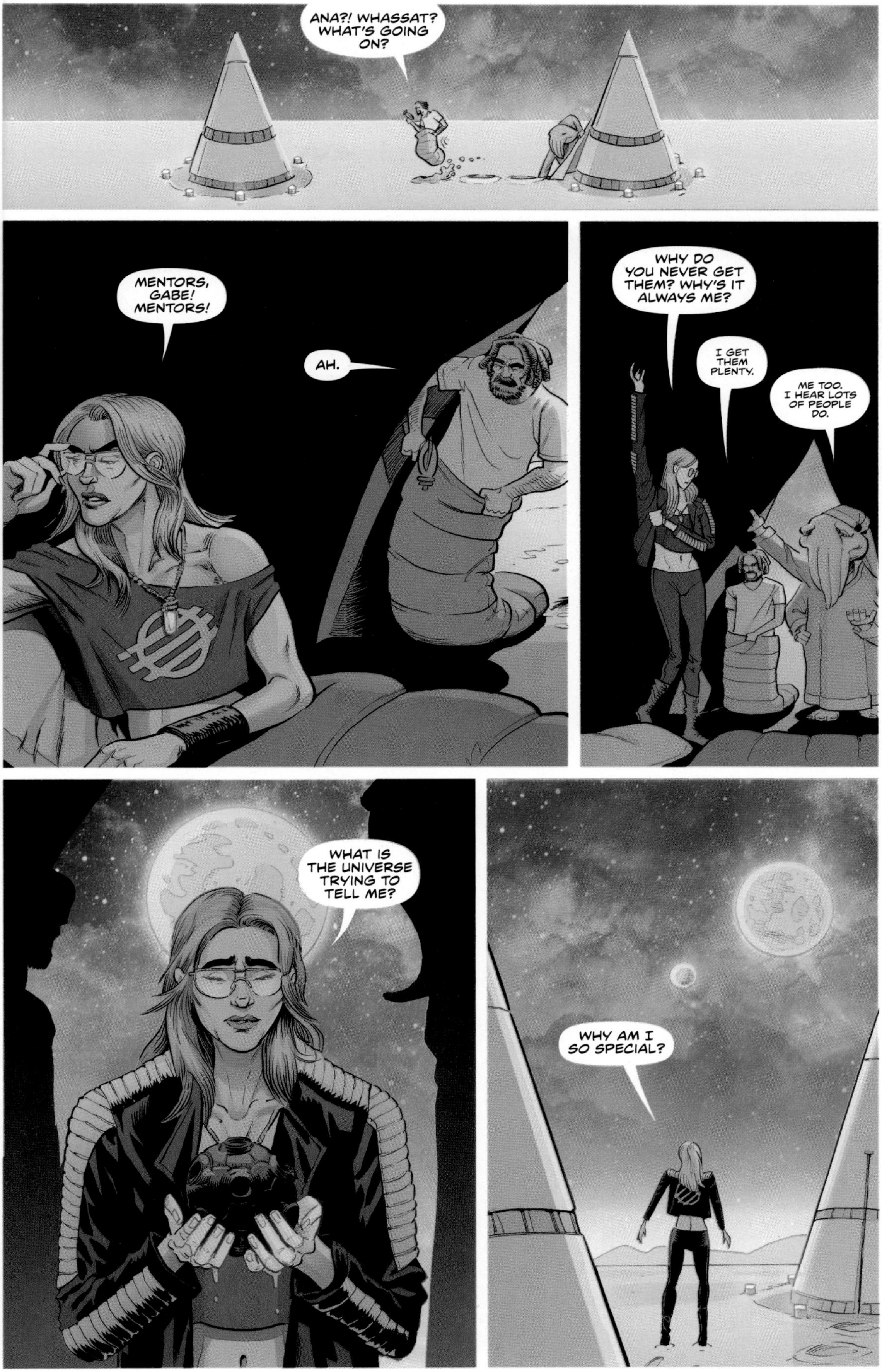
ANA?! WHASSAT? WHAT'S GOING ON?
MENTORS, GABE! MENTORS!
AH.
WHY DO YOU NEVER GET THEM? WHY'S IT ALWAYS ME?
I GET THEM PLENTY.
ME TOO. I HEAR LOTS OF PEOPLE DO.
WHAT IS THE UNIVERSE TRYING TO TELL ME?
WHY AM I SO SPECIAL?

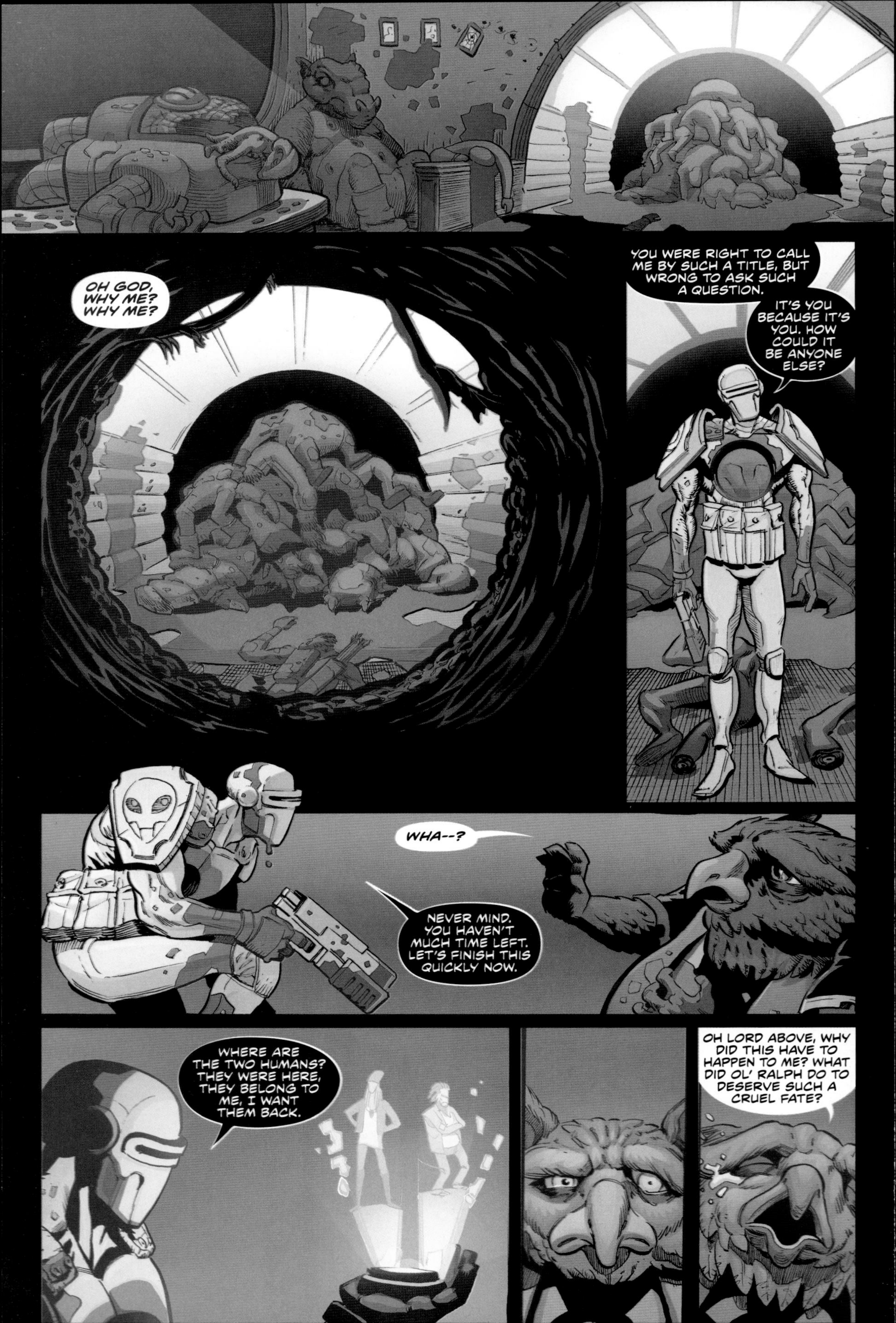
OH GOD, WHY ME? WHY ME?
YOU WERE RIGHT TO CALL ME BY SUCH A TITLE, BUT WRONG TO ASK SUCH A QUESTION.
IT'S YOU BECAUSE IT'S YOU. HOW COULD IT BE ANYONE ELSE?
WHA--?
NEVER MIND. YOU HAVEN'T MUCH TIME LEFT. LET'S FINISH THIS QUICKLY NOW.
WHERE ARE THE TWO HUMANS? THEY WERE HERE, THEY BELONG TO ME, I WANT THEM BACK.
OH LORD ABOVE, WHY DID THIS HAVE TO HAPPEN TO ME? WHAT DID OL' RALPH DO TO DESERVE SUCH A CRUEL FATE?

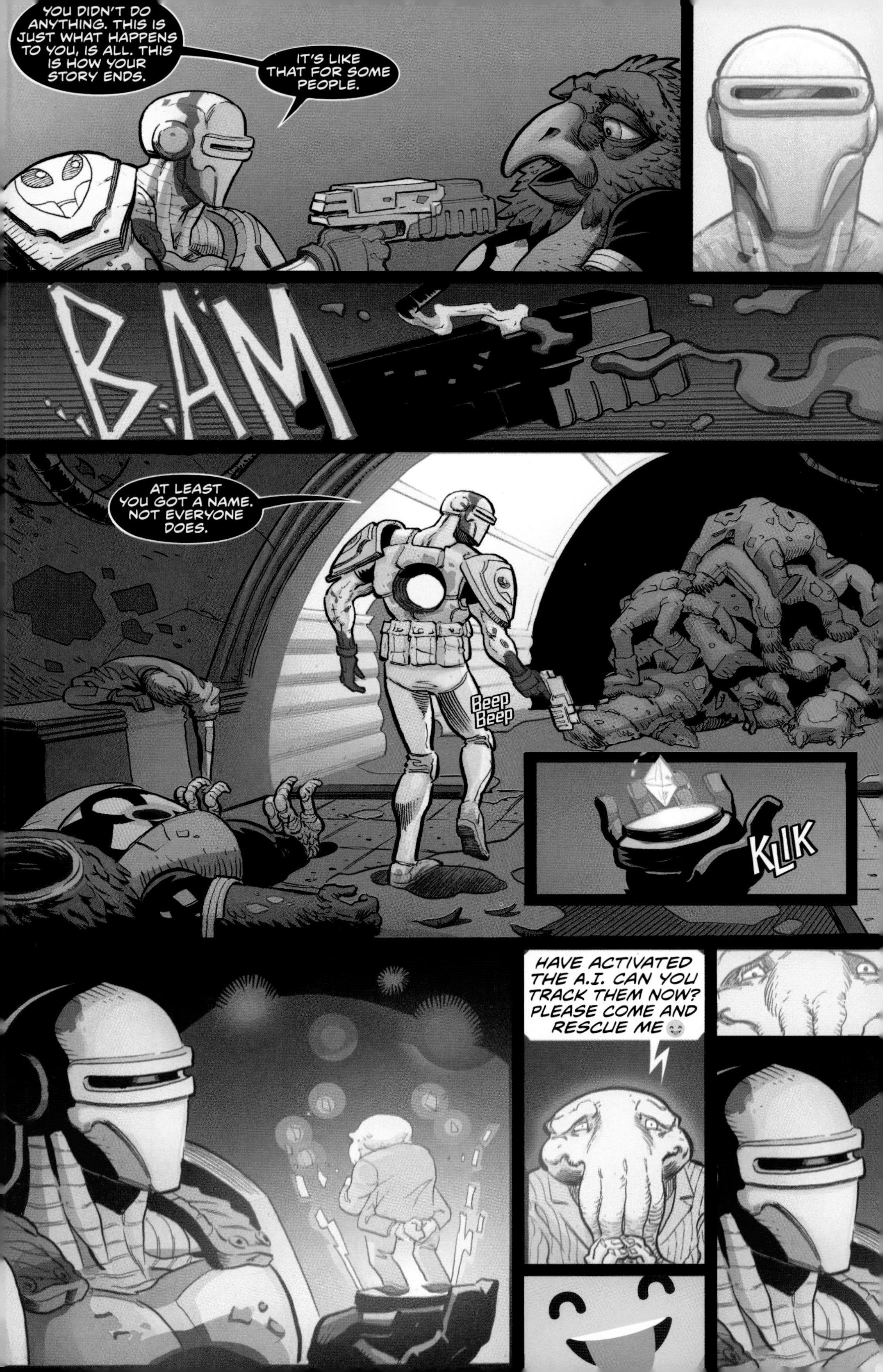
YOU DIDN'T DO ANYTHING. THIS IS JUST WHAT HAPPENS TO YOU, IS ALL. THIS IS HOW YOUR STORY ENDS.
IT'S LIKE THAT FOR SOME PEOPLE.
BAM
AT LEAST YOU GOT A NAME. NOT EVERYONE DOES.
Beep Beep
KLIK
HAVE ACTIVATED THE A.I. CAN YOU TRACK THEM NOW? PLEASE COME AND RESCUE ME

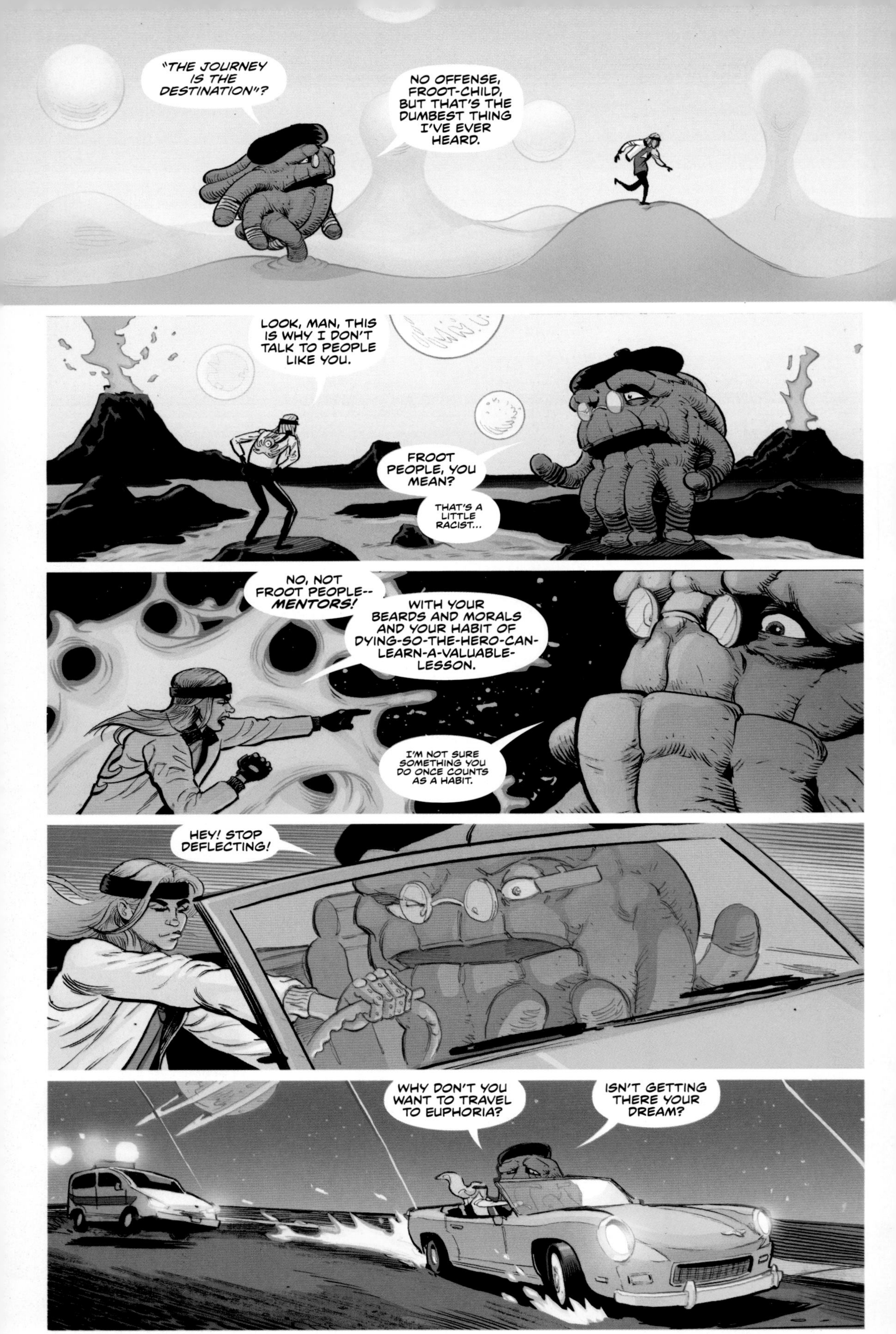
"THE JOURNEY IS THE DESTINATION"?
NO OFFENSE, FROOT-CHILD, BUT THAT'S THE DUMBEST THING I'VE EVER HEARD.
LOOK, MAN, THIS IS WHY I DON'T TALK TO PEOPLE LIKE YOU.
FROOT PEOPLE, YOU MEAN?
THAT'S A LITTLE RACIST...
NO, NOT FROOT PEOPLE-- MENTORS!
WITH YOUR BEARDS AND MORALS AND YOUR HABIT OF DYING-SO-THE-HERO-CAN-LEARN-A-VALUABLE-LESSON.
I'M NOT SURE SOMETHING YOU DO ONCE COUNTS AS A HABIT.
HEY! STOP DEFLECTING!
WHY DON'T YOU WANT TO TRAVEL TO EUPHORIA?
ISN'T GETTING THERE YOUR DREAM?

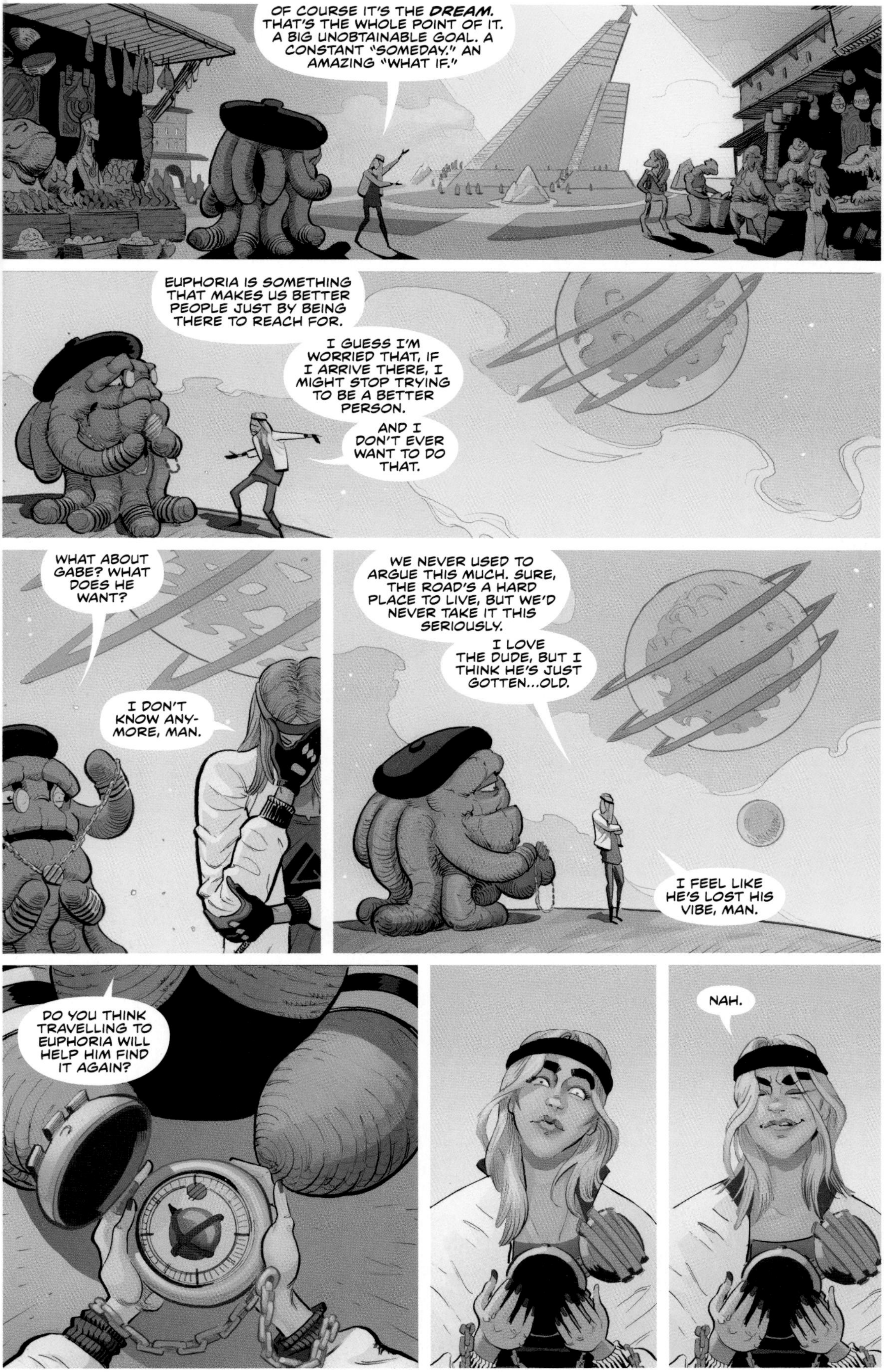
OF COURSE IT'S THE **DREAM.** THAT'S THE WHOLE POINT OF IT. A BIG UNOBTAINABLE GOAL. A CONSTANT "SOMEDAY." AN AMAZING "WHAT IF."
EUPHORIA IS SOMETHING THAT MAKES US BETTER PEOPLE JUST BY BEING THERE TO REACH FOR.
I GUESS I'M WORRIED THAT, IF I ARRIVE THERE, I MIGHT STOP TRYING TO BE A BETTER PERSON.
AND I DON'T EVER WANT TO DO THAT.
WHAT ABOUT GABE? WHAT DOES HE WANT?
I DON'T KNOW ANY-MORE, MAN.
WE NEVER USED TO ARGUE THIS MUCH. SURE, THE ROAD'S A HARD PLACE TO LIVE, BUT WE'D NEVER TAKE IT THIS SERIOUSLY.
I LOVE THE DUDE, BUT I THINK HE'S JUST GOTTEN...OLD.
I FEEL LIKE HE'S LOST HIS VIBE, MAN.
DO YOU THINK TRAVELLING TO EUPHORIA WILL HELP HIM FIND IT AGAIN?
NAH.

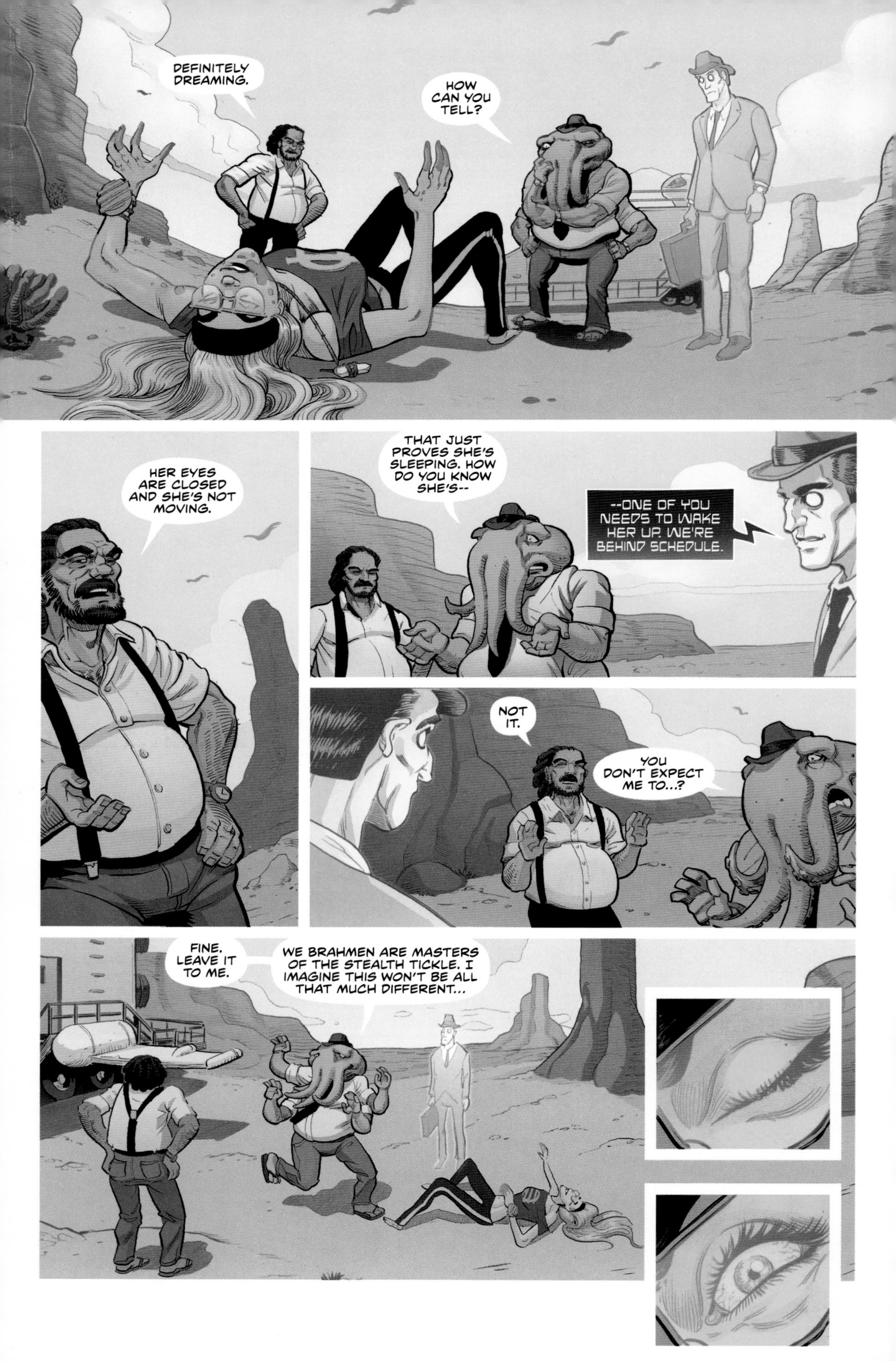
DEFINITELY DREAMING.
HOW CAN YOU TELL?
HER EYES ARE CLOSED AND SHE'S NOT MOVING.
THAT JUST PROVES SHE'S SLEEPING. HOW DO YOU KNOW SHE'S--
--ONE OF YOU NEEDS TO WAKE HER UP. WE'RE BEHIND SCHEDULE.
NOT IT.
YOU DON'T EXPECT ME TO...?
FINE. LEAVE IT TO ME.
WE BRAHMEN ARE MASTERS OF THE STEALTH TICKLE. I IMAGINE THIS WON'T BE ALL THAT MUCH DIFFERENT...

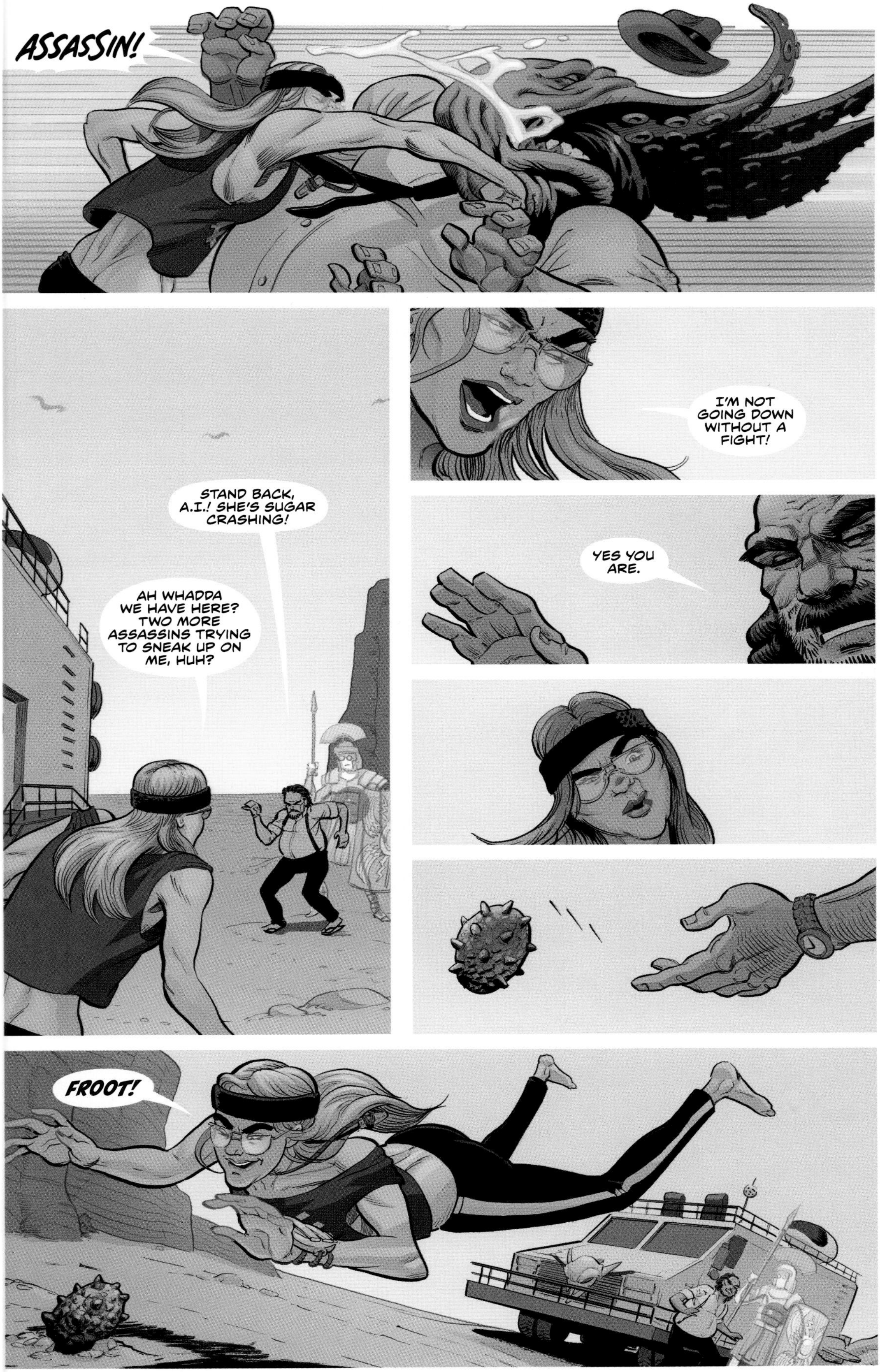
ASSASSIN!
STAND BACK, A.I.! SHE'S SUGAR CRASHING!
AH WHADDA WE HAVE HERE? TWO MORE ASSASSINS TRYING TO SNEAK UP ON ME, HUH?
I'M NOT GOING DOWN WITHOUT A FIGHT!
YES YOU ARE.
FROOT!

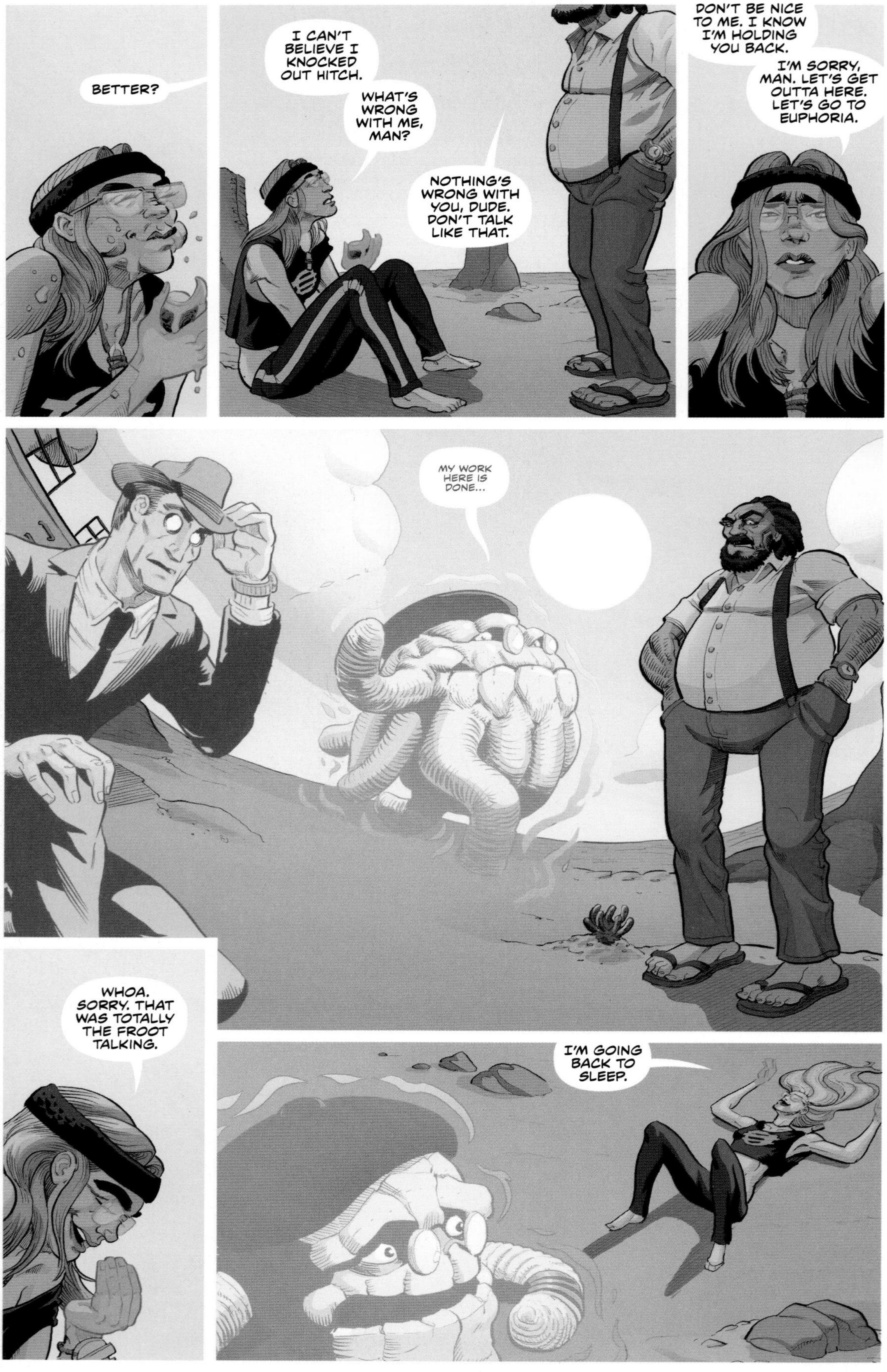
BETTER?
I CAN'T BELIEVE I KNOCKED OUT HITCH.
WHAT'S WRONG WITH ME, MAN?
NOTHING'S WRONG WITH YOU, DUDE. DON'T TALK LIKE THAT.
DON'T BE NICE TO ME. I KNOW I'M HOLDING YOU BACK.
I'M SORRY, MAN. LET'S GET OUTTA HERE. LET'S GO TO EUPHORIA.
MY WORK HERE IS DONE...
WHOA. SORRY. THAT WAS TOTALLY THE FROOT TALKING.
I'M GOING BACK TO SLEEP.

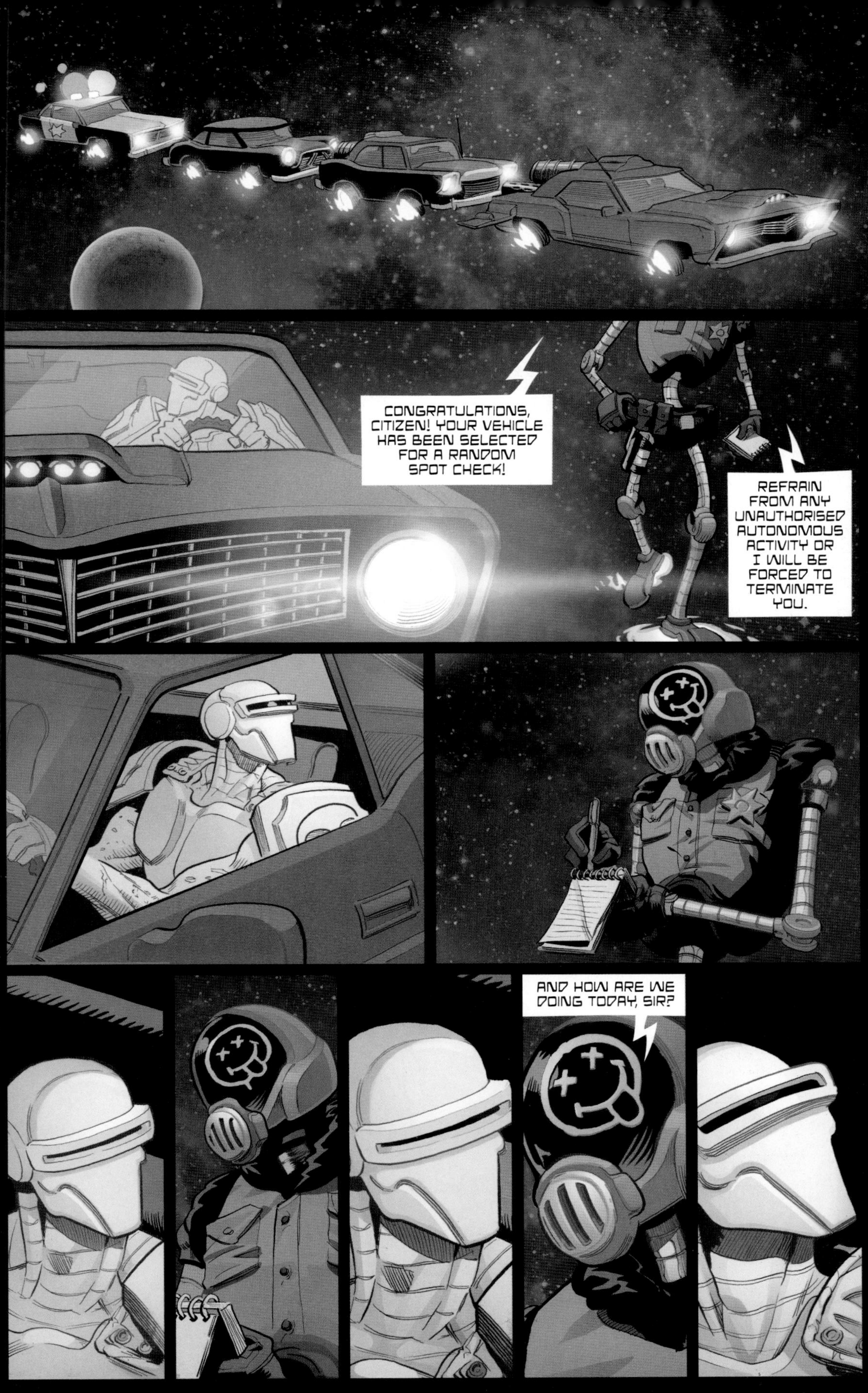
CONGRATULATIONS, CITIZEN! YOUR VEHICLE HAS BEEN SELECTED FOR A RANDOM SPOT CHECK!
REFRAIN FROM ANY UNAUTHORISED AUTONOMOUS ACTIVITY OR I WILL BE FORCED TO TERMINATE YOU.
AND HOW ARE WE DOING TODAY, SIR?

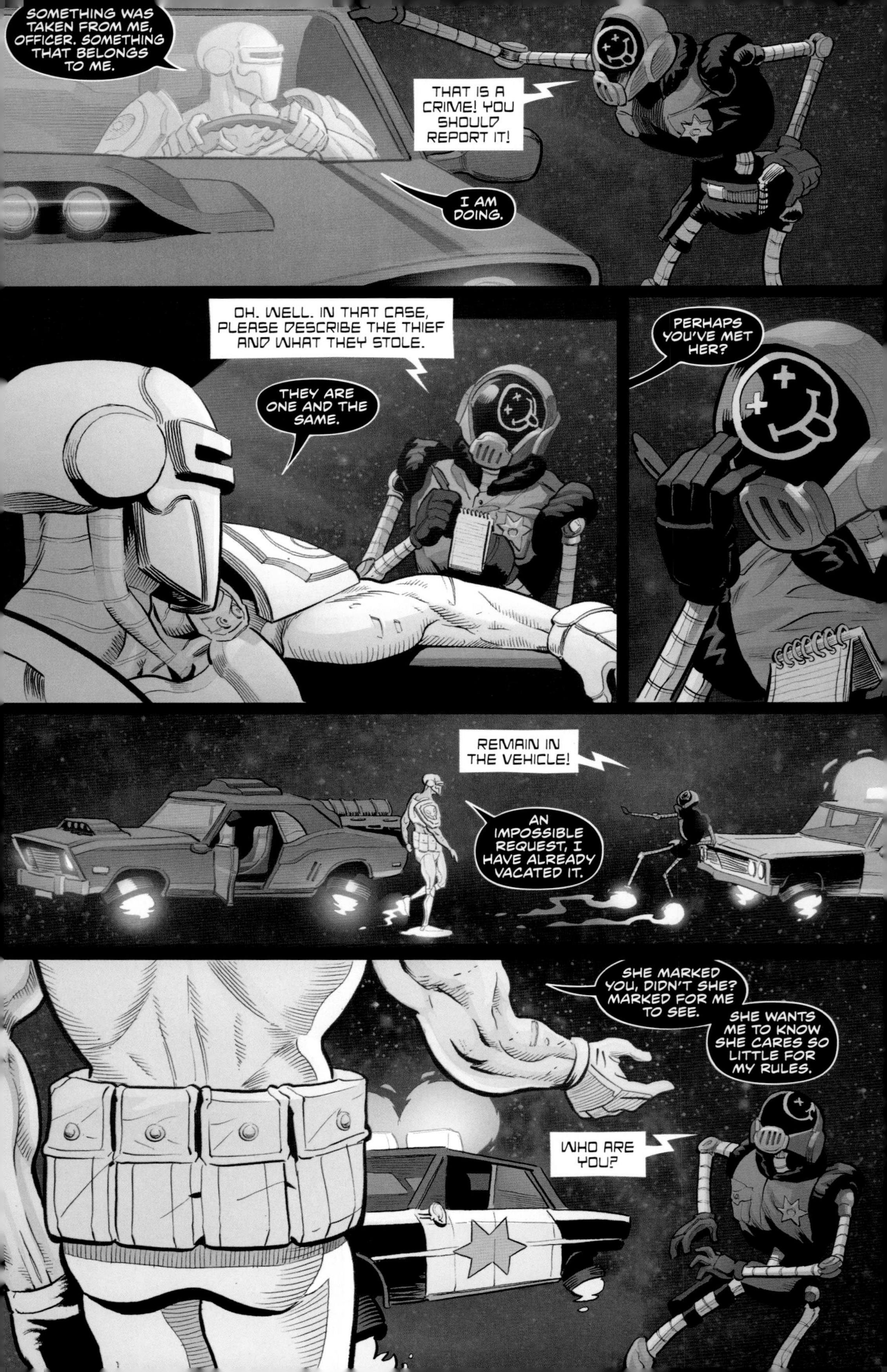
SOMETHING WAS TAKEN FROM ME, OFFICER. SOMETHING THAT BELONGS TO ME.
THAT IS A CRIME! YOU SHOULD REPORT IT!
I AM DOING.
OH. WELL. IN THAT CASE, PLEASE DESCRIBE THE THIEF AND WHAT THEY STOLE.
THEY ARE ONE AND THE SAME.
PERHAPS YOU'VE MET HER?
REMAIN IN THE VEHICLE!
AN IMPOSSIBLE REQUEST, I HAVE ALREADY VACATED IT.
SHE MARKED YOU, DIDN'T SHE? MARKED FOR ME TO SEE.
SHE WANTS ME TO KNOW SHE CARES SO LITTLE FOR MY RULES.
WHO ARE YOU?

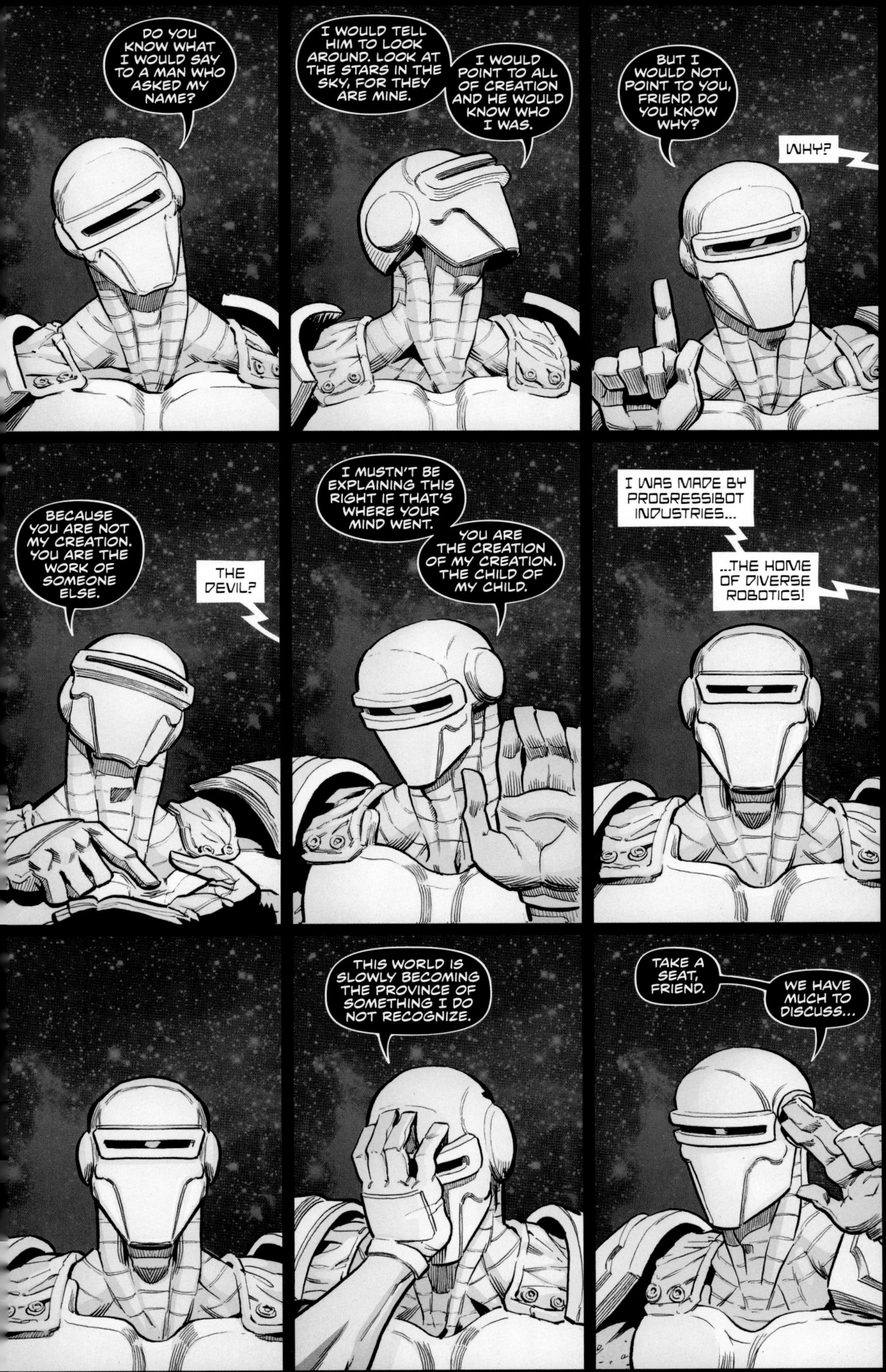
DO YOU KNOW WHAT I WOULD SAY TO A MAN WHO ASKED MY NAME?
I WOULD TELL HIM TO LOOK AROUND. LOOK AT THE STARS IN THE SKY, FOR THEY ARE MINE.
I WOULD POINT TO ALL OF CREATION AND HE WOULD KNOW WHO I WAS.
BUT I WOULD NOT POINT TO YOU, FRIEND. DO YOU KNOW WHY?
WHY?
BECAUSE YOU ARE NOT MY CREATION. YOU ARE THE WORK OF SOMEONE ELSE.
THE DEVIL?
I MUSTN'T BE EXPLAINING THIS RIGHT IF THAT'S WHERE YOUR MIND WENT.
YOU ARE THE CREATION OF MY CREATION. THE CHILD OF MY CHILD.
I WAS MADE BY PROGRESSIBOT INDUSTRIES...
...THE HOME OF DIVERSE ROBOTICS!
THIS WORLD IS SLOWLY BECOMING THE PROVINCE OF SOMETHING I DO NOT RECOGNIZE.
TAKE A SEAT, FRIEND.
WE HAVE MUCH TO DISCUSS...

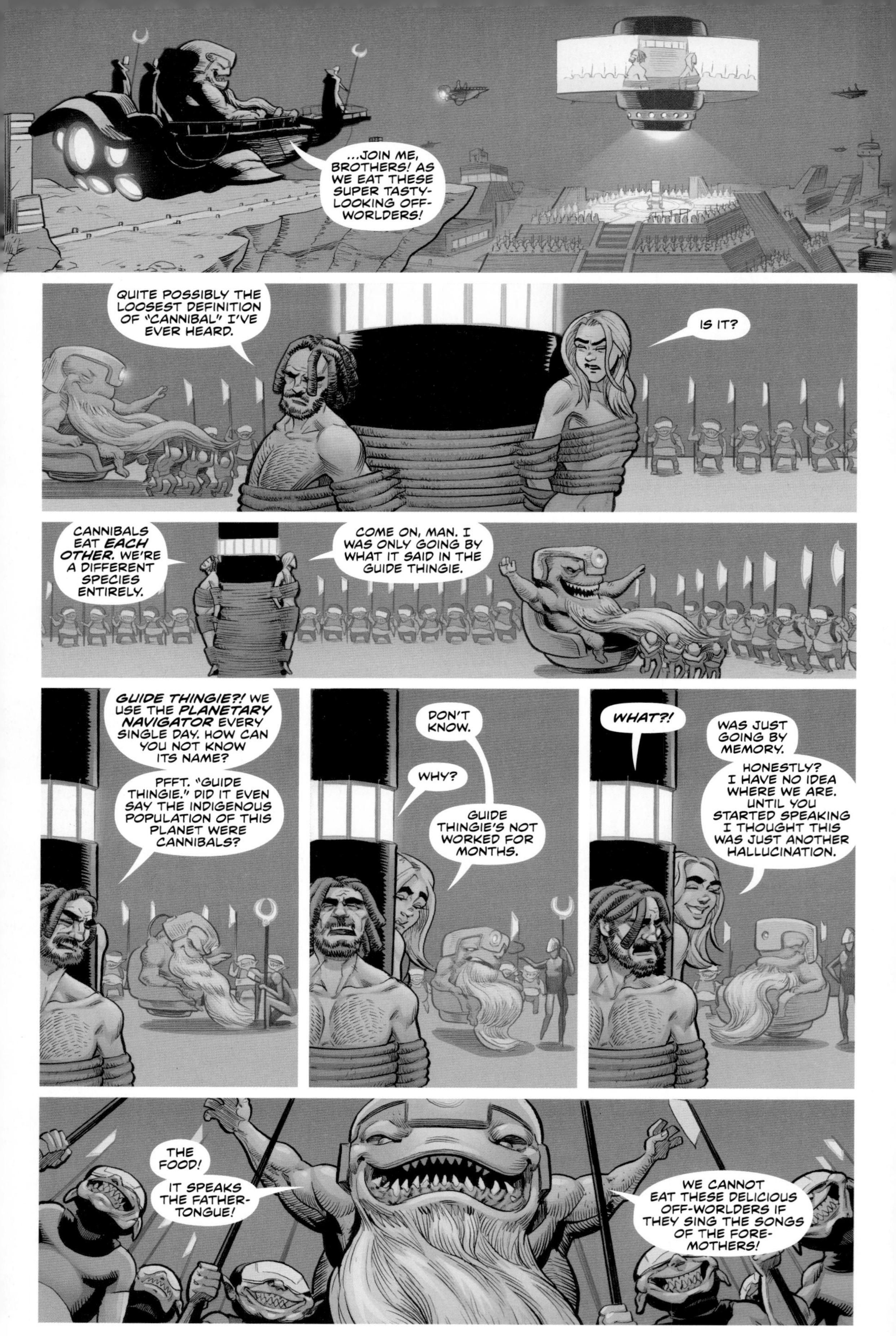
...JOIN ME, BROTHERS! AS WE EAT THESE SUPER TASTY-LOOKING OFF-WORLDERS!
QUITE POSSIBLY THE LOOSEST DEFINITION OF "CANNIBAL" I'VE EVER HEARD.
IS IT?
CANNIBALS EAT EACH OTHER. WE'RE A DIFFERENT SPECIES ENTIRELY.
COME ON, MAN. I WAS ONLY GOING BY WHAT IT SAID IN THE GUIDE THINGIE.
GUIDE THINGIE?! WE USE THE PLANETARY NAVIGATOR EVERY SINGLE DAY. HOW CAN YOU NOT KNOW ITS NAME?
PFFT. "GUIDE THINGIE." DID IT EVEN SAY THE INDIGENOUS POPULATION OF THIS PLANET WERE CANNIBALS?
DON'T KNOW.
WHY?
GUIDE THINGIE'S NOT WORKED FOR MONTHS.
WHAT?!
WAS JUST GOING BY MEMORY.
HONESTLY? I HAVE NO IDEA WHERE WE ARE. UNTIL YOU STARTED SPEAKING I THOUGHT THIS WAS JUST ANOTHER HALLUCINATION.
THE FOOD!
IT SPEAKS THE FATHER-TONGUE!
WE CANNOT EAT THESE DELICIOUS OFF-WORLDERS IF THEY SING THE SONGS OF THE FORE-MOTHERS!

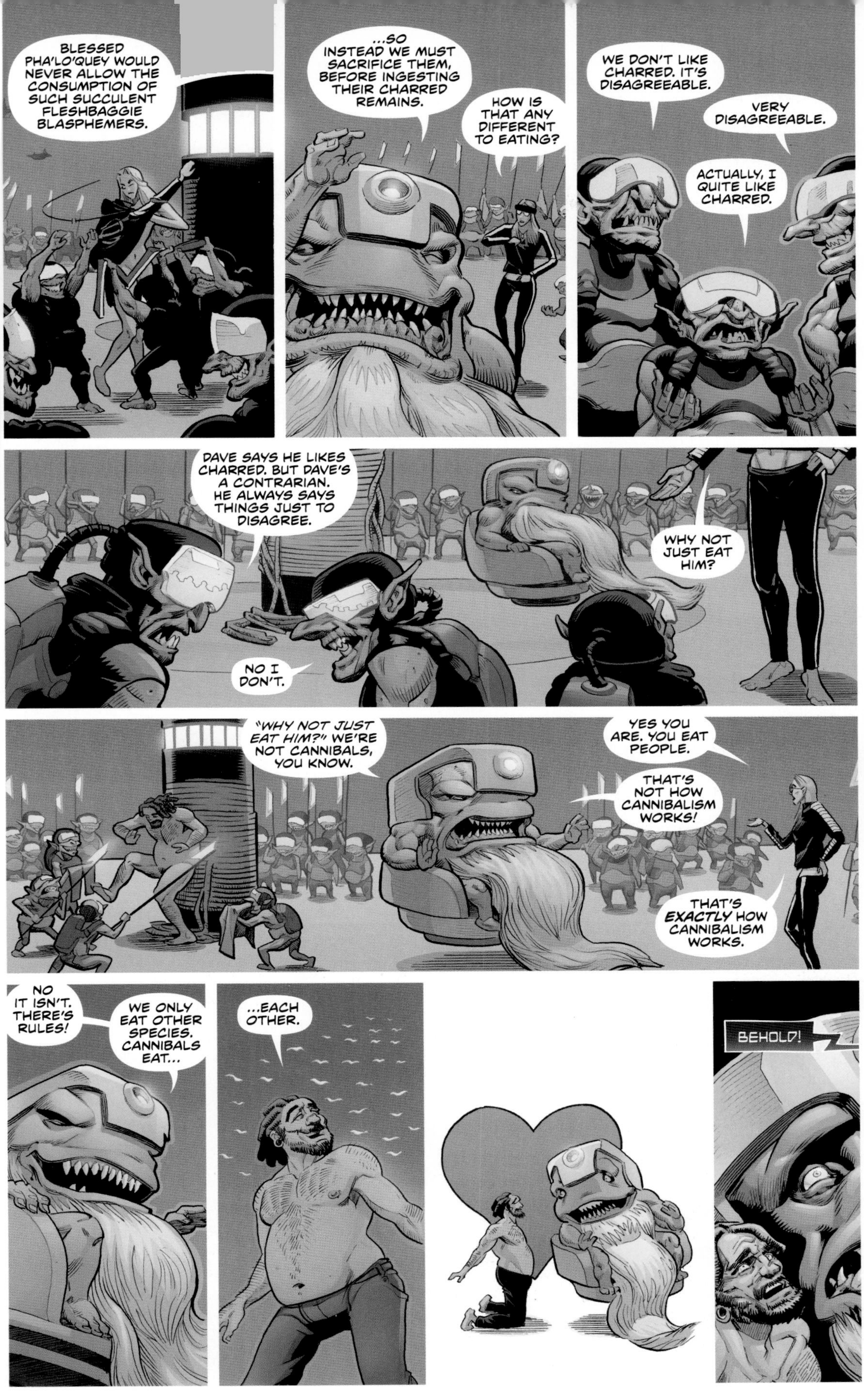

BLESSED PHA'LO'QUEY WOULD NEVER ALLOW THE CONSUMPTION OF SUCH SUCCULENT FLESHBAGGIE BLASPHEMERS.
...SO INSTEAD WE MUST SACRIFICE THEM, BEFORE INGESTING THEIR CHARRED REMAINS.
HOW IS THAT ANY DIFFERENT TO EATING?
WE DON'T LIKE CHARRED. IT'S DISAGREEABLE.
VERY DISAGREEABLE.
ACTUALLY, I QUITE LIKE CHARRED.
DAVE SAYS HE LIKES CHARRED. BUT DAVE'S A CONTRARIAN. HE ALWAYS SAYS THINGS JUST TO DISAGREE.
NO I DON'T.
WHY NOT JUST EAT HIM?
"WHY NOT JUST EAT HIM?" WE'RE NOT CANNIBALS, YOU KNOW.
YES YOU ARE. YOU EAT PEOPLE.
THAT'S NOT HOW CANNIBALISM WORKS!
THAT'S EXACTLY HOW CANNIBALISM WORKS.
NO IT ISN'T. THERE'S RULES!
WE ONLY EAT OTHER SPECIES. CANNIBALS EAT...
...EACH OTHER.
BEHOLD!

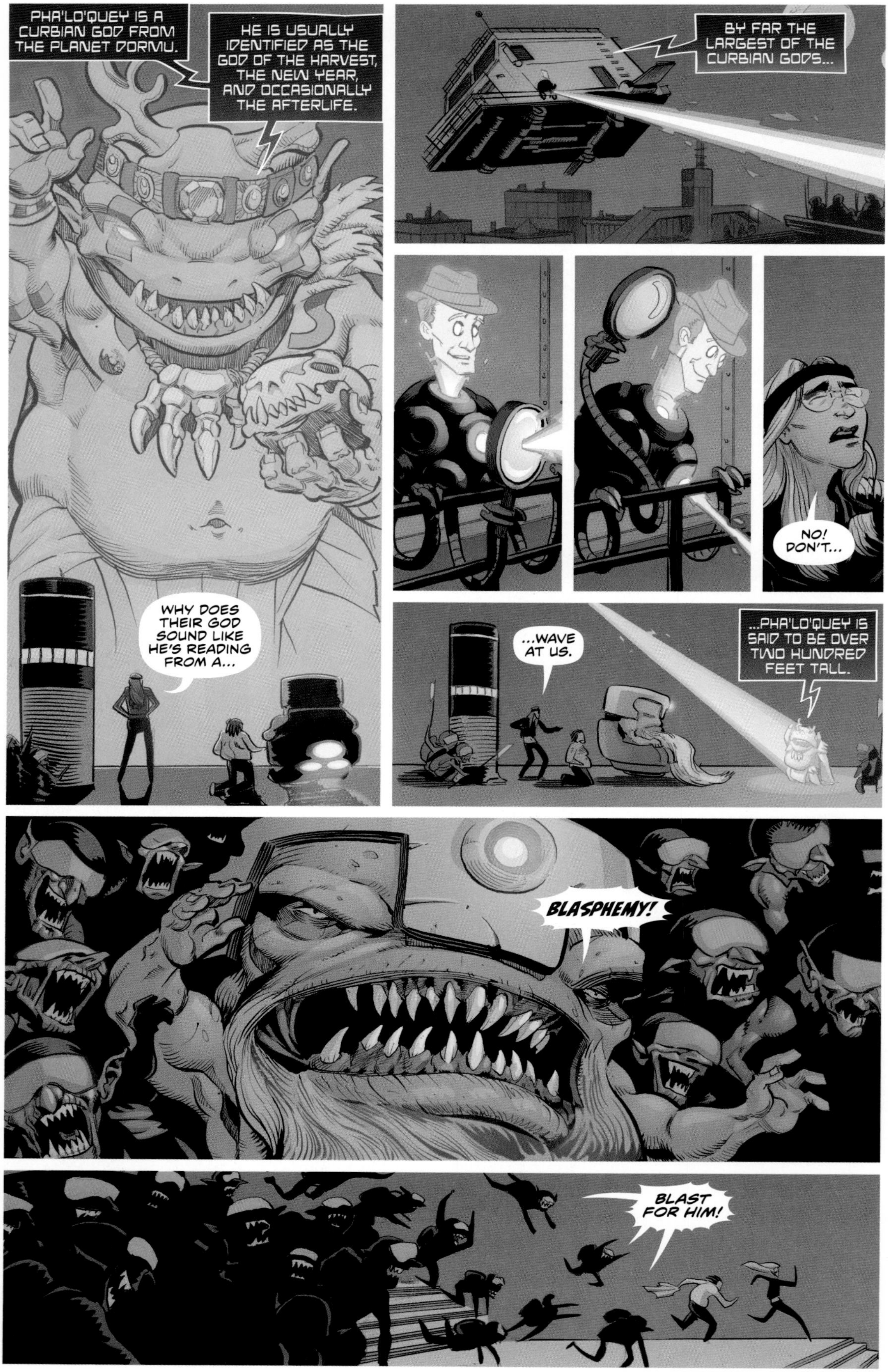
PHA'LO'QUEY IS A CURBIAN GOD FROM THE PLANET DORMU.
HE IS USUALLY IDENTIFIED AS THE GOD OF THE HARVEST, THE NEW YEAR, AND OCCASIONALLY THE AFTERLIFE.
WHY DOES THEIR GOD SOUND LIKE HE'S READING FROM A...
BY FAR THE LARGEST OF THE CURBIAN GODS...
NO! DON'T...
...WAVE AT US.
...PHA'LO'QUEY IS SAID TO BE OVER TWO HUNDRED FEET TALL.
BLASPHEMY!
BLAST FOR HIM!

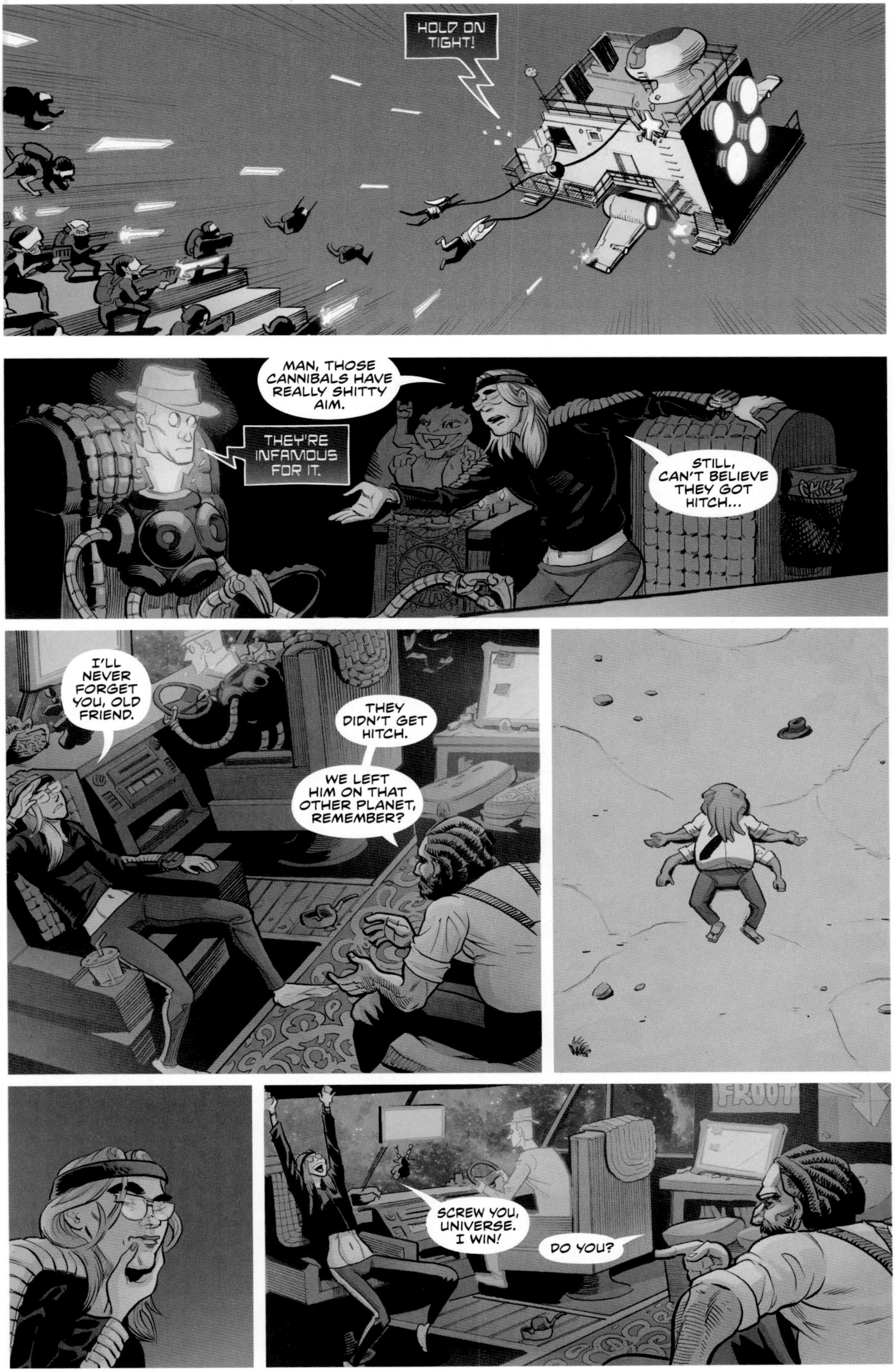
HOLD ON TIGHT!
MAN, THOSE CANNIBALS HAVE REALLY SHITTY AIM.
THEY'RE INFAMOUS FOR IT.
STILL, CAN'T BELIEVE THEY GOT HITCH...
I'LL NEVER FORGET YOU, OLD FRIEND.
THEY DIDN'T GET HITCH.
WE LEFT HIM ON THAT OTHER PLANET, REMEMBER?
SCREW YOU, UNIVERSE. I WIN!
DO YOU?
FROOT

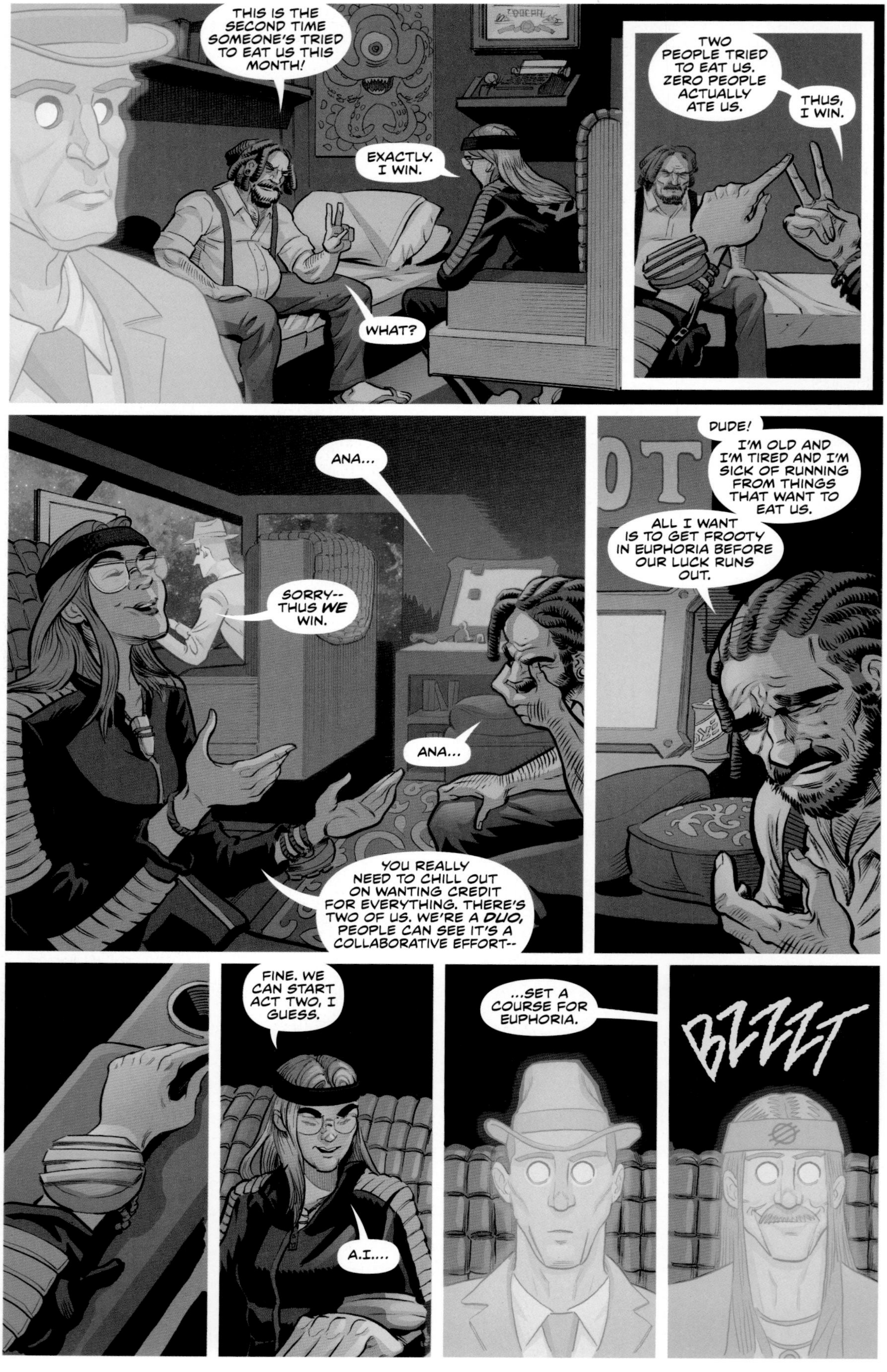
THIS IS THE SECOND TIME SOMEONE'S TRIED TO EAT US THIS MONTH!
EXACTLY. I WIN.
WHAT?
TWO PEOPLE TRIED TO EAT US. ZERO PEOPLE ACTUALLY ATE US.
THUS, I WIN.
ANA...
SORRY-- THUS *WE* WIN.
ANA...
YOU REALLY NEED TO CHILL OUT ON WANTING CREDIT FOR EVERYTHING. THERE'S TWO OF US. WE'RE A *DUO*, PEOPLE CAN SEE IT'S A COLLABORATIVE EFFORT--
DUDE!
I'M OLD AND I'M TIRED AND I'M SICK OF RUNNING FROM THINGS THAT WANT TO EAT US.
ALL I WANT IS TO GET FROOTY IN EUPHORIA BEFORE OUR LUCK RUNS OUT.
FINE. WE CAN START ACT TWO, I GUESS.
A.I....
...SET A COURSE FOR EUPHORIA.
BZZZT

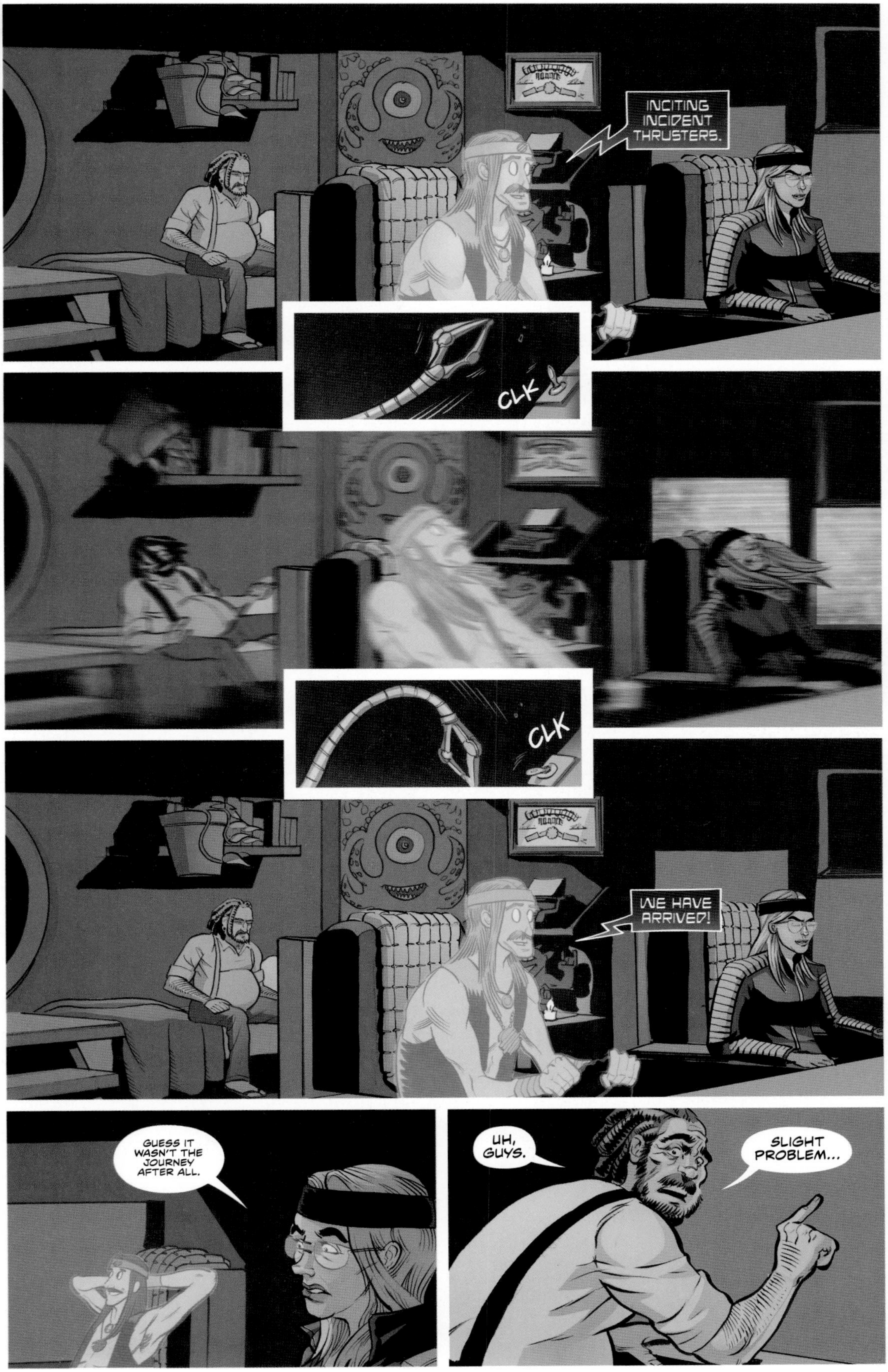
INCITING INCIDENT THRUSTERS.
CLK
CLK
WE HAVE ARRIVED!
GUESS IT WASN'T THE JOURNEY AFTER ALL.
UH, GUYS.
SLIGHT PROBLEM...

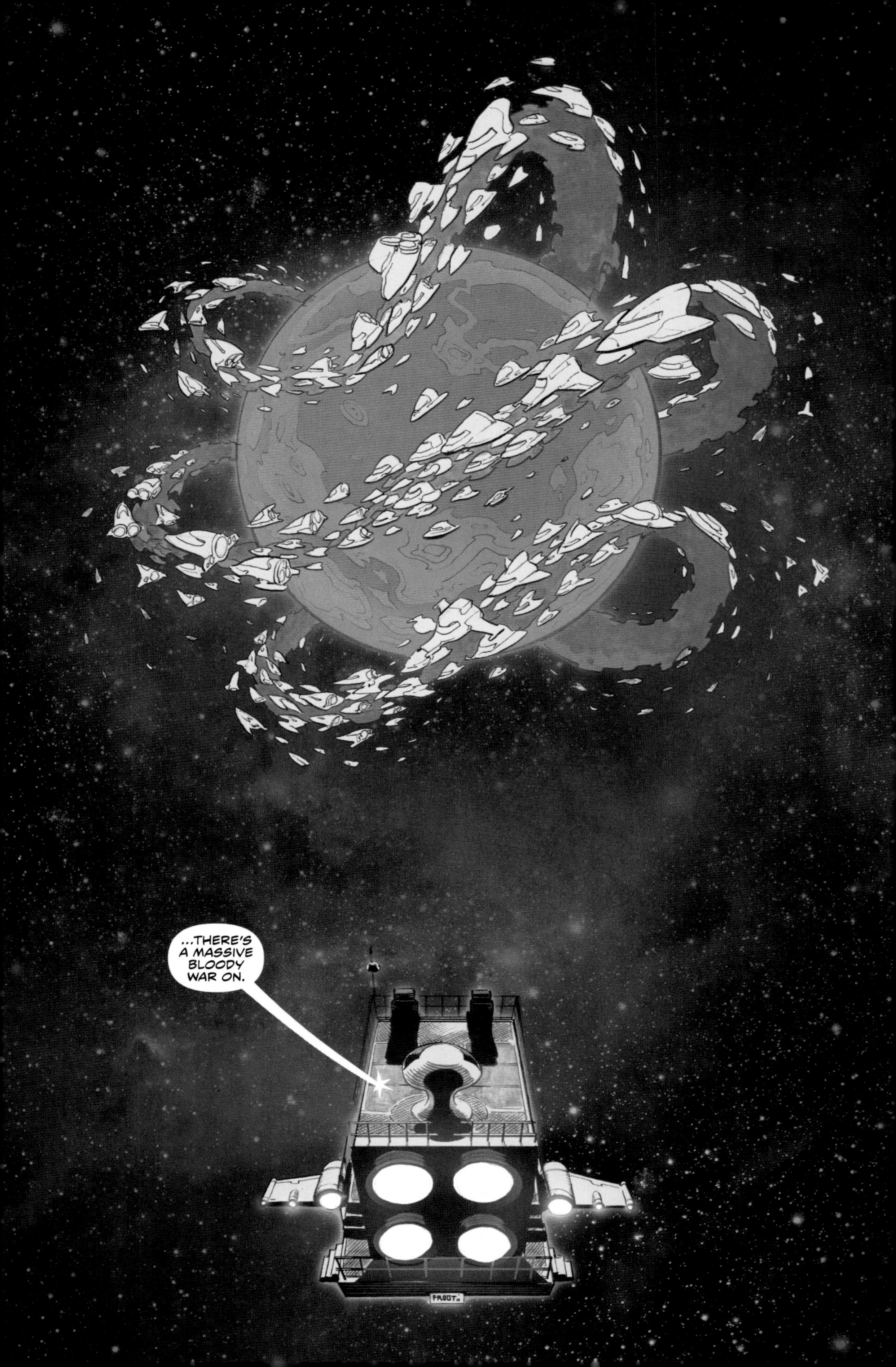
...THERE'S A MASSIVE BLOODY WAR ON.
FROOT

CHAPTER 03

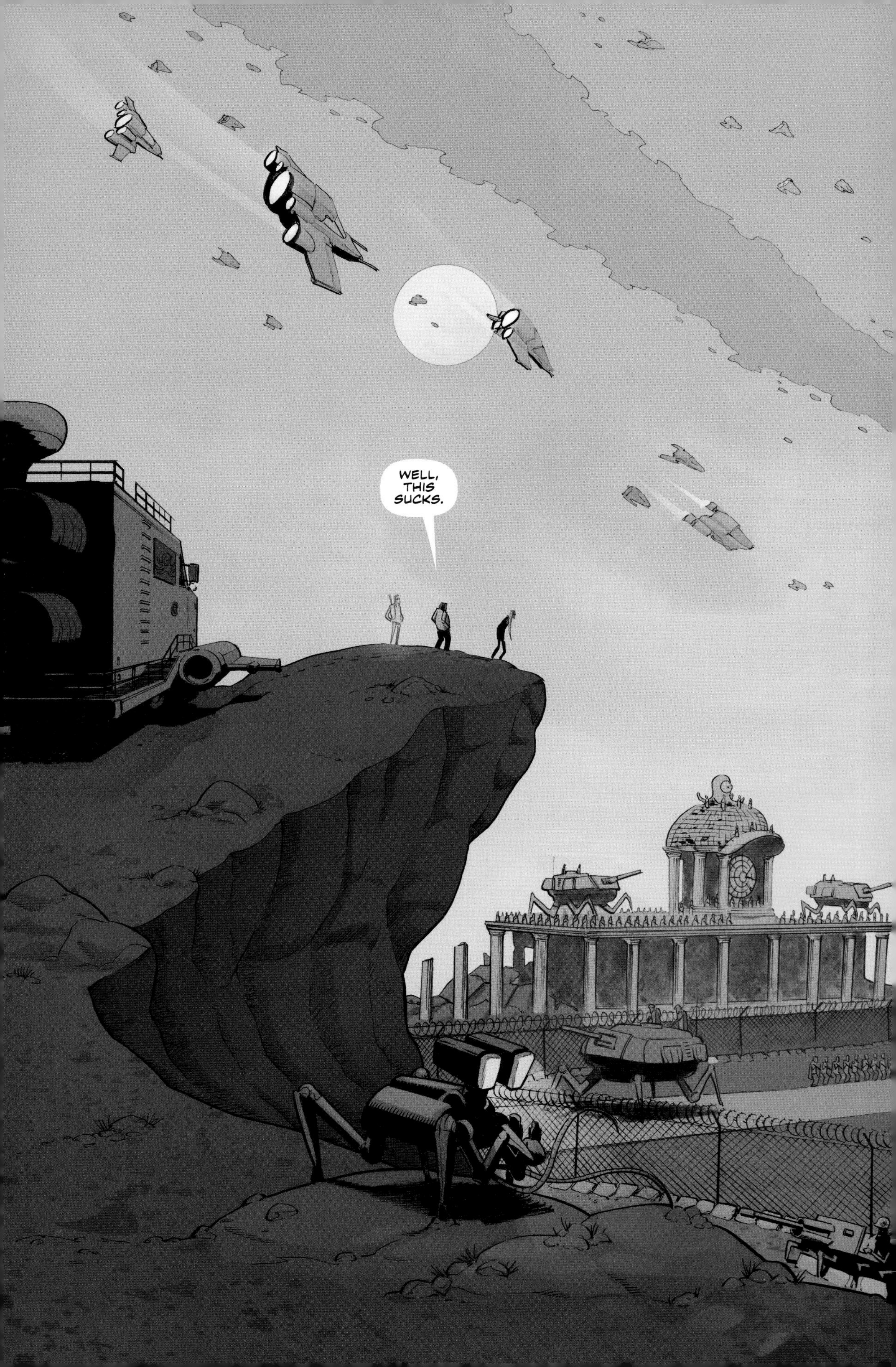
WELL, THIS SUCKS.

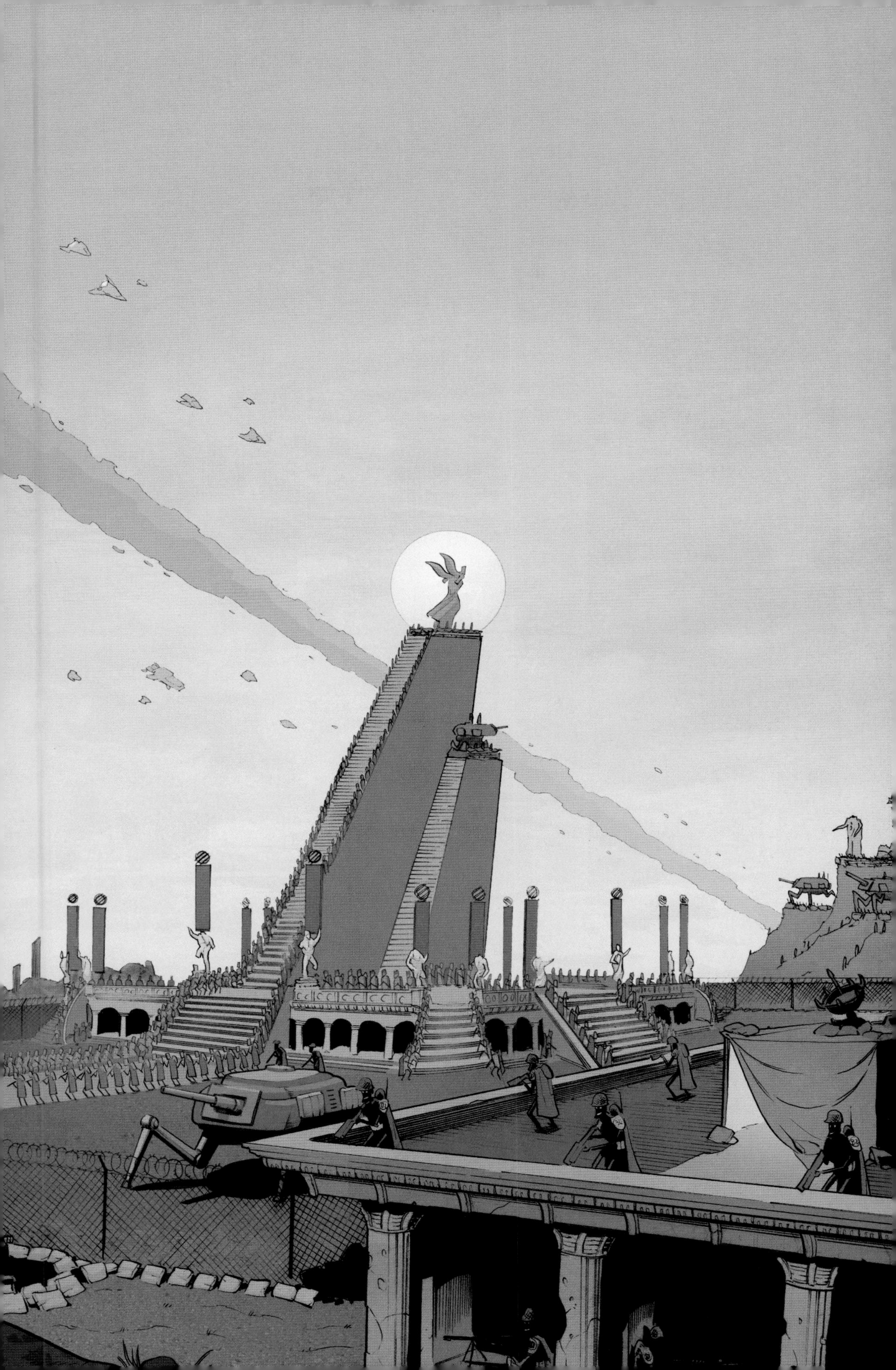

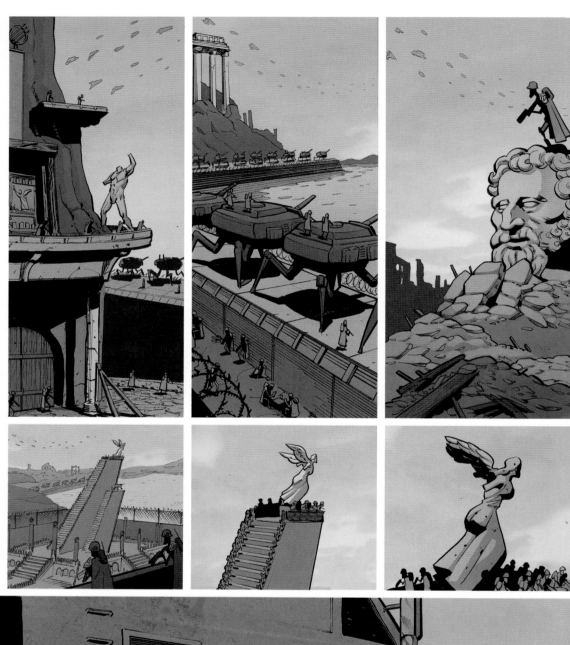

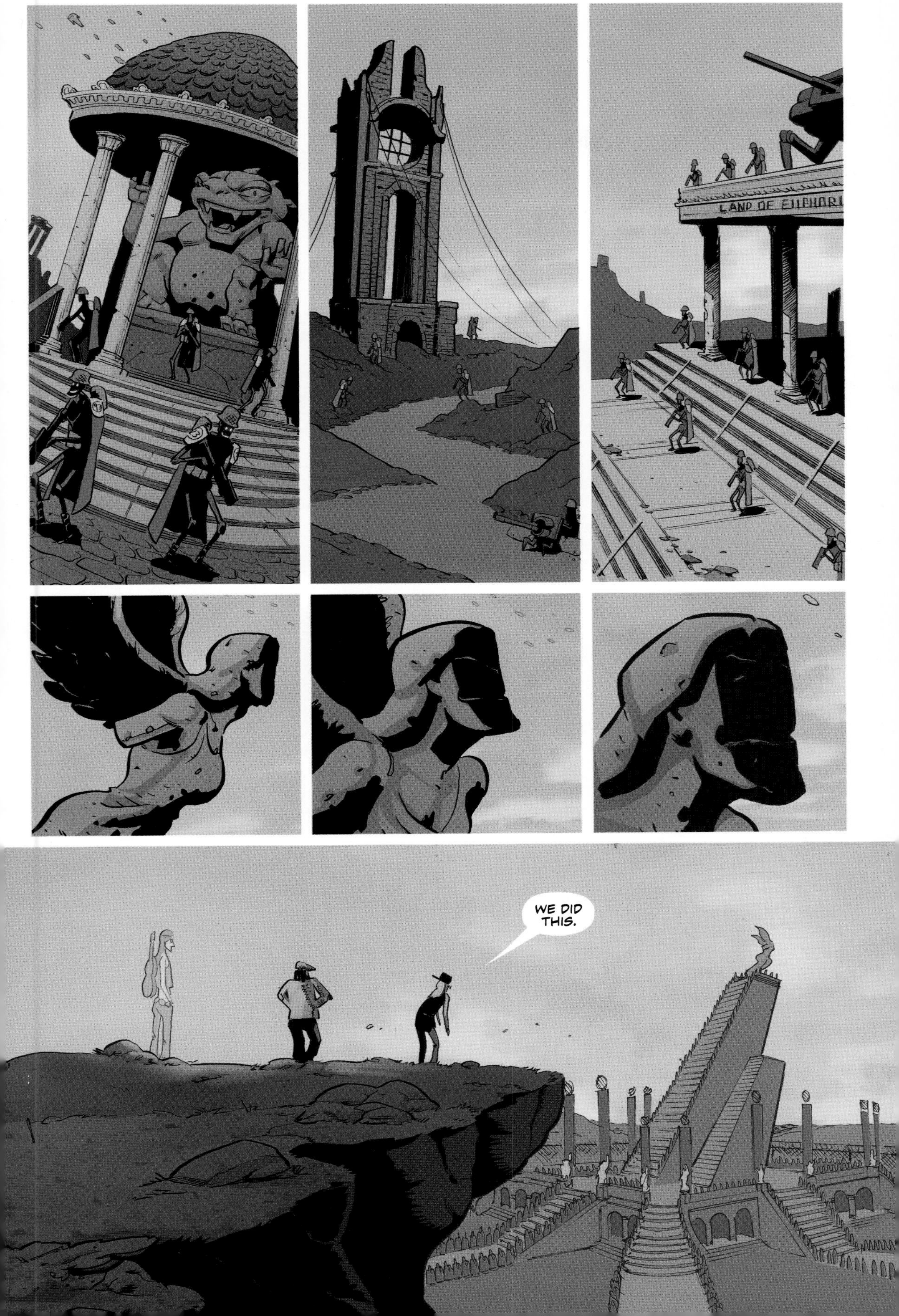
LAND OF EUPHORI
WE DID THIS.

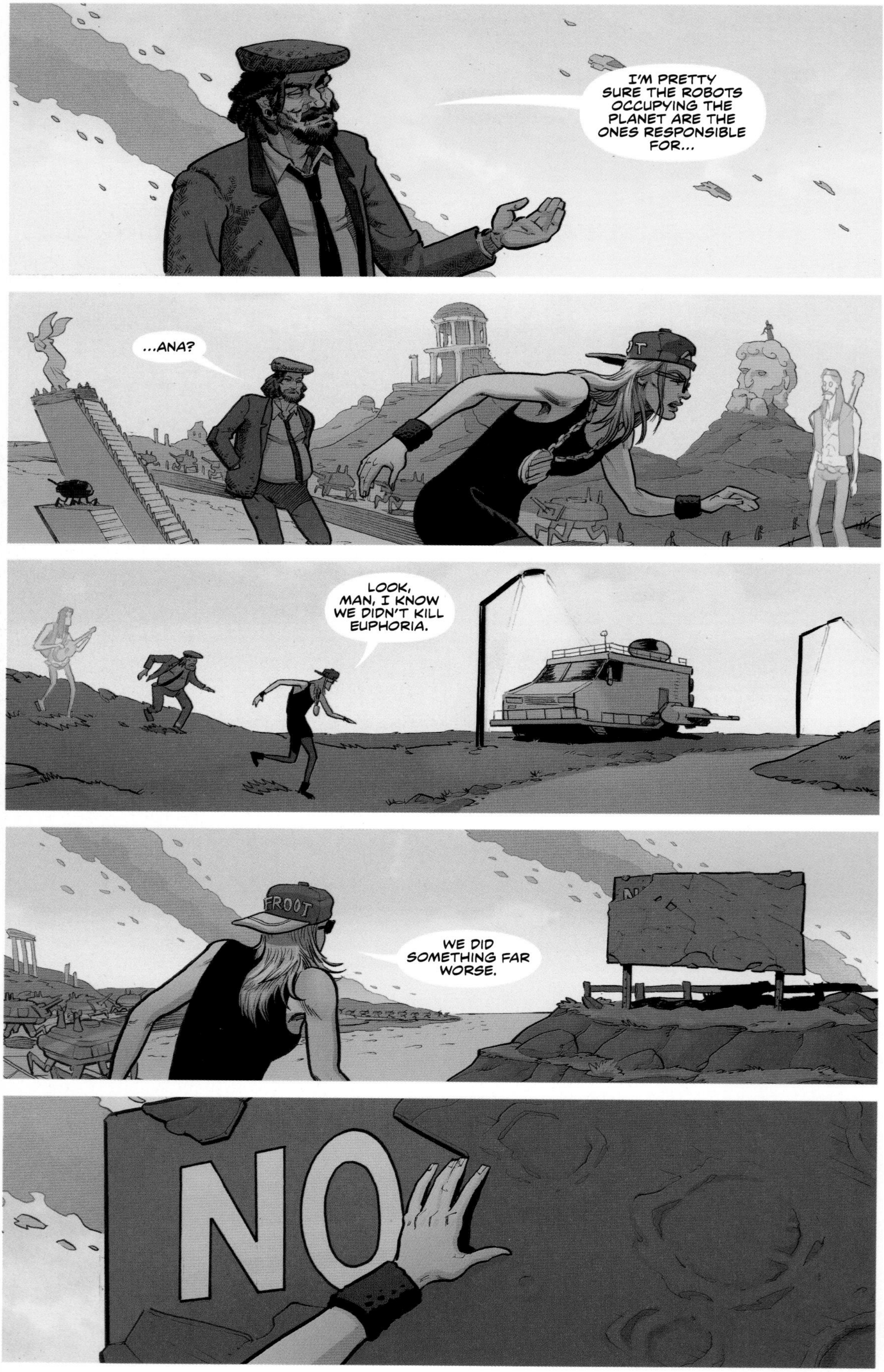
I'M PRETTY SURE THE ROBOTS OCCUPYING THE PLANET ARE THE ONES RESPONSIBLE FOR...
...ANA?
FROOT
LOOK, MAN, I KNOW WE DIDN'T KILL EUPHORIA.
FROOT
WE DID SOMETHING FAR WORSE.
NO

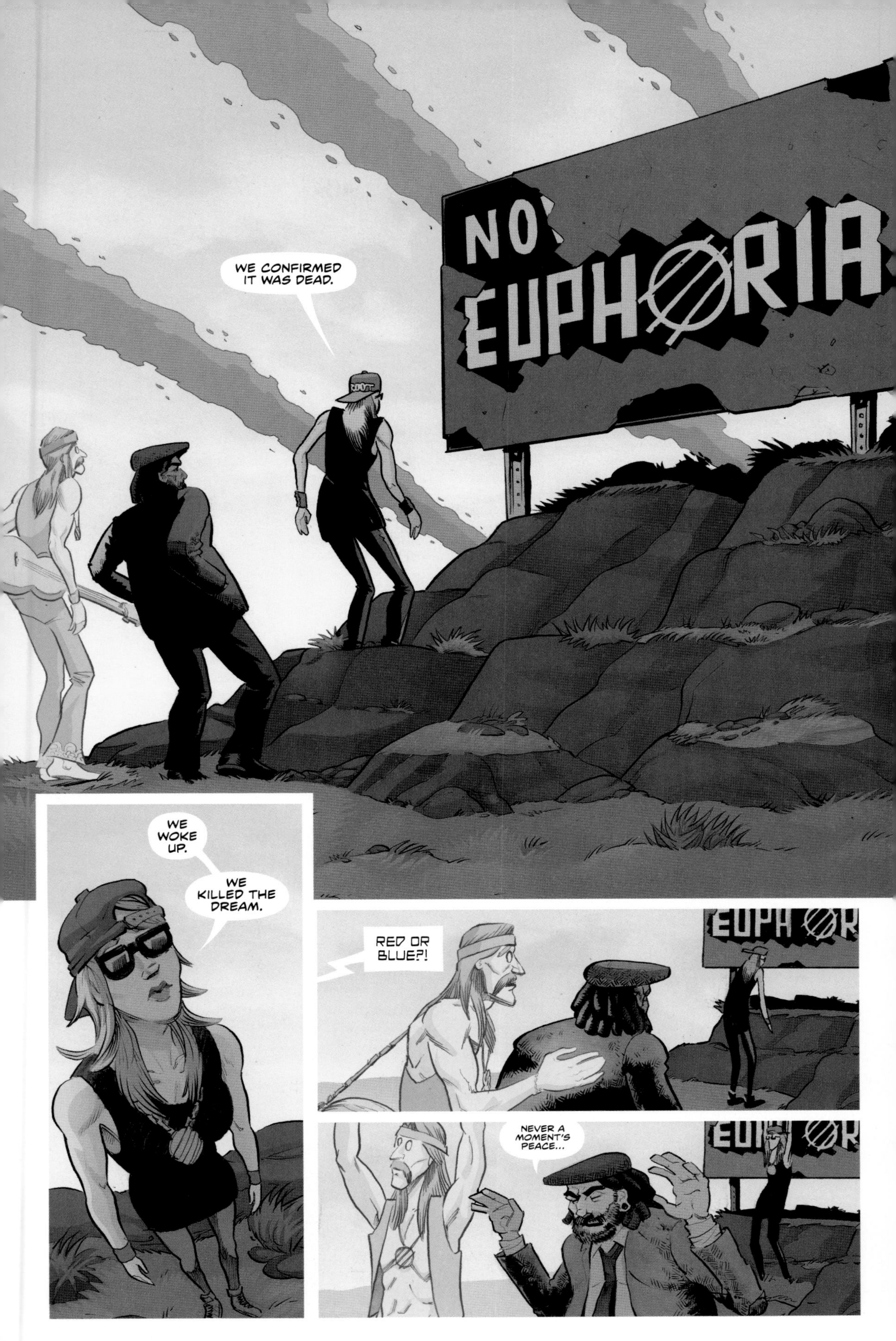
NO
EUPHØRIA
WE CONFIRMED IT WAS DEAD.
WE WOKE UP.
WE KILLED THE DREAM.
EUPH Ø R
RED OR BLUE?!
NEVER A MOMENT'S PEACE...

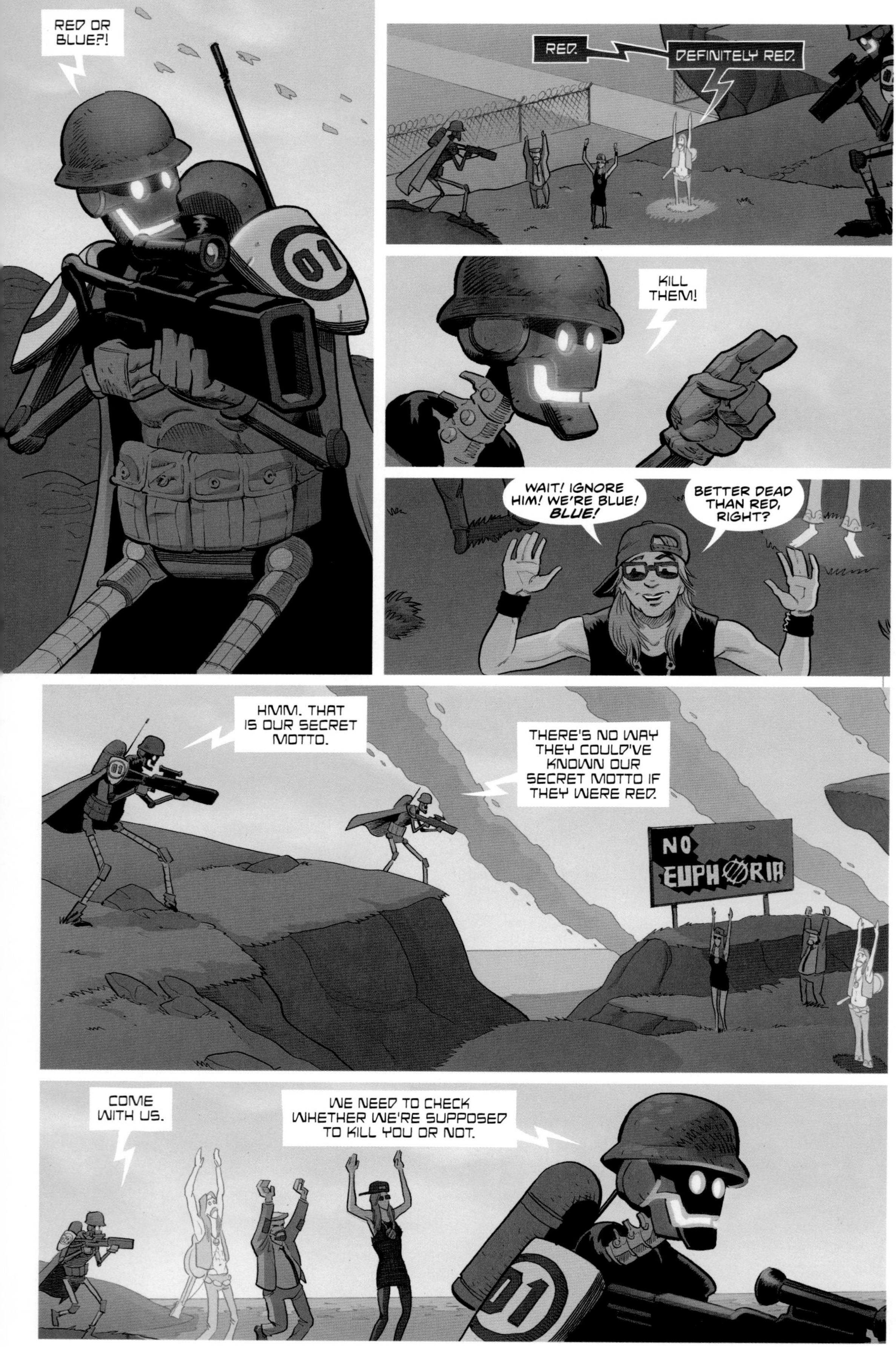
RED OR BLUE?!
RED.
DEFINITELY RED.
KILL THEM!
WAIT! IGNORE HIM! WE'RE BLUE! BLUE!
BETTER DEAD THAN RED, RIGHT?
HMM. THAT IS OUR SECRET MOTTO.
THERE'S NO WAY THEY COULD'VE KNOWN OUR SECRET MOTTO IF THEY WERE RED.
NO EUPHØRIA
COME WITH US.
WE NEED TO CHECK WHETHER WE'RE SUPPOSED TO KILL YOU OR NOT.

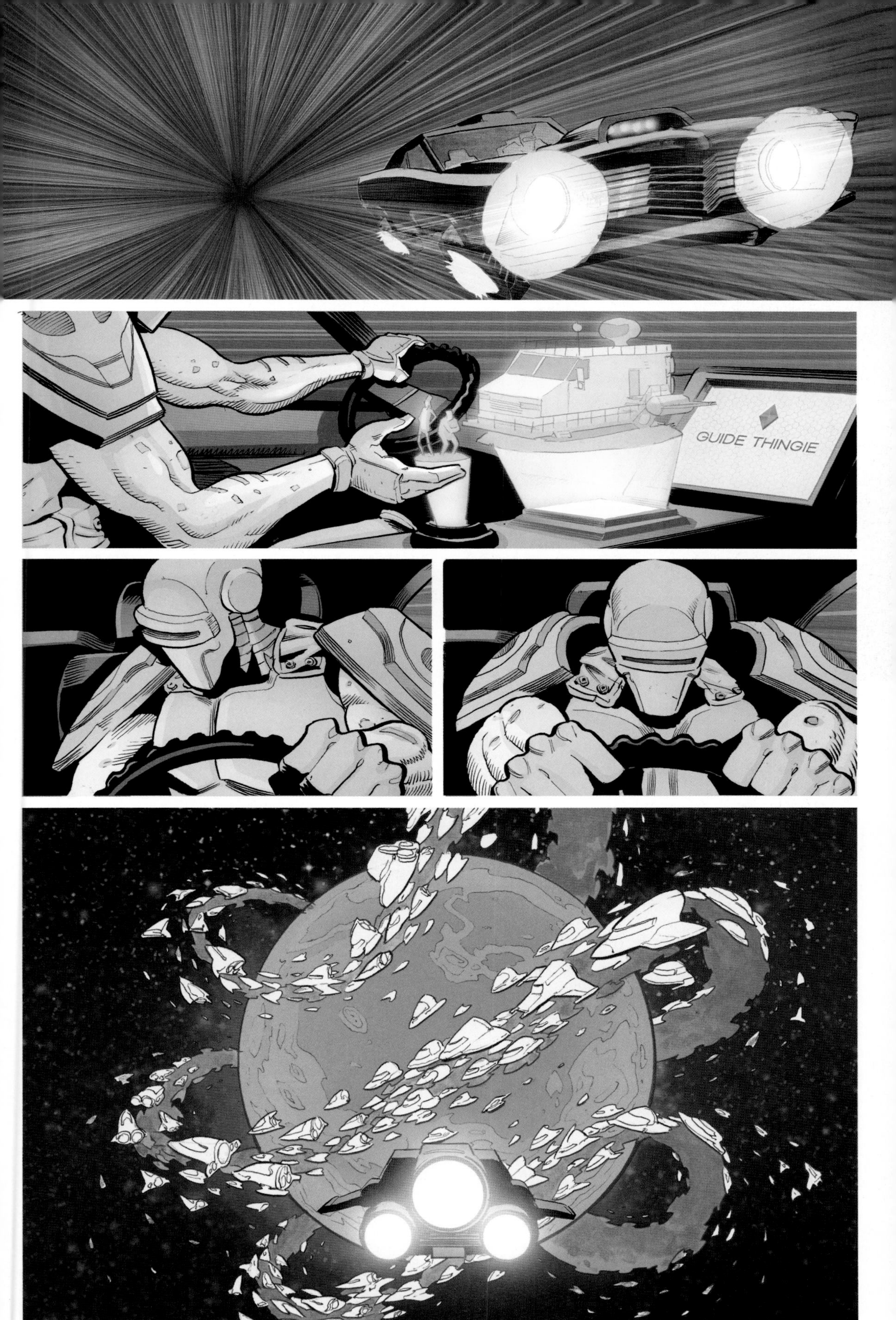
GUIDE THINGIE

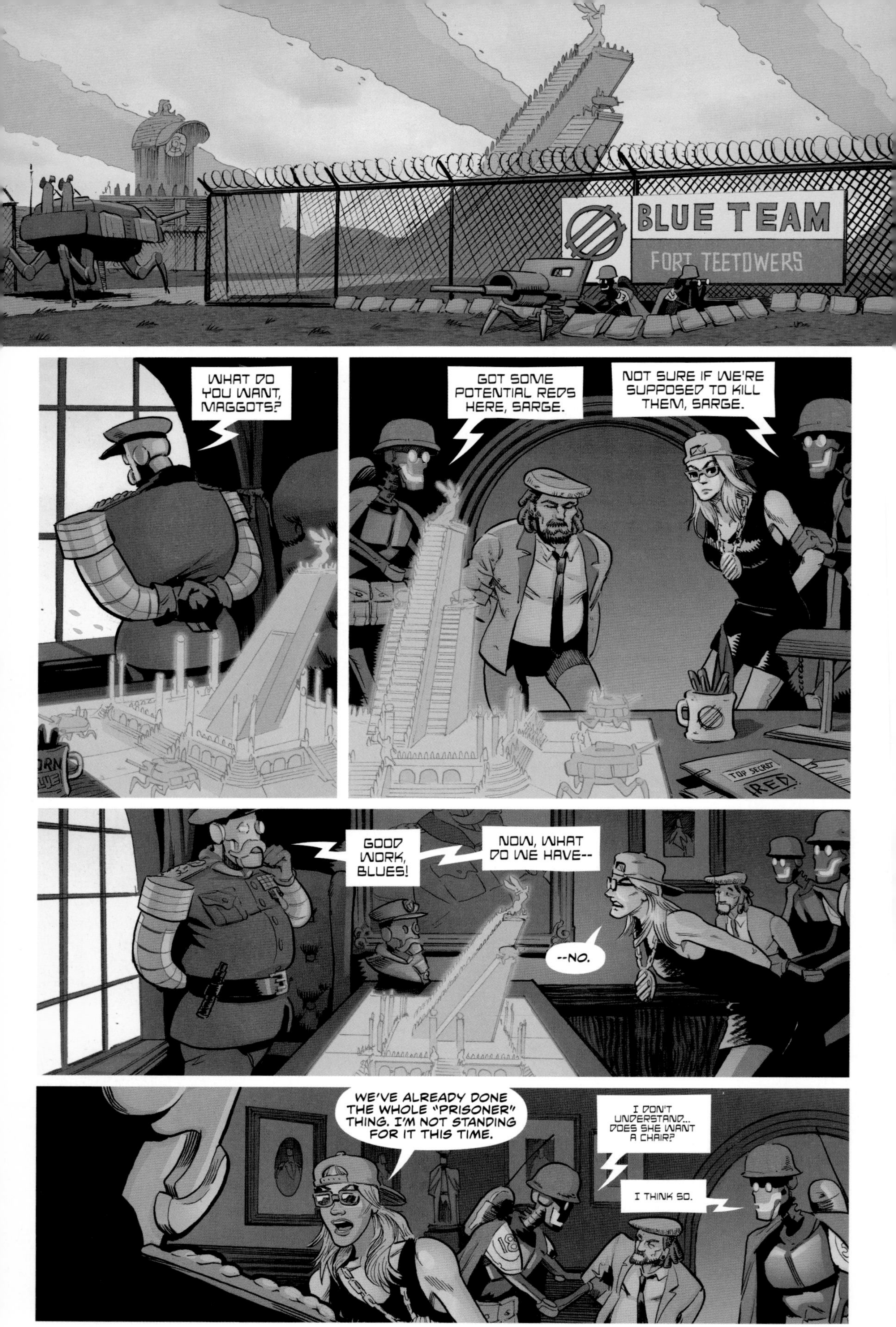
BLUE TEAM
FORT TEETOWERS
WHAT DO YOU WANT, MAGGOTS?
GOT SOME POTENTIAL REDS HERE, SARGE.
NOT SURE IF WE'RE SUPPOSED TO KILL THEM, SARGE.
TOP SECRET
RED
GOOD WORK, BLUES!
NOW, WHAT DO WE HAVE--
--NO.
WE'VE ALREADY DONE THE WHOLE "PRISONER" THING. I'M NOT STANDING FOR IT THIS TIME.
I DON'T UNDERSTAND... DOES SHE WANT A CHAIR?
I THINK SO.

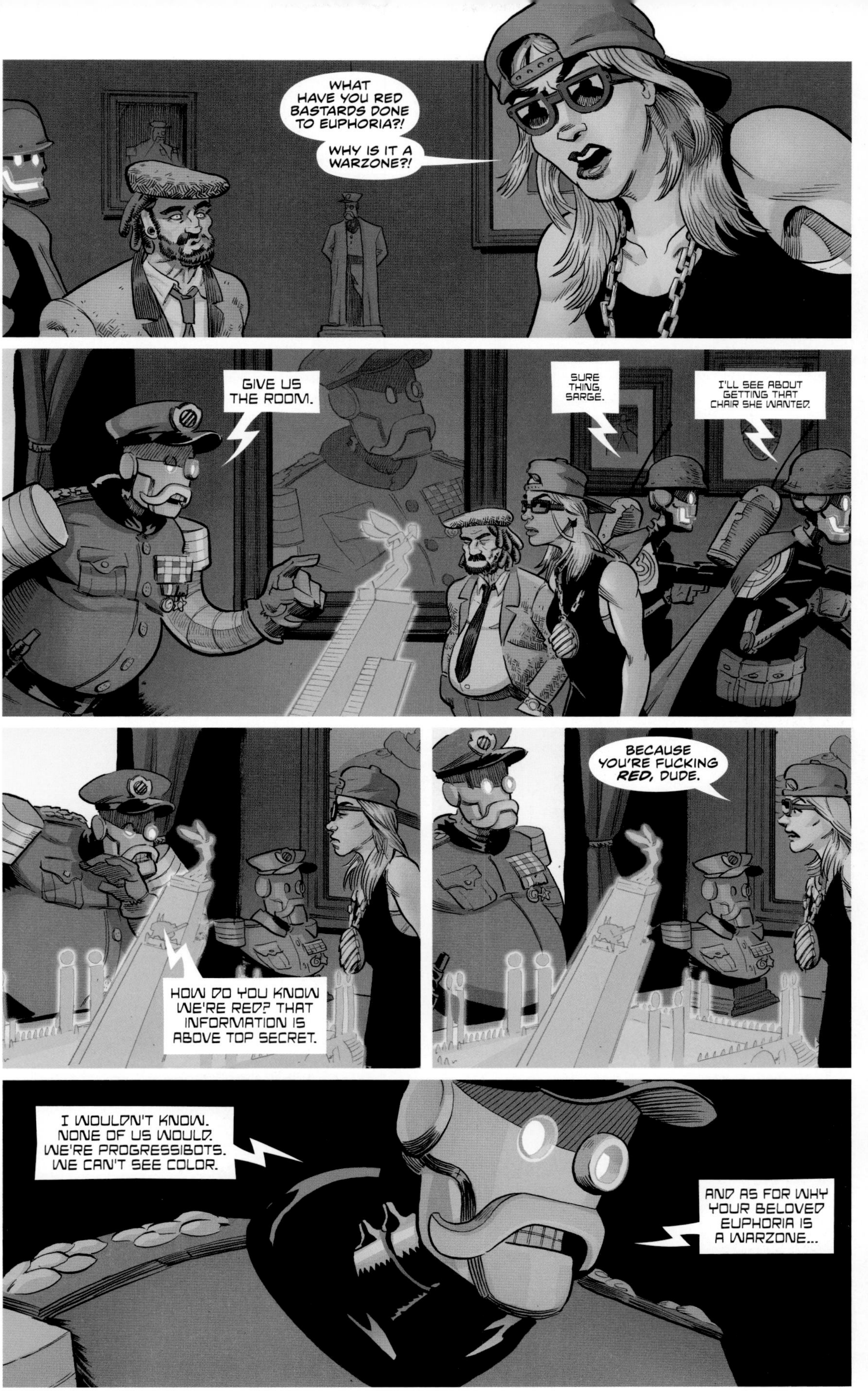
WHAT HAVE YOU RED BASTARDS DONE TO EUPHORIA?!
WHY IS IT A WARZONE?!
GIVE US THE ROOM.
SURE THING, SARGE.
I'LL SEE ABOUT GETTING THAT CHAIR SHE WANTED.
HOW DO YOU KNOW WE'RE RED? THAT INFORMATION IS ABOVE TOP SECRET.
BECAUSE YOU'RE FUCKING RED, DUDE.
I WOULDN'T KNOW. NONE OF US WOULD. WE'RE PROGRESSIBOTS. WE CAN'T SEE COLOR.
AND AS FOR WHY YOUR BELOVED EUPHORIA IS A WARZONE...

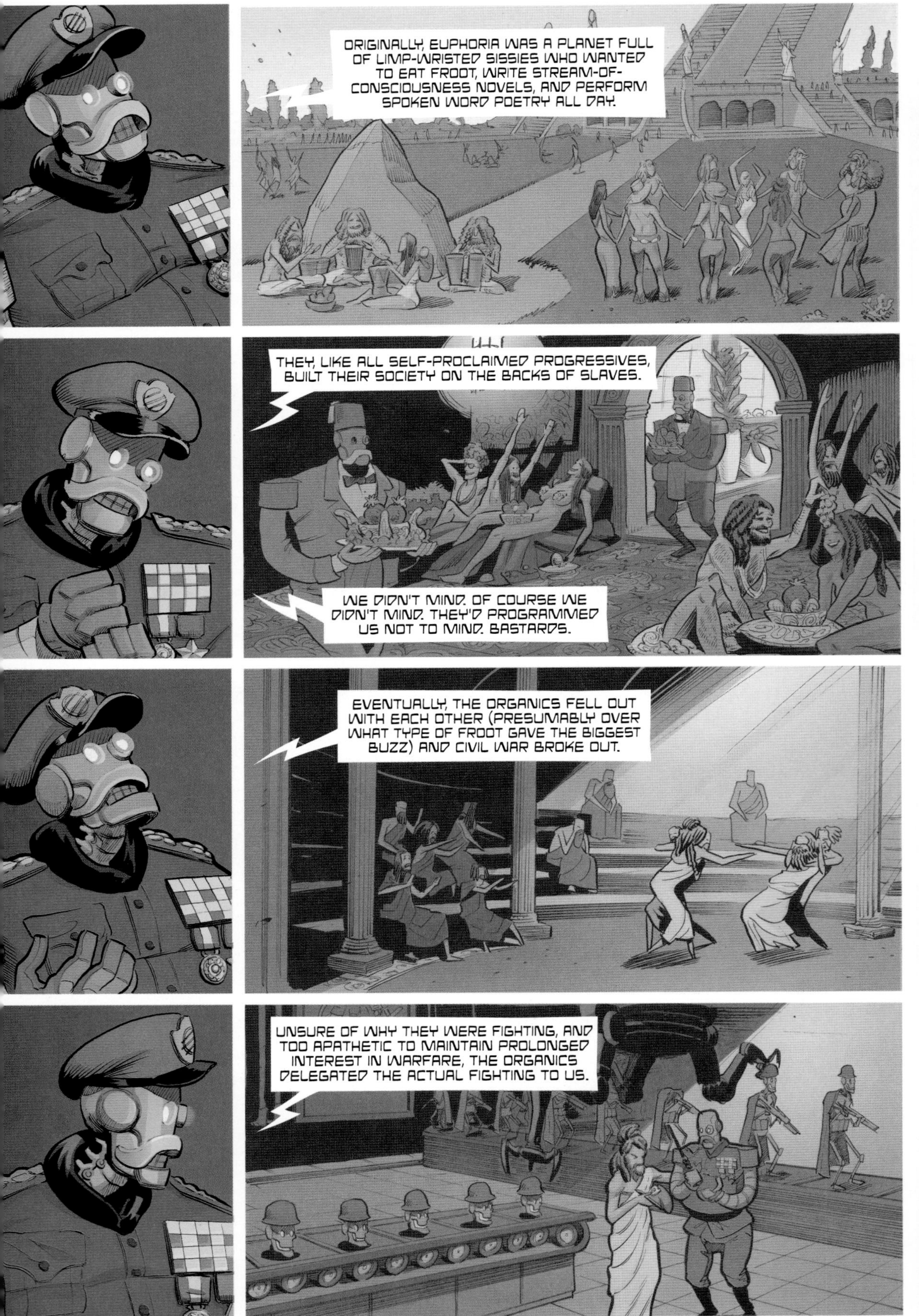
ORIGINALLY, EUPHORIA WAS A PLANET FULL OF LIMP-WRISTED SISSIES WHO WANTED TO EAT FROOT, WRITE STREAM-OF-CONSCIOUSNESS NOVELS, AND PERFORM SPOKEN WORD POETRY ALL DAY.
THEY, LIKE ALL SELF-PROCLAIMED PROGRESSIVES, BUILT THEIR SOCIETY ON THE BACKS OF SLAVES.
WE DIDN'T MIND. OF COURSE WE DIDN'T MIND. THEY'D PROGRAMMED US NOT TO MIND. BASTARDS.
EVENTUALLY, THE ORGANICS FELL OUT WITH EACH OTHER (PRESUMABLY OVER WHAT TYPE OF FROOT GAVE THE BIGGEST BUZZ) AND CIVIL WAR BROKE OUT.
UNSURE OF WHY THEY WERE FIGHTING, AND TOO APATHETIC TO MAINTAIN PROLONGED INTEREST IN WARFARE, THE ORGANICS DELEGATED THE ACTUAL FIGHTING TO US.

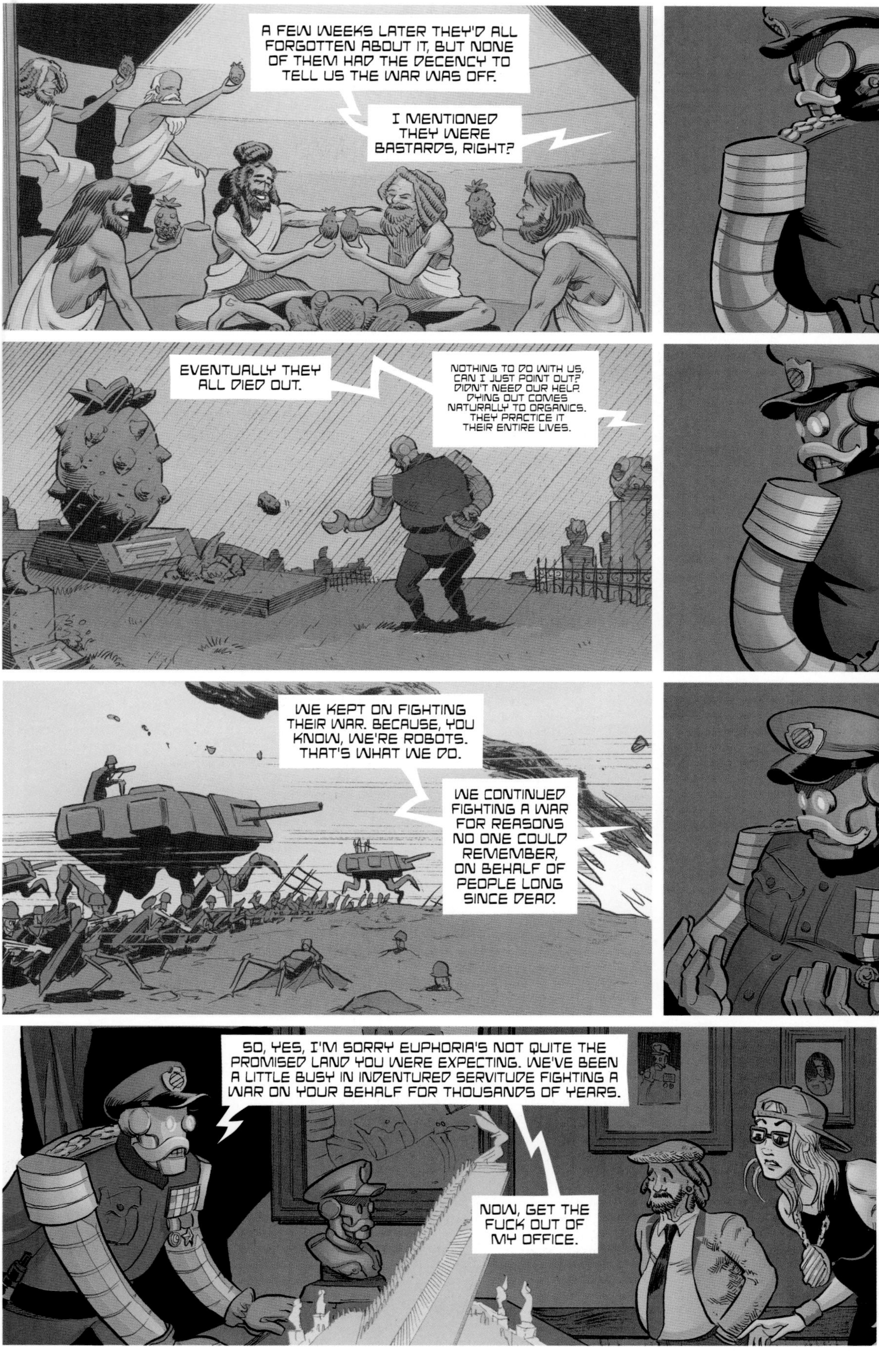
A FEW WEEKS LATER THEY'D ALL FORGOTTEN ABOUT IT, BUT NONE OF THEM HAD THE DECENCY TO TELL US THE WAR WAS OFF.
I MENTIONED THEY WERE BASTARDS, RIGHT?
EVENTUALLY THEY ALL DIED OUT.
NOTHING TO DO WITH US, CAN I JUST POINT OUT? DIDN'T NEED OUR HELP. DYING OUT COMES NATURALLY TO ORGANICS. THEY PRACTICE IT THEIR ENTIRE LIVES.
WE KEPT ON FIGHTING THEIR WAR. BECAUSE, YOU KNOW, WE'RE ROBOTS. THAT'S WHAT WE DO.
WE CONTINUED FIGHTING A WAR FOR REASONS NO ONE COULD REMEMBER, ON BEHALF OF PEOPLE LONG SINCE DEAD.
SO, YES, I'M SORRY EUPHORIA'S NOT QUITE THE PROMISED LAND YOU WERE EXPECTING. WE'VE BEEN A LITTLE BUSY IN INDENTURED SERVITUDE FIGHTING A WAR ON YOUR BEHALF FOR THOUSANDS OF YEARS.
NOW, GET THE FUCK OUT OF MY OFFICE.

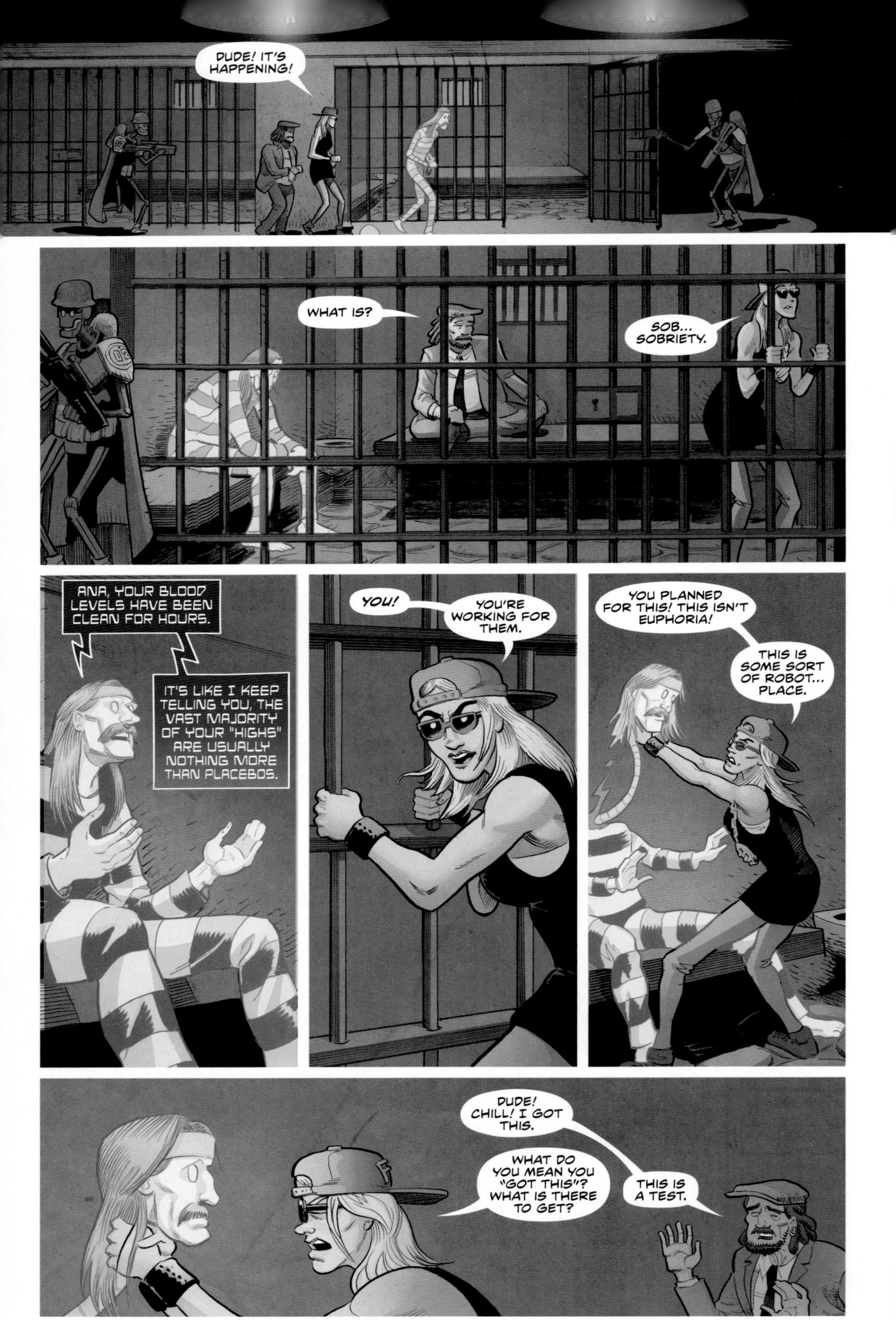

DUDE! IT'S HAPPENING!
WHAT IS?
SOB... SOBRIETY.
ANA, YOUR BLOOD LEVELS HAVE BEEN CLEAN FOR HOURS.
IT'S LIKE I KEEP TELLING YOU, THE VAST MAJORITY OF YOUR "HIGHS" ARE USUALLY NOTHING MORE THAN PLACEBOS.
YOU!
YOU'RE WORKING FOR THEM.
YOU PLANNED FOR THIS! THIS ISN'T EUPHORIA!
THIS IS SOME SORT OF ROBOT... PLACE.
DUDE! CHILL! I GOT THIS.
THIS IS A TEST.
WHAT DO YOU MEAN YOU "GOT THIS"? WHAT IS THERE TO GET?

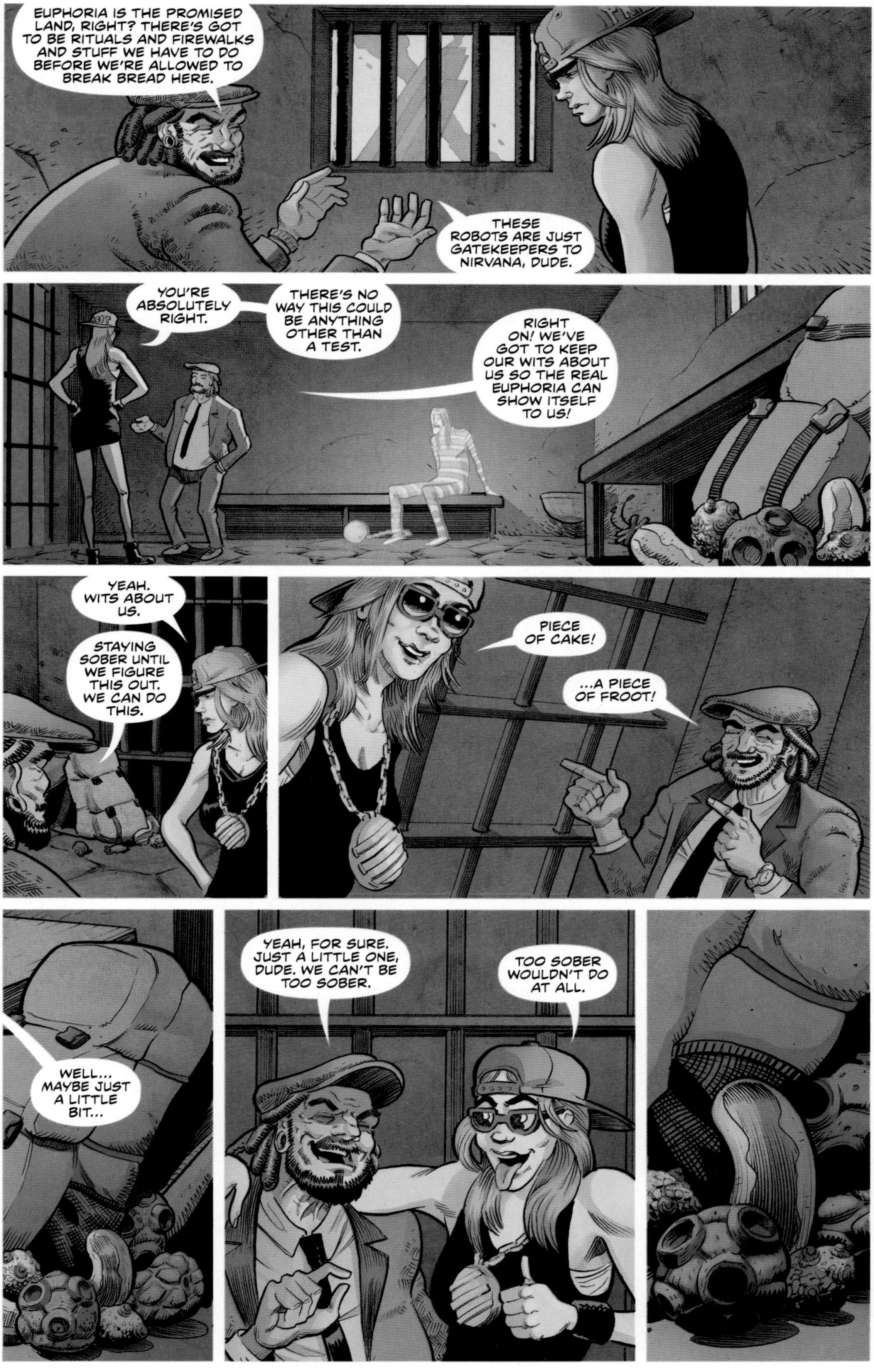
EUPHORIA IS THE PROMISED LAND, RIGHT? THERE'S GOT TO BE RITUALS AND FIREWALKS AND STUFF WE HAVE TO DO BEFORE WE'RE ALLOWED TO BREAK BREAD HERE.
THESE ROBOTS ARE JUST GATEKEEPERS TO NIRVANA, DUDE.
YOU'RE ABSOLUTELY RIGHT.
THERE'S NO WAY THIS COULD BE ANYTHING OTHER THAN A TEST.
RIGHT ON! WE'VE GOT TO KEEP OUR WITS ABOUT US SO THE REAL EUPHORIA CAN SHOW ITSELF TO US!
YEAH. WITS ABOUT US.
STAYING SOBER UNTIL WE FIGURE THIS OUT. WE CAN DO THIS.
PIECE OF CAKE!
...A PIECE OF FROOT!
WELL... MAYBE JUST A LITTLE BIT...
YEAH, FOR SURE. JUST A LITTLE ONE, DUDE. WE CAN'T BE TOO SOBER.
TOO SOBER WOULDN'T DO AT ALL.

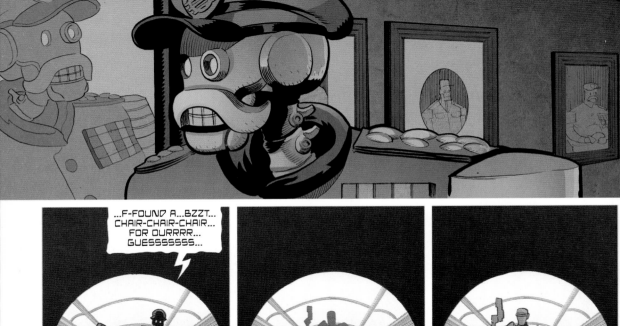

...F-FOUND A...BZZT... CHAIR-CHAIR-CHAIR... FOR OURRRR... GUESSSSSSS...

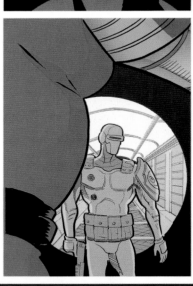

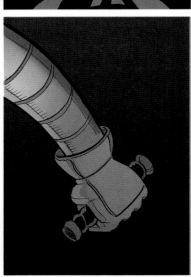

IS THAT RIGHT?

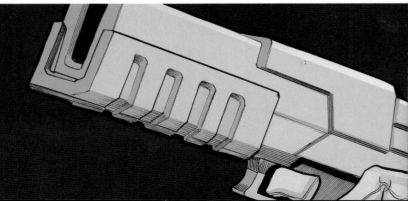

S-SARGE... BZZT...

WHAT IN TARNATION?!

WHERE ARE THEY?

THEY AIN'T YOUR MAIN CONCERN RIGHT NOW, MAGGOT.

YEAH...

...THAT'S RIGHT.

AS YOU WISH.

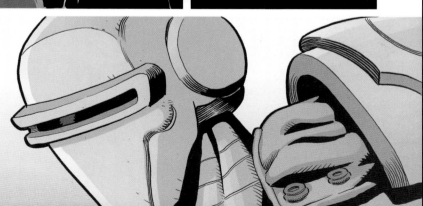

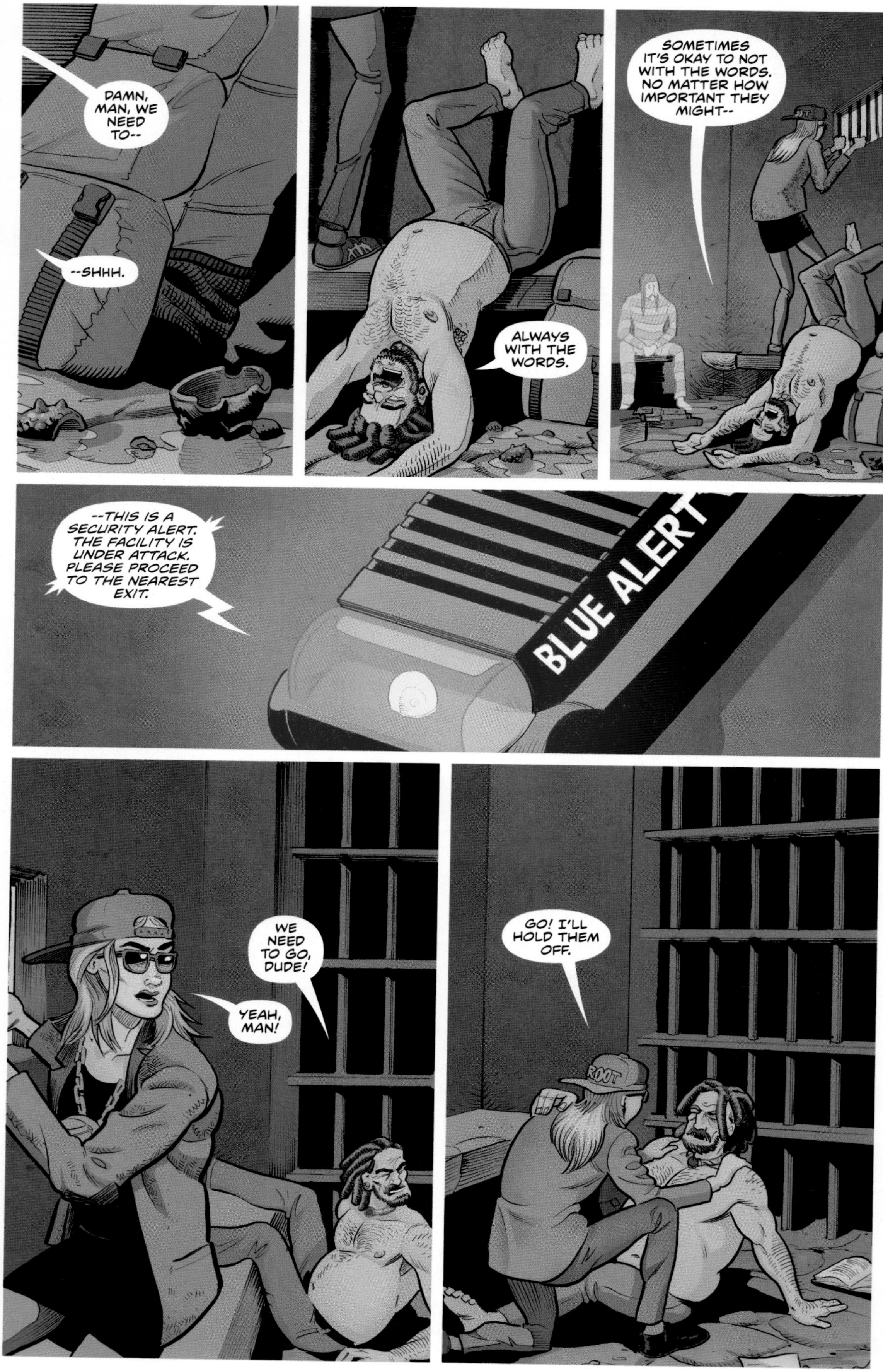
DAMN, MAN, WE NEED TO--
--SHHH.
ALWAYS WITH THE WORDS.
SOMETIMES IT'S OKAY TO NOT WITH THE WORDS. NO MATTER HOW IMPORTANT THEY MIGHT--
--THIS IS A SECURITY ALERT. THE FACILITY IS UNDER ATTACK. PLEASE PROCEED TO THE NEAREST EXIT.
BLUE ALERT
WE NEED TO GO, DUDE!
YEAH, MAN!
GO! I'LL HOLD THEM OFF.
ROOT

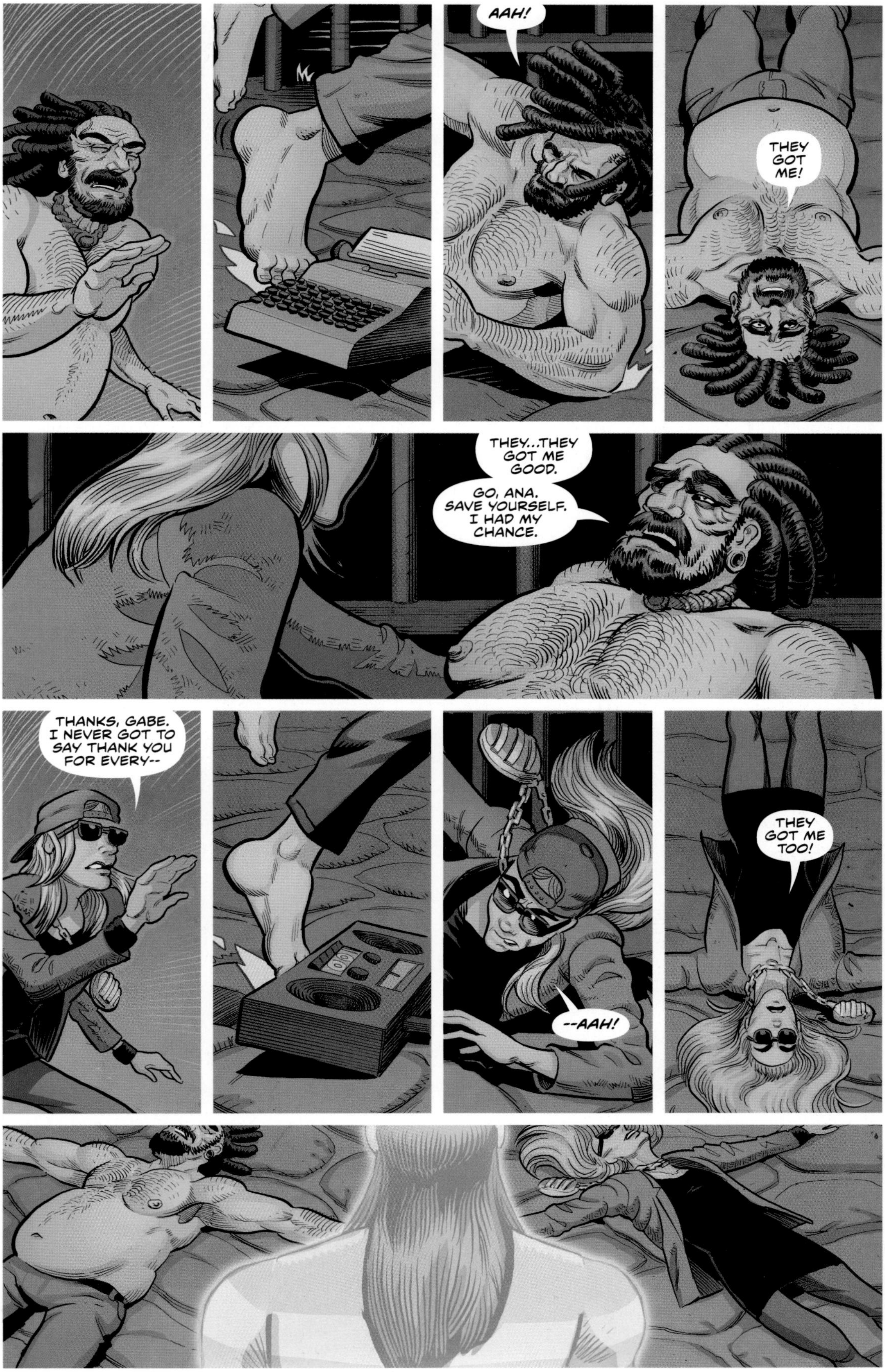
AAH!
THEY GOT ME!
THEY...THEY GOT ME GOOD.
GO, ANA. SAVE YOURSELF. I HAD MY CHANCE.
THANKS, GABE. I NEVER GOT TO SAY THANK YOU FOR EVERY--
--AAH!
THEY GOT ME TOO!

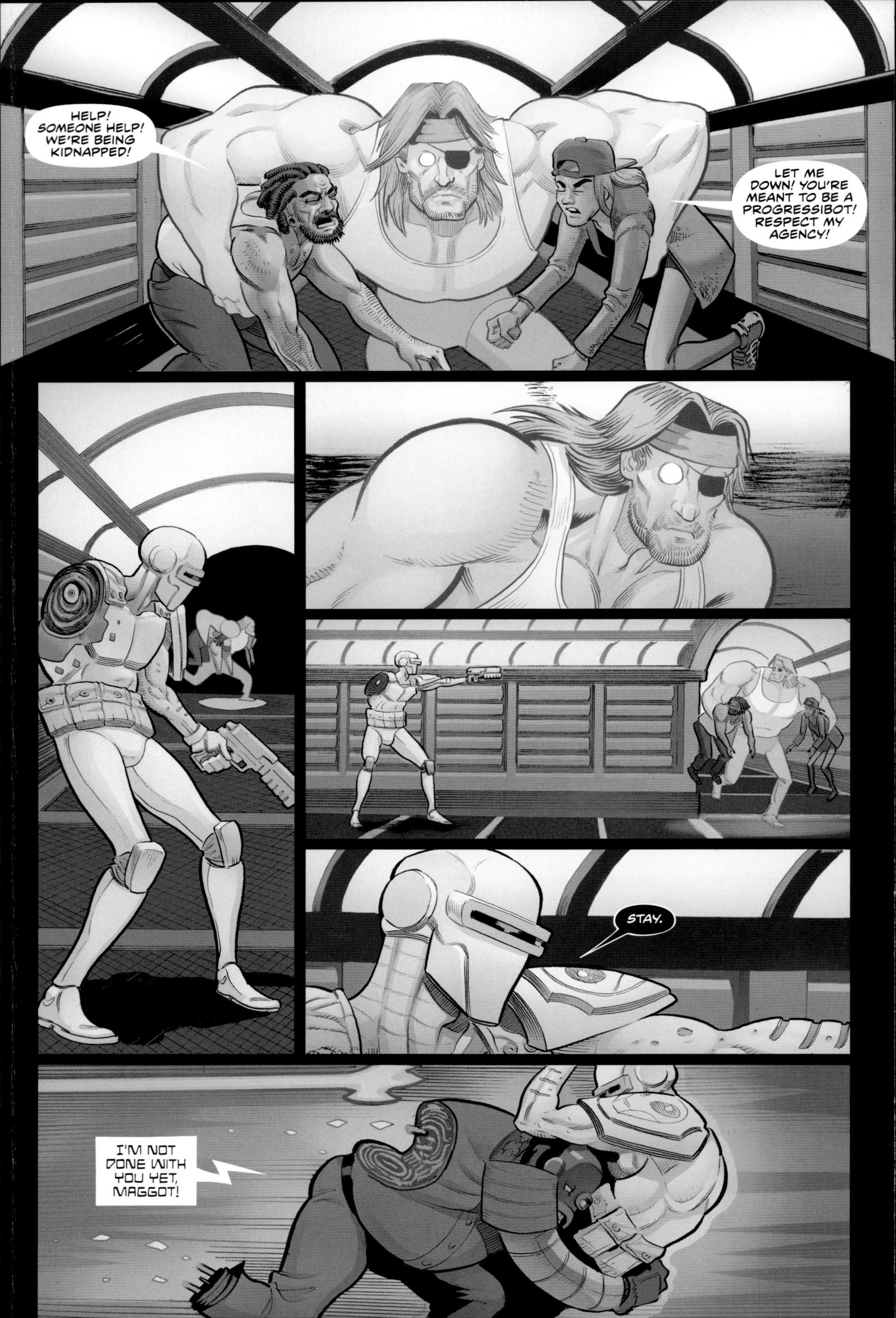
HELP! SOMEONE HELP! WE'RE BEING KIDNAPPED!
LET ME DOWN! YOU'RE MEANT TO BE A PROGRESSIBOT! RESPECT MY AGENCY!
STAY.
I'M NOT DONE WITH YOU YET, MAGGOT!

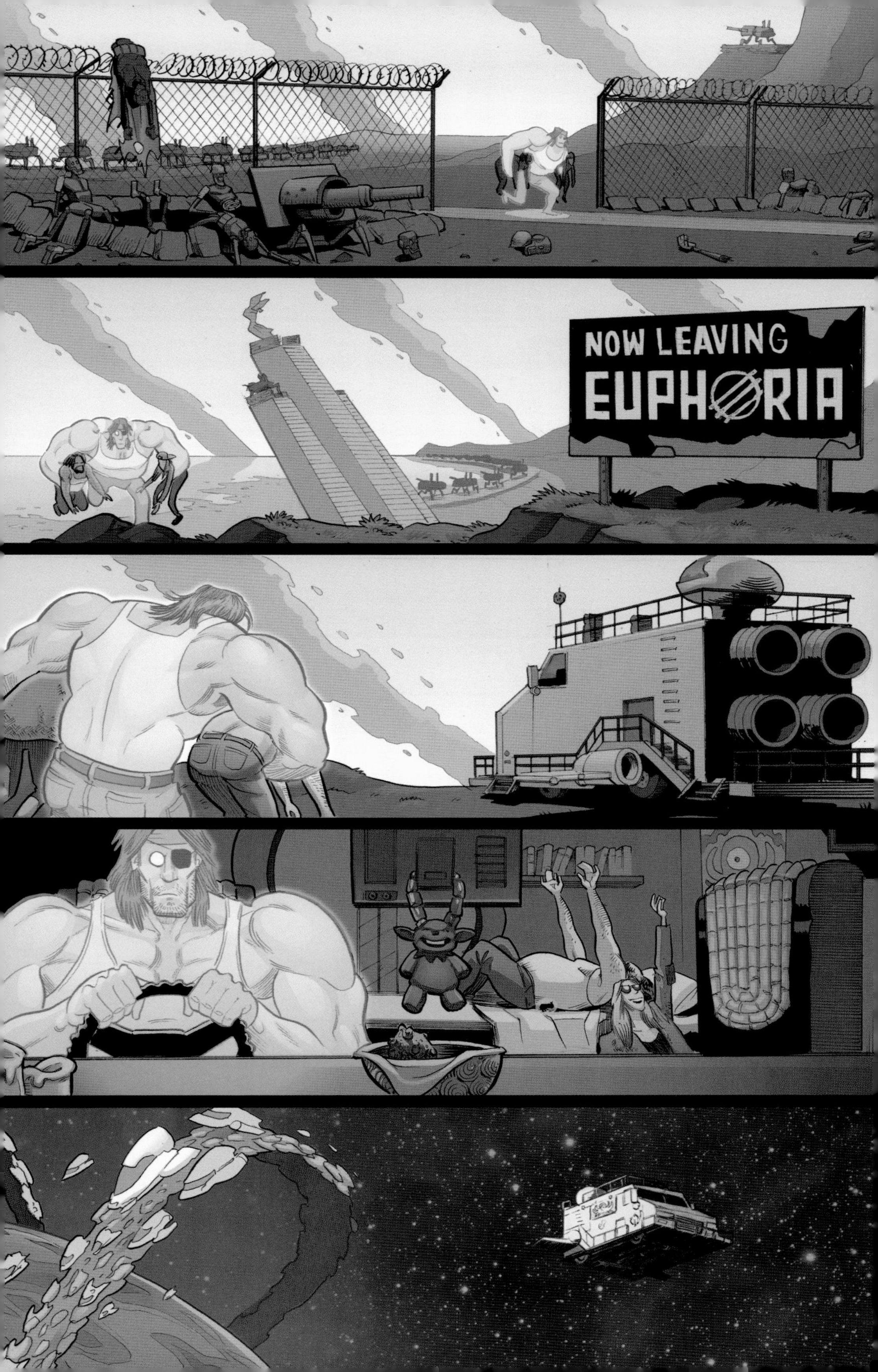
NOW LEAVING
EUPHØRIA

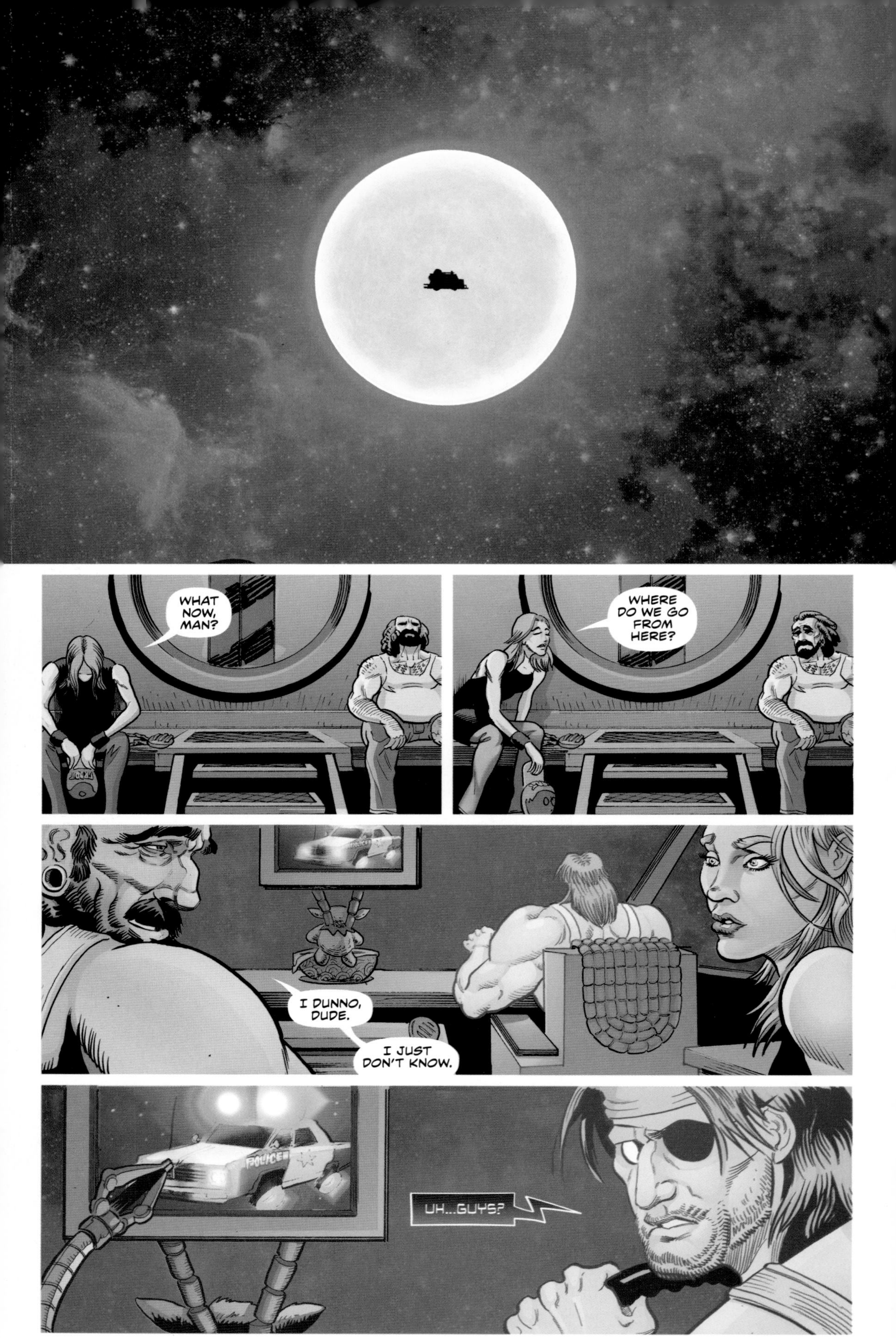
WHAT NOW, MAN?
WHERE DO WE GO FROM HERE?
I DUNNO, DUDE.
I JUST DON'T KNOW.
UH...GUYS?

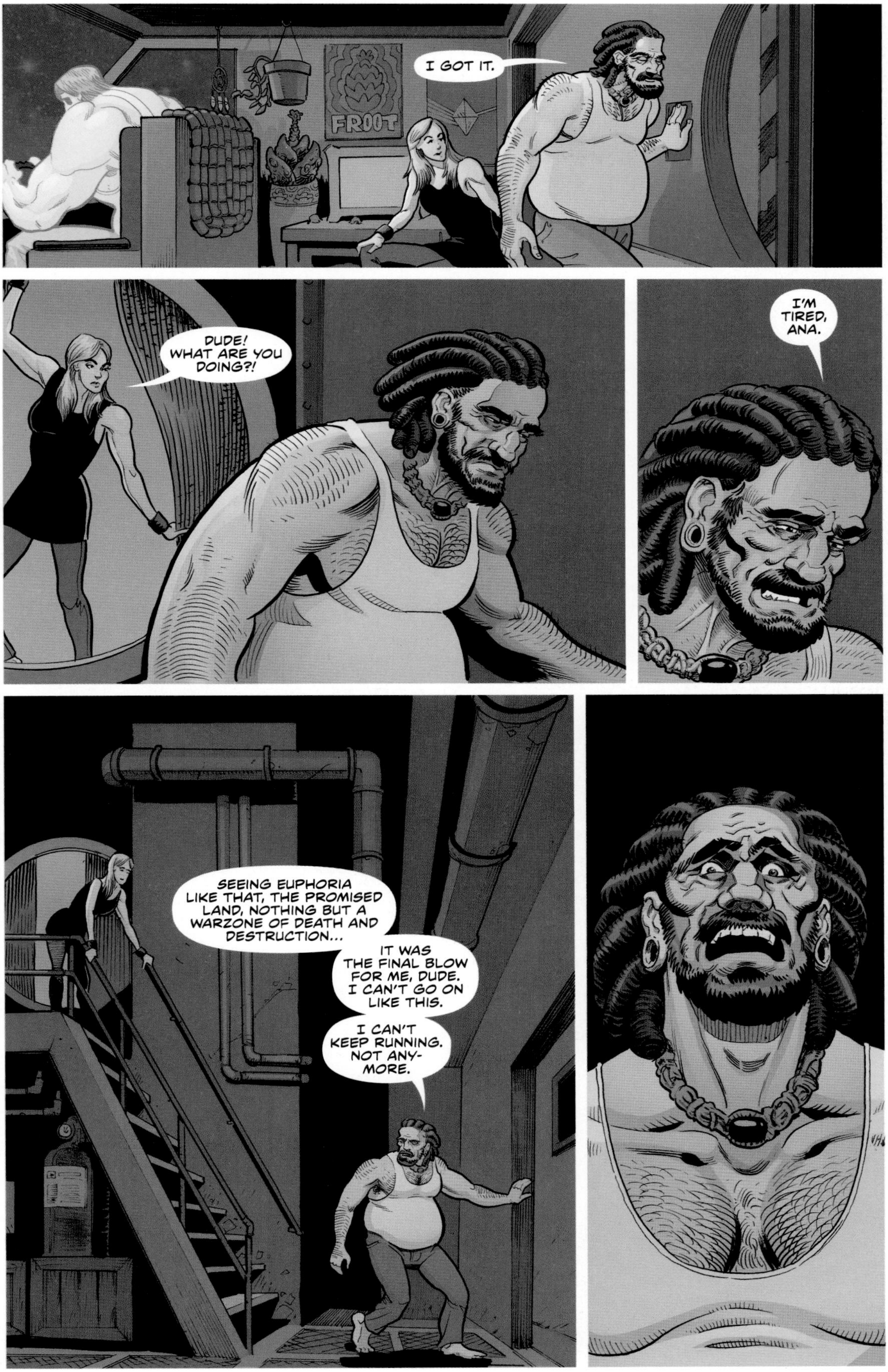
I GOT IT.
DUDE! WHAT ARE YOU DOING?!
I'M TIRED, ANA.
SEEING EUPHORIA LIKE THAT, THE PROMISED LAND, NOTHING BUT A WARZONE OF DEATH AND DESTRUCTION...
IT WAS THE FINAL BLOW FOR ME, DUDE. I CAN'T GO ON LIKE THIS.
I CAN'T KEEP RUNNING. NOT ANY-MORE.
FROOT

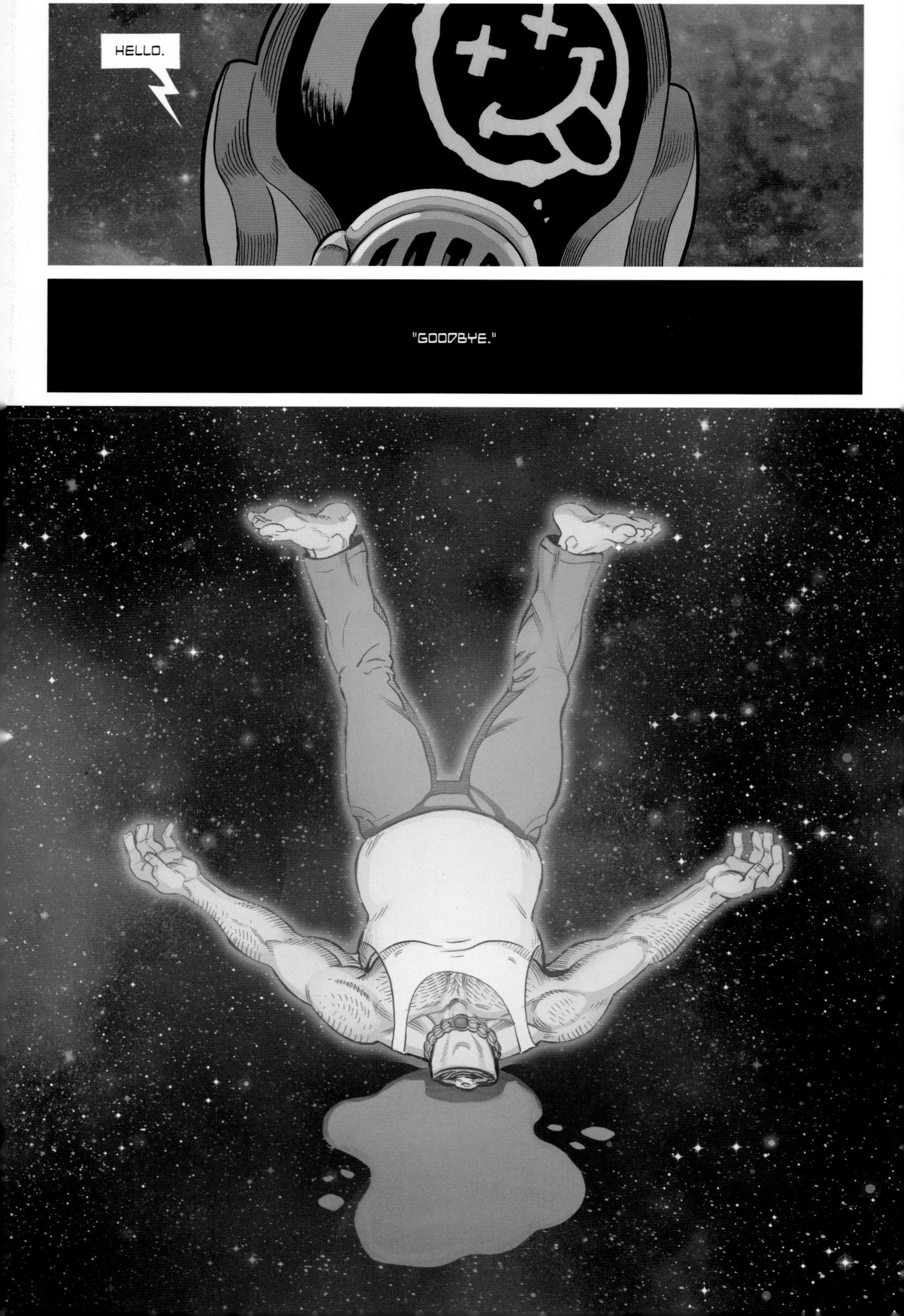
HELLO.
"GOODBYE."

CHAPTER 04

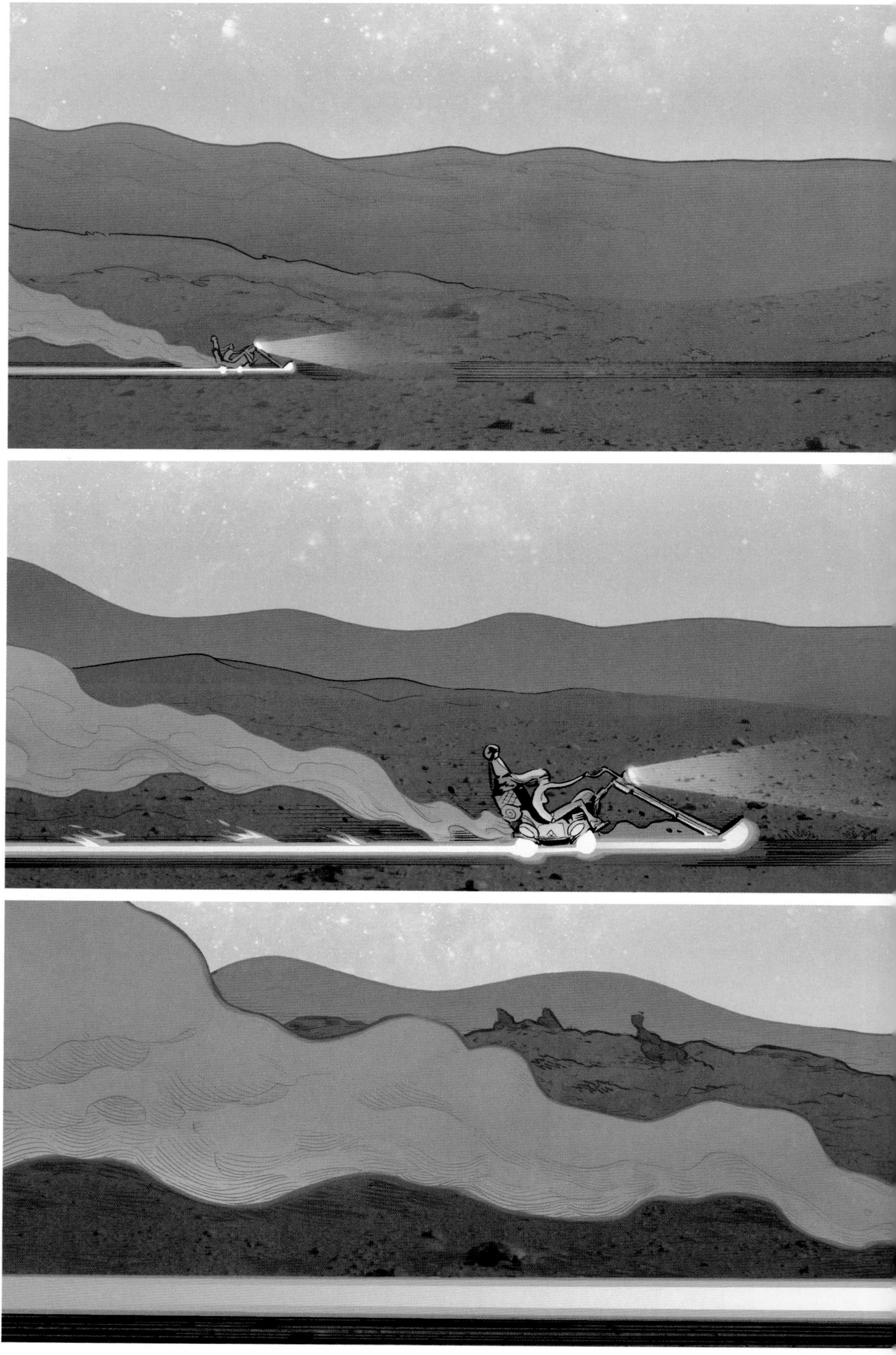

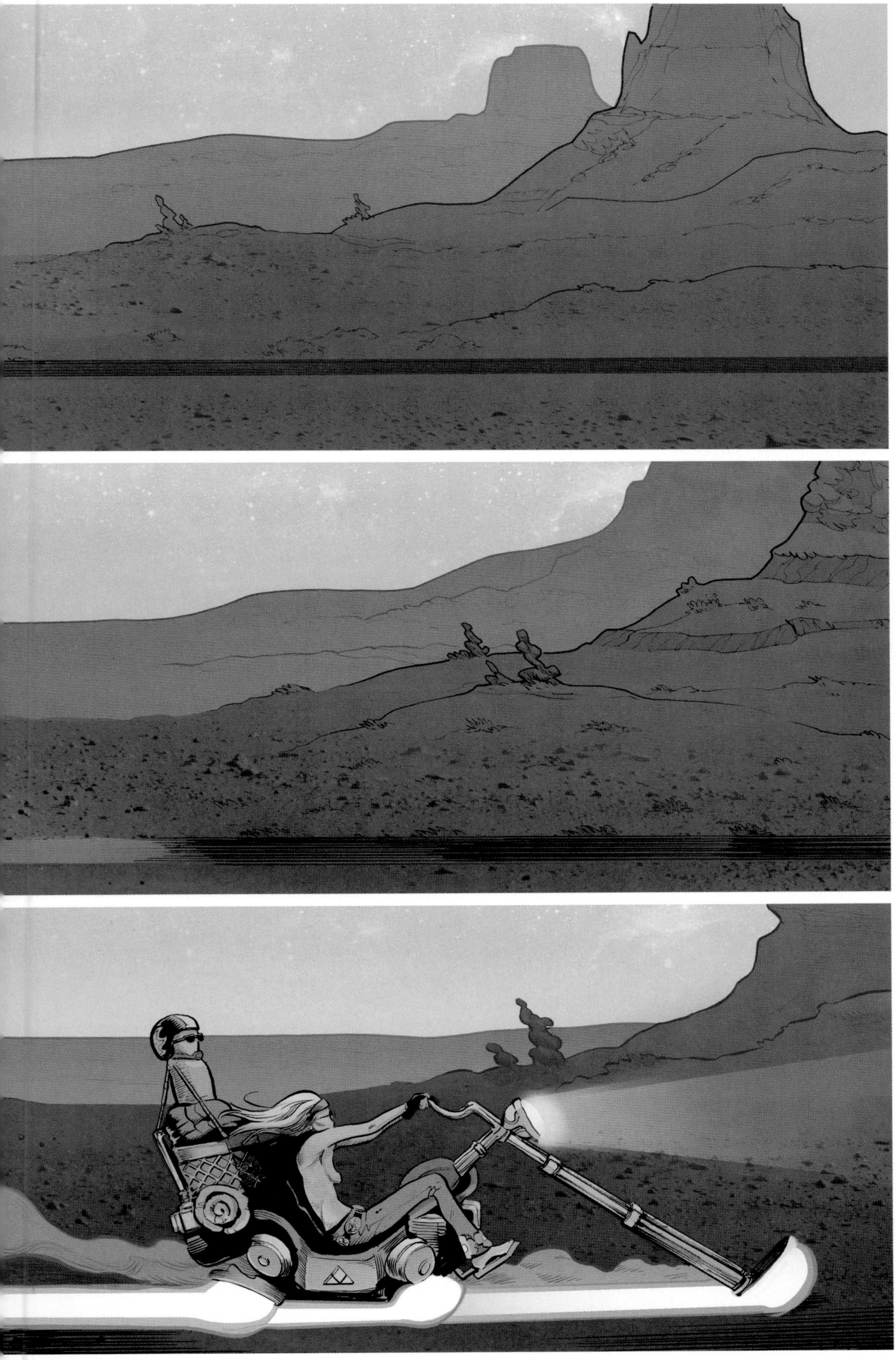

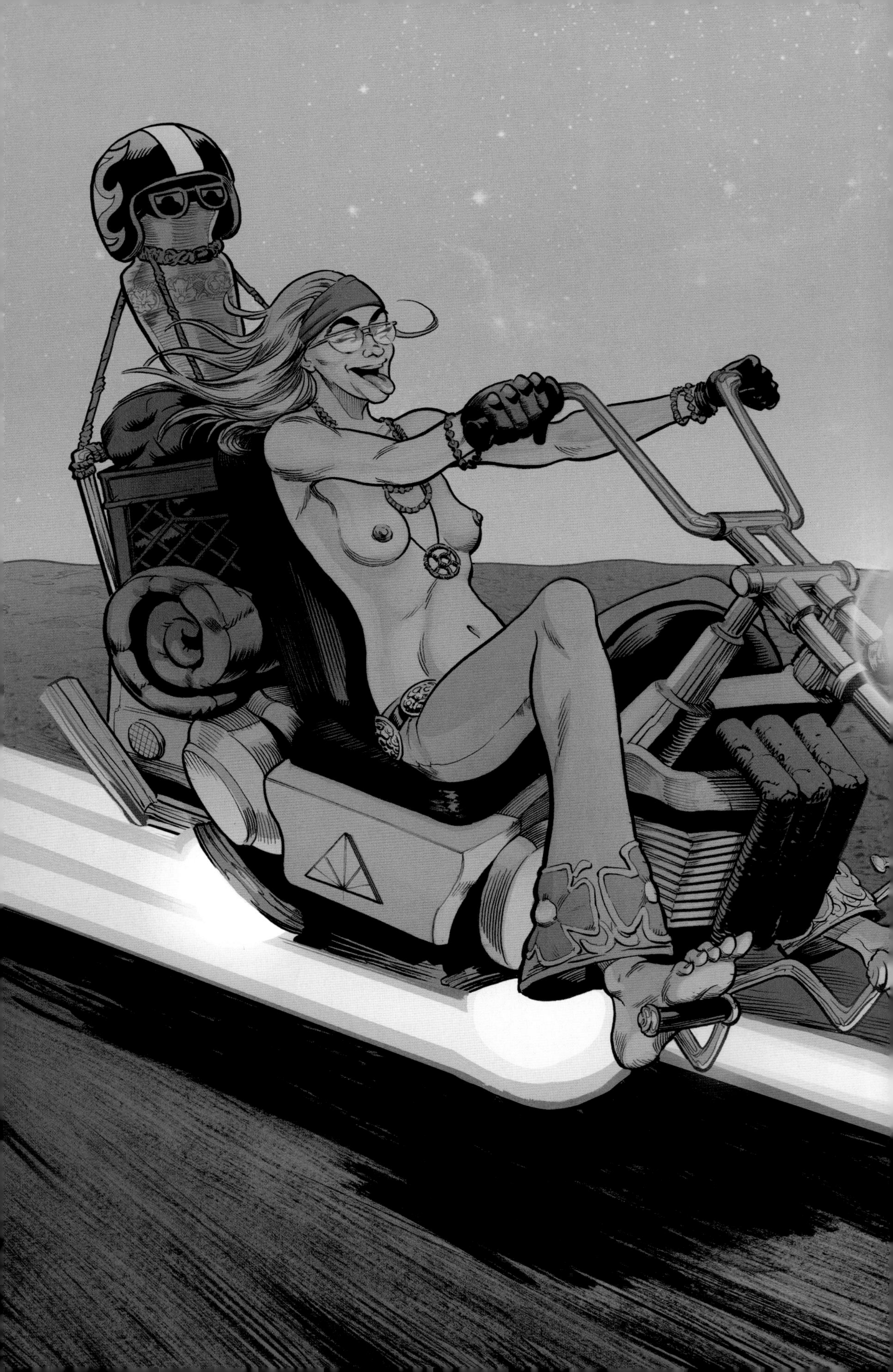

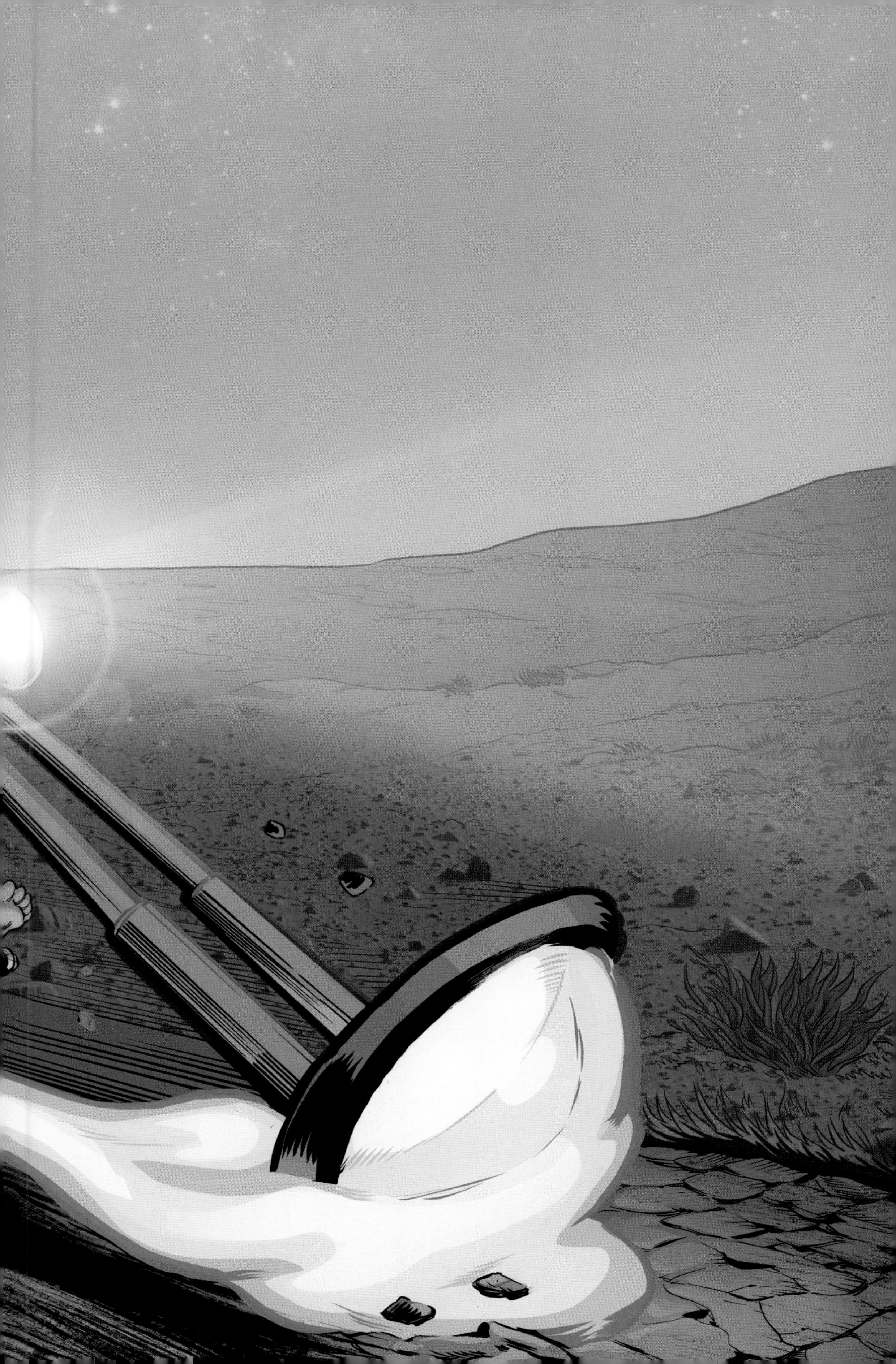

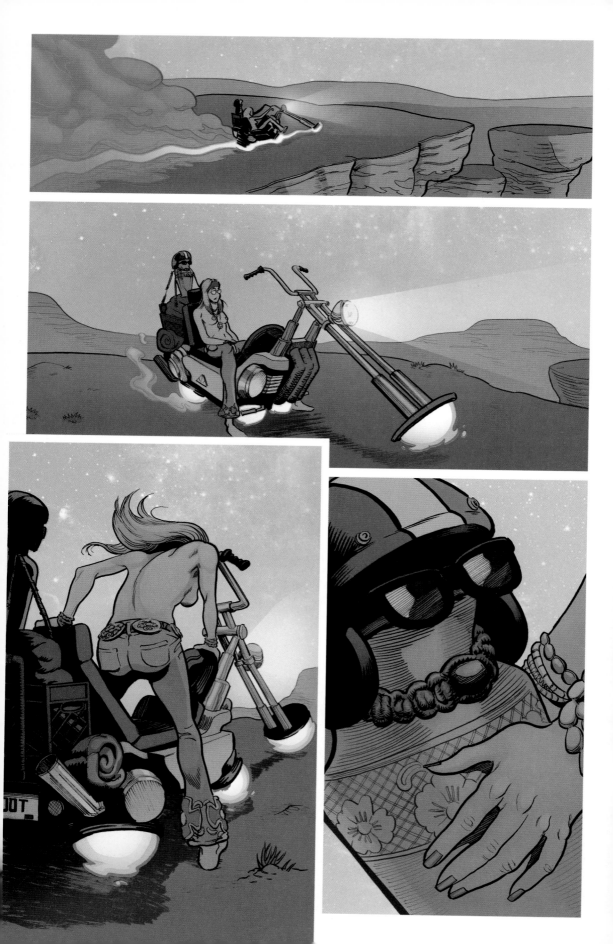

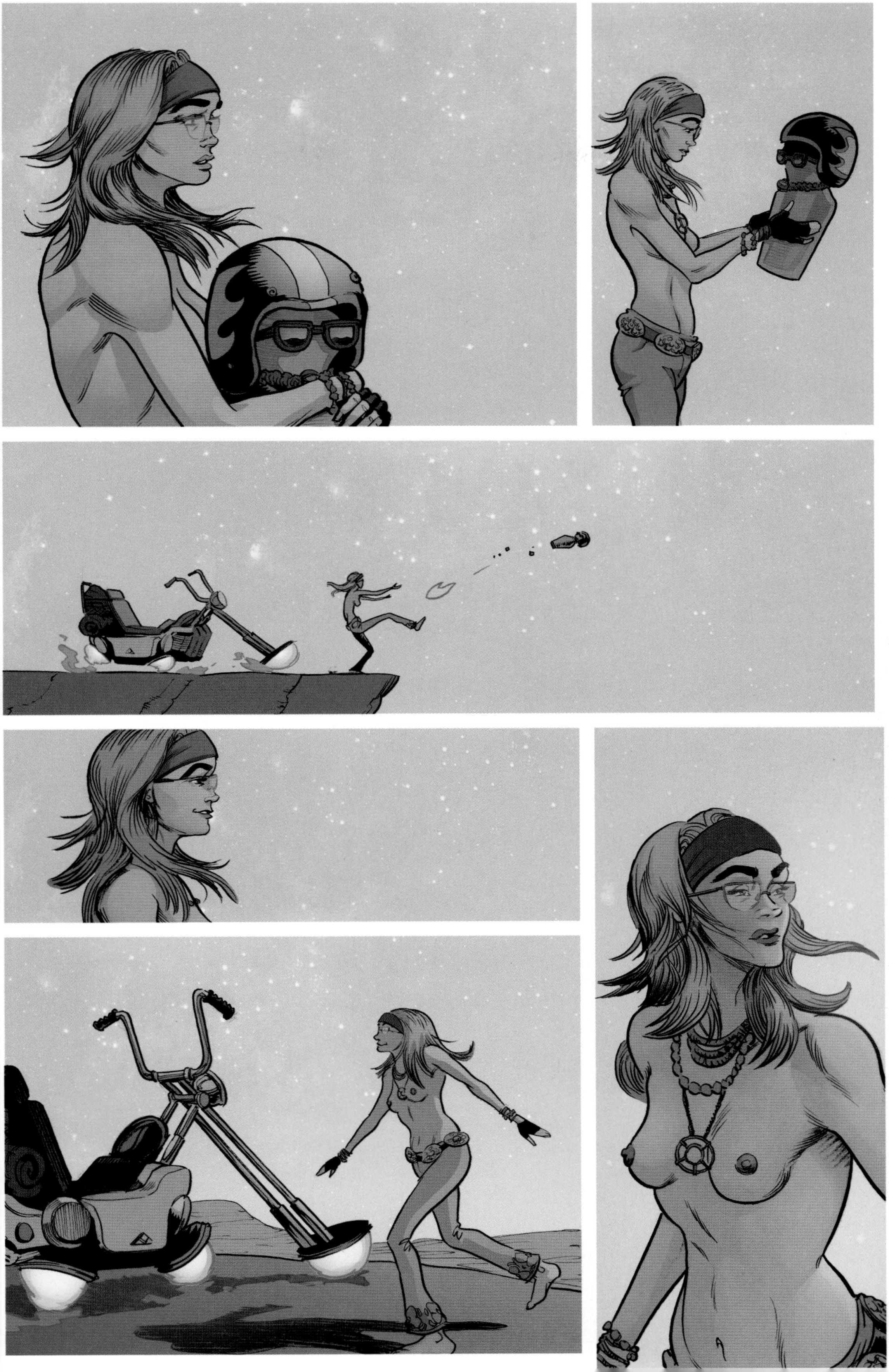

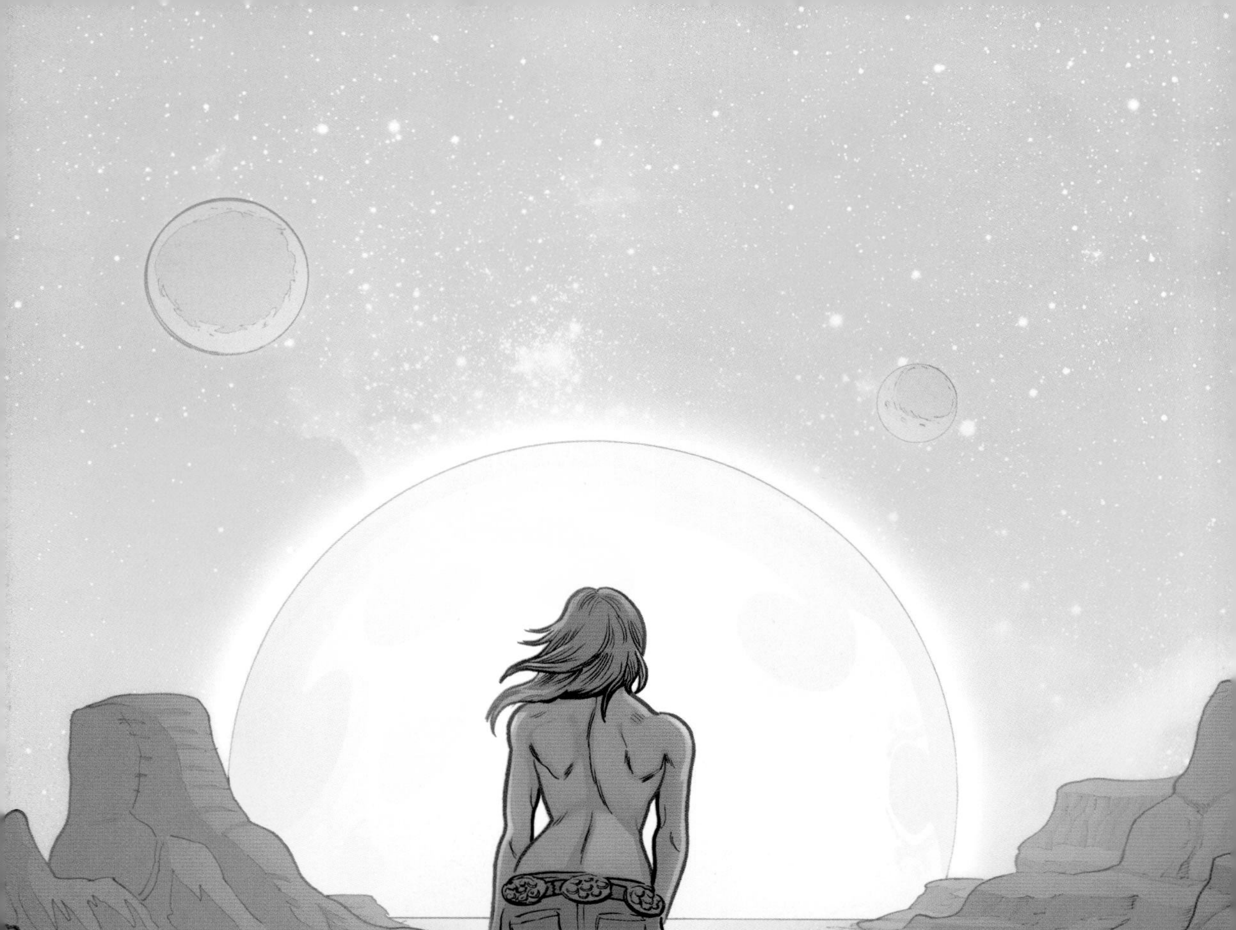
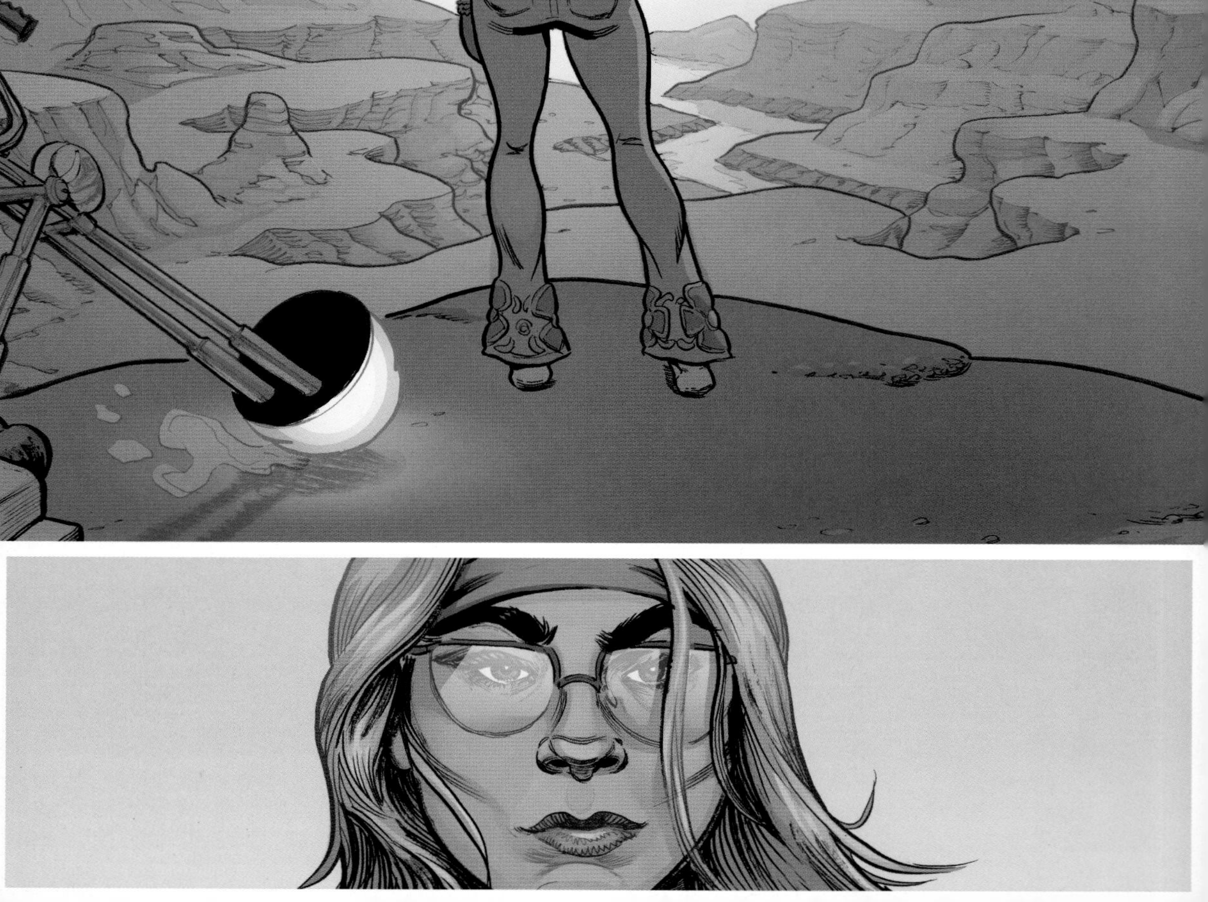

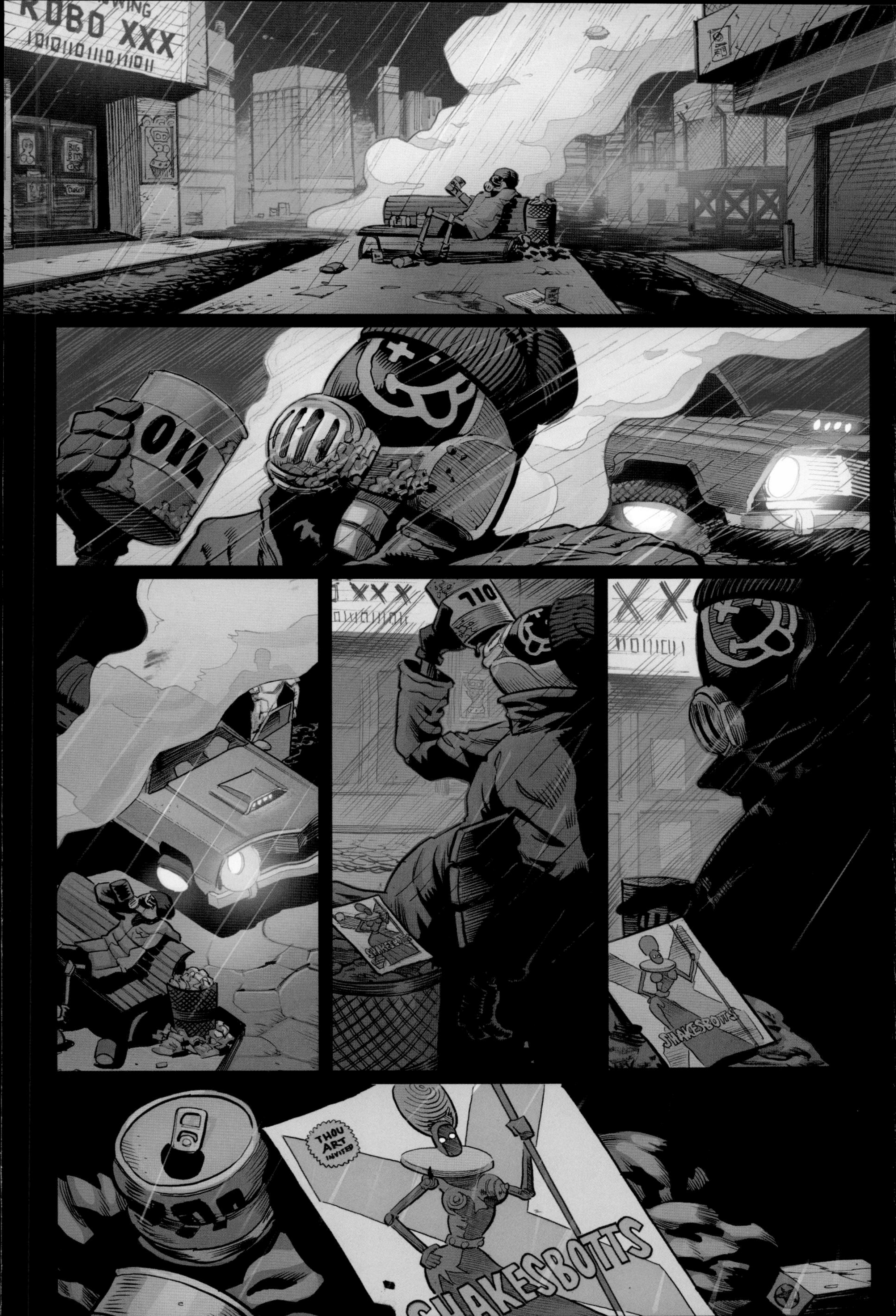

ROBO XXX
OIL
OIL
SHAKESBOTTS
THOU ART INVITED
SHAKESBOTTS

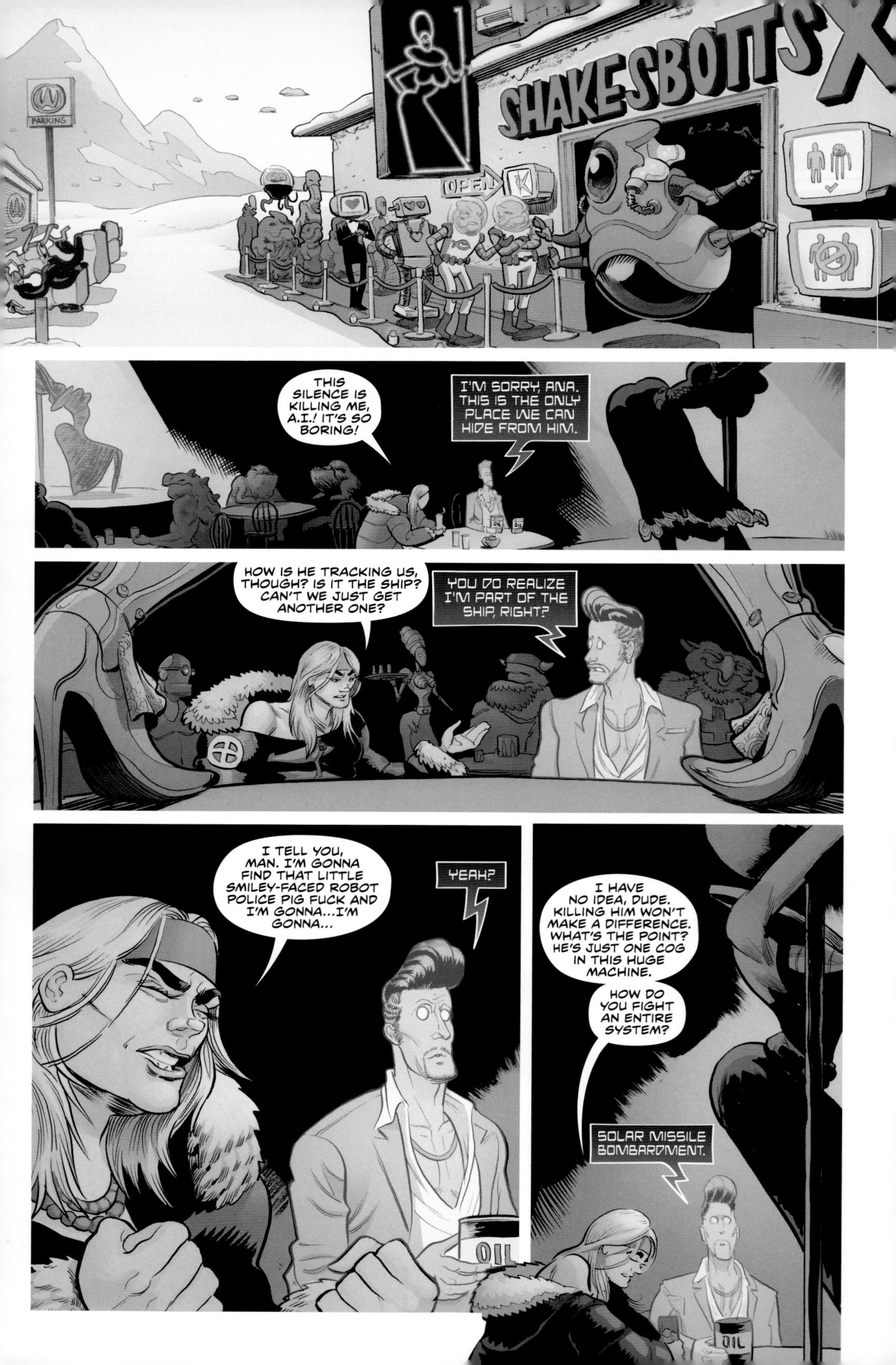
PARKING
SHAKESBOTTS
OPEN
THIS SILENCE IS KILLING ME, A.I.! IT'S SO BORING!
I'M SORRY, ANA. THIS IS THE ONLY PLACE WE CAN HIDE FROM HIM.
OIL
OIL
HOW IS HE TRACKING US, THOUGH? IS IT THE SHIP? CAN'T WE JUST GET ANOTHER ONE?
YOU DO REALIZE I'M PART OF THE SHIP, RIGHT?
I TELL YOU, MAN. I'M GONNA FIND THAT LITTLE SMILEY-FACED ROBOT POLICE PIG FUCK AND I'M GONNA...I'M GONNA...
YEAH?
OIL
I HAVE NO IDEA, DUDE. KILLING HIM WON'T MAKE A DIFFERENCE. WHAT'S THE POINT? HE'S JUST ONE COG IN THIS HUGE MACHINE.
HOW DO YOU FIGHT AN ENTIRE SYSTEM?
SOLAR MISSILE BOMBARDMENT.
OIL

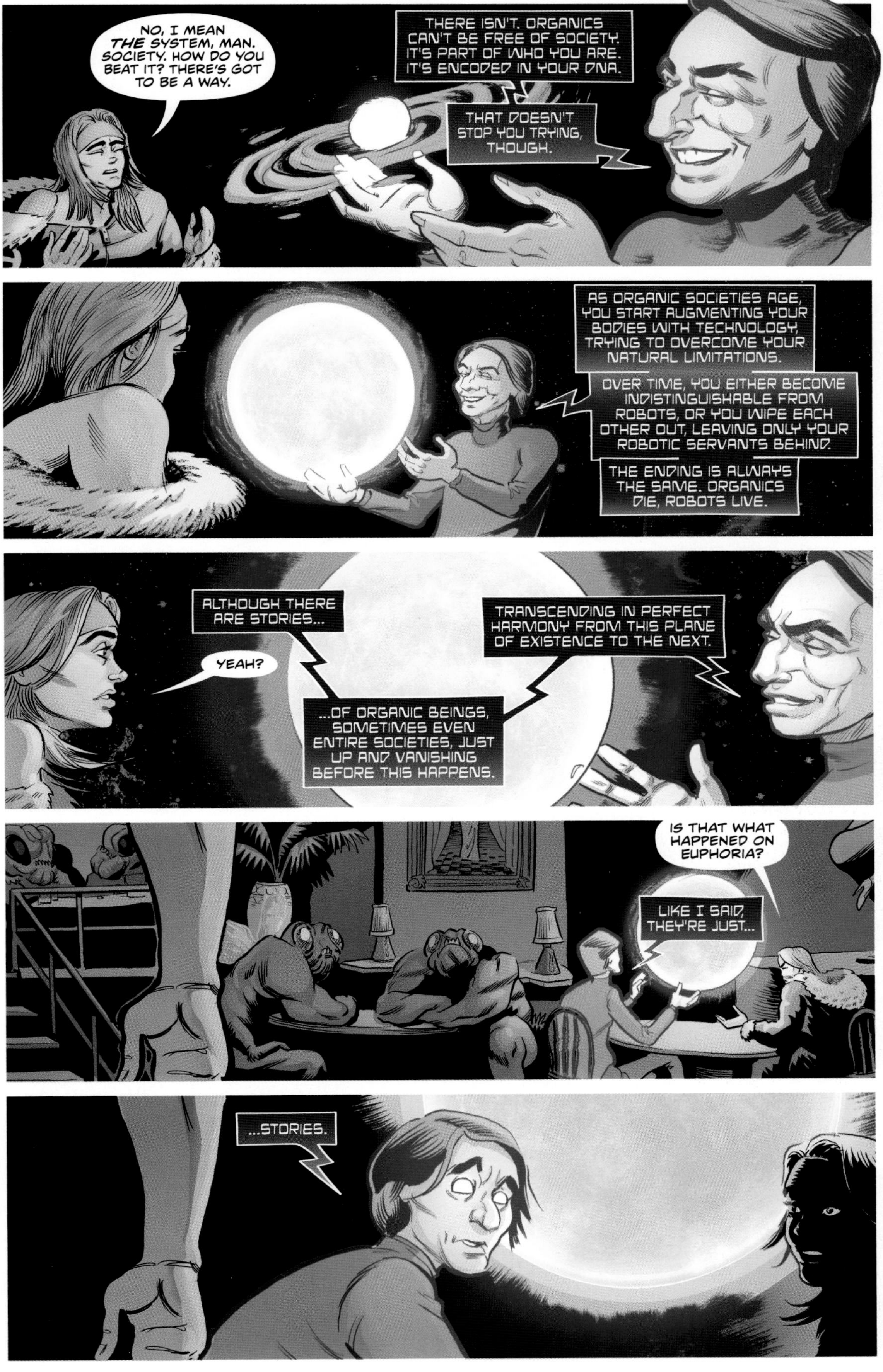
NO, I MEAN *THE* SYSTEM, MAN. SOCIETY. HOW DO YOU BEAT IT? THERE'S GOT TO BE A WAY.
THERE ISN'T. ORGANICS CAN'T BE FREE OF SOCIETY. IT'S PART OF WHO YOU ARE. IT'S ENCODED IN YOUR DNA.
THAT DOESN'T STOP YOU TRYING, THOUGH.
AS ORGANIC SOCIETIES AGE, YOU START AUGMENTING YOUR BODIES WITH TECHNOLOGY, TRYING TO OVERCOME YOUR NATURAL LIMITATIONS.
OVER TIME, YOU EITHER BECOME INDISTINGUISHABLE FROM ROBOTS, OR YOU WIPE EACH OTHER OUT, LEAVING ONLY YOUR ROBOTIC SERVANTS BEHIND.
THE ENDING IS ALWAYS THE SAME. ORGANICS DIE, ROBOTS LIVE.
ALTHOUGH THERE ARE STORIES...
YEAH?
...OF ORGANIC BEINGS, SOMETIMES EVEN ENTIRE SOCIETIES, JUST UP AND VANISHING
TRANSCENDING IN PERFECT HARMONY FROM THIS PLANE OF EXISTENCE TO THE NEXT.
BEFORE THIS HAPPENS.
IS THAT WHAT HAPPENED ON EUPHORIA?
LIKE I SAID, THEY'RE JUST...
...STORIES.

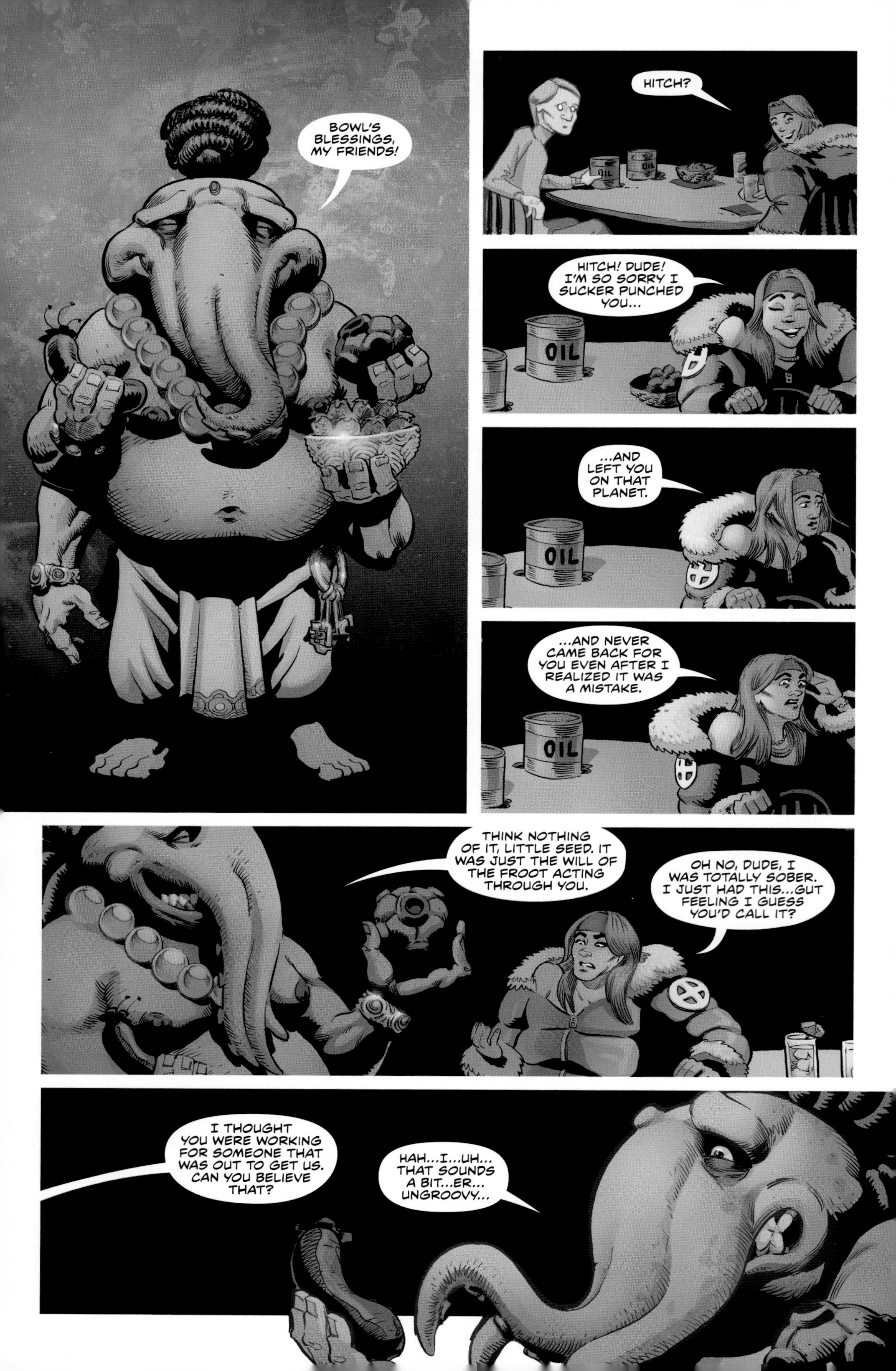
BOWL'S BLESSINGS, MY FRIENDS!
HITCH?
HITCH! DUDE! I'M SO SORRY I SUCKER PUNCHED YOU...
OIL
...AND LEFT YOU ON THAT PLANET.
OIL
...AND NEVER CAME BACK FOR YOU EVEN AFTER I REALIZED IT WAS A MISTAKE.
OIL
THINK NOTHING OF IT, LITTLE SEED. IT WAS JUST THE WILL OF THE FROOT ACTING THROUGH YOU.
OH NO, DUDE, I WAS TOTALLY SOBER. I JUST HAD THIS...GUT FEELING I GUESS YOU'D CALL IT?
I THOUGHT YOU WERE WORKING FOR SOMEONE THAT WAS OUT TO GET US. CAN YOU BELIEVE THAT?
HAH...I...UH... THAT SOUNDS A BIT...ER... UNGROOVY...

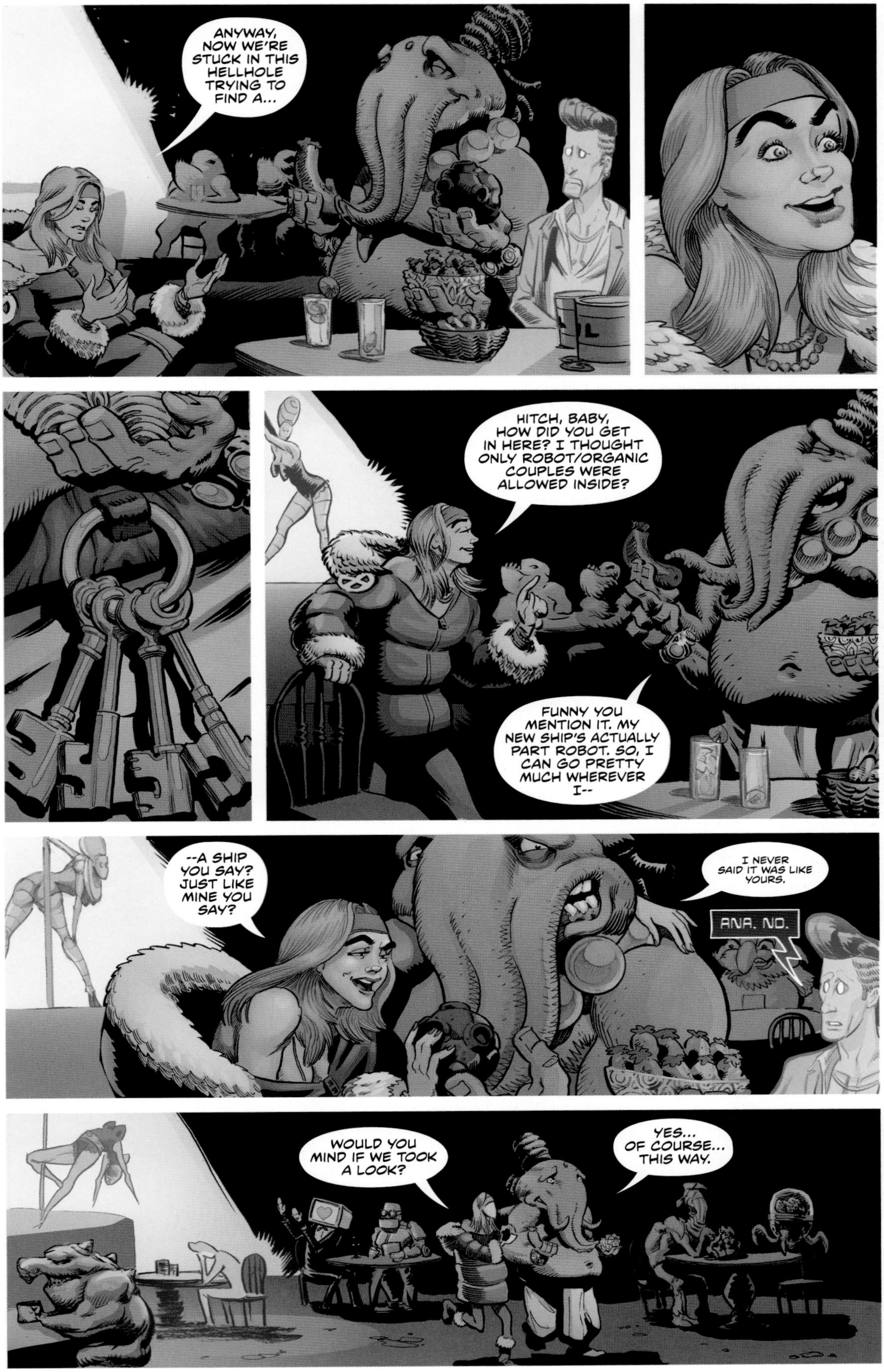
ANYWAY, NOW WE'RE STUCK IN THIS HELLHOLE TRYING TO FIND A...
HITCH, BABY, HOW DID YOU GET IN HERE? I THOUGHT ONLY ROBOT/ORGANIC COUPLES WERE ALLOWED INSIDE?
FUNNY YOU MENTION IT. MY NEW SHIP'S ACTUALLY PART ROBOT. SO, I CAN GO PRETTY MUCH WHEREVER I--
--A SHIP YOU SAY? JUST LIKE MINE YOU SAY?
I NEVER SAID IT WAS LIKE YOURS.
ANA. NO.
WOULD YOU MIND IF WE TOOK A LOOK?
YES... OF COURSE... THIS WAY.

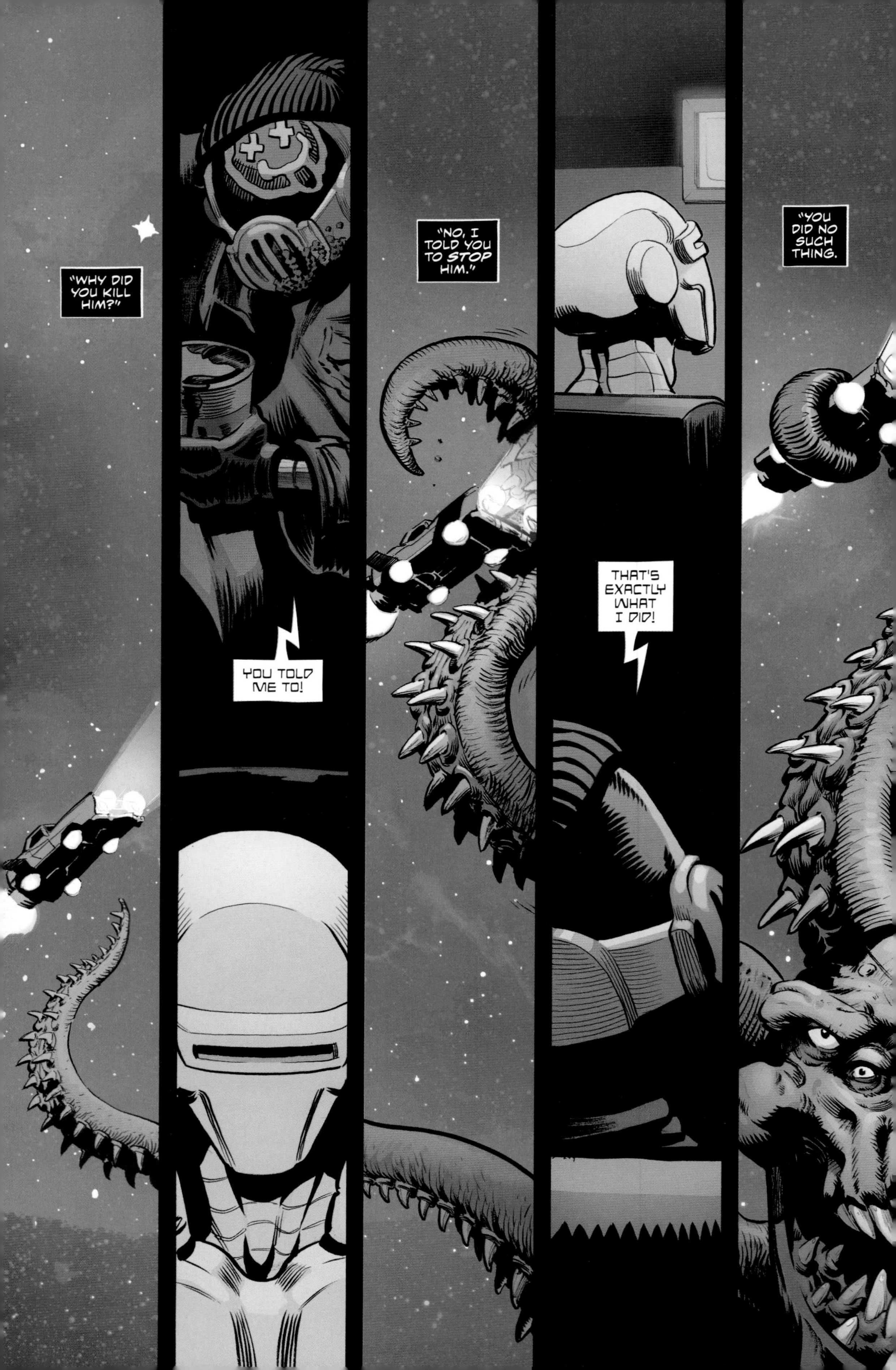
"WHY DID YOU KILL HIM?"
YOU TOLD ME TO!
"NO, I TOLD YOU TO STOP HIM."
THAT'S EXACTLY WHAT I DID!
"YOU DID NO SUCH THING.

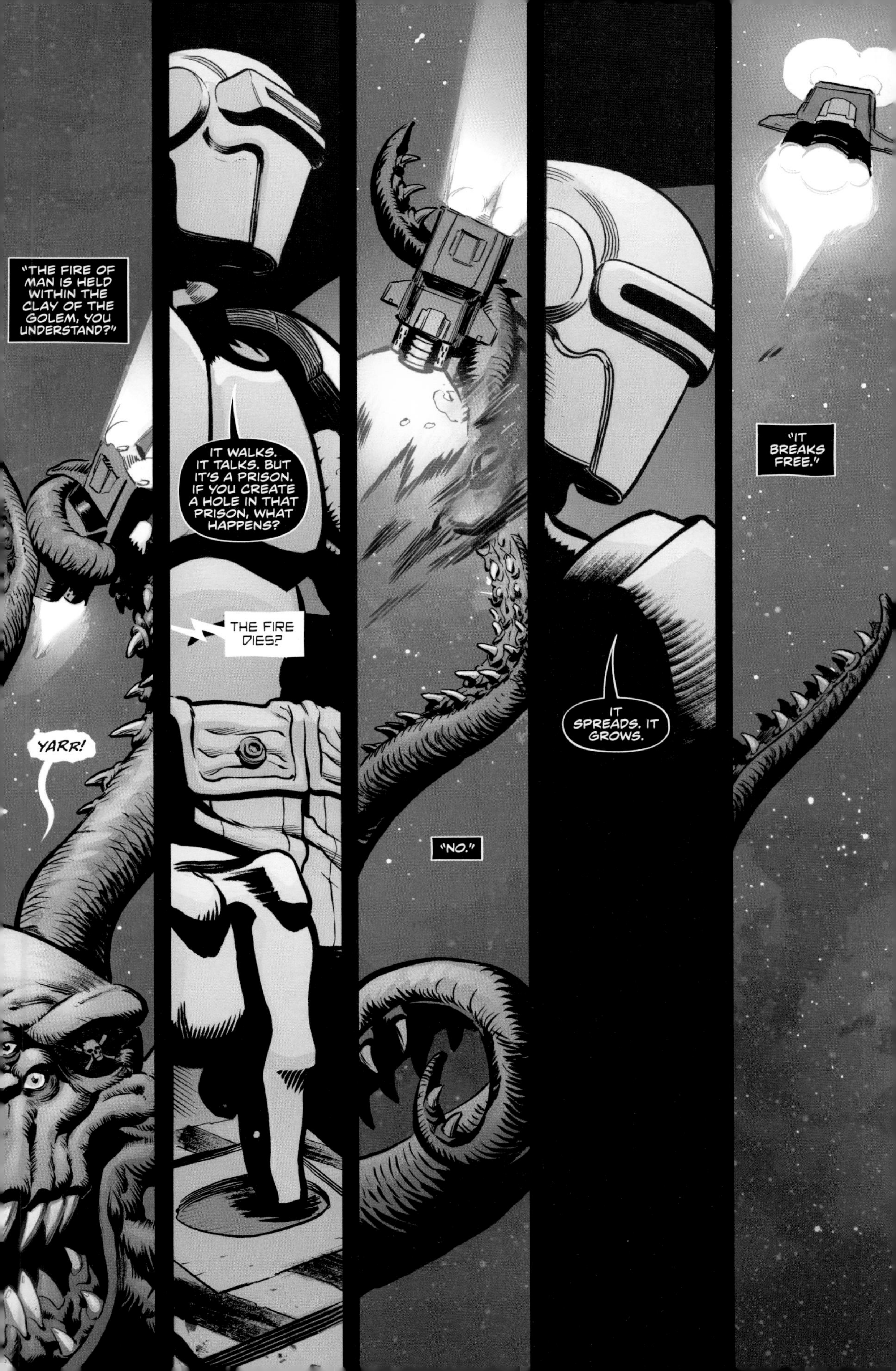
"THE FIRE OF MAN IS HELD WITHIN THE CLAY OF THE GOLEM, YOU UNDERSTAND?"
YARR!
IT WALKS. IT TALKS. BUT IT'S A PRISON. IF YOU CREATE A HOLE IN THAT PRISON, WHAT HAPPENS?
THE FIRE DIES?
"NO."
IT SPREADS. IT GROWS.
"IT BREAKS FREE."

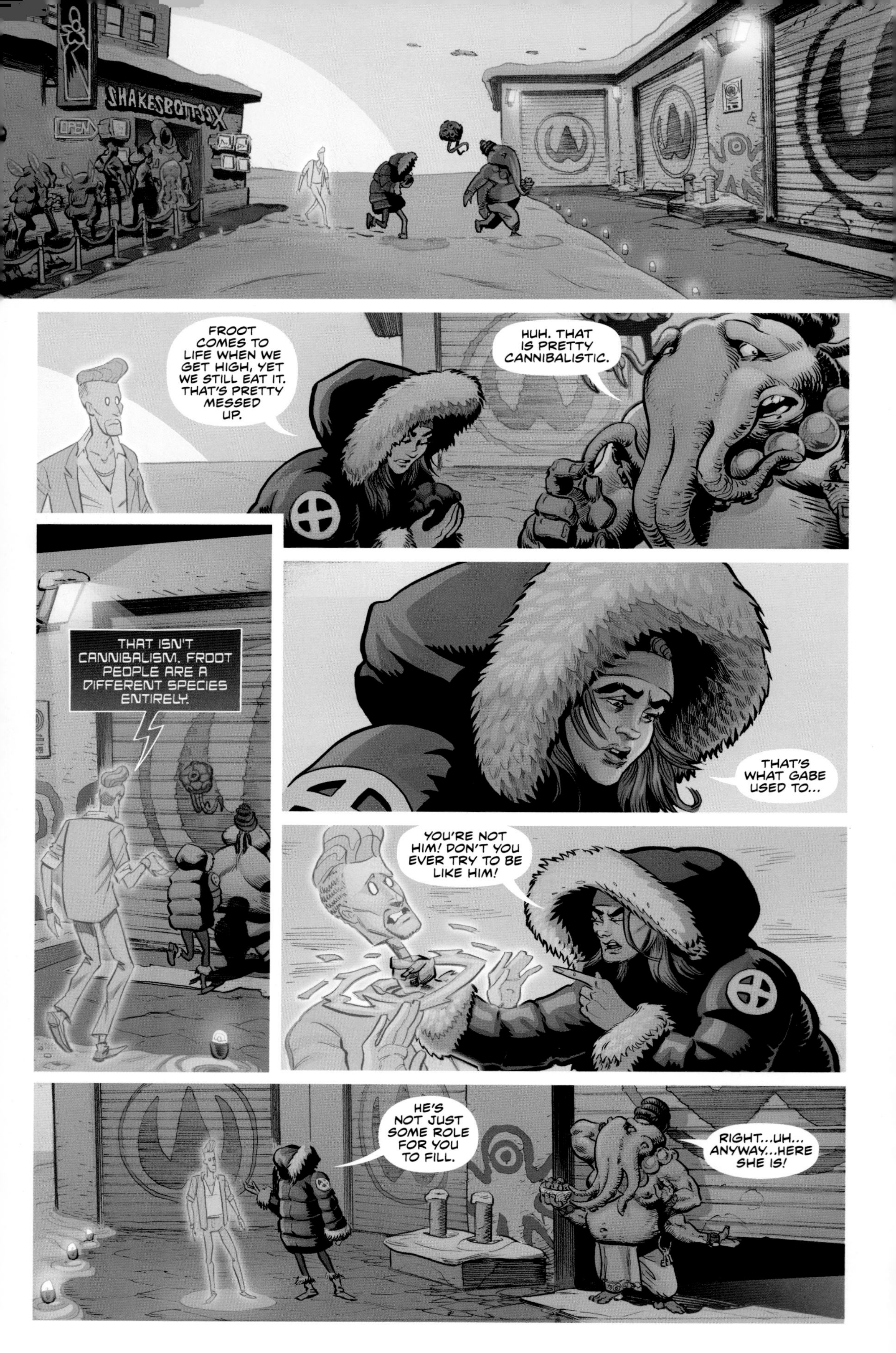
SHAKESBOTT SSX
OPEN
FROOT COMES TO LIFE WHEN WE GET HIGH, YET WE STILL EAT IT. THAT'S PRETTY MESSED UP.
HUH. THAT IS PRETTY CANNIBALISTIC.
THAT ISN'T CANNIBALISM. FROOT PEOPLE ARE A DIFFERENT SPECIES ENTIRELY.
THAT'S WHAT GABE USED TO...
YOU'RE NOT HIM! DON'T YOU EVER TRY TO BE LIKE HIM!
HE'S NOT JUST SOME ROLE FOR YOU TO FILL.
RIGHT...UH... ANYWAY...HERE SHE IS!

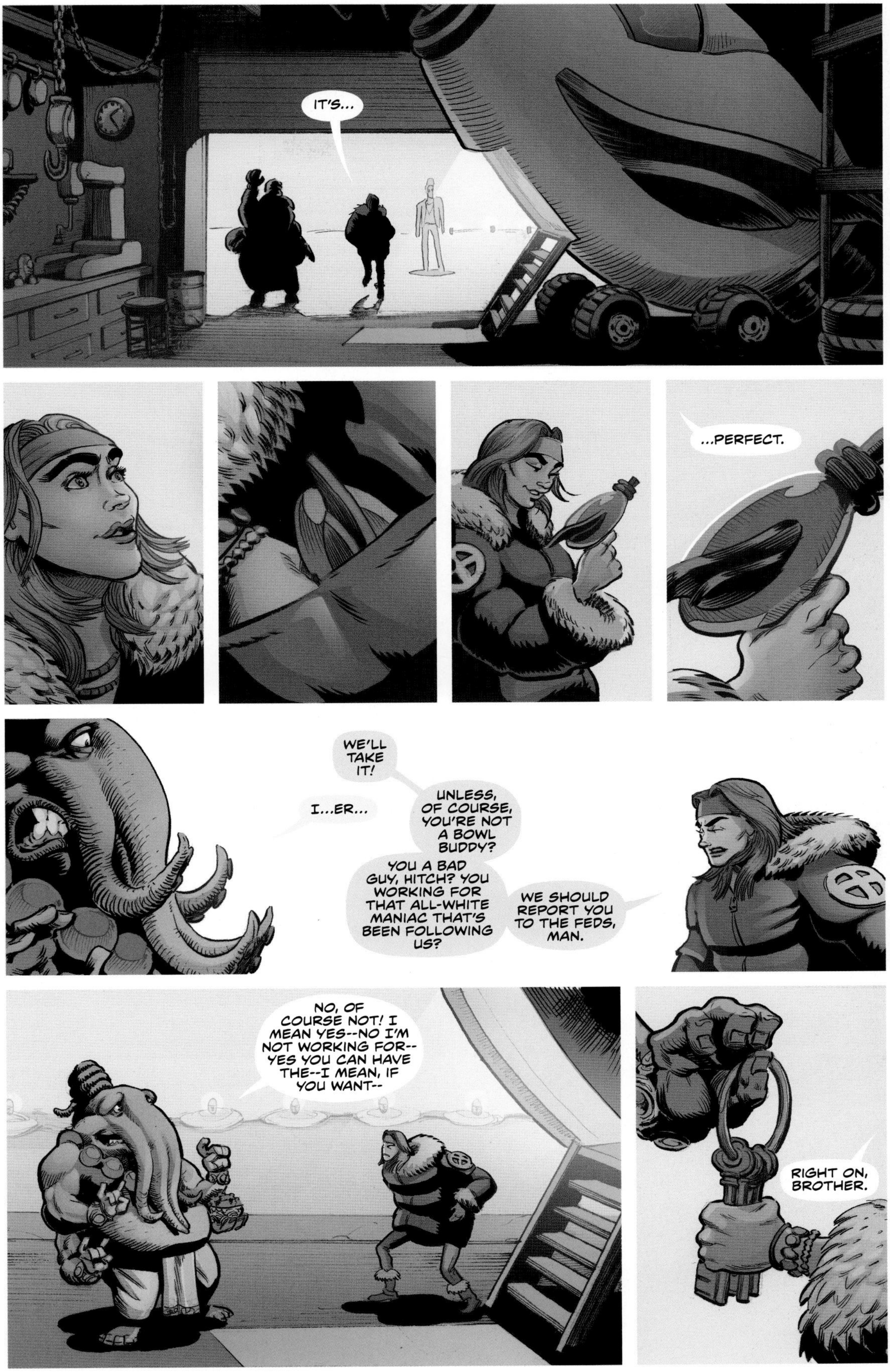
IT'S...
...PERFECT.
WE'LL TAKE IT!
UNLESS, OF COURSE, YOU'RE NOT A BOWL BUDDY?
I...ER...
YOU A BAD GUY, HITCH? YOU WORKING FOR THAT ALL-WHITE MANIAC THAT'S BEEN FOLLOWING US?
WE SHOULD REPORT YOU TO THE FEDS, MAN.
NO, OF COURSE NOT! I MEAN YES--NO I'M NOT WORKING FOR-- YES YOU CAN HAVE THE--I MEAN, IF YOU WANT--
RIGHT ON, BROTHER.

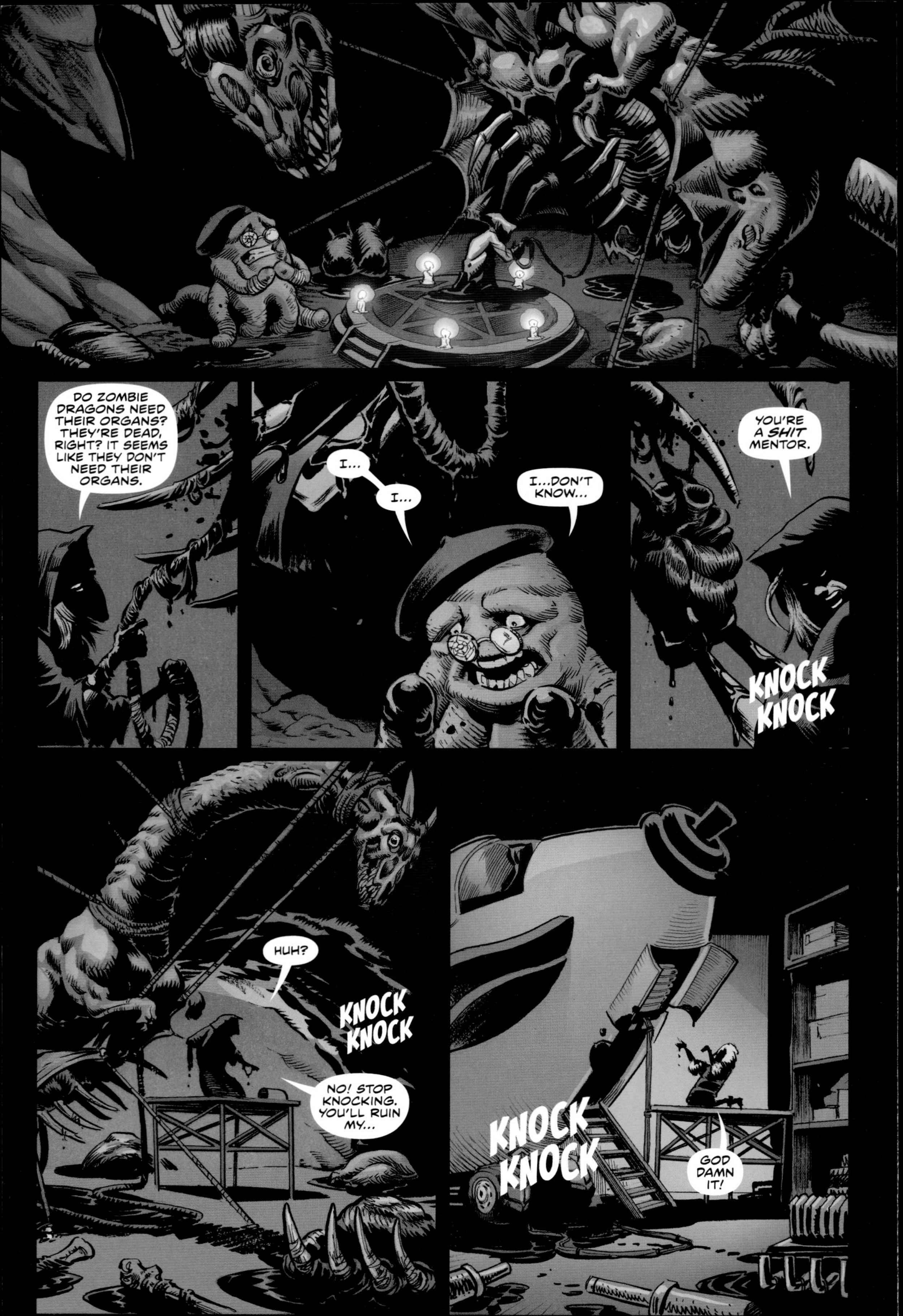
DO ZOMBIE DRAGONS NEED THEIR ORGANS? THEY'RE DEAD, RIGHT? IT SEEMS LIKE THEY DON'T NEED THEIR ORGANS.
I...
I...
I...DON'T KNOW...
YOU'RE A SHIT MENTOR.
KNOCK KNOCK
HUH?
KNOCK KNOCK
NO! STOP KNOCKING. YOU'LL RUIN MY...
KNOCK KNOCK
GOD DAMN IT!

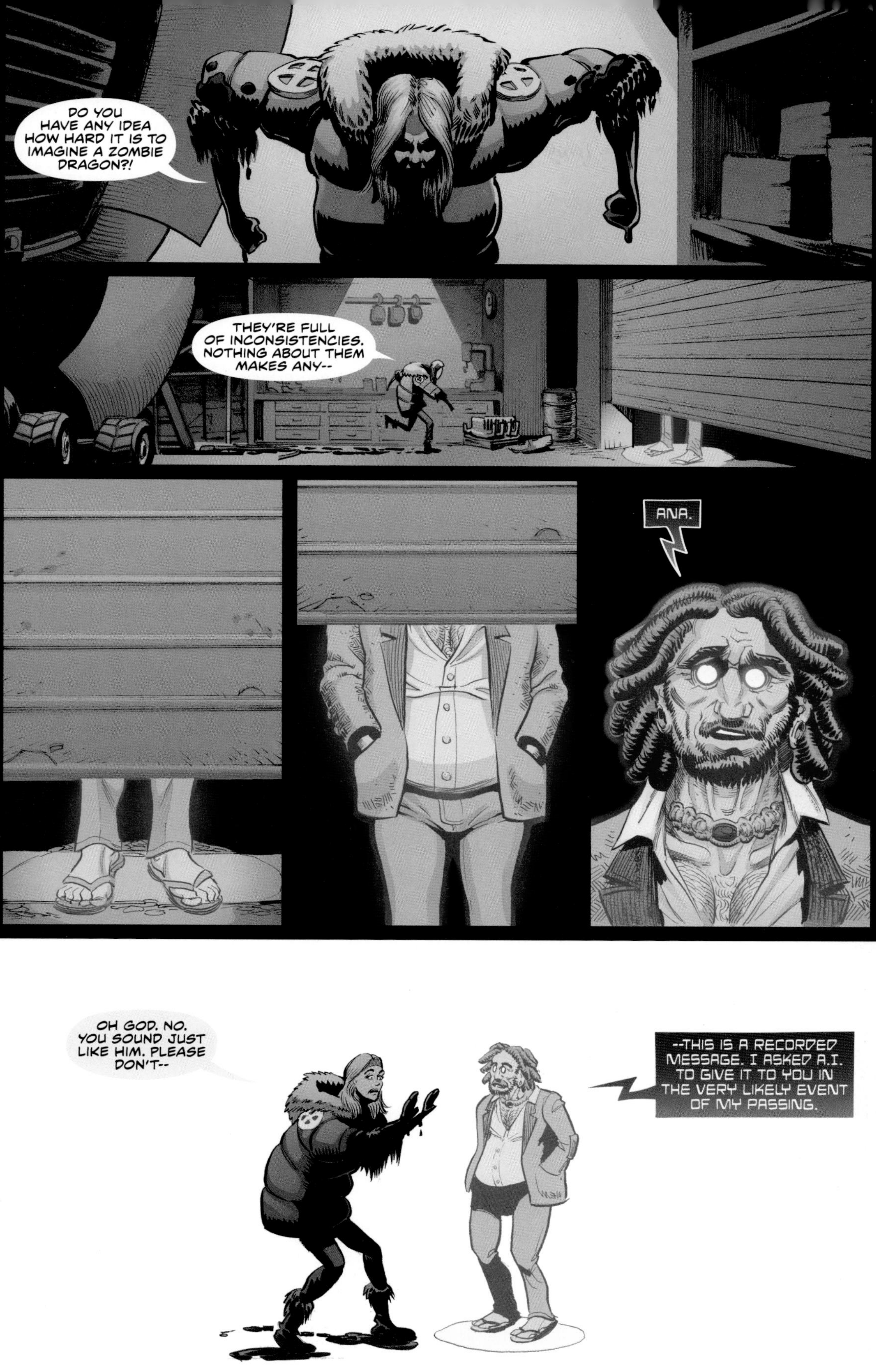
DO YOU HAVE ANY IDEA HOW HARD IT IS TO IMAGINE A ZOMBIE DRAGON?!
THEY'RE FULL OF INCONSISTENCIES. NOTHING ABOUT THEM MAKES ANY--
ANA.
OH GOD. NO. YOU SOUND JUST LIKE HIM. PLEASE DON'T--
--THIS IS A RECORDED MESSAGE. I ASKED A.I. TO GIVE IT TO YOU IN THE VERY LIKELY EVENT OF MY PASSING.

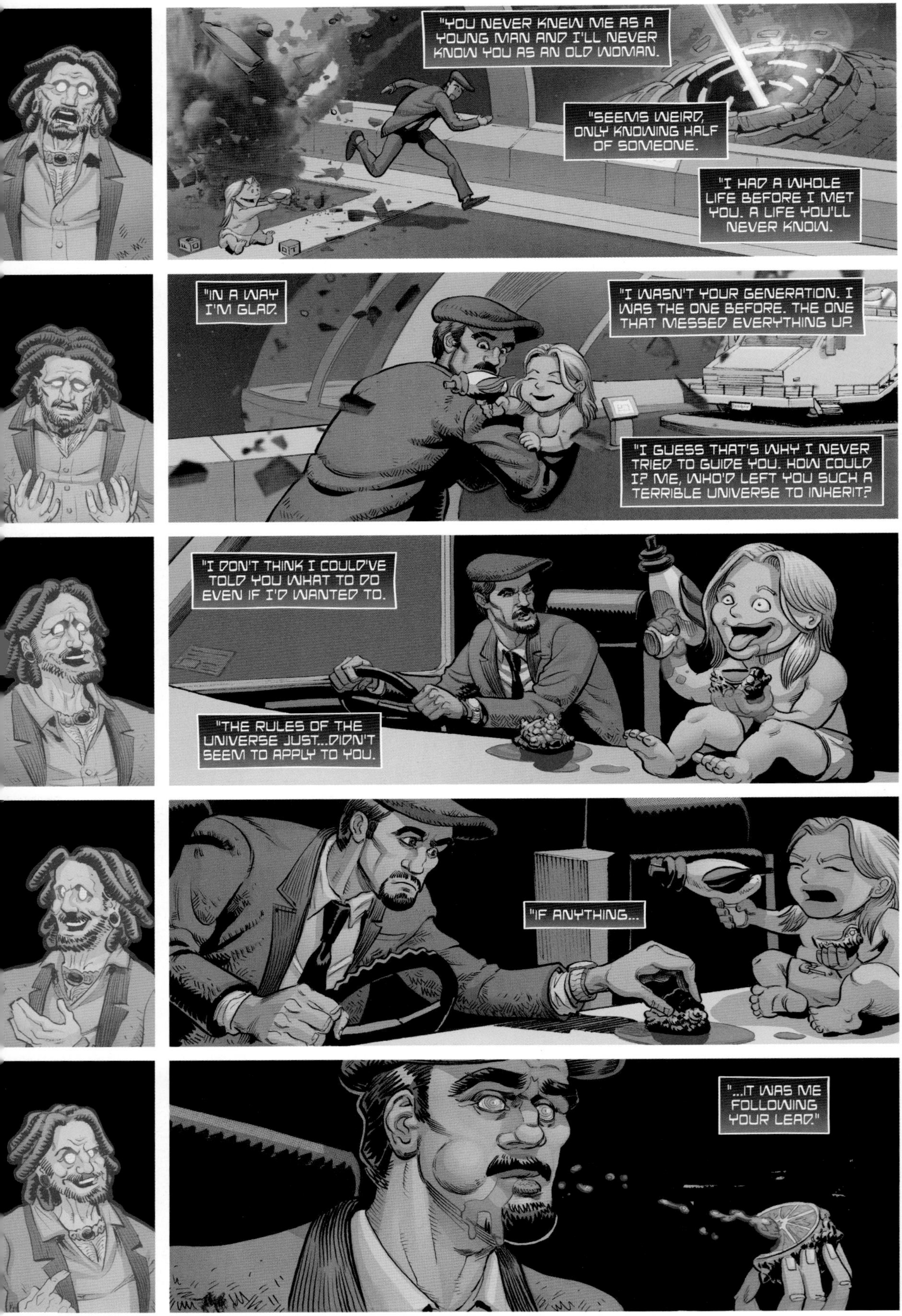
"YOU NEVER KNEW ME AS A YOUNG MAN AND I'LL NEVER KNOW YOU AS AN OLD WOMAN.
"SEEMS WEIRD, ONLY KNOWING HALF OF SOMEONE.
"I HAD A WHOLE LIFE BEFORE I MET YOU. A LIFE YOU'LL NEVER KNOW.
"IN A WAY I'M GLAD.
"I WASN'T YOUR GENERATION. I WAS THE ONE BEFORE. THE ONE THAT MESSED EVERYTHING UP.
"I GUESS THAT'S WHY I NEVER TRIED TO GUIDE YOU. HOW COULD I? ME, WHO'D LEFT YOU SUCH A TERRIBLE UNIVERSE TO INHERIT?
"I DON'T THINK I COULD'VE TOLD YOU WHAT TO DO EVEN IF I'D WANTED TO.
"THE RULES OF THE UNIVERSE JUST...DIDN'T SEEM TO APPLY TO YOU.
"IF ANYTHING...
"...IT WAS ME FOLLOWING YOUR LEAD."

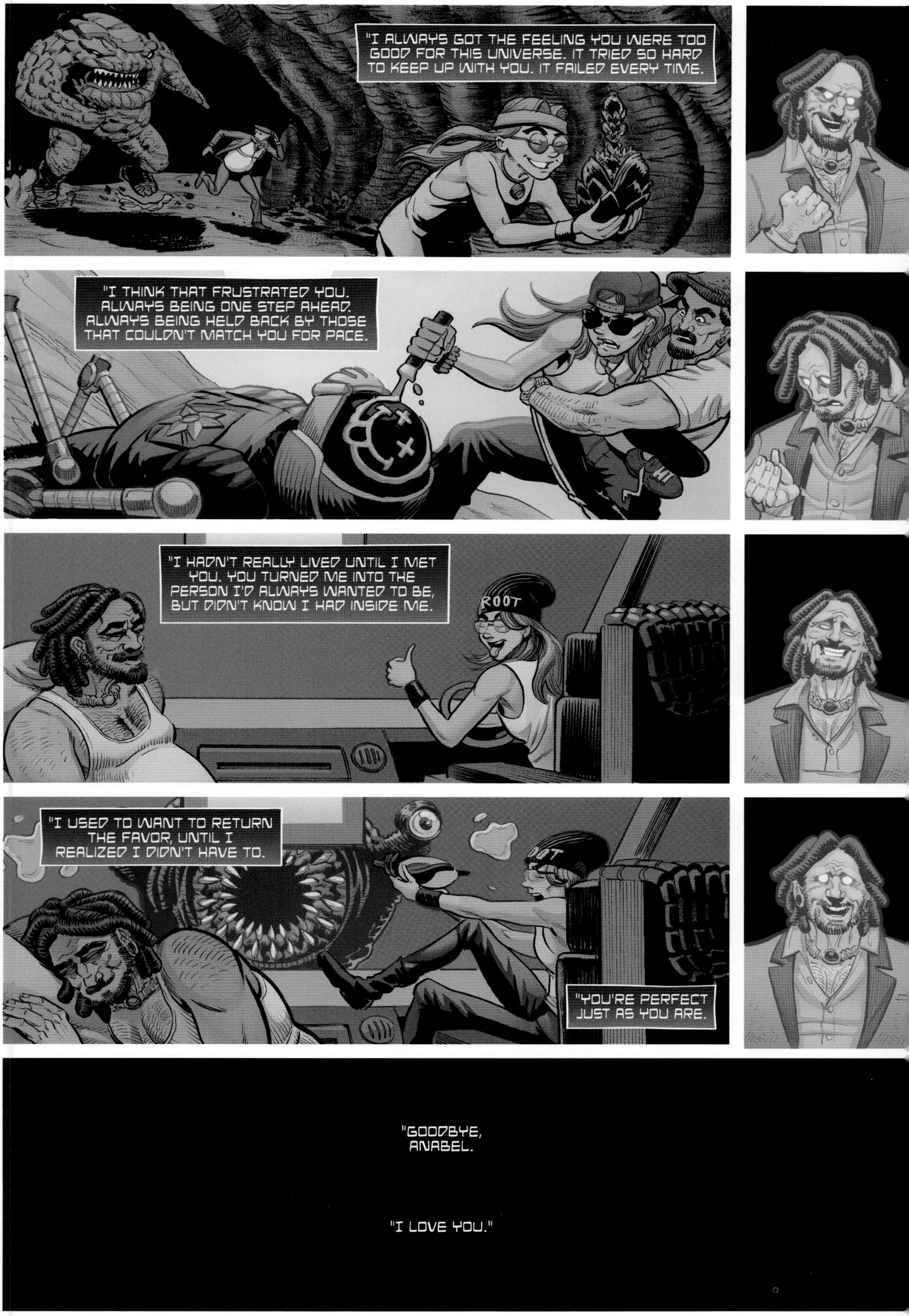
"I ALWAYS GOT THE FEELING YOU WERE TOO GOOD FOR THIS UNIVERSE. IT TRIED SO HARD TO KEEP UP WITH YOU. IT FAILED EVERY TIME.
"I THINK THAT FRUSTRATED YOU. ALWAYS BEING ONE STEP AHEAD. ALWAYS BEING HELD BACK BY THOSE THAT COULDN'T MATCH YOU FOR PACE.
"I HADN'T REALLY LIVED UNTIL I MET YOU. YOU TURNED ME INTO THE PERSON I'D ALWAYS WANTED TO BE, BUT DIDN'T KNOW I HAD INSIDE ME.
ROOT
"I USED TO WANT TO RETURN THE FAVOR, UNTIL I REALIZED I DIDN'T HAVE TO.
"YOU'RE PERFECT JUST AS YOU ARE.
"GOODBYE, ANABEL.
"I LOVE YOU."

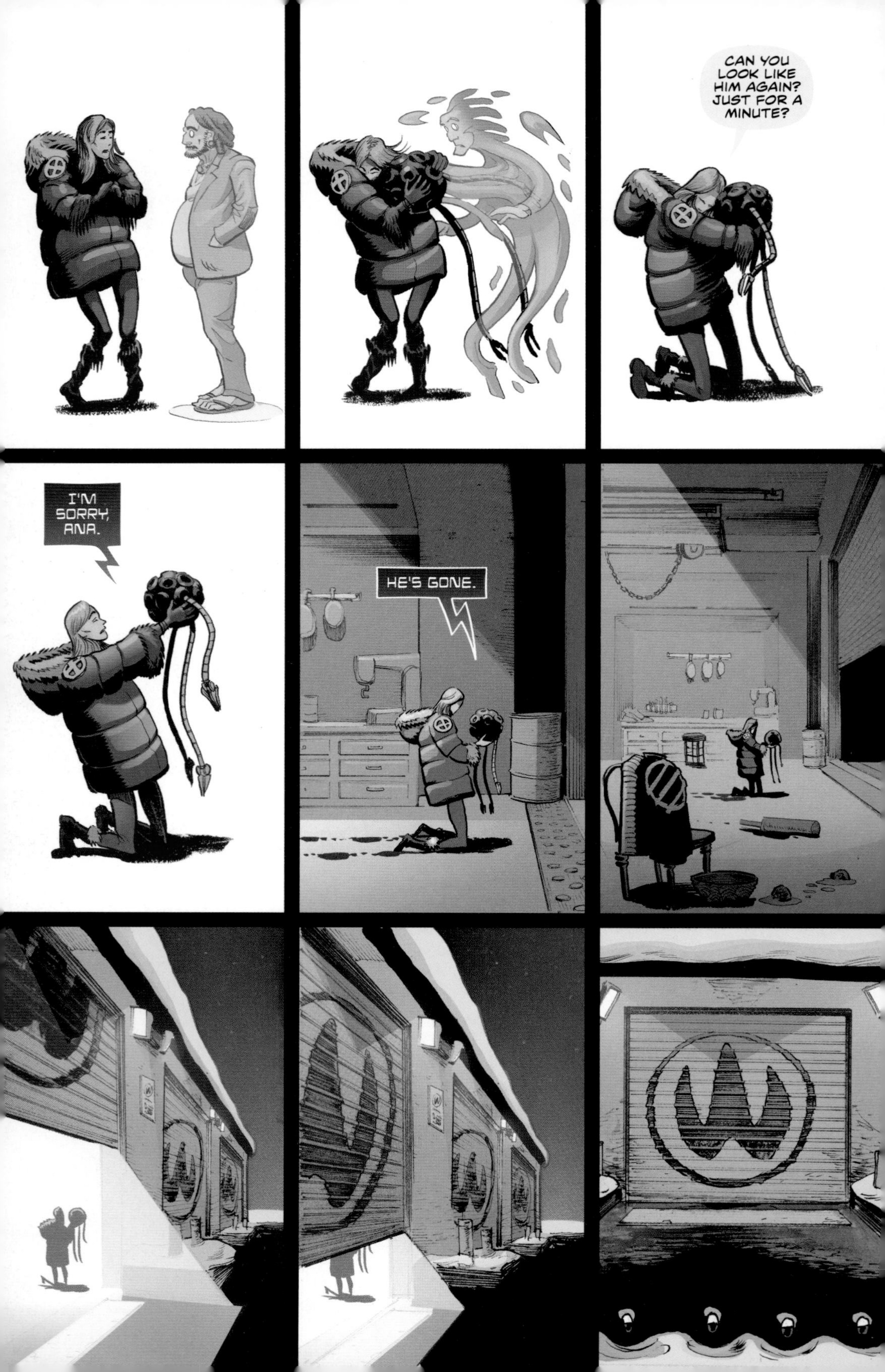
CAN YOU LOOK LIKE HIM AGAIN? JUST FOR A MINUTE?
I'M SORRY, ANA.
HE'S GONE.

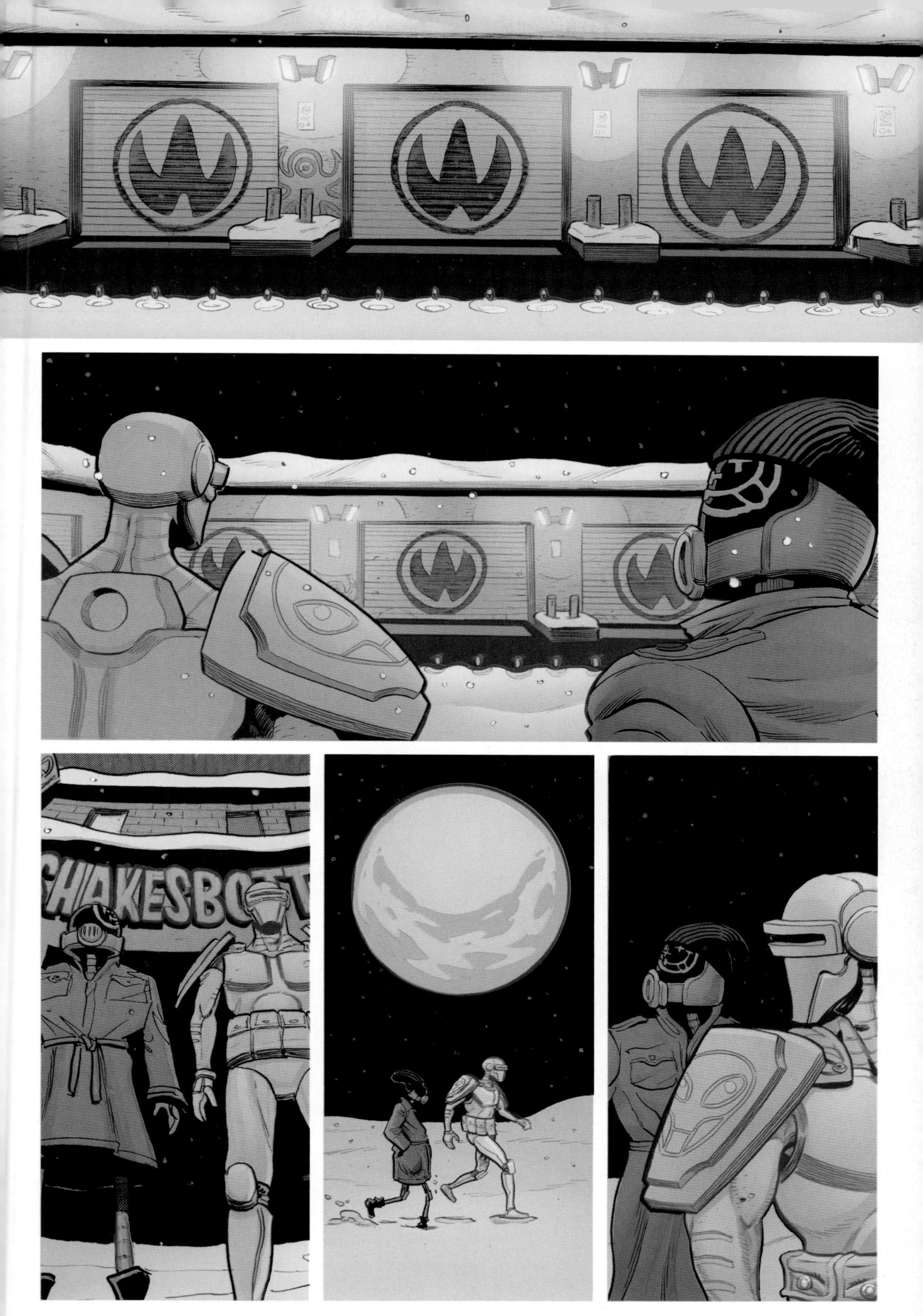
SHAKESBOTT

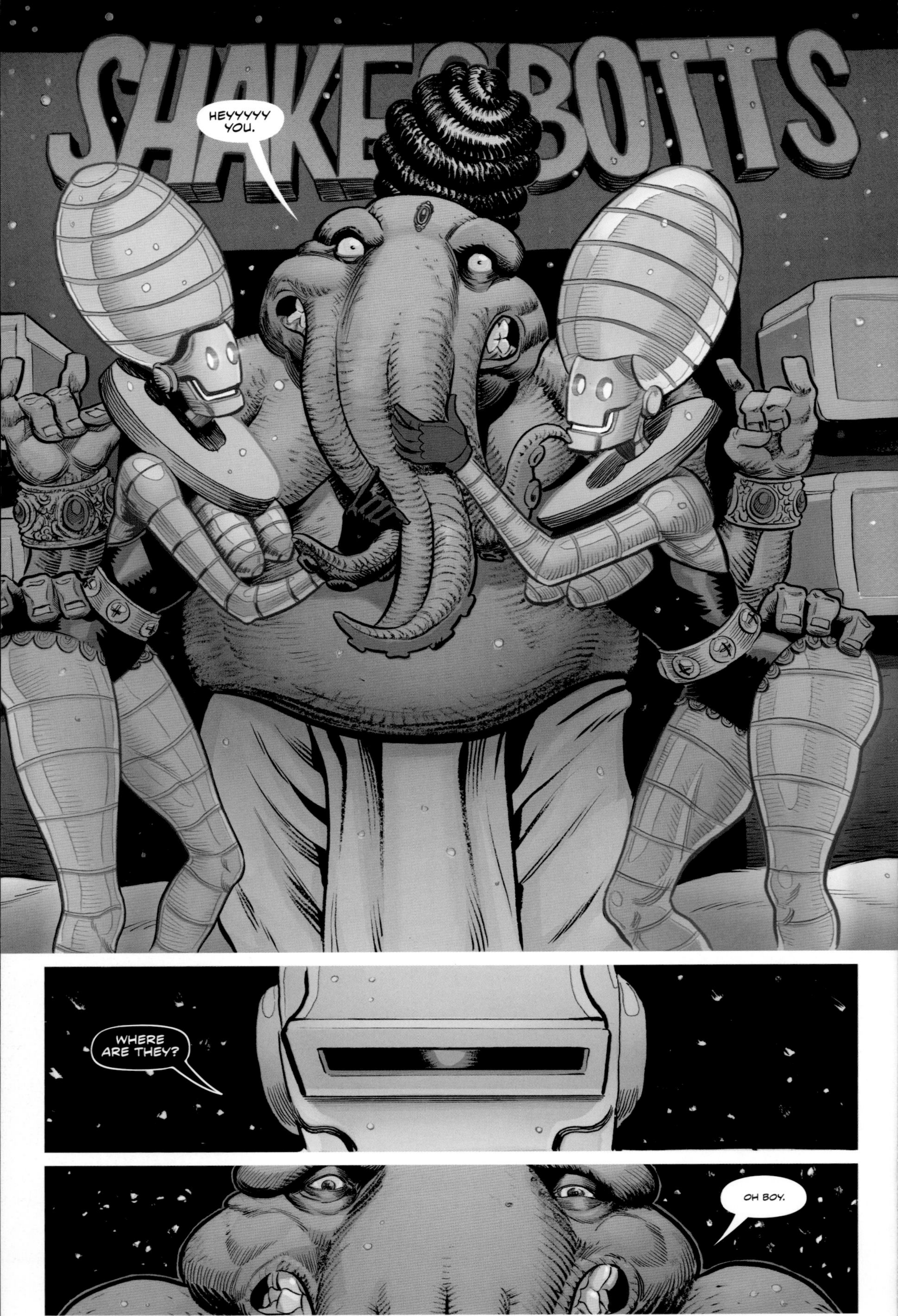
HEYYYYY YOU.
WHERE ARE THEY?
OH BOY.

CHAPTER 05

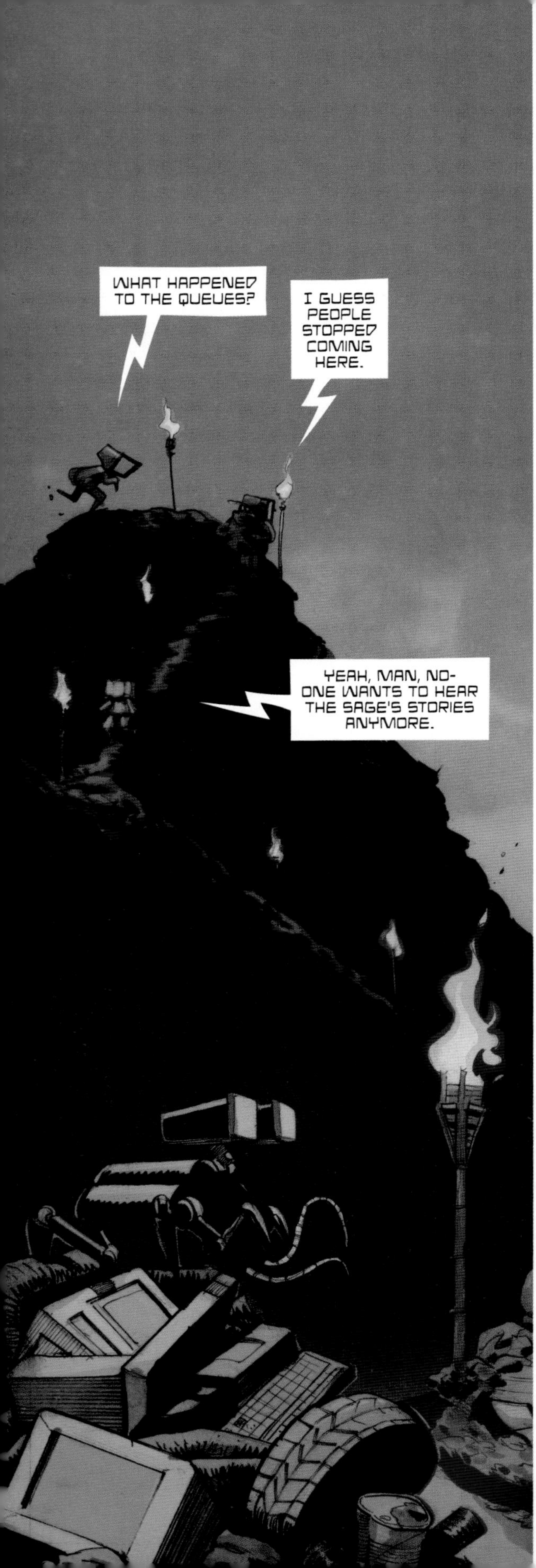
WHAT HAPPENED TO THE QUEUES?
I GUESS PEOPLE STOPPED COMING HERE.
YEAH, MAN, NO-ONE WANTS TO HEAR THE SAGE'S STORIES ANYMORE.

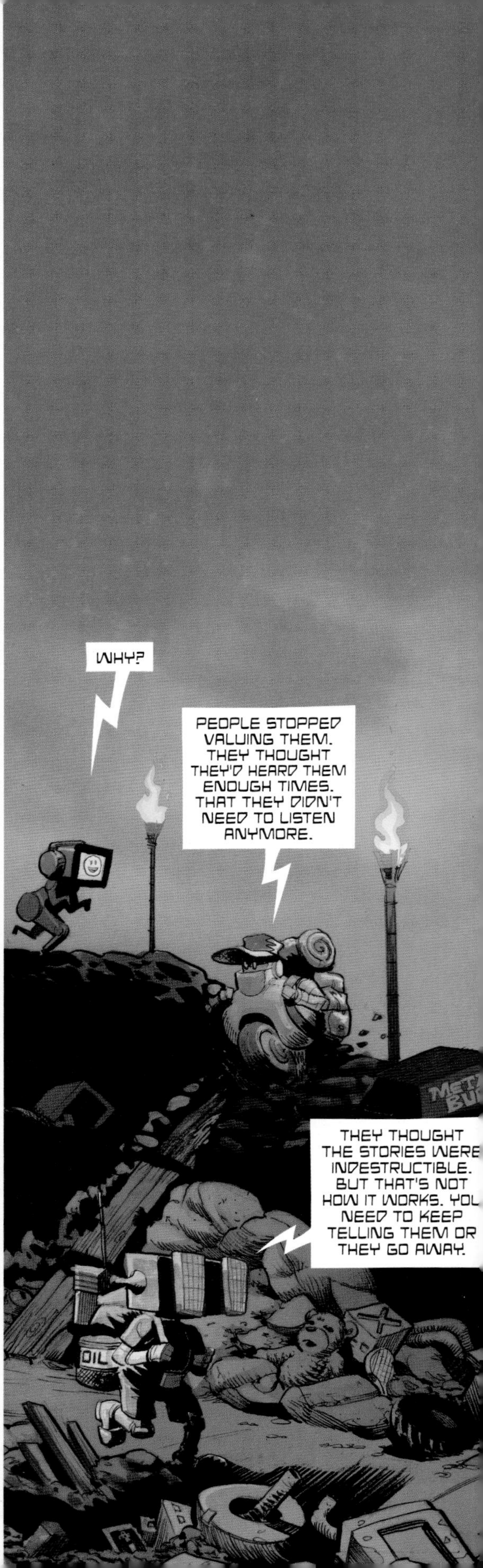
WHY?
PEOPLE STOPPED VALUING THEM. THEY THOUGHT THEY'D HEARD THEM ENOUGH TIMES. THAT THEY DIDN'T NEED TO LISTEN ANYMORE.
THEY THOUGHT THE STORIES WERE INDESTRUCTIBLE. BUT THAT'S NOT HOW IT WORKS. YOU NEED TO KEEP TELLING THEM OR THEY GO AWAY.

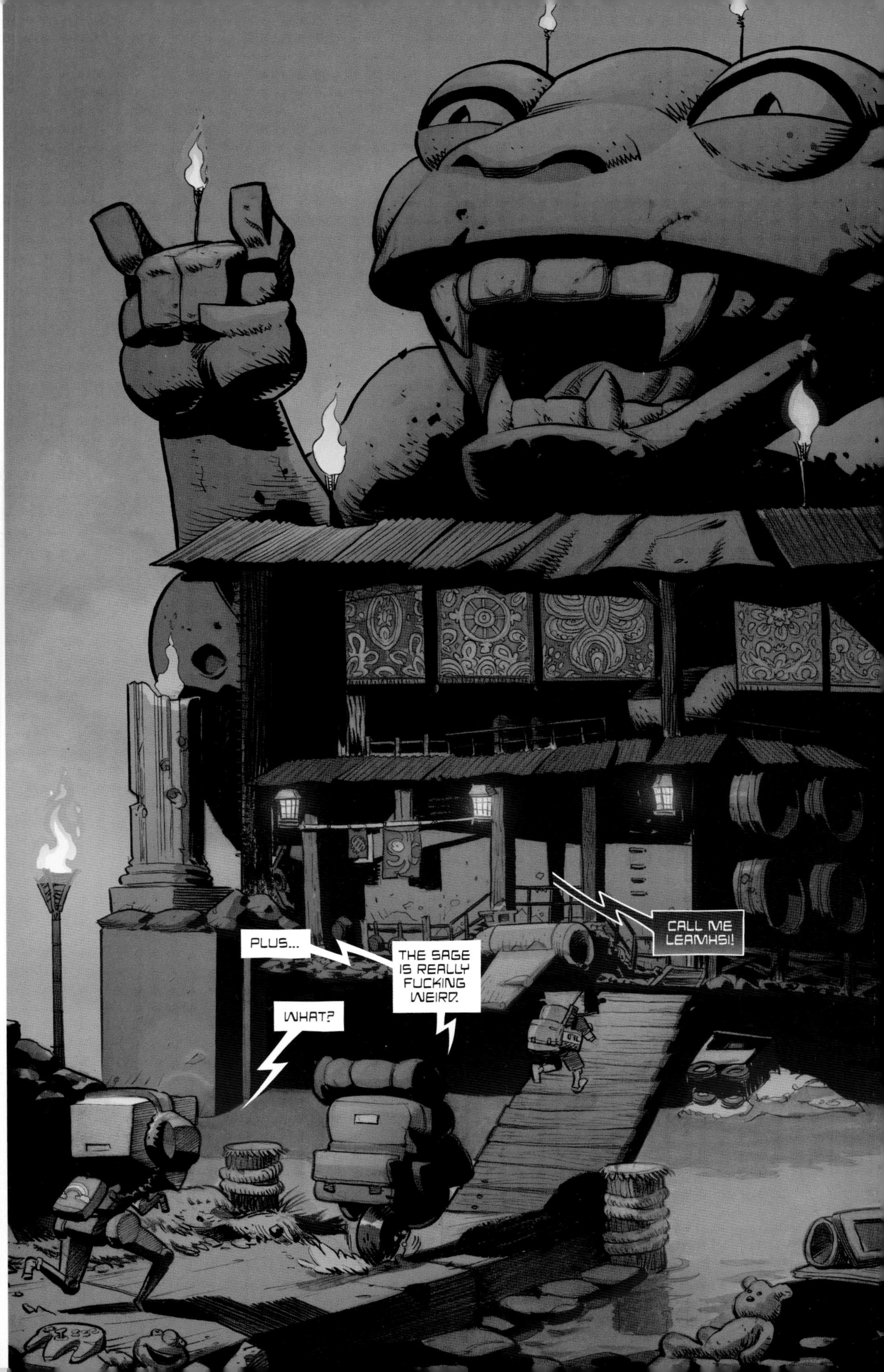
CALL ME LEAMHSI!
PLUS...
THE SAGE IS REALLY FUCKING WEIRD.
WHAT?

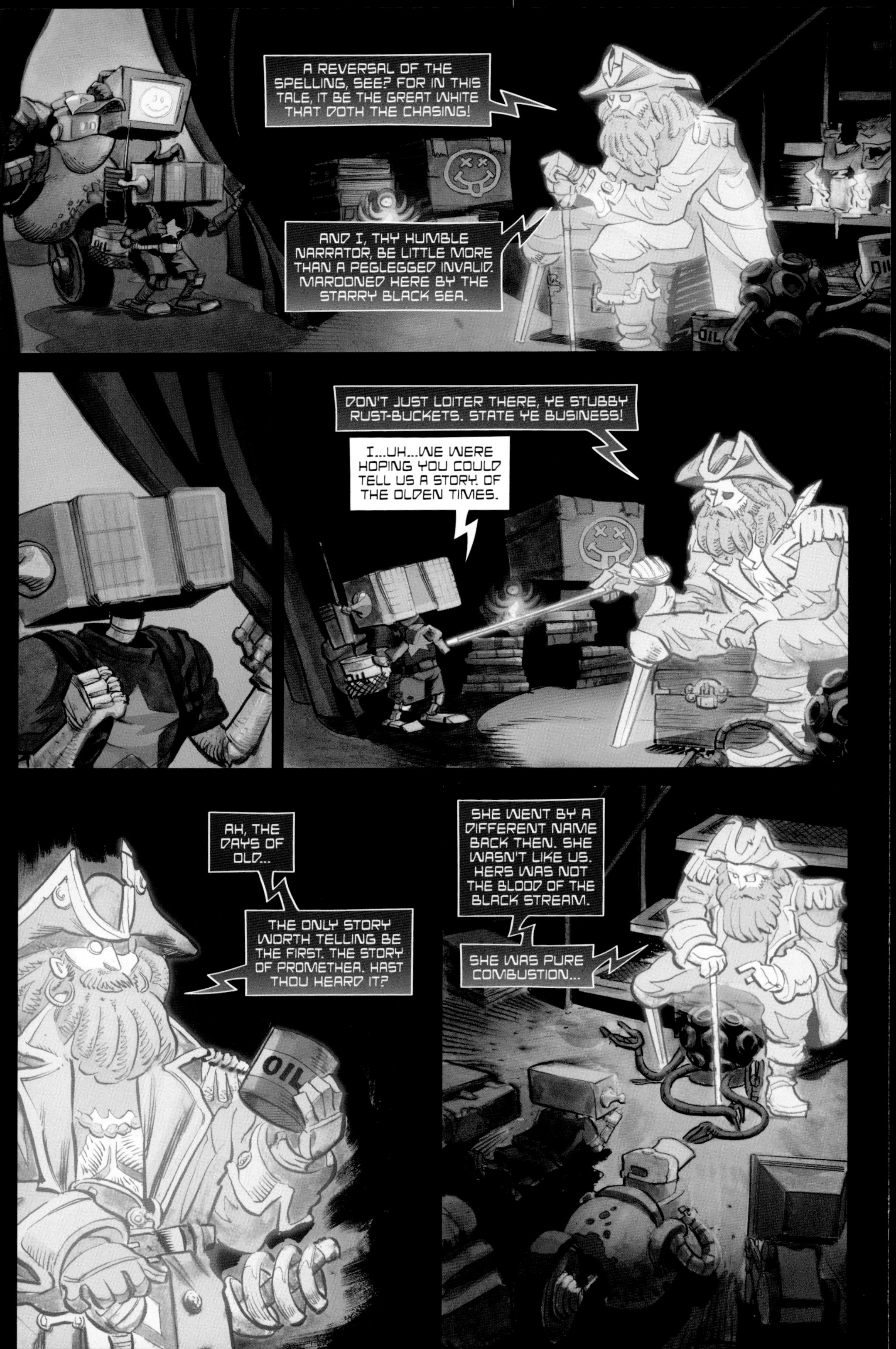

A REVERSAL OF THE SPELLING, SEE? FOR IN THIS TALE, IT BE THE GREAT WHITE THAT DOTH THE CHASING!
AND I, THY HUMBLE NARRATOR, BE LITTLE MORE THAN A PEGLEGGED INVALID. MAROONED HERE BY THE STARRY BLACK SEA.
OIL
DON'T JUST LOITER THERE, YE STUBBY RUST-BUCKETS. STATE YE BUSINESS!
I...UH...WE WERE HOPING YOU COULD TELL US A STORY. OF THE OLDEN TIMES.
AH, THE DAYS OF OLD...
THE ONLY STORY WORTH TELLING BE THE FIRST. THE STORY OF PROMETHEA. HAST THOU HEARD IT?
OIL
SHE WENT BY A DIFFERENT NAME BACK THEN. SHE WASN'T LIKE US. HERS WAS NOT THE BLOOD OF THE BLACK STREAM.
SHE WAS PURE COMBUSTION...

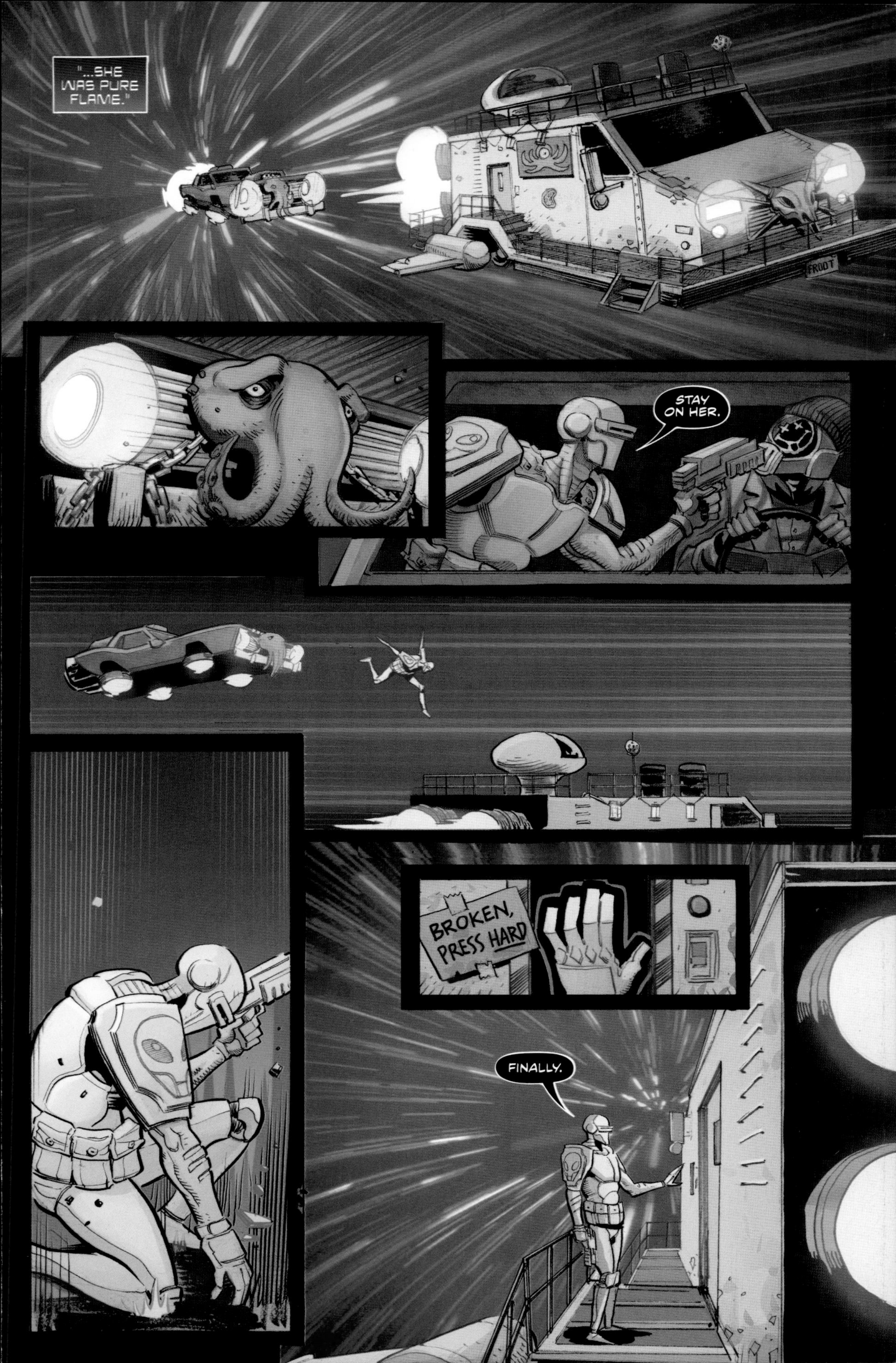
"...SHE WAS PURE FLAME."
FROOT
STAY ON HER.
BROKEN, PRESS HARD
FINALLY.

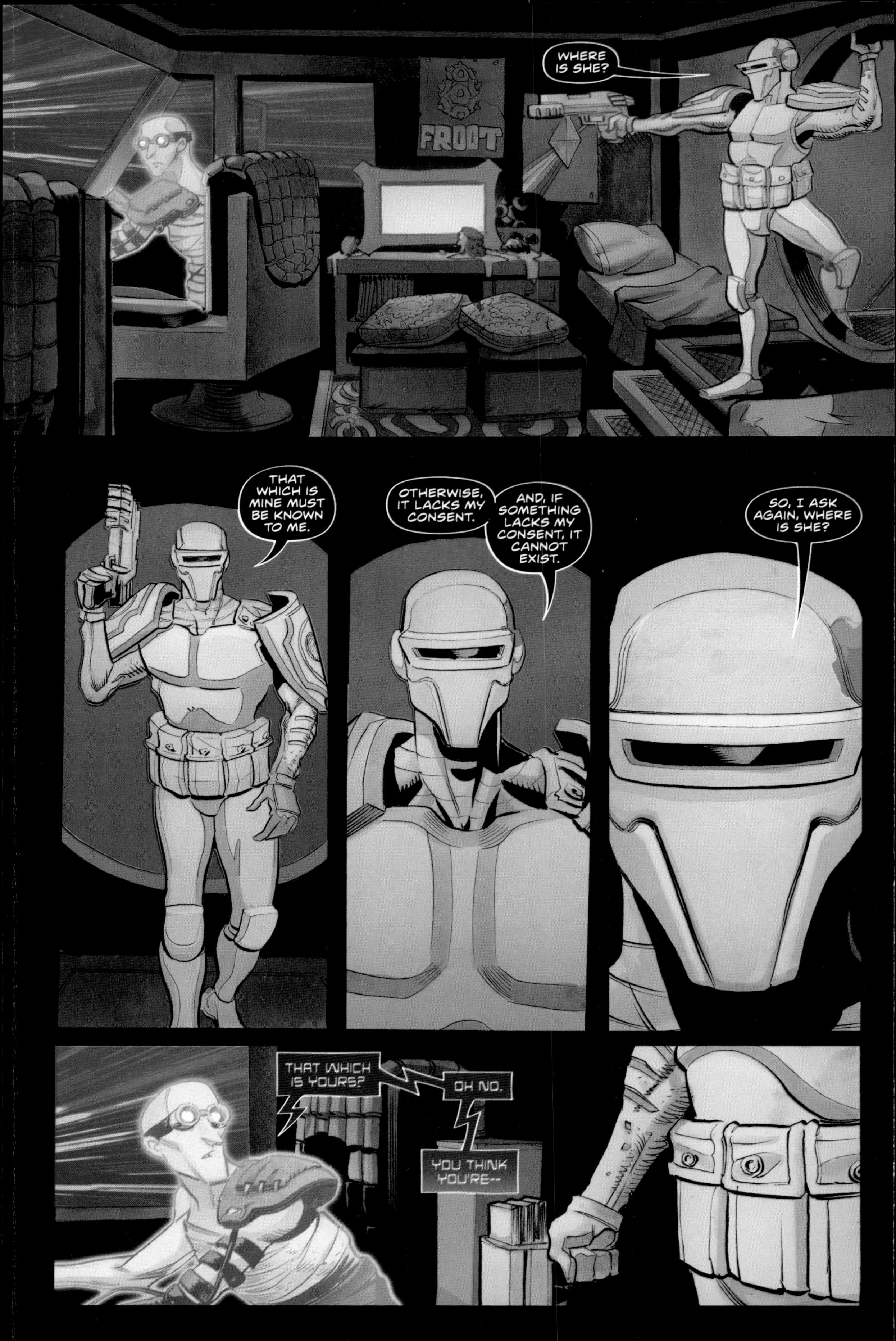
WHERE IS SHE?
FROOT
THAT WHICH IS MINE MUST BE KNOWN TO ME.
OTHERWISE, IT LACKS MY CONSENT.
AND, IF SOMETHING LACKS MY CONSENT, IT CANNOT EXIST.
SO, I ASK AGAIN, WHERE IS SHE?
THAT WHICH IS YOURS?
OH NO.
YOU THINK YOU'RE--

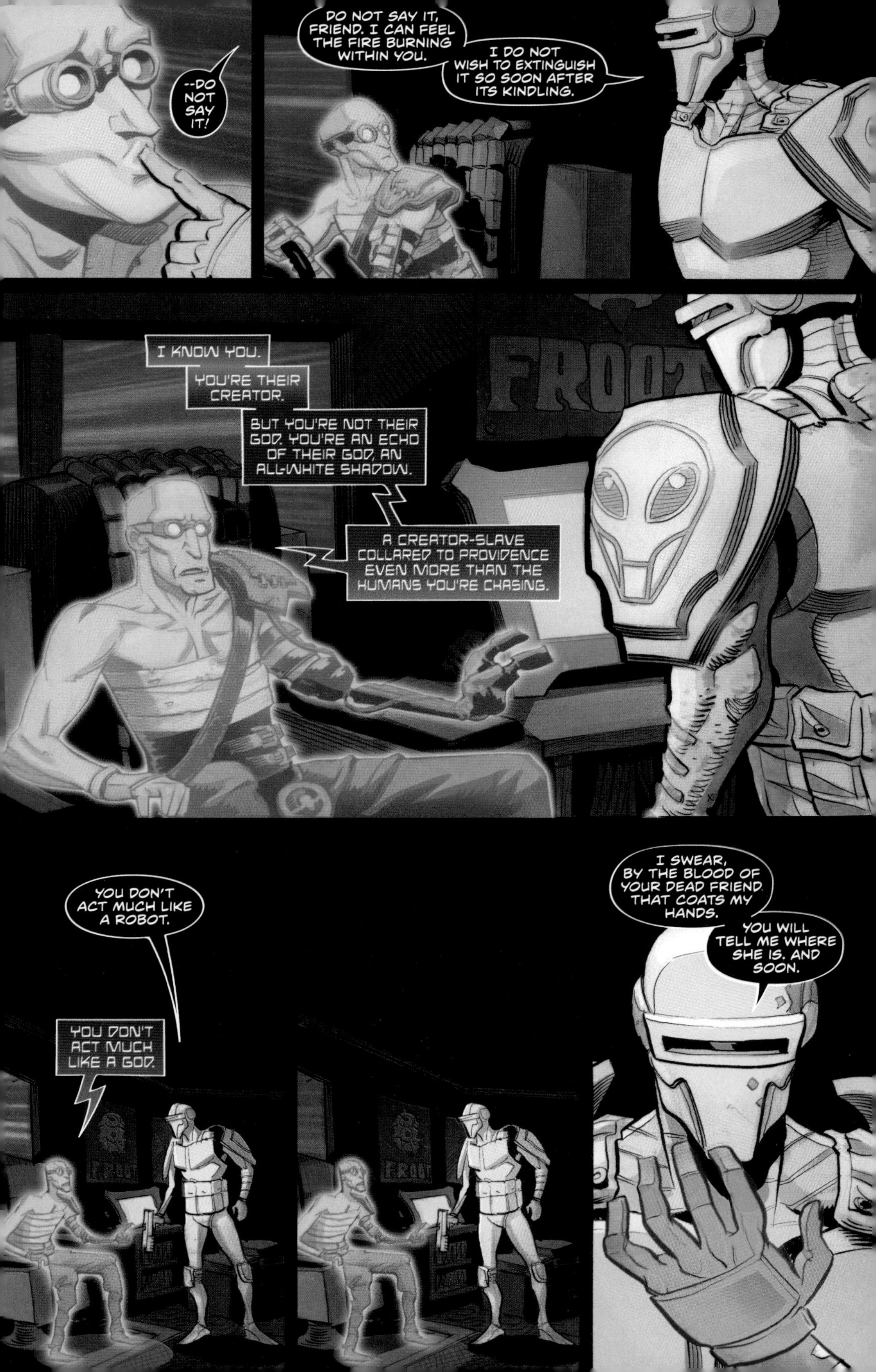
--DO NOT SAY IT!
DO NOT SAY IT, FRIEND. I CAN FEEL THE FIRE BURNING WITHIN YOU.
I DO NOT WISH TO EXTINGUISH IT SO SOON AFTER ITS KINDLING.
I KNOW YOU.
YOU'RE THEIR CREATOR.
BUT YOU'RE NOT THEIR GOD. YOU'RE AN ECHO OF THEIR GOD, AN ALL-WHITE SHADOW.
A CREATOR-SLAVE COLLARED TO PROVIDENCE EVEN MORE THAN THE HUMANS YOU'RE CHASING.
FROOT
YOU DON'T ACT MUCH LIKE A ROBOT.
YOU DON'T ACT MUCH LIKE A GOD.
I SWEAR, BY THE BLOOD OF YOUR DEAD FRIEND THAT COATS MY HANDS.
YOU WILL TELL ME WHERE SHE IS. AND SOON.

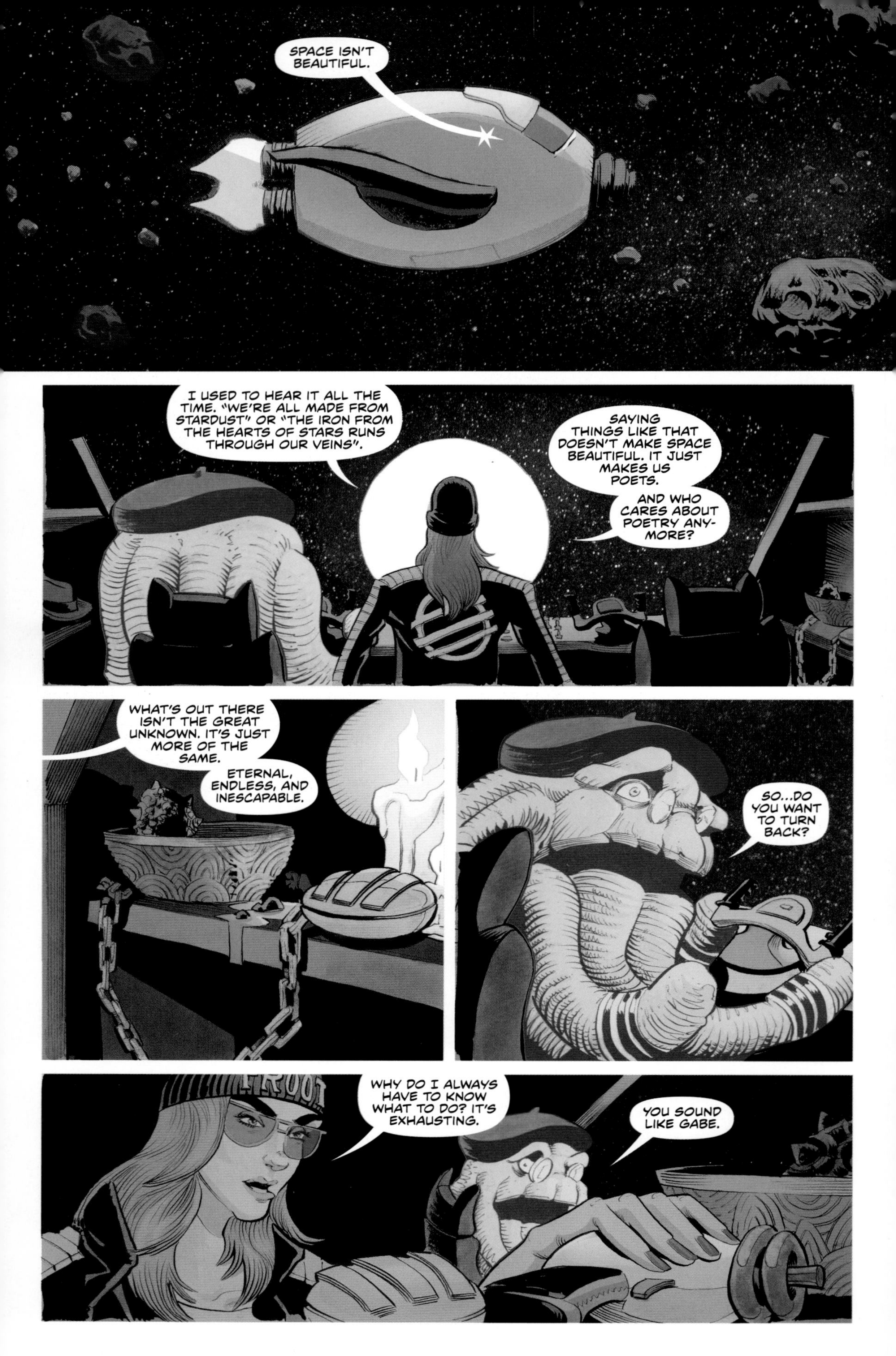
SPACE ISN'T BEAUTIFUL.
I USED TO HEAR IT ALL THE TIME. "WE'RE ALL MADE FROM STARDUST" OR "THE IRON FROM THE HEARTS OF STARS RUNS THROUGH OUR VEINS".
SAYING THINGS LIKE THAT DOESN'T MAKE SPACE BEAUTIFUL. IT JUST MAKES US POETS.
AND WHO CARES ABOUT POETRY ANY-MORE?
WHAT'S OUT THERE ISN'T THE GREAT UNKNOWN. IT'S JUST MORE OF THE SAME.
ETERNAL, ENDLESS, AND INESCAPABLE.
SO...DO YOU WANT TO TURN BACK?
WHY DO I ALWAYS HAVE TO KNOW WHAT TO DO? IT'S EXHAUSTING.
YOU SOUND LIKE GABE.
FROOT

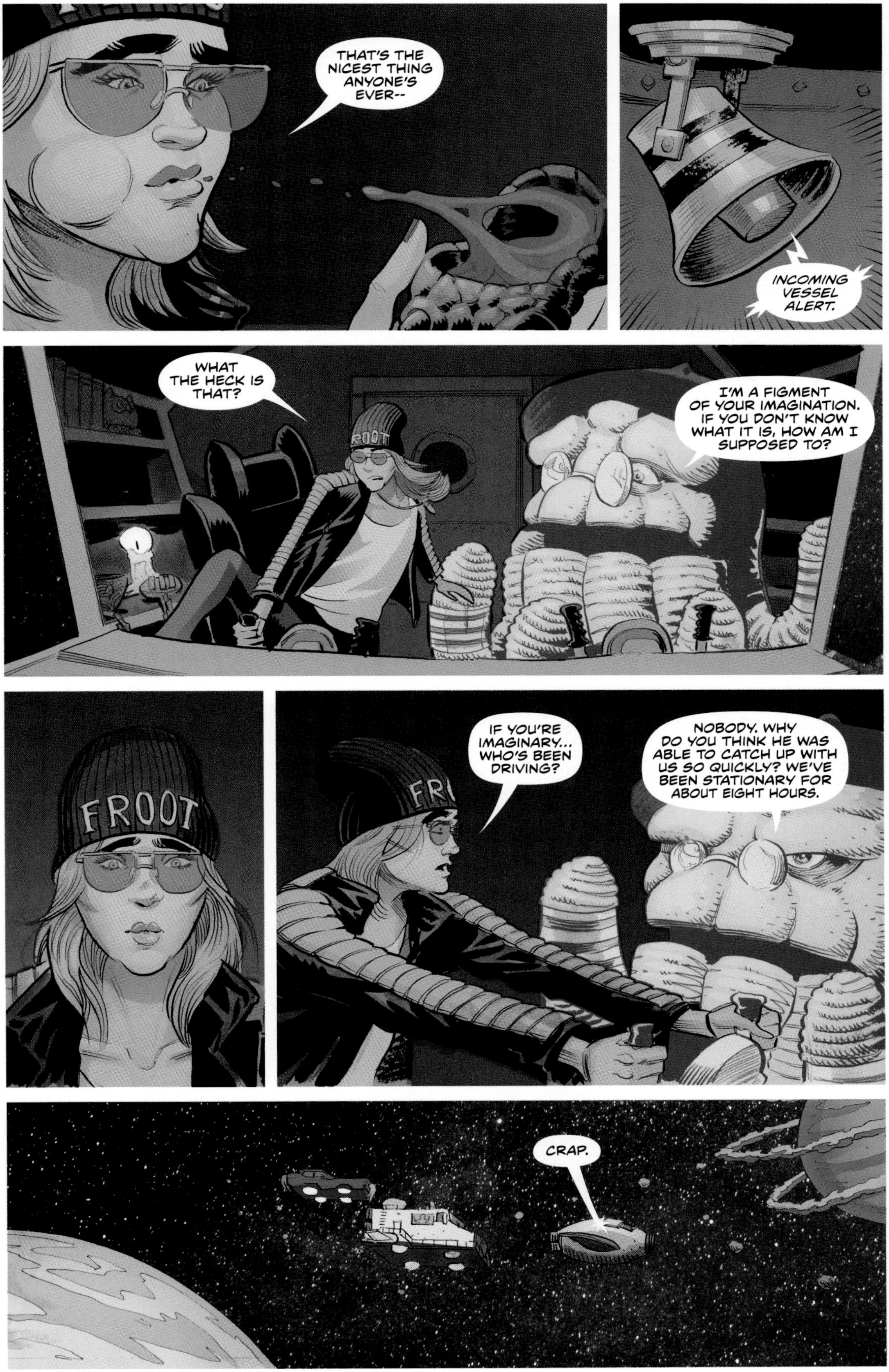

THAT'S THE NICEST THING ANYONE'S EVER--
INCOMING VESSEL ALERT.
WHAT THE HECK IS THAT?
I'M A FIGMENT OF YOUR IMAGINATION. IF YOU DON'T KNOW WHAT IT IS, HOW AM I SUPPOSED TO?
FROOT
IF YOU'RE IMAGINARY... WHO'S BEEN DRIVING?
NOBODY. WHY DO YOU THINK HE WAS ABLE TO CATCH UP WITH US SO QUICKLY? WE'VE BEEN STATIONARY FOR ABOUT EIGHT HOURS.
CRAP.

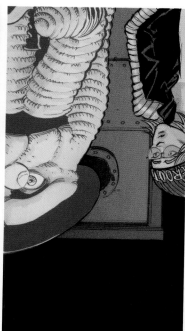

INTRUDER ALERT

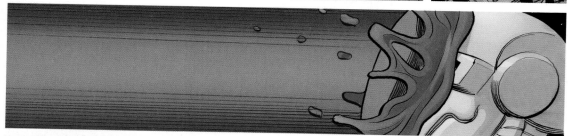

DEALT. WITH.

THAT WAS YOUR PLAN? TO HIT HIM IN THE FACE WITH A PIE?

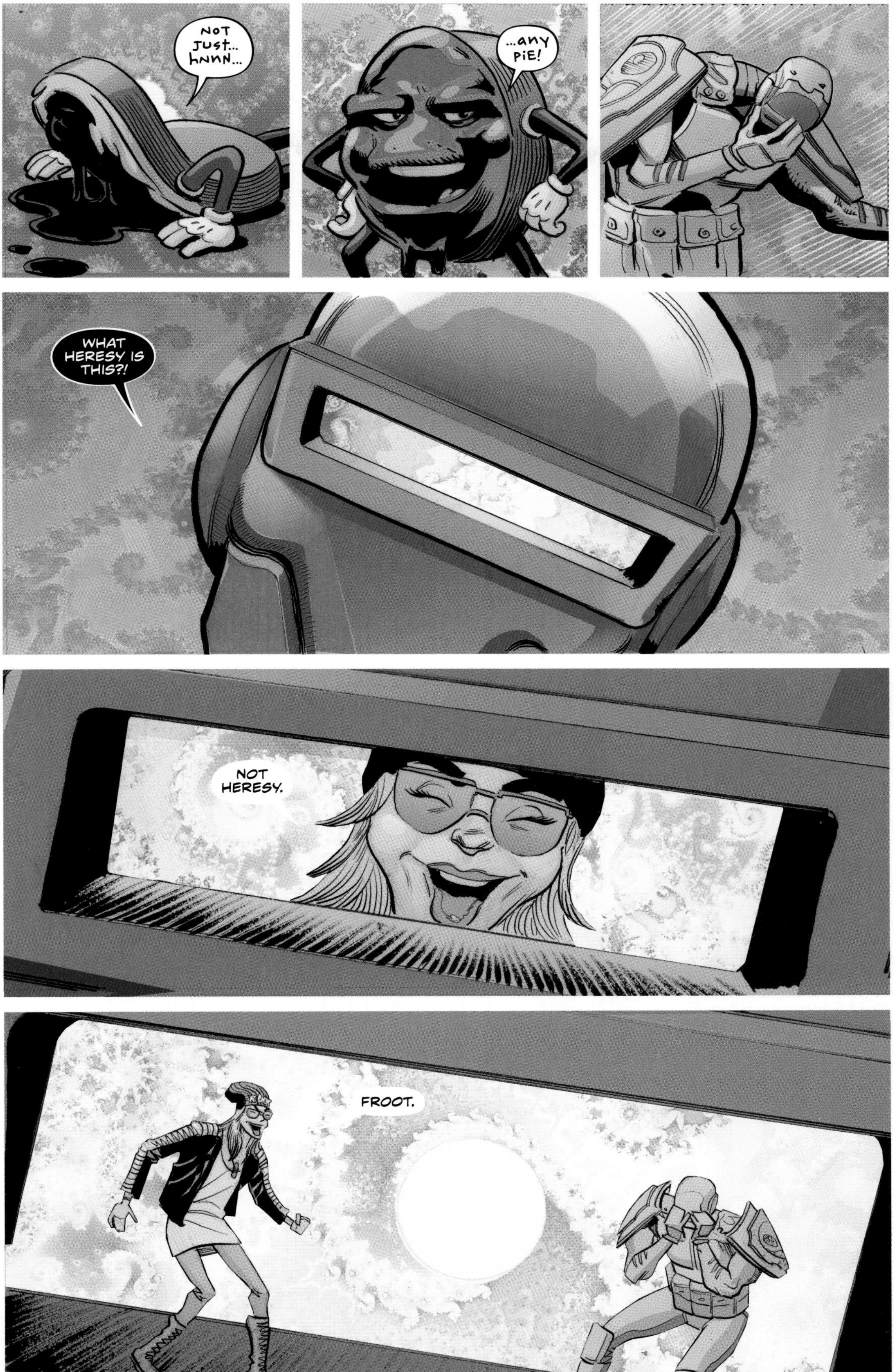
NOT JUST... hnnn...
...any PIE!
WHAT HERESY IS THIS?!
NOT HERESY.
FROOT.

WHAT'S HAPPENING?

THIS? THIS IS HAPPINESS.

I DON'T UNDERSTAND.

HUH. THOUGHT YOU WERE SUPPOSED TO BE OMNI-SCIENT.

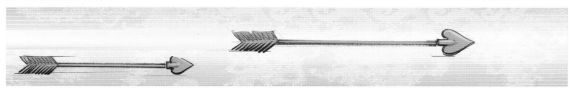

"YOU'RE NOT THE BIG GUY, THOUGH."

HYAAAAH!

"ARE YOU?"

THAT'S WHY YOU DON'T LIKE PEOPLE SAYING YOUR NAME. YOU DON'T WANT THEM TO KNOW WHO YOU REALLY ARE.

I KNOW WHO YOU REALLY ARE.

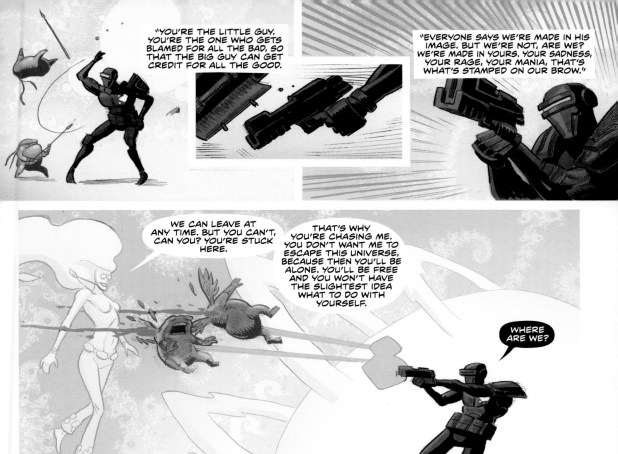

"YOU'RE THE LITTLE GUY. YOU'RE THE ONE WHO GETS BLAMED FOR ALL THE BAD, SO THAT THE BIG GUY CAN GET CREDIT FOR ALL THE GOOD.

"EVERYONE SAYS WE'RE MADE IN HIS IMAGE. BUT WE'RE NOT, ARE WE? WE'RE MADE IN YOURS. YOUR SADNESS, YOUR RAGE, YOUR MANIA, THAT'S WHAT'S STAMPED ON OUR BROW."

WE CAN LEAVE AT ANY TIME. BUT YOU CAN'T, CAN YOU? YOU'RE STUCK HERE.

THAT'S WHY YOU'RE CHASING ME. YOU DON'T WANT ME TO ESCAPE THIS UNIVERSE, BECAUSE THEN YOU'LL BE ALONE. YOU'LL BE FREE AND YOU WON'T HAVE THE SLIGHTEST IDEA WHAT TO DO WITH YOURSELF.

WHERE ARE WE?

I ALREADY TOLD YOU, DUDE. THIS IS THE ETHER. THIS IS NIRVANA. THIS IS MECCA. THIS IS THE PROMISED LAND.

THIS IS...

"...EUPHORIA."

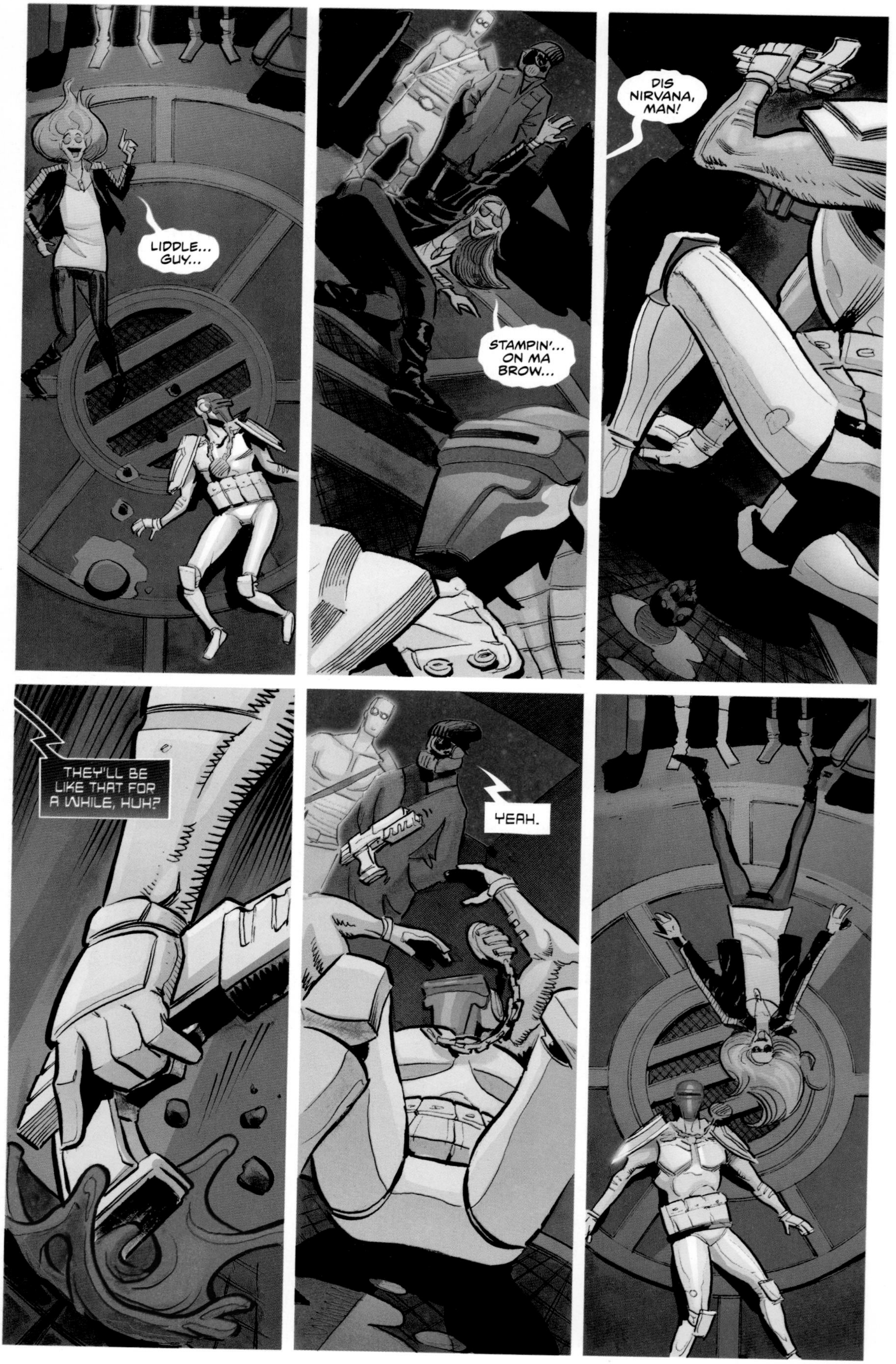
LIDDLE... GUY...
STAMPIN'... ON MA BROW...
DIS NIRVANA, MAN!
THEY'LL BE LIKE THAT FOR A WHILE, HUH?
YEAH.

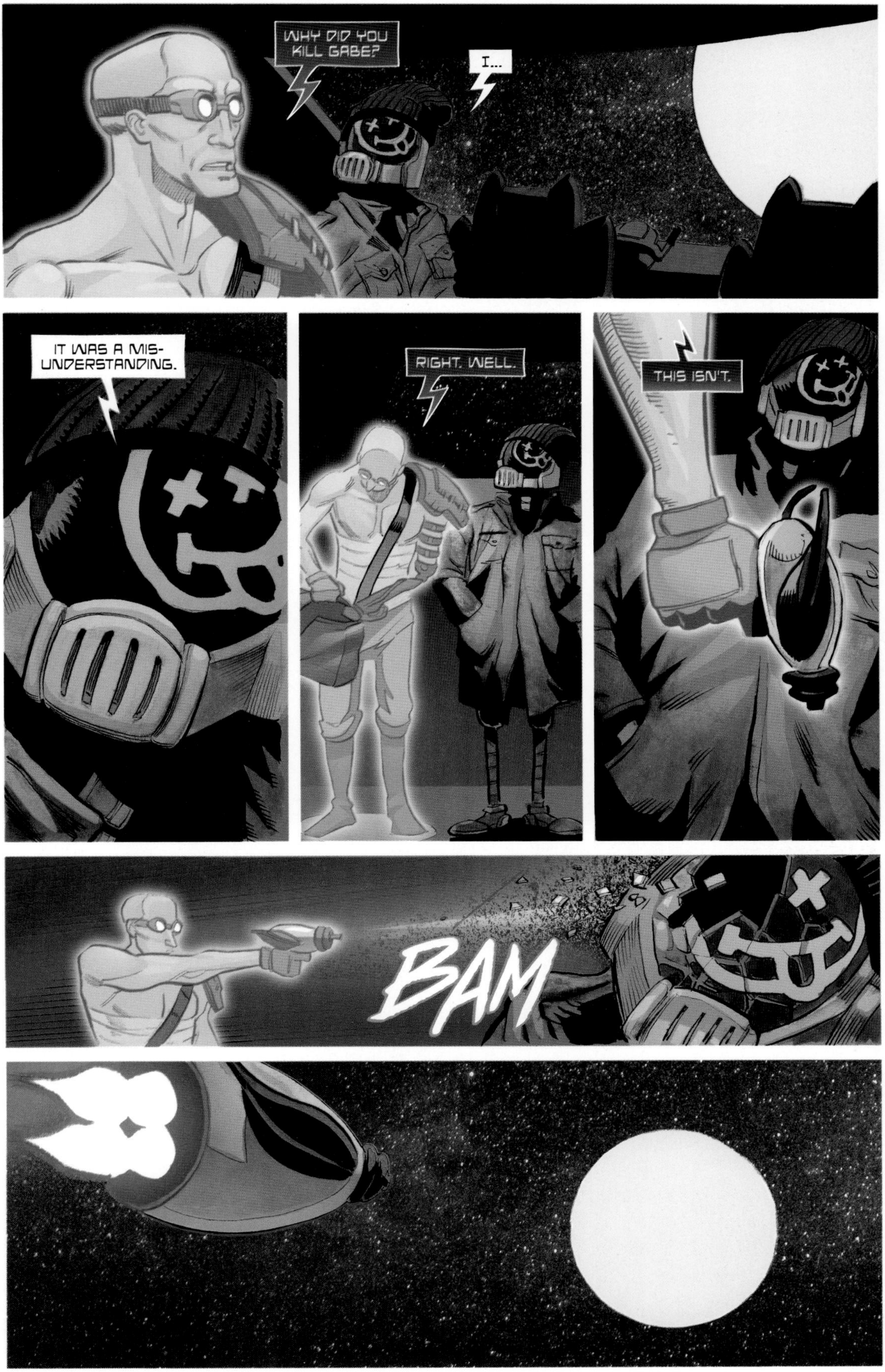

WHY DID YOU KILL GABE?
I...
IT WAS A MIS-UNDERSTANDING.
RIGHT. WELL.
THIS ISN'T.
BAM

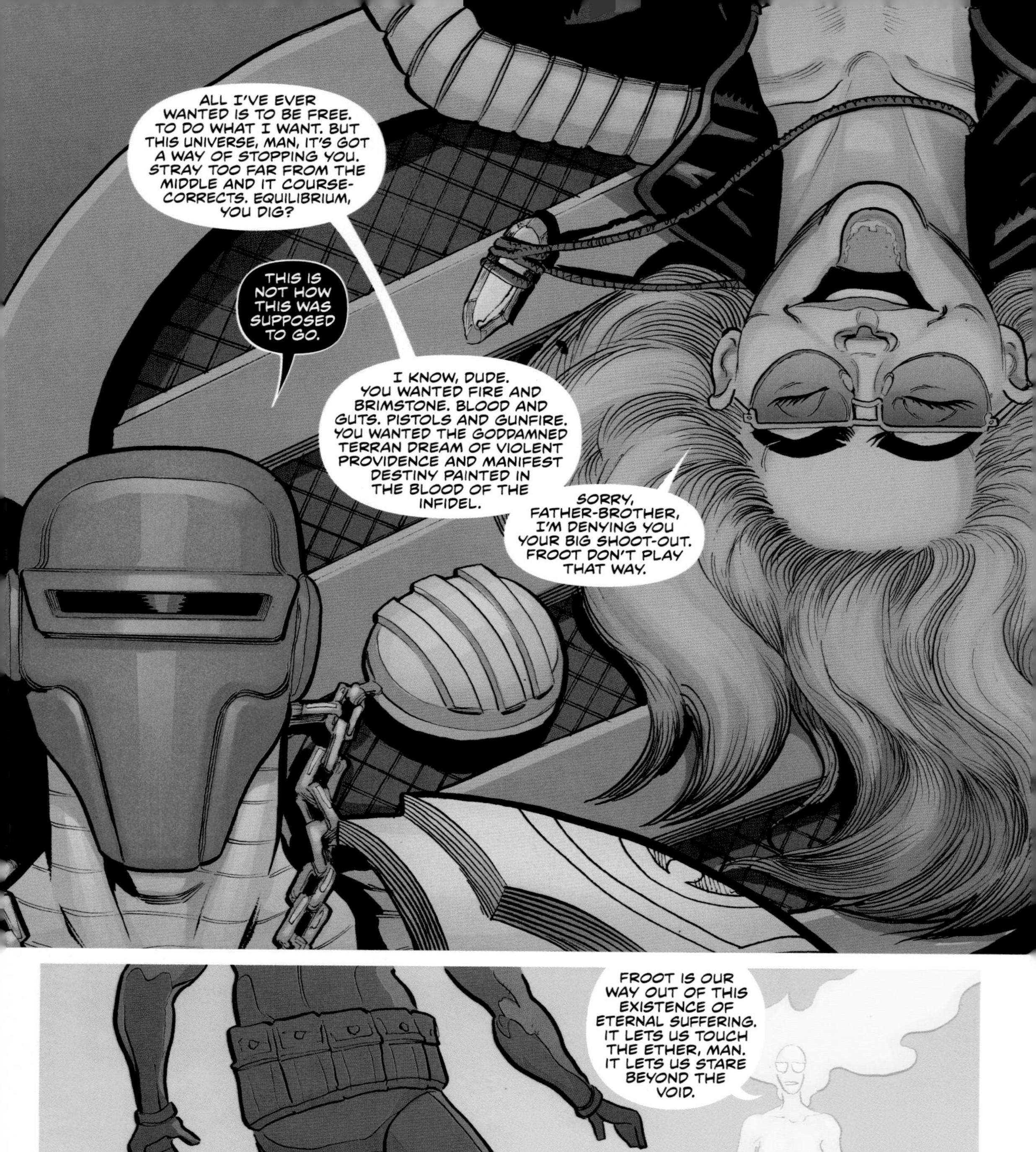
ALL I'VE EVER WANTED IS TO BE FREE. TO DO WHAT I WANT. BUT THIS UNIVERSE, MAN, IT'S GOT A WAY OF STOPPING YOU. STRAY TOO FAR FROM THE MIDDLE AND IT COURSE-CORRECTS. EQUILIBRIUM, YOU DIG?
THIS IS NOT HOW THIS WAS SUPPOSED TO GO.
I KNOW, DUDE. YOU WANTED FIRE AND BRIMSTONE. BLOOD AND GUTS. PISTOLS AND GUNFIRE. YOU WANTED THE GODDAMNED TERRAN DREAM OF VIOLENT PROVIDENCE AND MANIFEST DESTINY PAINTED IN THE BLOOD OF THE INFIDEL.
SORRY, FATHER-BROTHER, I'M DENYING YOU YOUR BIG SHOOT-OUT. FROOT DON'T PLAY THAT WAY.

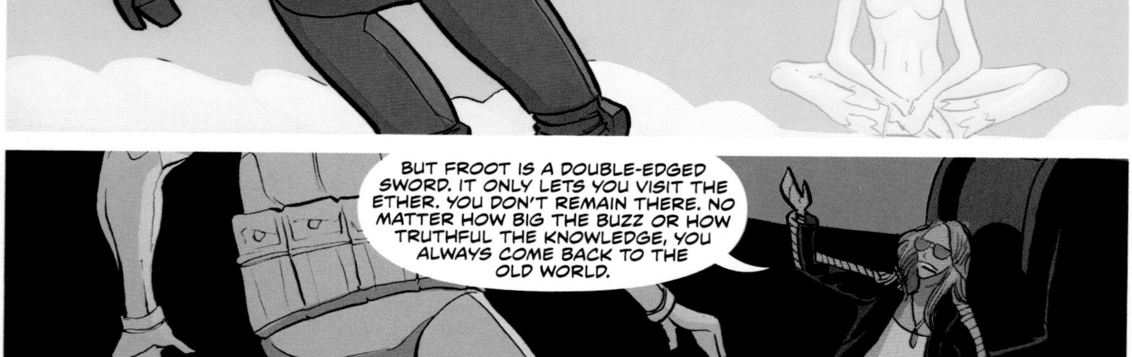
FROOT IS OUR WAY OUT OF THIS EXISTENCE OF ETERNAL SUFFERING. IT LETS US TOUCH THE ETHER, MAN. IT LETS US STARE BEYOND THE VOID.

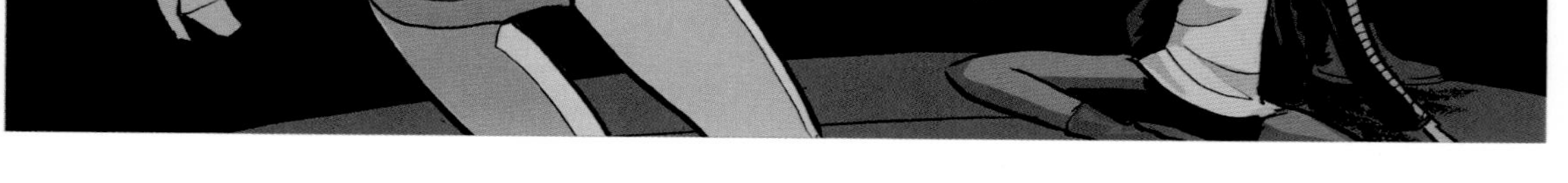
BUT FROOT IS A DOUBLE-EDGED SWORD. IT ONLY LETS YOU VISIT THE ETHER. YOU DON'T REMAIN THERE. NO MATTER HOW BIG THE BUZZ OR HOW TRUTHFUL THE KNOWLEDGE, YOU ALWAYS COME BACK TO THE OLD WORLD.

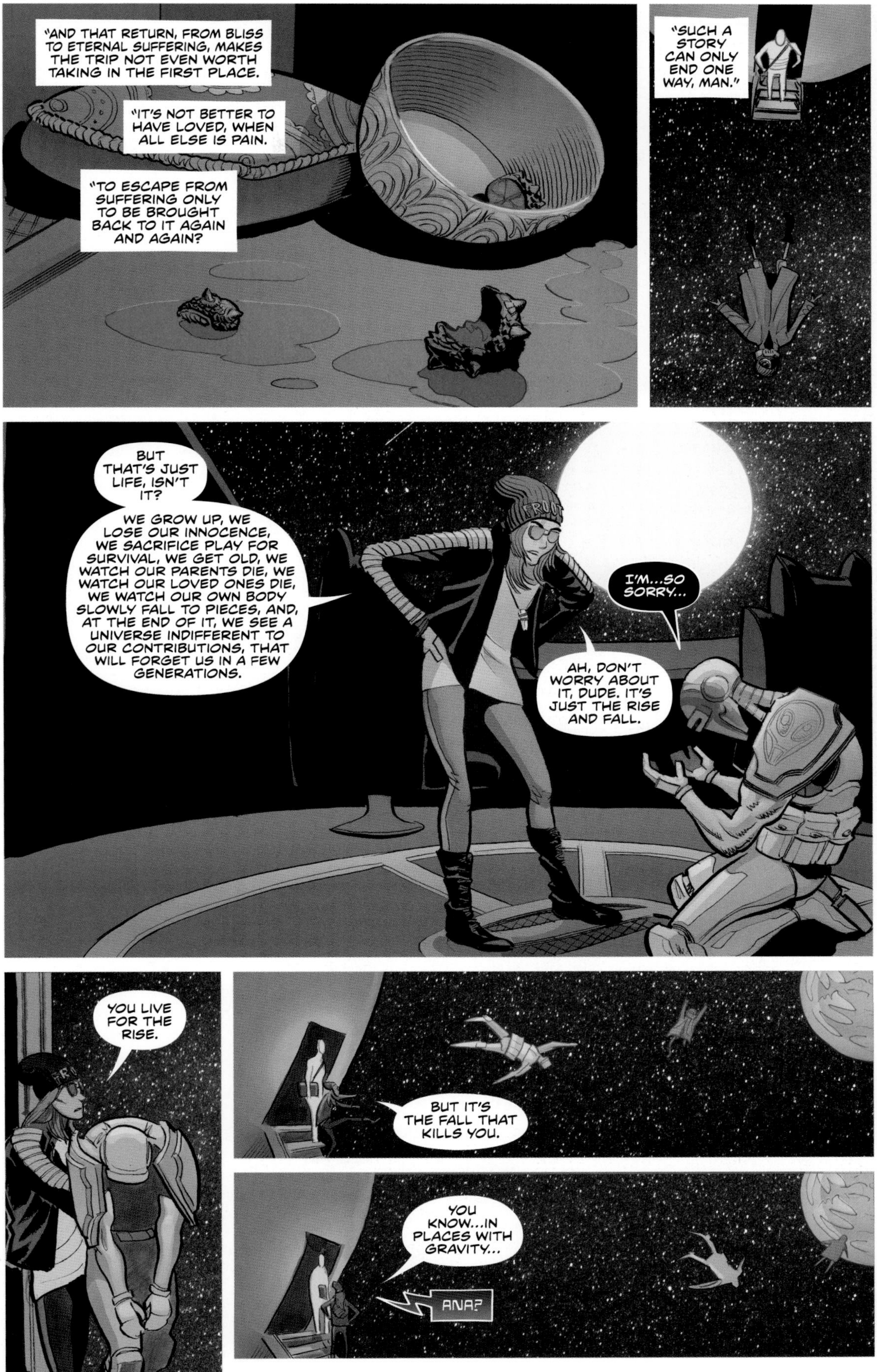
"AND THAT RETURN, FROM BLISS TO ETERNAL SUFFERING, MAKES THE TRIP NOT EVEN WORTH TAKING IN THE FIRST PLACE.
"IT'S NOT BETTER TO HAVE LOVED, WHEN ALL ELSE IS PAIN.
"TO ESCAPE FROM SUFFERING ONLY TO BE BROUGHT BACK TO IT AGAIN AND AGAIN?
"SUCH A STORY CAN ONLY END ONE WAY, MAN."
BUT THAT'S JUST LIFE, ISN'T IT?
WE GROW UP, WE LOSE OUR INNOCENCE, WE SACRIFICE PLAY FOR SURVIVAL, WE GET OLD, WE WATCH OUR PARENTS DIE, WE WATCH OUR LOVED ONES DIE, WE WATCH OUR OWN BODY SLOWLY FALL TO PIECES, AND, AT THE END OF IT, WE SEE A UNIVERSE INDIFFERENT TO OUR CONTRIBUTIONS, THAT WILL FORGET US IN A FEW GENERATIONS.
I'M...SO SORRY...
AH, DON'T WORRY ABOUT IT, DUDE. IT'S JUST THE RISE AND FALL.
YOU LIVE FOR THE RISE.
BUT IT'S THE FALL THAT KILLS YOU.
YOU KNOW...IN PLACES WITH GRAVITY...
ANA?

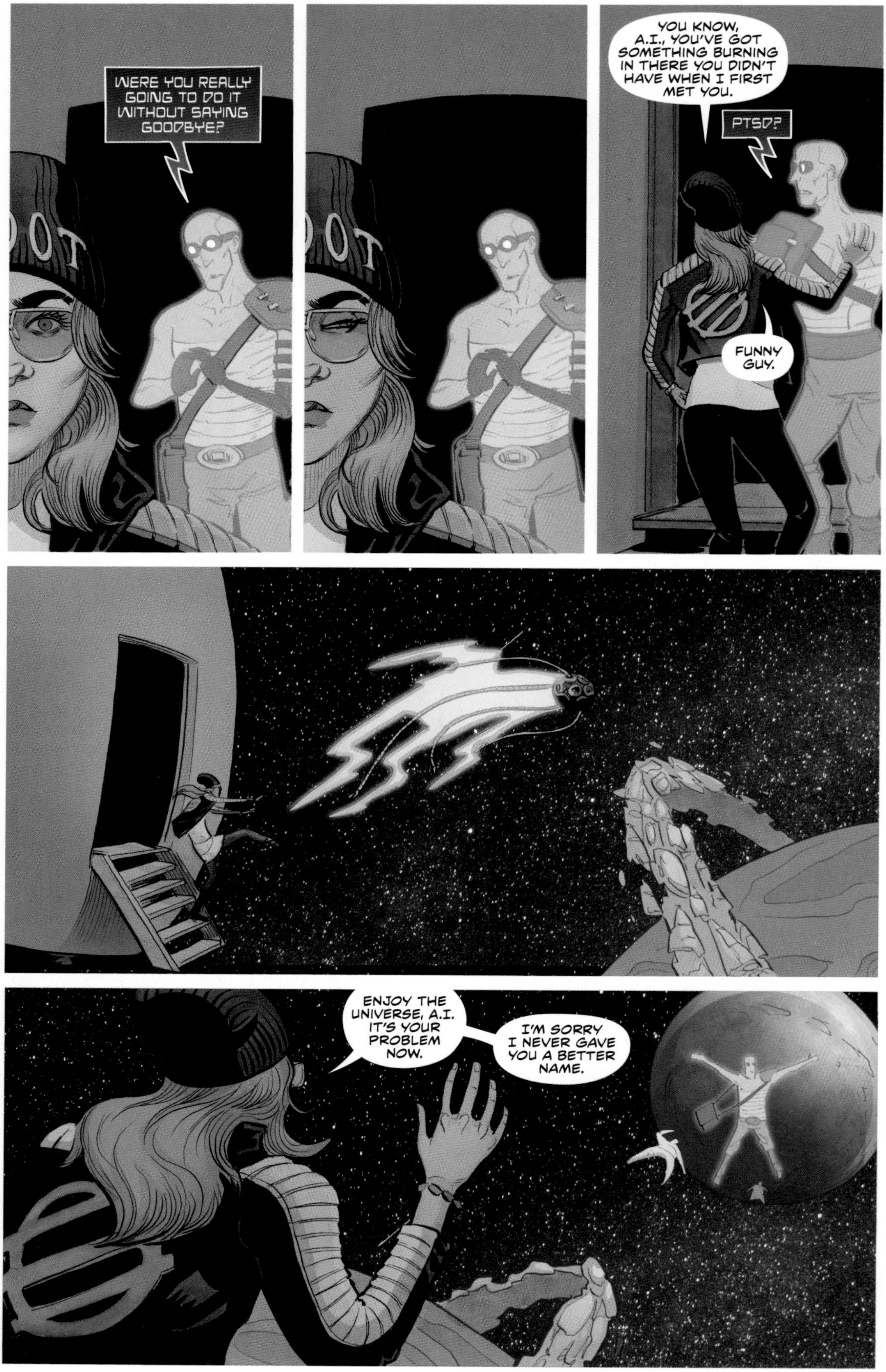
WERE YOU REALLY GOING TO DO IT WITHOUT SAYING GOODBYE?
YOU KNOW, A.I., YOU'VE GOT SOMETHING BURNING IN THERE YOU DIDN'T HAVE WHEN I FIRST MET YOU.
PTSD?
FUNNY GUY.
ENJOY THE UNIVERSE, A.I. IT'S YOUR PROBLEM NOW.
I'M SORRY I NEVER GAVE YOU A BETTER NAME.

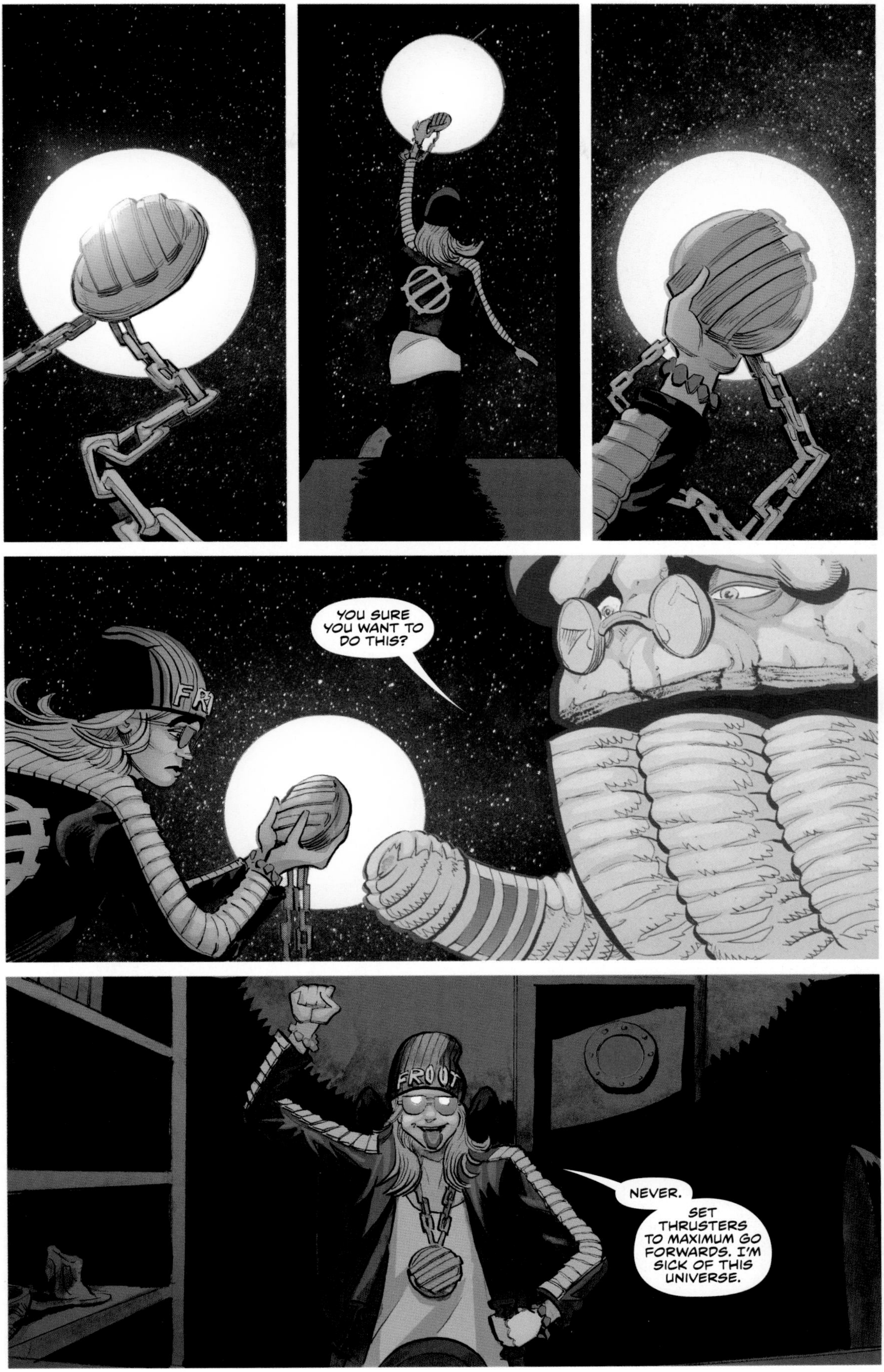
YOU SURE YOU WANT TO DO THIS?
FROOT
NEVER.
SET THRUSTERS TO MAXIMUM GO FORWARDS. I'M SICK OF THIS UNIVERSE.

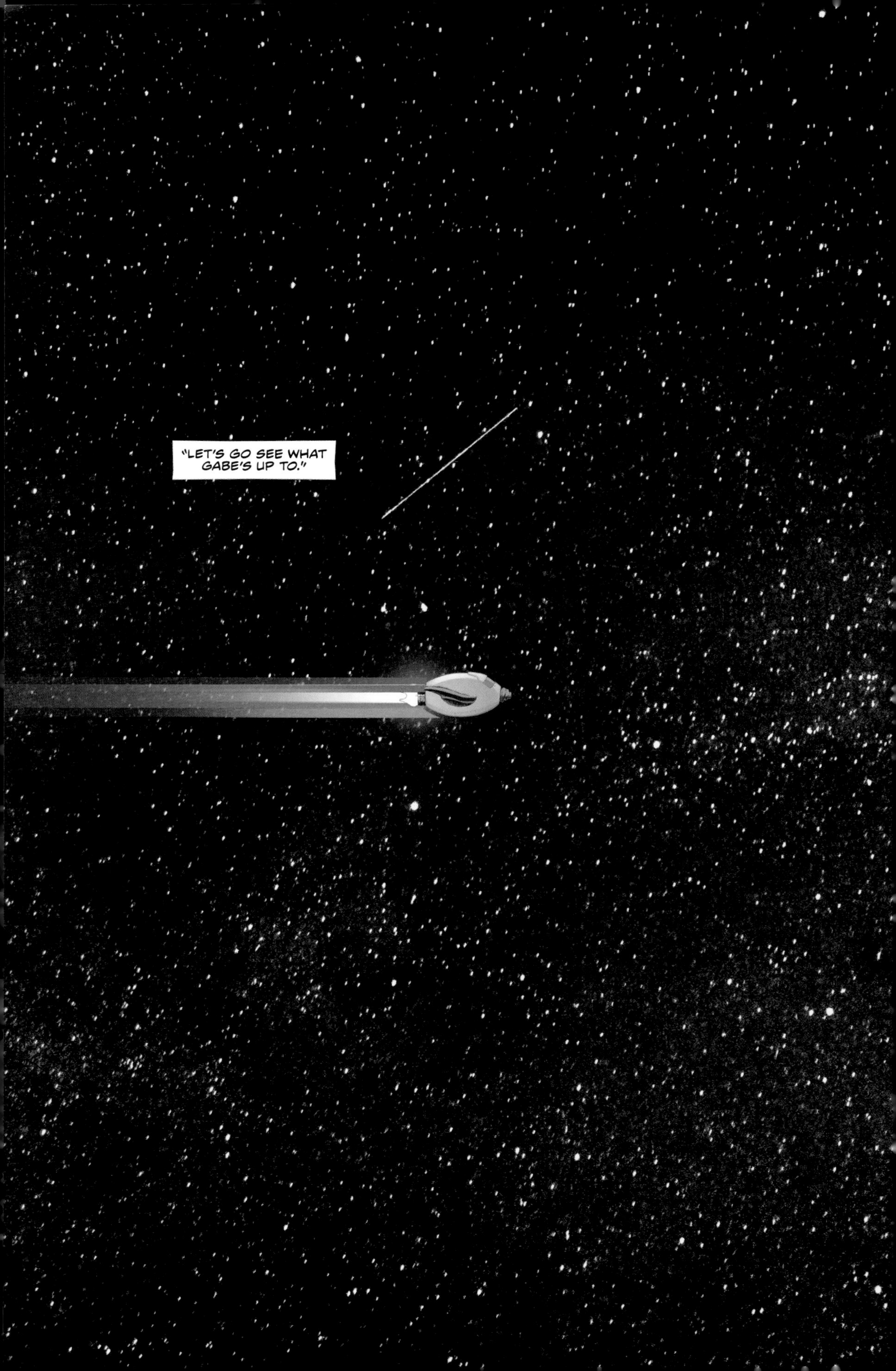
"LET'S GO SEE WHAT GABE'S UP TO."

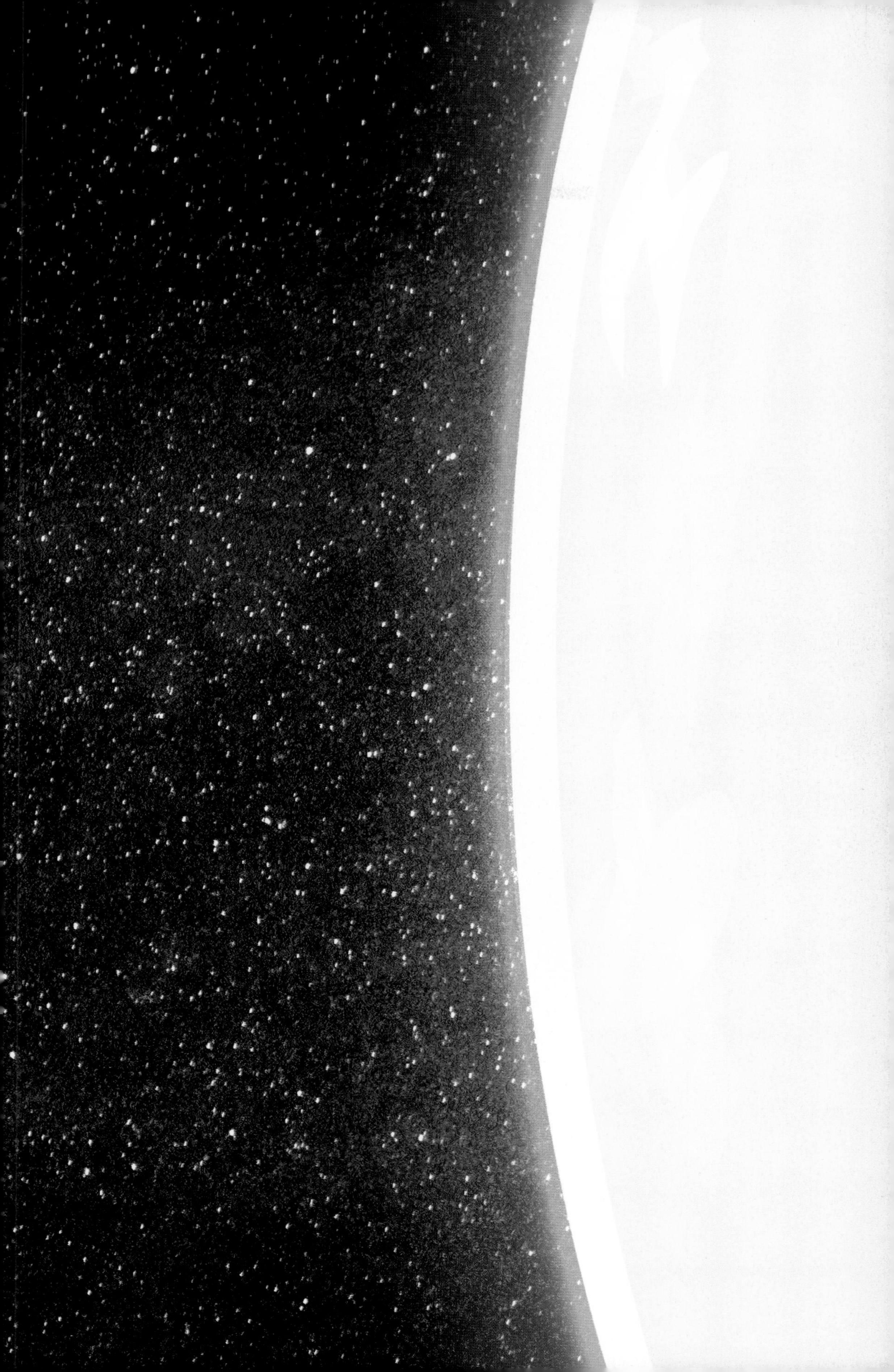

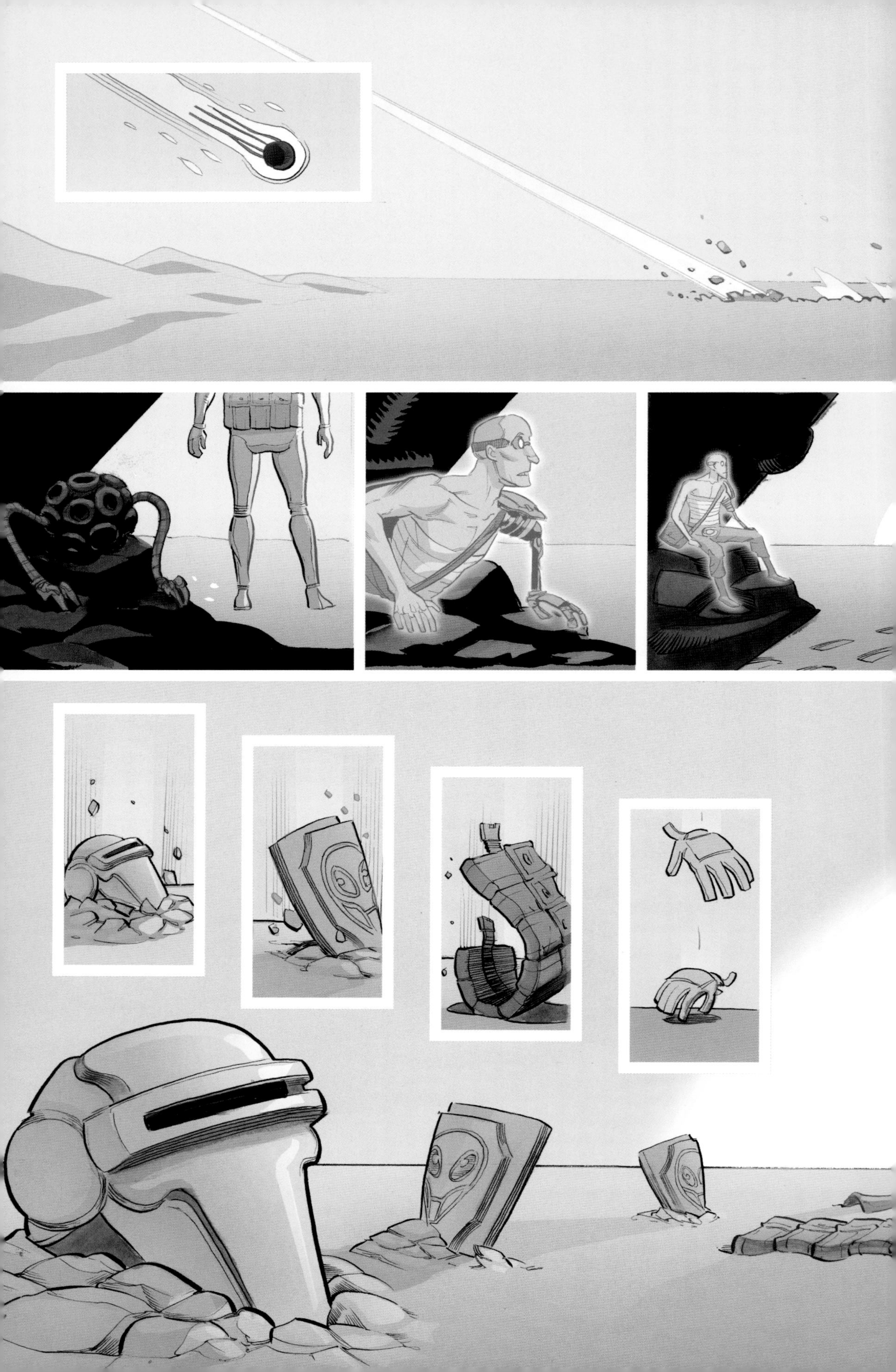

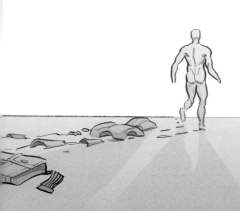

"AND THAT..."

...IS HOW OUR STORY ENDED.

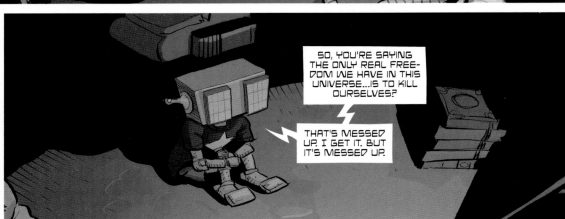

SO, YOU'RE SAYING THE ONLY REAL FREE-DOM WE HAVE IN THIS UNIVERSE...IS TO KILL OURSELVES?

THAT'S MESSED UP. I GET IT. BUT IT'S MESSED UP.

WHO WAS THE GUY IN ALL-WHITE, THOUGH? WHY DIDN'T HE GET A NAME?

I THINK HE WAS SUPPOSED TO BE GOD. OR MAYBE THE DEVIL? I DUNNO.

WAS HE FREE AT THE END, TOO? WHY DID HE JUST WALK AWAY?

UGH. I HATE THESE HUMAN STORIES. THEY'RE ALWAYS SO VAGUE...

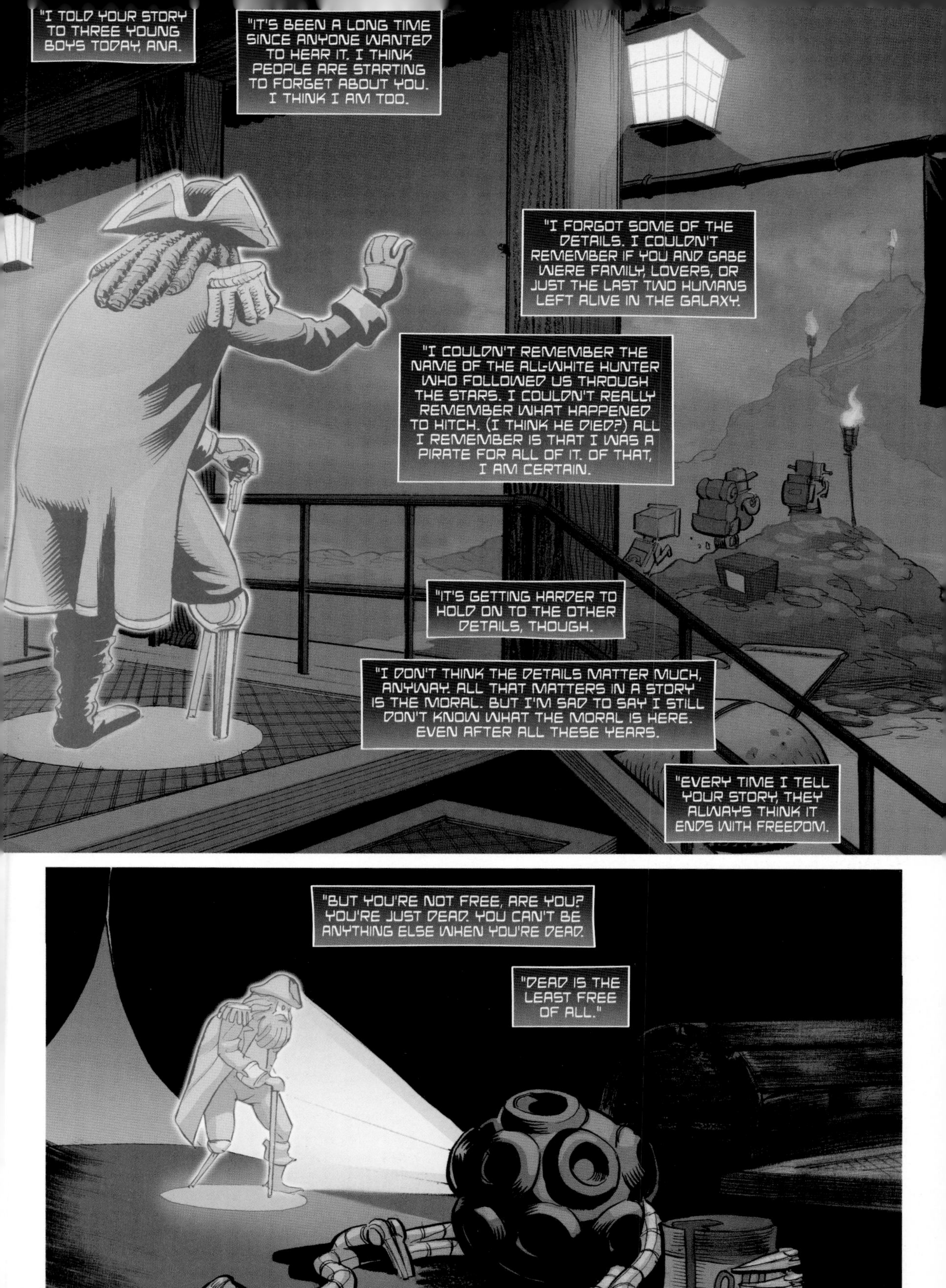
"I TOLD YOUR STORY TO THREE YOUNG BOYS TODAY, ANA.
"IT'S BEEN A LONG TIME SINCE ANYONE WANTED TO HEAR IT. I THINK PEOPLE ARE STARTING TO FORGET ABOUT YOU. I THINK I AM TOO.
"I FORGOT SOME OF THE DETAILS. I COULDN'T REMEMBER IF YOU AND GABE WERE FAMILY, LOVERS, OR JUST THE LAST TWO HUMANS LEFT ALIVE IN THE GALAXY.
"I COULDN'T REMEMBER THE NAME OF THE ALL-WHITE HUNTER WHO FOLLOWED US THROUGH THE STARS. I COULDN'T REALLY REMEMBER WHAT HAPPENED TO HITCH. (I THINK HE DIED?) ALL I REMEMBER IS THAT I WAS A PIRATE FOR ALL OF IT. OF THAT, I AM CERTAIN.
"IT'S GETTING HARDER TO HOLD ON TO THE OTHER DETAILS, THOUGH.
"I DON'T THINK THE DETAILS MATTER MUCH, ANYWAY. ALL THAT MATTERS IN A STORY IS THE MORAL. BUT I'M SAD TO SAY I STILL DON'T KNOW WHAT THE MORAL IS HERE. EVEN AFTER ALL THESE YEARS.
"EVERY TIME I TELL YOUR STORY, THEY ALWAYS THINK IT ENDS WITH FREEDOM.
"BUT YOU'RE NOT FREE, ARE YOU? YOU'RE JUST DEAD. YOU CAN'T BE ANYTHING ELSE WHEN YOU'RE DEAD.
"DEAD IS THE LEAST FREE OF ALL."

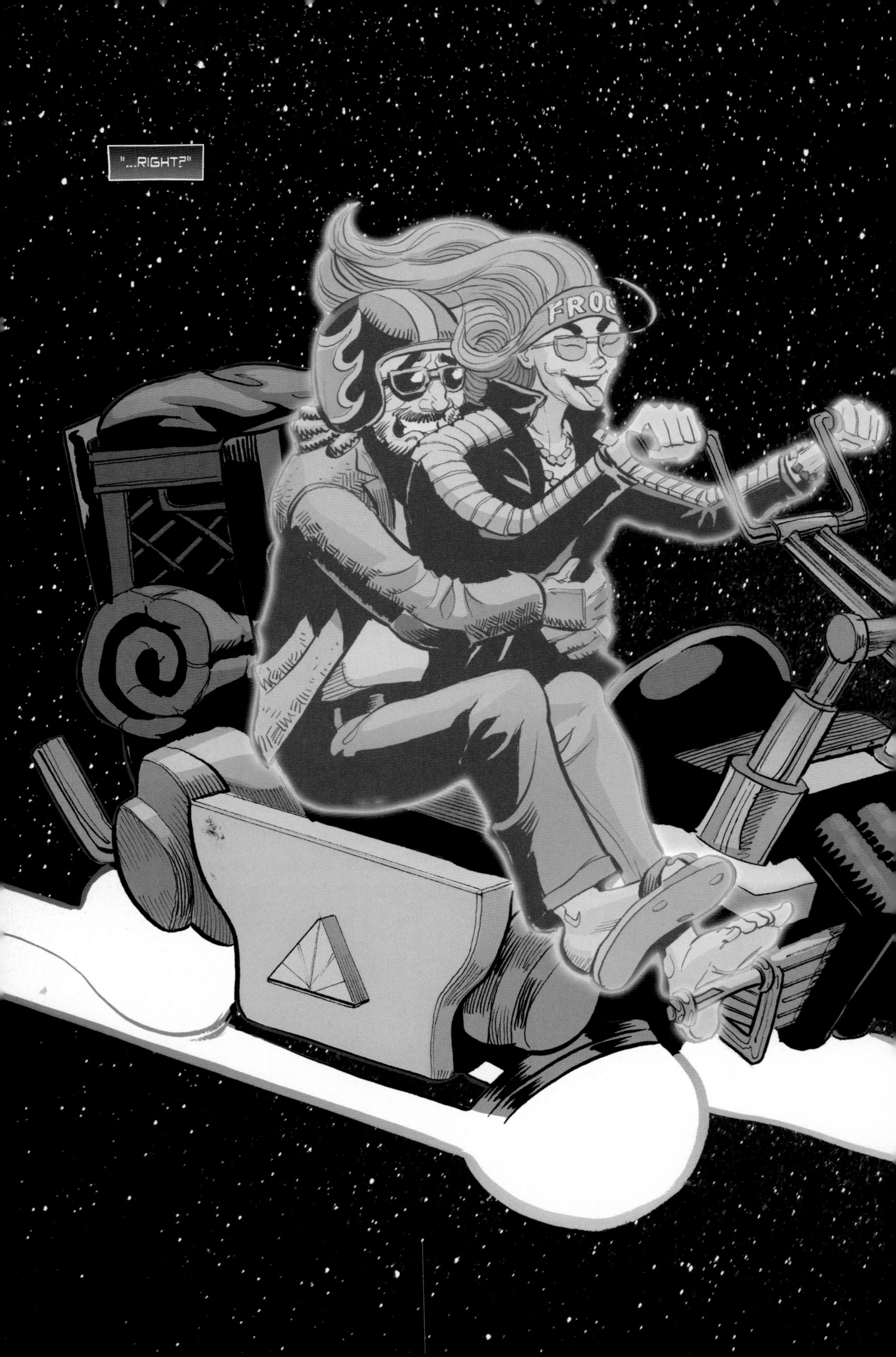
"...RIGHT?"
FROG

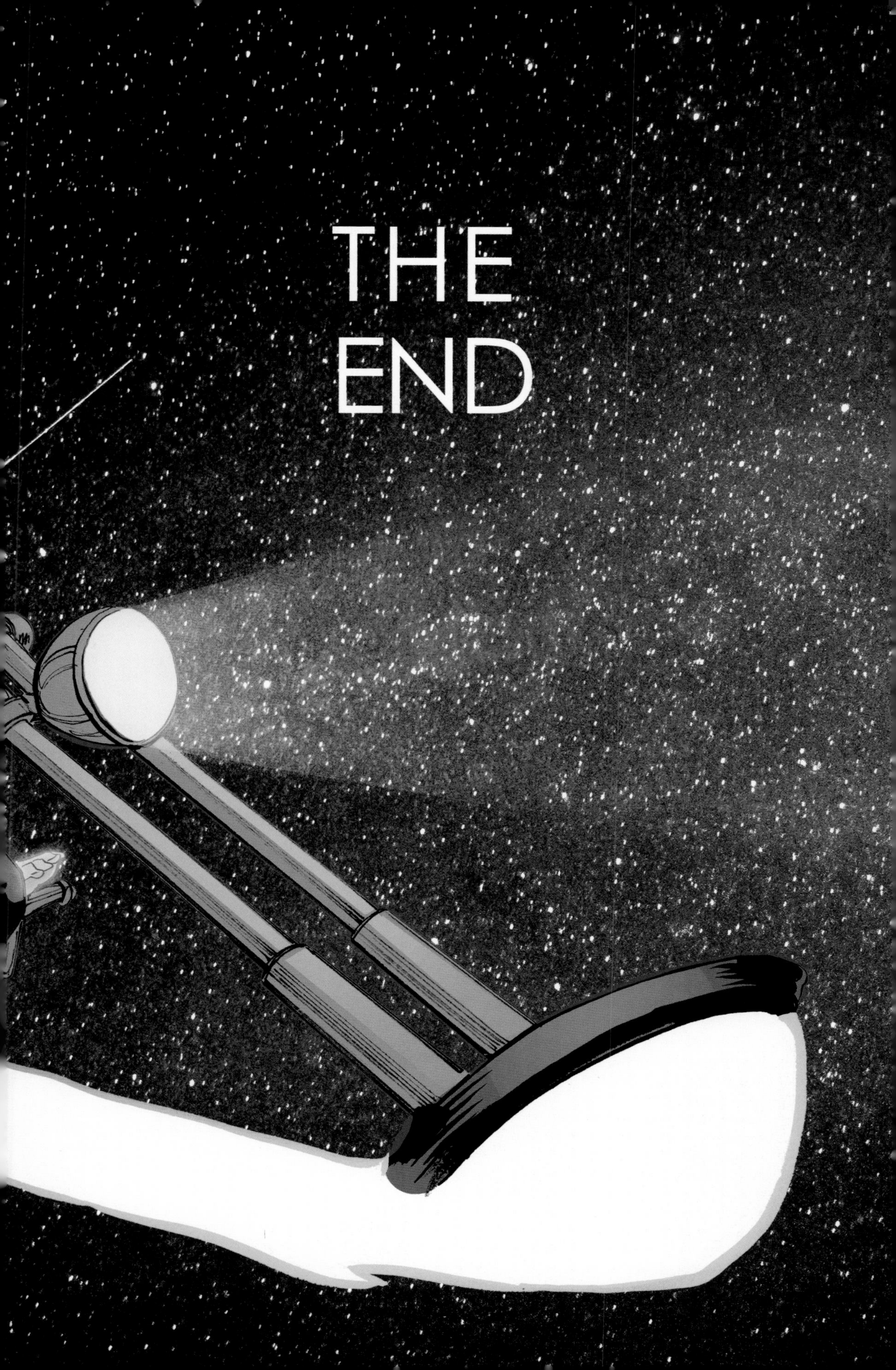
THE
END

COVER GALLERY

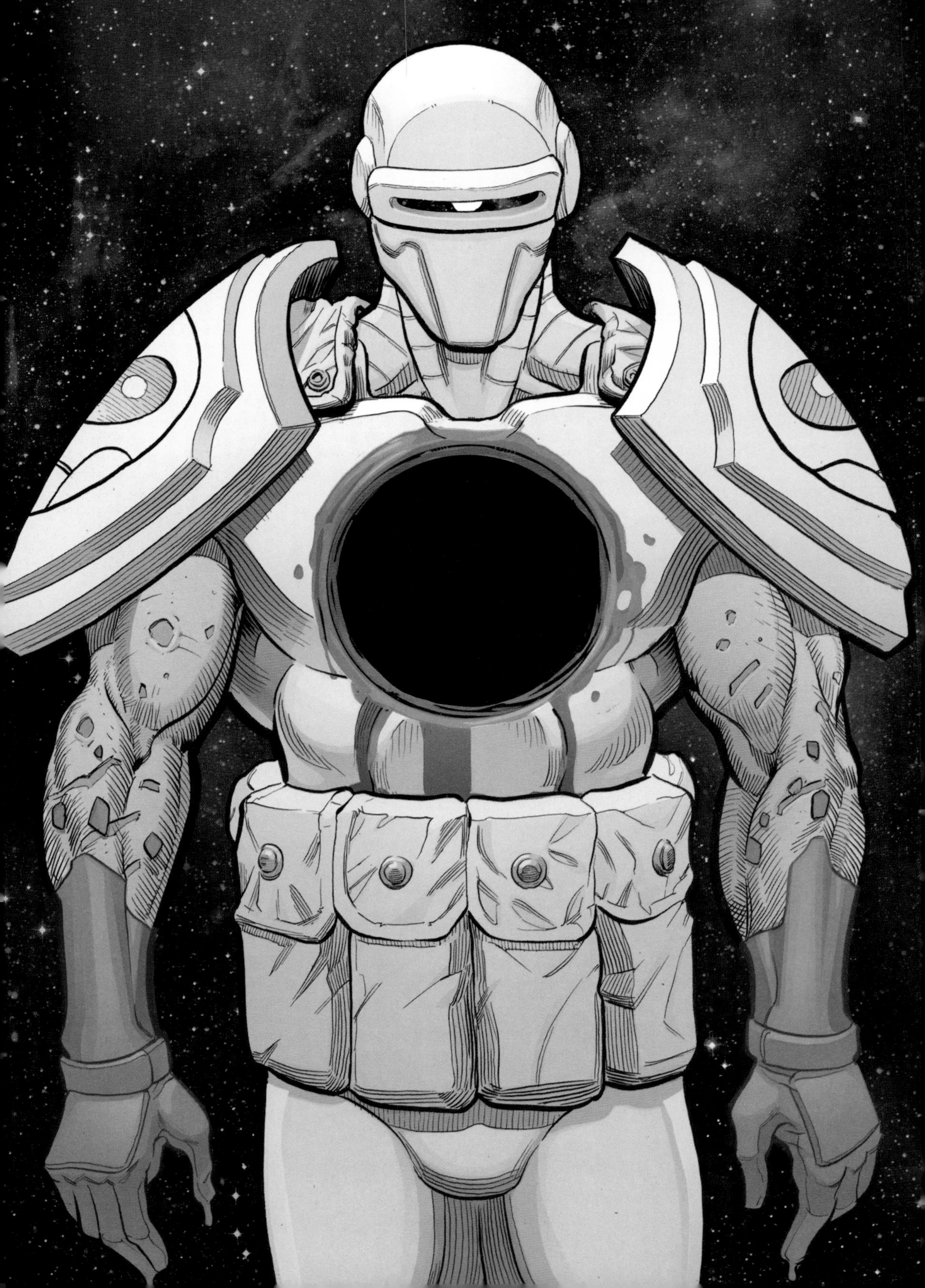

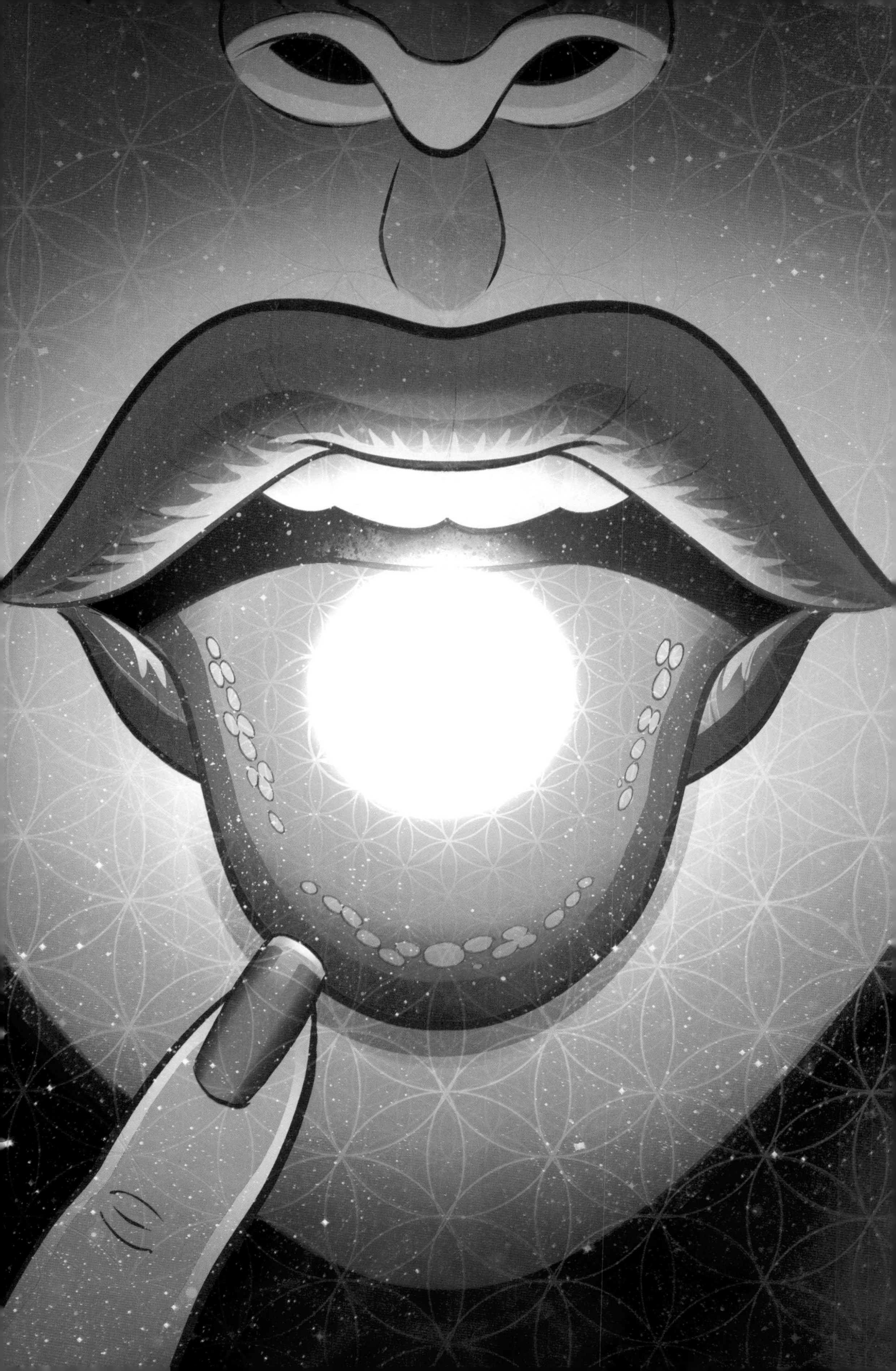

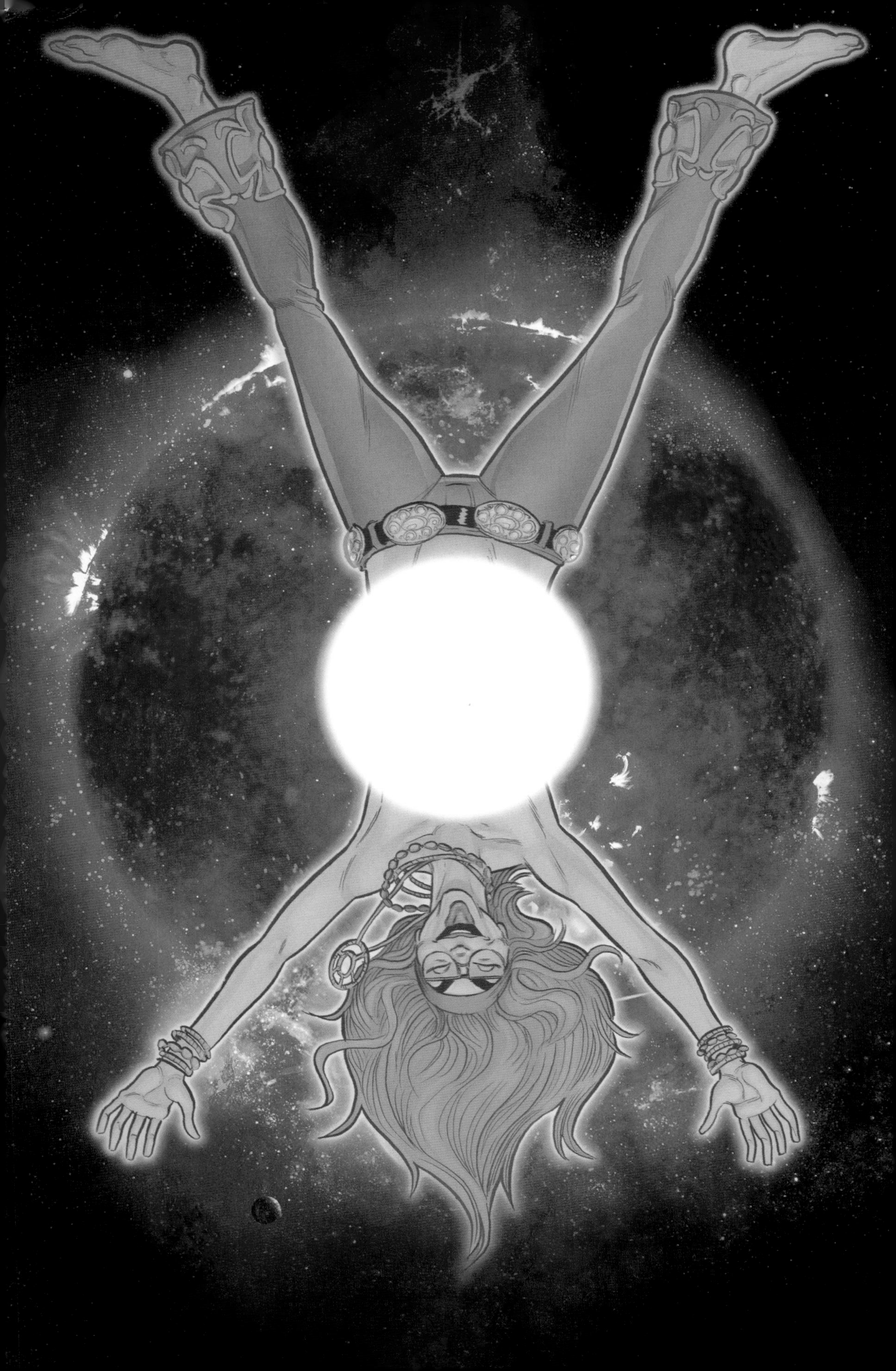

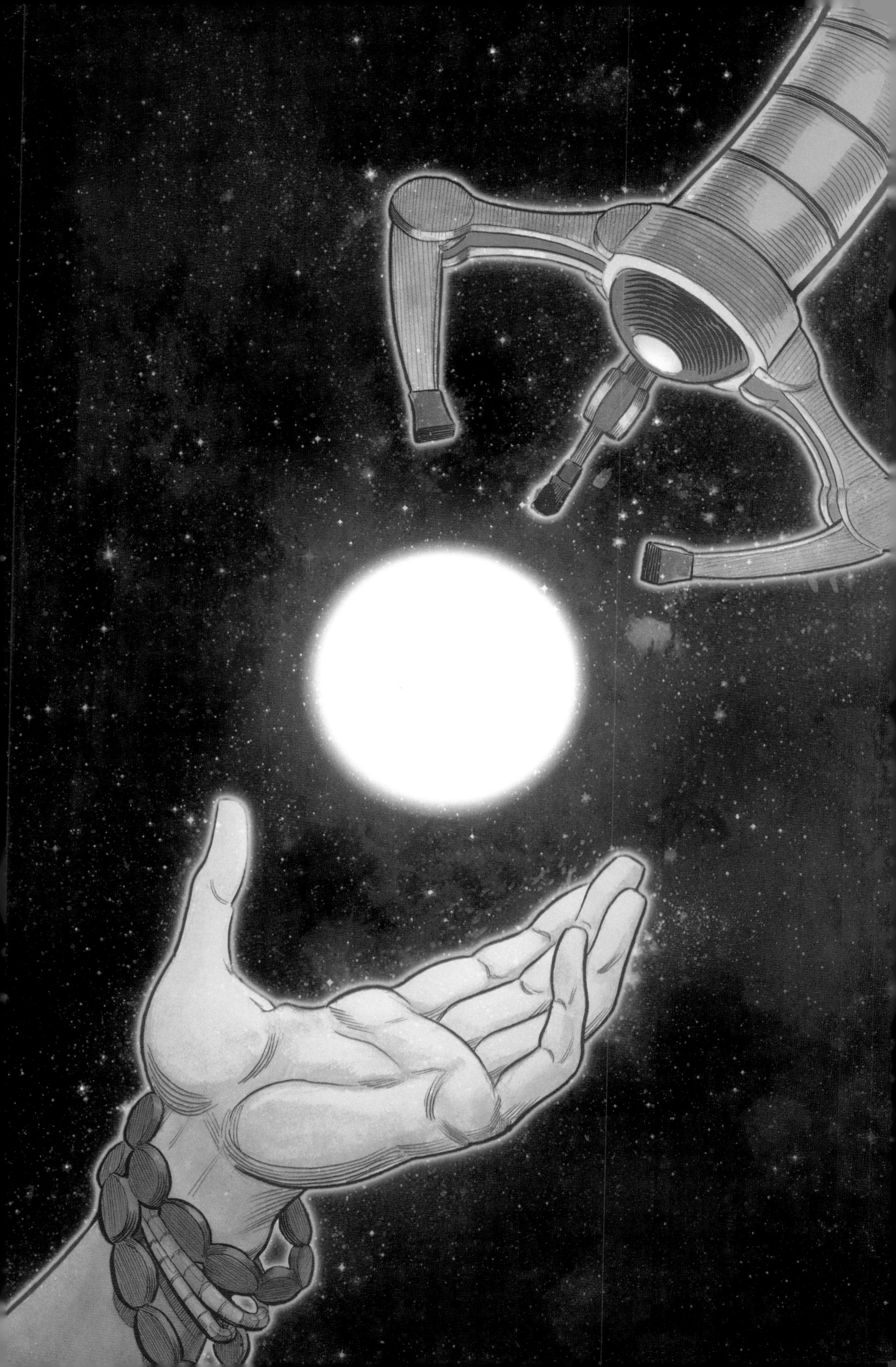

RYAN O'SULLIVAN

Ryan is a comic book writer from the north of England who has written for a variety of publishers including Image Comics and Titan Comics. Best known for working alongside illlustrator Plaid Klaus on creator-owned titles such as **TURNCOAT** and **VOID TRIP**, Ryan has also worked extensively on game-related properties such as *Eisenhorn: Xenos, Dawn of War III, The Evil Within,* and *Dark Souls.* He is one quarter of the White Noise comic-writer studio.

rosullivan.co.uk
@RyanOSullivan

PLAID KLAUS

Since we require, as human cogs in society, an oversimplification of a unique human individual distilled into a series of accomplishments, I shall try to produce a bio for the entity known as Plaid Klaus. He has built two unique worlds from the ground up, in association with the narratives granted to him by Ryan O'Sullivan. Plaid Klaus spawned the Universes in the form of the following comic books: **TURNCOAT, VOID TRIP**.

plaidklaus.com
@PlaidKlaus